The Oracle's Bridge

Book 1 of The Bridges of Magic Series

Stacy Hall

The Oracle's Bridge

Bridges of Magic, Book One

Cover design by 100 Covers

Website: stacyhallauthor.com

First published 2026

Published by Stacy Hall

Mooroopna, Victoria, Australia

1st Paperback edition - 2026 ISBN: 978-1-7646560-0-9

1st Hardcover edition - 2026 ISBN: 978-1-7646560-1-6

Contents

For Mum,
you always said you'd read one of my books someday.
Here it is ready for you. Finally.

For Dad,
the kind of support that never announces itself
and never wavers.

For Tanya,
who never once said, "can we talk about something else?"
even when you absolutely wanted to.

For Cassie, Jesse, Tatum, and Tia,
everything worth finishing, I finish for you all.

Lastly, For every reader who needed a quest
before they could find their way home.

The Unknown Lands
Lormir Island
Daramoor Island
Aelith's Shore
Eldoria
Fairy Grove
Drakenholt
Pack Grraall
Teela's Hut
Strave's Village
Vrill's Tower
Treast
TALNARESS
VELTAK

PART ONE

Quest for a King

Prologue

Acrid smoke scratched at Kael's throat, a lesser evil than the surrounding chaos. Staring through a shattered window, the alcove's stone pressed cold against his shoulders. The air clawed its way down his throat with each breath.

Flames prowled along the defenceless sides of the Royal Palace of Talnaress with the hunger of a predator. Soot now blackened the marble that once gleamed white with deep-cut carvings.

Night air tore through the city, thick with smoke and the sweetness of decay riding under it. Screams pierced the darkness. High notes that cracked and broke, then cut to nothing. A chorus of agony rang through the devastated courtyards, then faded to a terrible silence.

Kael had fought in border skirmishes. But these screams made his fingers tremble. His hand moved to the hilt of his sword.

Barok Tana's forces moved through the palace as if the defenders were nothing more than obstacles to step around. In under an hour, the defences fell. They manoeuvred through narrow streets. Their blades and stone fists found every gap in armour, every unguarded throat. Each strike left silence where moments before had been defiant shouts. This wasn't a battle. It was a slaughter.

Golems, hulking monstrosities of sand and stone twisted by dark magic, marched through the city and onto the palace grounds. Their bodies shimmered in the moonlight. Granite fists shattered timber, marble, and armour, sending shards flying.

Decay hung thick in the air. Rotting figures draped in the tattered remnants of clothing stalked the streets and corridors. Viscous fluid dripped from ruined eye sockets. Catching firelight. Gleaming copper trailing down bone-white faces.

Steel clattered, useless against stone bodies. The undead continued to push forward, even when missing limbs. The attack had come so fast that no one had time to arm themselves with anything more than what they carried.

King Caelric fell as his sword was torn from his hand. The nobleman, with his kind smile and booming laugh, was defending Queen Elendra. Her elegant silver gown ran crimson. The queen's gaze snapped from shadow to shadow. Her hand reached for the king's arm. Fingers closed on empty air as he fell forward. Each swing bought seconds. No more.

The king fell. Blood spread across the white marble. The queen's cry rose above the din of battle. High notes that cracked, then broke as a shadow descended upon her. Quick. Deadly. Her eyes searched for an escape that would never come.

Golems pinned Kael and his squad; they could not reach the king and queen. The constructs loomed over them, cold rolling off their bodies in waves, stone fists crashing down. The undead surged forward.

His comrades fell all around him. Janken's defiant yell was cut short, overwhelmed in a mass of stone limbs. Markal fell beside him, sword jammed in a skeletal ribcage. Stone fists hurled another against the wall, the crack of armour on stone lost in the roar around them. Kael's knees buckled. Stone scraped his palms as he caught himself. His gaze fixed on the opposite wall. Stone.

Cracks. Old mortar crumbling between blocks. His fingers traced the sword hilt's grooves. One, two, three. One, two, three.

He stumbled back, then darted through a gap into a corridor. Each step faltered where his comrades had fallen. Heat blistered his skin as he pushed deeper. Flames roared around him, drowning out everything else. The sickening sweetness of blood clung to his nostrils. Copper tang coated his tongue. He ducked into an alcove; the coldness emanating from a passing golem prickled his skin. A tremor shook the ground as another section of the palace collapsed. He edged deeper into the shadowy alcove, inching closer to the small, dusty window.

Buildings crumbling. People running in all directions. Bodies in the streets. The distant bell's rhythm changed. Steady tolls became erratic clanging. Faster, louder, missing beats as if the ringer's hands shook. Burning corridors. Fallen comrades. The Queen's terrified eyes.

He shook his head and pushed himself off the wall. His spine straightened. His grip shifted on the hilt of his sword, fingers finding the familiar grooves.

He entered a narrow passage where smoke clung to his throat and stung his eyes. A Magician gripped his Powerstaff tight, beads of sweat trickling down his temples. Like distant thunder, the blows of two massive golems hammered against an iridescent barrier, blocking their way at the end of the passage.

The Magician turned to Kael, chest heaving, words forced between gasps. He thrust his arm toward a door, hand trembling. "Through that door. I don't know..." Another impact drove him to one knee. "...how long this barrier will hold."

Cearan. The breath left him. His hands steadied. His breathing sharpened. He moved toward the door.

He burst into the room. Boots crunched over shattered bits of stone and splintered wood. Charred wood and melted wax hung heavy in the air. A small cradle sat amid the debris, its polished wood pale and clean against the ash.

It rocked with the rhythm of gentle motion. There inside lay a sleeping baby. Tiny. Serene. Wrapped in a silken blanket embroidered with the royal crest.

Kael's breath caught. Prince Dreese, the infant heir to the throne of Veltak. Untouched by the destruction ravaging the palace. Warmth radiated through the blanket. The baby's tiny fingers curled against the blanket. Kael's breathing changed. Deliberate inhales. Controlled. His jaw set. His hands moved with sudden certainty, lifting the prince and cradling the infant against his chest. The kingdom's future weighed so little, yet everything depended on this small life.

As he returned to the passageway, Cearan was there. Their eyes met, wide and questioning.

"Back that way." Cearan's voice cracked with strain. He glanced towards the golems trapped in the corridor behind them. "Go." He gripped his Powerstaff tighter.

He lifted the staff high. The protective shield that had been shimmering faintly in front of the golems flickered out of existence. They advanced with heavy, thunderous steps.

Just as their feet touched the ground in the corridor, a brilliant flash erupted from the tip of the Powerstaff, casting a blinding light throughout the tunnel. The ceiling overhead creaked and trembled. Then collapsed with a thunderous noise. Rocks and debris created an impassable wall of rubble.

Kael shielded the baby's face with the edge of his undershirt from the dense, swirling dust. They staggered away, eyes watering, coughing it from their lungs. Against his chest, a small sound. Thin. Frightened. The prince stirred in his arms, a single whimper swallowed almost before it began. Cearan swayed, breath coming in shallow gasps. The Powerstaff nearly slipped from fingers slick with sweat and trembling from the magical strain. He gripped tighter, knuckles bone-white against dark wood, and blinked away the grey creeping at the edges of his vision.

Behind them, stone fists hammered against the rubble, testing its strength. The dull thunder of impacts drove them forward faster.

They sprinted through narrow, dimly lit corridors. Their footsteps echoed against stone walls, the sound bouncing off the eerie silence. The turbulence of battle lay mostly behind now, and they encountered only a scattering of Barok Tana's troops, their presence more like spectres than threats.

A lone figure. A human clad in a tattered robe. His dark eyes darted, unfocused, as he clutched a large, gleaming crystal in shaking hands. His voice cracked. "Flame!" The word split into two syllables, high and wavering. The crystal unleashed a rope of searing fire that shot forward, crackling and twisting through the air.

Cearan moved with his Powerstaff already aloft. He channelled his energy through it, creating an invisible barrier that met the fiery attack. The flame rebounded with furious intensity back towards its caster, as if striking a mirror. The man's scream pierced the air. High, thin, cutting short. In under a heartbeat, the flames had consumed him, leaving nothing but a pile of ash that scattered with the breeze of their passing.

They stepped into the grand hall, where the king and queen lay motionless on the cold marble floor. Moonlight streamed through the stained-glass windows, casting coloured patterns over their still forms. Cearan paused. He looked at the king's face, then away. His hand tightened on his Powerstaff until the wood creaked.

With trembling fingers, he picked up the king's ornate sword, firelight reflecting off the blade. "Your son will need this." His voice caught as he spoke. He bowed, his spine straight despite exhaustion, and held the position for three slow heartbeats before straightening. "Goodbye, my liege," he said before turning his attention to the fallen scabbard near the Queen, its leather worn but still regal. Sheathing the sword, he attached it to his belt.

Kael bowed, his spine straight despite exhaustion, and held the position for three slow heartbeats before straightening. They hurried into another shadowy corridor. They navigated the labyrinthine passages, each footfall echoing too loud, breath coming too fast to catch. Each corner brought only stone, shadow, and the echo of their own boots.

The bell grew louder. Faster. The sound drove into Kael's skull like hammer blows. Footsteps thundered somewhere in the corridors above, stone grinding against stone as more golems converged. They had minutes at most before being found. Perhaps less.

They reached a doorway concealed behind a faded tapestry, which opened into a long-forgotten servant's tunnel. Mildew thick enough to taste coated the back of Kael's throat. The air pressed down, stale and still. Cobwebs hung in sheets from the low ceiling, their strands heavy with decades of accumulated dust. Brick crumbled beneath his hand when he steadied himself against the wall, sharp fragments that bit into his palm.

Cearan moved ahead. A pale blue light bloomed from the crystal atop his Powerstaff, painting the crumbling brick walls in shades of ice and bone. Enough to move by. No more.

Halfway through, the tunnel convulsed. The tremor started beneath their feet, travelling up through the ancient stone. Dust fell from the ceiling in choking clouds, and somewhere in the blackness from behind came the grinding scrape of stone against stone. Kael didn't look back. Couldn't afford to. Prince Dreese's weight against his chest was the only thing that mattered. They pushed through ghostly curtains that caught at their faces like grasping fingers, sticky threads catching in their hair and eyelashes.

The fires had taken the sky, turning it orange and black. Smoke stung their eyes. Each breath scraped their throats raw. Ash covered everything. Their clothes, their skin, grinding between their teeth.

The bell had stopped ringing; the screams were gone. But the silence was worse. It meant the city had fallen. Resistance crushed beneath stone and shadow, leaving only the distant, rhythmic scrape of metal on cobblestone. Too steady to be a coincidence, too distant to confirm their fears.

Cearan adjusted his cloak, the fabric whispering around him. "We must head to the docks and get out of this city. The prince must survive!"

Kael nodded, his jaw tightening as he glanced at the crumbling rooftops silhouetted against the orange glow. "I know a shortcut through less-travelled alleyways. If the warehouses hold, we should remain mostly unseen," he said as he scanned the shadows for movement. A shape jerked forward. Too tall, limbs bending at wrong angles, moving with a purpose no wind could give debris. He passed the prince to Cearan and unsheathed his sword, its blade catching the firelight. He led the way, each step deliberate on the soot-slicked cobblestones.

They wove through the tangled streets, sidestepping fallen bricks, shattered glass, and the occasional body. In the corner of Kael's vision, shapes moved. Angular, deliberate, too coordinated to be survivors fleeing. When he turned his head, there was nothing but drifting smoke. Behind them, the scraping sound continued, closer now. Or perhaps it was only the settling of destroyed buildings. The death throes of a conquered city. Neither man spoke. The scraping continued.

They slipped into narrow back alleys, making their way through the chaos in shadow, avoiding the flickering glow of distant fires that painted the night sky. More shapes appeared ahead. Tall figures beyond the smoke, moving with the slow certainty of things that understood nothing about exhaustion. Kael's hand tightened around his sword's hilt as they quickened their pace and veered down a narrower street. The route to the docks lengthened with each detour, each moment bringing something closer. Whether Barok's living forces or something worse, they couldn't afford to discover.

Every shadow might conceal bone-white faces and rusted blades, or might conceal nothing at all.

Heat rolled toward them in waves as they approached the warehouse row. The roar of flames drowned out all other sounds, including the metallic scraping that had kept their pace too fast to breathe. With no alternative and something closing in on their trail, they made their way down the perilous street with desperate care.

Halfway down the street, a warehouse groaned. They stopped. Sparks showered across the cobblestones. Cearan shielded the sleeping prince with his robe. Behind them, another section crashed down, blocking their retreat. Fire now surrounded them. Through the smoke at their backs, shapes emerged with terrible clarity.

A dozen skeletal soldiers stood beyond the fire. Oozing eye sockets gleamed in the firelight. Rusted blades hung at their sides. Waiting. Patient as the grave itself. They did not rush forward. They waited. All the time death offered, was theirs. The fire crackled between hunter and prey, an impassable barrier that held them back.

Kael's eyes darted around the chaos, seeking a way out through the swirling smoke and towering debris. The undead remained motionless beyond the flames, a silent jury bearing witness. Roaring heat blocked every path forward.

Cearan, his robes singed and ash-dusted, closed his eyes. His lips moved in silent prayer to a magic greater than his own. A wind swept through that carried no trace of the burning city. Clean. Cold. Air with a taste like mountain stone. The inferno before them flared white-hot, then died to embers in three heartbeats.

The fire that had blocked them from behind remained, burning hotter than before. It still held the skeletal soldiers back.

Kael grabbed Cearan by the arm. He guided him and the prince he carried away from the dying embers, refusing to look back at the waiting soldiers trapped beyond the flames. They sprinted down the street, the cobblestones slick with soot, until they reached the end of the block. There, a narrow alley led toward the docks. At the water's edge, dilapidated boats listed in their moorings, their hulls half-submerged. Among the wrecks, a lone fishing boat bobbed with the rhythm of the tide.

They clambered aboard, the boards groaning under their weight, salt crystals crunching beneath their boots. The sun had found the horizon. Kael turned to Cearan, his gaze darting toward the horizon as he spoke, his hands already reaching for the ship's ropes. "Take the prince below deck, out of sight. I have sailed vessels like this before."

"Very well," Cearan enveloped the infant in his cloak. "You have done well. The Grandmaster asked me to thank you for your service, Kael." He held Kael's gaze for one beat, jaw tight, then descended without another word.

Kael untied the mooring rope, his fingers moving through the frayed fibres. With a firm grip, he hoisted the sail upward. Its canvas billowed as it caught the brisk sea breeze, snapping taut against the brightening sky. The boat lurched forward, slicing through the water as they left the blazing city behind. Salt spray kissed his face, sharp and clean after hours of breathing ash and death.

Kael's face stung from the saltwater. The city shrank into shadows at the horizon's edge. His family. His friends. Somewhere in that smoke and ash, were they able to escape and go into hiding? Or had they met a worse fate? Each breath scraped. Saltwater or smoke. He couldn't tell anymore. The horizon blurred.

Prince Dreese slept below deck, safe for this heartbeat. But Barok Tana controlled the palace, the roads, and every path back to the capital. They'd escaped with an infant heir and a stolen fishing boat. No army. No allies. No plan.

How did you protect the future of a kingdom when you had nowhere left to run?

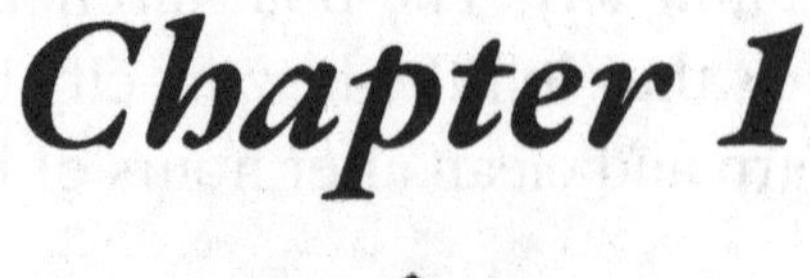

Chapter 1

The Calling

The message globe's flash and resonating chime jolted Stric awake. Stone walls caught its glow, angular shadows leaping across sparse furnishings. Brighter the sphere pulsed, louder the chime, demanding attention.

"Receive." The word scraped past his dry throat, rough and audible. Energy flickered. Before his doorway, the air shimmered, giving way to an elderly magician's image. Silver hair fell down the figure's back, blending with the flowing beard that framed his face.

Stric's fingers found the bedframe's edge. The cold iron, solid under his palm. The magician's ornate robes bore runic symbols marking council rank. He pushed himself upright. Council members don't message in the middle of the night with pleasant news.

The magician's brow furrowed, eyes sharp and unyielding, locked onto him. Each breath required conscious effort. The voice arrived. Each word clipped and precise. "Stric Deamara." The magician paused, letting the weight settle on the young man's shoulders. "You're summoned to appear before us at once. Proceed to the nearest porter!"

The message concluded, and the elderly magician's image faded, plunging the room back into darkness. Stric's voice cut through the silence: "Light on." The lighting crystal embedded in the ceiling flared to life, throwing sharp shadows against the stone walls. He leapt from his bed. His fingers closed on the plain blue apprentice robes where he had left them, draped over the wooden chair.

Stric wrestled the robe over his head. The sleeve caught. He yanked it free, with no thought of seams tearing. His fingers fumbled with the purple sash, silk slipping through sweating palms. Could this be a test?

Footsteps ringing off stone walls, he hurried towards the transporter. A deafening thud reverberated through the halls. Beneath him, the ground trembled. From hidden cracks above, ancient dust drifted down, settling on his tongue, coating his throat. Something colossal had struck the academy's shields. Air refused to reach his lungs properly. What is happening? This is no test! His legs moved without conscious thought, boots pounding against polished stone. The hallway stretched longer with each step.

Skidding to a stop at the porter's alcove, he heard hinges creak behind him. Doors swinging open, urgent voices following. The sounds reached him as if through water. He pressed his hand to the activation crystal's cool surface. Smooth stone. Real. Another distant explosion as the floor jumped beneath his boots. He tried to swallow. Couldn't.

"Council Hall!" His voice rang through the hall before he vanished, leaving the academy in Treast behind.

After the briefest glimpse of swirling colours, Stric materialised in Talnaress, standing in the foyer of the council hall. Mosaics covered the marble floor, their tiles worn smooth at the threshold, whispering tales of magic and valour. Tall arched windows allowed weak moonlight to filter through. At the chamber's end, two massive doors carved with swirling runic patterns hummed with silent vigilance.

The doors swung open without a sound, their polished surfaces catching slivers of light as they revealed the cavernous room beyond. A voice boomed from within, each syllable striking against the stone.

"Stric Deamara, enter!"

The moment his boots touched the stone threshold, a tremor vibrated through his soles. The subsequent thud resonated through the hall. Talnaress was also under siege.

The council hall stretched out before him. Vast. Hollow. Its emptiness emphasised by the absence of adornments and the gathering darkness. At the centre, a massive table bearing scratches and stains, memories of countless debates carved into worn wood. Around it stood thirteen chairs. Eight vacant.

Five occupied. Three physical bodies bent under impossible strain, two projections flickering like dying candles, translucent robes clinging to exhausted frames. Every eye turned to him.

A dozen steps separated him from the table.

Blood trickled from Master Dalit's nose, a thin crimson line against pale skin. His hands trembled; one gripped the edge of the table, his knuckles white against the ancient wood. The other held his Powerstaff, the crystal atop it pulsing with an irregular rhythm. Bright. Dim. Bright. Responding to each impact that shook the hall. The projection beside him wavered, its edges blurring like smoke in the wind.

"What in the seven hells is going on?" The words tore free before Stric could stop them.

"Calm yourself. We need your head clear." Master Dalit's voice carried steadily despite his condition. He raised his hand, the gesture unhurried despite the blood still tracking down his chin. The Powerstaff's crystal pulsed once, bright. Warmth spread from Stric's chest outward, like heat from the crystals blazing on every staff in the room. Tension eased from his shoulders, fists unclenched, breath deepening.

"Forgive the necessity. Time is short." His gaze swept across the table. He met each gathered magician's eyes, receiving subtle nods in return.

Another impact struck. Master Dalit's other hand shot to his Powerstaff. The crystal blazed white-hot as he channelled magic into the shields protecting the hall. His face paled, shoulders sagging under the strain. Blood dripped onto robes he had no time to wipe. The two other council members swayed, their own Powerstaffs flaring as they poured energy into the failing wards.

"Barok struck everywhere at once." Teesa's projection flickered, edges bleeding translucent. "The palace. Every garrison." Her voice thinned. "Here..."

Distant screams filtered through the magical link. Flames roared behind her fading form.

"... the academy is burning."

Her projection wavered more violently, its edges growing translucent, as the background chaos became visible through her fading form. Distant sounds filtered through. Screams, explosions, the roar of flames consuming the academy.

Another thud rang through the hall. Ancient dust sifted from stonework cracks. The floor quivered with violent tremors. The three magicians staggered as one, Powerstaffs blazing as they reinforced the shields that groaned under the assault. Master Alban gasped, sweat beading on his brow despite the cool chamber. The councillor beside him went bone-white, blood trickling from her own nose now as she poured her remaining strength into the wards.

"Grandmaster Vrill has a task for you." Master Dalit continued, voice steady despite the chaos, despite the blood, despite the exhaustion that carved deeper lines into his aged face. "A task critical to Veltak's future."

Master Dalit's gaze swept over him. Stric's hand found the purple sash at his waist. The silk, still slightly damp from his sweating palms during the run. Silence stretched.

"Vrill requested you for this mission." Master Dalit's eyebrows knitted as he studied the young recruit. "He believes your past gives you a unique strength or skill." His voice had a quality Stric recognised. The flat precision of a man committed to a task he hadn't made his own peace with.

His throat worked. He turned his head from one council member to another, searching their faces for some sign that this was an elaborate jest. "But what could he want from me, a mere apprentice?" The words came out smaller than he'd intended. Questions about my past. Not now. Not tonight.

"Only the Grandmaster knows. It's for him to tell." Master Alban leaned forward as he spoke. His gaze found Stric and did not move.

"We trust his word." Teesa's projection wavered, its form growing translucent. "Do you?" Her voice drifted softly in the dimly lit chamber, background flames showing through her translucent image.

"Of course, I trust his words, masters." The words climbed higher with each syllable, cracking on the last.

He straightened. "And I shall do whatever is required of me."

"Do you wil..." White light erupted around Master Teesa's image. The sound reached them, crashing and roaring, a scream cut short. Then she vanished, leaving only empty space where her projection had flickered moments before.

The academy had fallen.

Master Dalit's hand fell from his Powerstaff to grip the table's edge. His eyes closed. The councillor beside him bowed her head, lips moving in silent prayer for the fallen. Master Alban's jaw clenched, the only outward sign of grief they could afford. A heartbeat of stillness held them. Acknowledgement. Mourning. Farewell.

A thunderous thud rang through the grand hall, louder and more insistent than before, shaking the room's very foundations.

The remaining projection on the left side of the table guttered and vanished entirely without warning. Gone, severed by whatever catastrophe had claimed that section of the academy.

Only the three physical council members remained, all gripping their Powerstaffs with both hands, crystals blazing then dimming as shields absorbed impacts that should have shattered this wing. Master Dalit's knees buckled. He steadied himself on the edge of the table, leaving a red handprint on the scarred wood.

"If you agree to accept this, we shall send you to meet with the Grandmaster." Master Alban's voice rang off the stone walls. His own Powerstaff pulsed, crystal struggling to maintain brightness.

Stric stood near the centre of the grand circular table, eyes fixed on the masters surrounding him. His shoulders sagged, then straightened. "I am..." His voice started strong, then wavered. Clearing his throat, he tried again. "I am ready!"

A murmur moved through the masters' ranks, dry as the dust still sifting from the walls, as some exchanged wary glances, their scepticism hidden behind exhausted faces. Dalit's hand tightened once on his Powerstaff. Then they rose from their high-backed chairs, movements synchronised despite the strain.

Together, they stretched their arms forward, raising their Powerstaffs. A low hum filled the air. A vibration gathered in Stric's chest and raised the hair on his arms as their magic built. Their voices mingled, the incantation moving through stone and bone as the power built. The spell's power grew, swirling around him in light and shadow that reflected in the master's eyes.

Magic surged, wrapping Stric in brilliant light that spilled around him, casting long shadows that moved across the stone floor. A louder thud rang out. Stone splintered somewhere in the hall. He didn't look. Couldn't afford to. A single anguished cry, the last thing he carried. His form flickered as if caught in a shimmering mirage. The cold of the hall was still on his face when the stone let go beneath him.

This teleportation differed from the swift blink he'd known at the academy. Stric remained aware.

Though his fingers were gone, tingling spread from phantom fingertips to absent toes. The sensation crept across nonexistent skin while a low hum buzzed through his scattered being. Consciousness persisted through the void. Billions of particles swirling around some essential nucleus that still recognised itself as him.

The wrongness twisted through him like fever-dream logic. Where his stomach should exist, nausea churned. Where his heart belonged, phantom beats hammered rapid and erratic. Before he could examine the wrongness of existing as scattered particles while still holding coherent thoughts, his scattered particles coalesced, pulling together with a forceful snap. He stood upright, gravity pulling solid ground beneath his feet.

Teleportation magic had carried him far beyond the Academy halls, depositing him in a tower sanctum he'd never seen. The air tasted different here. Cleaner, with a hint of pine and a cold mountain breeze.

Sunlight streamed through the dust-thick air. Beneath his boots, shattered crystals crunched like dry leaves. Ancient tomes lay buried on the table, their yellowed pages fluttering to the floor.

Stric surveyed the chaos. Shattered crystals. Scattered tomes. No enemies. No bodies. No Grandmaster. Had the Masters sent him to the wrong place? Or had he arrived too late? Had destruction already swept through?

"Forgive the chaos." A voice emerged from the shadows.

Stric turned, spine straightening before conscious thought. Shadows peeled away, revealing Grandmaster Vrill. His tall frame draped in white robes marked with ink stains and ash. Sky-blue eyes.

Stric's gaze dropped to the Powerstaff in his hand. The crystal pulsed through the spectrum too fast.

Vrill gestured at the scattered crystals, the tumbled books. "I've spent weeks trying to find Barok's plans." He stepped forward, movements precise despite the exhaustion carved into every line. "They found us. Everything that could be done has been done. Except this." He paused, hand tightening on his Powerstaff. "Give me a moment." He turned and moved back into the alcove. "Then we can talk."

The shadows swallowed him again. A glow bathed the alcove, casting flickering patterns on the cold stone walls. Vrill's fingers danced over a crystal ball atop a carved pedestal, its cloudy surface beginning to shine. Tendrils of light wove together inside the sphere. A city consumed by flames appeared, the image focusing on the outskirts.

Two figures raced through burning streets. A royal guard at the forefront, dull armour reflecting flickering flames. Close behind. A middle-aged magician carried an infant swaddled in silk. The child slept peacefully, a tiny hand curled around the blanket's fold.

Behind him, Vrill stood in the alcove, his gaze sharp and unwavering, fixed on the glowing crystal ball. His lips moved in a precise, unbroken rhythm, shaping the syllables of an ancient incantation. The crystal's light shifted with each word, brightening and darkening against the alcove walls.

The pair skidded to a halt as the building beside them groaned and buckled, sending a shower of fiery debris that blocked their way. A deafening crash jolted them as another building crumbled behind them. Flames leapt hungrily, cutting off any escape and locking them within a blistering inferno.

Vrill raised his Powerstaff higher; the crystal atop it glowed brightly. His magic reached across the distance, the Grandmaster's power doing what the other magicians could not: containing the flames that threatened to trap them.

The flames died. The path opened. The guard's eyes widened as they exchanged glances, then continued on their way. Reaching the end of the block, they veered away from the inferno and raced down another street, their feet pounding against the cobblestones. At the street's end, a dock stretched into the water. Broken sails and cracked hulls stood everywhere, but close to the end, a small fishing boat, untouched, bobbed gently in the harbour.

In the crystal, pale light caught the harbour water. They scrambled aboard. The Grandmaster murmured, "Thank him for me." The magician leaned in to speak to the royal guard, then nodded and disappeared below deck, out of sight. Vrill held his hands over the crystal ball for a moment longer before he withdrew them. The crystal's surface clouded from its edges inward. The light went flat.

He sagged against the pedestal, catching himself with a hand that shook. His Powerstaff dimmed, its crystal pulsing irregularly.

"All will be well again, young Stric." The Grandmaster's eyes held steady on his, unblinking, though exhaustion weighted every word. "Now, let me tidy up, and I can address some of your questions." With a sweep of his hand, the books vanished, parchment rustled into nothingness, and crystals twinkled before disappearing without a sound, leaving the surfaces pristine.

Stric had time to gasp before his perch vanished beneath him. Arms windmilling, he teetered forward but caught himself with a quick step.

"We do not have much time. This tower is hidden deep in the northern forest. It has been my sanctuary for my research for decades," Vrill said, gesturing to the stone walls around them. "Barok's troops will have torn apart the Academy and the council hall. By now, they realise I'm not there. Barok has been here; he will figure it out."

"But we have time to share a quick meal before we must part ways." Vrill's mouth shaped the curve of a smile, his hands still locked around the Powerstaff. He gestured towards the table, now laden with ripe fruit, honeyed sweetness mixing with the yeasty scent of bread still warm from the oven. The sharp tang of aged cheese made Stric's mouth water.

The silver platter. Ripe fruit. Fresh bread. His body insisted it was time for the morning meal. But he'd just left moonlit Talnaress. Minutes ago.

Sunlight streamed through Vrill's tower window.

Dust motes drifted in the honey-coloured light, each speck distinct in the still air. How long had it been since the mysterious summons had jolted him awake? Darkness still sat in his bones.

The Grandmaster's voice reached him. Its calm authority left no room for doubt. "You've been awake for many hours now, much of it spent in transit around our planet, fragmented into a billion pieces as you teleported here. I had to confuse any potential trackers trying to follow the teleportation trail. Giving me time to prepare. Keeping them from finding me prematurely."

Stric nodded, his breath catching. "Grandmaster, I was conscious. For the first time, I was aware of the journey."

The Grandmaster gave Stric a gentle smile and waved dismissively. "Please call me Vrill." Warmth filled his eyes as he slumped into a chair, gesturing to the seat across from him. "No formality here, my friend." He studied Stric's bewildered expression. "You felt the journey, didn't you? Most teleports happen too fast to notice, like a blink. But vast distances?" He shook his head. "You experience every moment."

"Thank you, Grand... Vrill." Stric's voice cracked as he accepted the chair, its high back curling around him like a protective shell. His robe rustled against the polished wood as he sank down.

A distant explosion rumbled through the forest, muffled by distance but unmistakable. Vrill's hand went to his Powerstaff, knuckles white around the wood. The crystal blazed a brilliant blue, magic pouring into wards that groaned under the impact. His face paled, sweat trickling down his temples. "Barok is here, attacking my wards." He shook his head, jaw tight. "We don't have long before..." Another explosion, closer this time. "Eat. You'll need strength."

The ward light flickered in the stone above them. Each word from Vrill pressed the cold closer, and Stric shifted.

"Barok Tana." Vrill's fingers stilled on the table's scarred surface. "We exiled him three years ago to Lormir Island, where magic dies." His voice caught. "We thought him powerless."

Stric set the bread down.

"He returned." Vrill leaned forward. "Creating golems. Raising the dead." His eyes met Stric's. "Our fallen will march against their brothers."

"We never saw him coming."

Two impacts in rapid succession. The tower rocked. Vrill lurched to his feet, Powerstaff blazing. His body swayed, breath coming in gasps, the crystal atop the staff flickering. Bright. Dim. Struggling. Blood trickled from his nose. He wiped it, leaving a red smear across his white beard. He collapsed back into his chair, catching himself. His Powerstaff remained gripped in a white-knuckled hand, crystal pulsing irregularly.

The words landed like a stone dropped into still water. The Guild. Wards layered over every major city. Detection spells woven into the Academy's foundations. And Barok had simply walked through it all.

"How?" The question scraped out. "How does an exiled man on a magic-dead island come back and destroy everything in a single night without anyone seeing?"

"He has discovered a way to mask his magic, his intent. Last night, he caught us all off guard. Our wards held no power against an enemy we couldn't see coming."

Vrill leaned forward, voice dropping. "Veltak lies in ruins. The Academy in ashes. The palace has been overthrown. Barok has slain the King and Queen, and our fellow magicians face being hunted like beasts." He paused, drawing a breath that shook once before steadying. His mouth found the shape of a smile, though his eyes stayed fixed somewhere past Stric's shoulder. "The newborn Prince Dreese escaped before the palace fell. We watched him being secreted away to safety. But he cannot return for many years, when he is old enough to take his rightful place as heir."

Windows shattered. Glass exploded inward, glittering shards raining onto the floor. Icy wind rushed through the breach. Vrill's Powerstaff erupted with light so bright Stric had to shield his eyes. The Grandmaster stood, both hands on the staff, magic pouring through him in a torrent.

His whole body trembled with effort. Blood flowed from his nose, spattering onto white robes. Wards screamed. A high, crystalline note rose higher, then held an impossible pitch.

He held. The assault paused.

Vrill sagged, catching himself on a staff that dimmed. His breathing came ragged.

Again, Vrill paused, his stained robes whispering against the chair as he rose, spine straight and gaze unwavering. "The prince will be safe, far from Barok's reach."

The sweet smell of the ripe fruit wrapped around him, nothing like the yeast and gruel scent of academy mornings. Pelter's gap-toothed grin. Eldena's laughter in the practice halls.

Gone now. All of it.

Vrill pointed at him. "I have watched over you since you arrived at the Academy, Stric. Since the night you were found in those woods." Vrill's eyes held his. Stric couldn't read what was in them. "The Oracle called out to me in dreams when you came to us. They showed me your coming victory, though I confess I did not understand the vision until it was almost too late. Not until tonight did the meaning become clear."

He leaned forward slightly. "You, Stric, have been foreseen. The Oracle showed me you possess something Veltak cannot survive without."

Vrill's eyes held his. The weight of those words pressed against his chest, heavy as the tower stones above them.

"You must find Prince Dreese, restore the royal bloodline, and counter Barok's dark sorcery. Only then can you bring light back to Veltak." Pausing to allow Stric to digest what had been said, Vrill gazed into his eyes intently. "Will you take up this burden and become Veltak's beacon?"

Stric rubbed the back of his neck. "I..." Words caught on themselves, his voice climbing higher with each syllable until he cleared his throat and tried again. "I don't know what I can do, Vrill. But if there's any hope, I'll do all I can." He cast an anxious glance towards Vrill. "But why me? How am I supposed to find a hidden baby and place him on the throne?"

Vrill smiled, his eyes steady and assured. "This will be answered in time. You are more capable than you know." His voice was quiet. Certain. "But right now, we must put you somewhere far from Barok and even further from the prince."

"Follow me." He strode toward a door concealed in the shadows. Stric caught sight of intricate runes carved into the archway. The hair on his arms had risen before he knew why.

Vrill pushed the door open, and bright golden light spilled over them from the chamber. Stric shielded his eyes, a slow smile forming as warmth spread through him. He trailed behind Vrill into the chamber. Inside its barren walls, each footstep amplified like a bell in a cavern. In the centre of the room lay a void, an area where light was absorbed.

"This is my most guarded secret." Vrill's words bounced off the cold stone walls, reverberating through the vast emptiness of the chamber. "This," he gestured to the darkness at the room's heart, "is a Timesling. With it, you can traverse days, months, and in your case, years into the future. You can journey to a time when Dreese is mature enough to rule and when our enemy has forgotten about the Guild's threat."

Stric's eyes widened. Power from the magic it held tingled over his skin. He turned to face Vrill, his brows knitted together. "I thought magical time travel was impossible." His voice was a whisper, as if afraid to give life to the idea.

"The sling itself is crafted and propelled by magic." Vrill gestured towards the Timesling. "But time itself answers to no magic. It answers only to the ancient laws woven into creation's foundation." He leaned in, his blue eyes reflecting the darkness of the void. "There exists a truth older than the Guild, older than the vampyre civilisations: the further and faster one travels through nature's fabric, the slower time's river flows for the traveller. Magic only provides the journey. The sling hurls you across vast distances, distances so great that time itself bends around your passage."

Stric stared into the void. Years. The word settled over him like winter frost. Pelter's gap-toothed grin would age into something unrecognisable. Eldena would become someone he'd never know. The Academy's corridors. Already ash. Already forgotten by everyone except him. He'd step out into a world where his name meant nothing, where the faces he'd memorised had been claimed by time.

"Everyone I know..." His voice barely carried across the chamber. "They'll all be..."

"Gone or changed beyond recognition." Vrill's words held no comfort, only truth. "You will be a ghost stepping into a future that has forgotten you ever existed. This is the price."

The darkness beckoned. Patient. Inevitable.

Three impacts came in rapid succession. The tower shook so violently that cracks spider-webbed across the walls, stone grinding against stone. Vrill staggered, Powerstaff blazing as the wards absorbed punishment. His knees buckled. He caught himself on the doorframe, both hands gripping the staff.

Stric swallowed hard. The Timesling's darkness pulled at him like deep water beckoning from a cliff's edge. He wiped his hand across his damp forehead.

"Vrill." Stric's voice came quieter than the tower's groaning stones. "How am I supposed to find a hidden prince and face... I'm just an apprentice? I can't..."

He stopped. Started again. "I'm not ready."

Something shifted in Vrill's face. The set of his jaw eased. The lines around his eyes deepened. Grief, perhaps. "No one could be ready for what I ask." His voice carried the exhaustion of centuries. "I am sending a boy to do the work of legends. I know this," he gripped his Powerstaff tighter. "But the Oracle showed me your face, Stric. Not mine. Not the council's. Yours. I do not understand why. I know only that if you do not go, Veltak dies in darkness."

Another impact shook the tower. Closer.

"Forgive me." Vrill's words cracked like breaking ice. Vrill held out his hand. A book materialised against his palm. His lips twitched into a brief, reassuring smile. "Take my Powerstaff and this book, Talnar. They will guide and assist you. They will give you everything you need."

Stric accepted them. The Powerstaff's tip dipped before he caught its balance, the wood pressing cold and unfamiliar into his palm. Too heavy. His wrist dropped with it before he steadied his grip. Talnar's leather binding felt warm, as though it had been held moments before. The book hummed with contained knowledge, centuries of wisdom pressed between covers. In his grip, these objects transformed from tools into a legacy. Into burden.

Vrill's Powerstaff. The Grandmaster's own weapon, carried through how many confrontations? How many councils? The wood pulsed against his fingers, recognising new hands with something like reluctance.

"I don't know how to find him." The words tumbled out. "The prince. I don't know where to start, or what I'm supposed to do when I get there, or..."

"Talnar will show you the path." Vrill's hand settled on his shoulder. "Trust the book. Trust yourself." His grip tightened. "And Stric? When you find him... tell Prince Dreese that his people never stopped fighting. That we held the line so he might have a chance to reclaim what was stolen."

A ground-trembling thud filled the space in the stone chamber. Dust rained down from hidden cracks. A loose stone dislodged from high on the wall, rattling downward before bouncing across the floor. The sound echoed, then died.

Vrill's face went snow white. The tower's wards groaned audibly, pitch rising to a desperate whine. "We are running out of time." Every corner pulsed alive with threat, reflecting Vrill's whispered fear. Stone itself vibrated. "Barok is inside the tower! You must go now!"

The void waited. Patient as death. Dark as forgetting.

Stric turned back once. A last glimpse of Vrill's ancient face, exhausted, resolute. The Grandmaster, who had watched over him since the night in the woods. Who had seen him in prophecy and chosen him despite everything. Behind Vrill, the tower's walls spider-webbed with cracks. The light filtering through shattered windows seemed already distant, already belonging to a world he was leaving behind.

"Vrill..."

"Go!" The command cracked like thunder.

Stric turned to face the darkness. Cold radiated from the void's heart. A cold beyond temperature. Absence. The absence of time, of place, of everything he'd known. His boot lifted. Hovered. The boundary between now and the future shimmered before him like heat on summer stone.

He stepped into the enveloping darkness, and the present released him into the unknown.

Vrill began murmuring a spell. A hum of building magic filled the room, resonating through his bones, the words ancient and powerful. Stric turned, intending to speak, but before he could utter a sound, his surroundings blurred.

The world of Veltak fell away beneath him.

Chapter 2

Through Time and Forest

The tower's darkness folded around Stric like a closing fist. The Timesling pulled, a force beyond resistance, and his green-and-grey world dwindled into a pinprick of light, swallowed by the vastness of space. Cosmic energies twisted through his stomach and scrambled his thoughts as colours clashed around him. His stomach dropped and held, no up and no down. Something moved through his lungs that wasn't quite air.

The path the Timesling carved through the between-worlds stretched before him, a wound through creation that sealed behind his passage, irreversible. Stars swelled from distant pinpricks to blazing suns, each trailing rings of light and spinning worlds that rushed past. His breath caught. Each pulse pressed against his chest until his ribs compressed, the breath squeezed thin.

Ahead, thick blackness crept along the horizon, swallowing his view inch by inch. The void encroached, devouring the light of the celestial dancers around him. Behind, one point of light held its ground. Cold and very far away.

The gathering shadows pulled at him. His breath caught, held.

For a heartbeat, the darkness was aware. Not empty, but watching. Waiting. As if something ancient slept in that void between moments, something that fed on endings. The sensation passed, but the wrongness lingered like oil on water.

His hand tightened on the Powerstaff, knuckles white against the cosmic void, yet his shoulders leaned forward.

Emptiness wrapped around him, thicker than the weightiest cloak. Each inhale scraped, sharp and icy against his throat. The endless void swallowed sight, swallowed time, moments expanding and contracting like a sleeping giant's breath. Space filled his lungs instead of air. Each heartbeat took years, or seconds. He couldn't find the difference.

Vrill's words rose through the inky blackness. "Our fellow magicians are being hunted like beasts."

Empty chairs at childhood tables. Pelter's gap-toothed grin over their morning gruel. Eldena's laughter in the practice halls. Academy corridors blazing bright with torchlight, shoulder bumps of camaraderie, whispered conspiracies shared over meals, hands clasped in celebration.

Ribs pressed inward. Each breath scraped shallow and quick. The darkness pressed closer, thick as water rising.

Just when the void threatened to swallow him whole. A flicker.

A lone star pierced through the oppressive void, its silvery luminescence swelling with each heartbeat until light again surrounded him. The emptiness had held him in its timeless grip for eternities or moments. He couldn't say. An hour, perhaps. A week. His body remembered nothing but the endless dark.

The star swelled. Stric turned his face toward it before he'd decided to. Suns wheeled back into view. Stric released a slow breath, willing his focus to remain on the beauty before him.

Familiar azure blues and rugged greens resolved below him. His shoulders dropped. His lungs expanded, drawing deeper breaths as if the air itself welcomed him back.

The flowing storm of colour ceased. The Timesling thrust him into stillness. A dense canopy filtered dappled sunlight onto the forest floor. Damp air clung to his skin. Unseen animals chattered while birds whose calls he had no name for echoed through undergrowth greener than anything he'd known. Every direction offered sights beyond his imagination.

Stric's grip tightened around the Powerstaff and the book. He hesitated before stepping onto unfamiliar ground, his breath racing. Pushing aside a large fern, he made his way to a moss-covered log that had succumbed to gravity, its bark worn smooth with time.

The forest pressed close. He had been lost before. Confused and alone, with no clear path ahead. But those other memories, fragmented and distant, belonged to a different life. One he'd learned not to examine too closely.

He settled onto the log, leaning the Powerstaff against its sturdy form and setting down the ancient tome, its leather cover warm from his journey. He glanced back at where he had landed. His back locked, as rigid as the log beneath him.

Dense foliage filled the space where the Timesling's shadow should have stood.

"Oh, terrific!" His fists clenched until his knuckles turned white. "I'm probably on the wrong planet or something, and my only way off it has vanished." He scanned the undergrowth, the canopy, the moss-covered trunks, before his shoulders sagged. Even if the Timesling stood before him, he wouldn't know the incantation to activate it.

Vrill said I would be sent into the future. Bark beneath his palm felt more real than anything else, its rough edges and weathered grooves carved by seasons he'd never witnessed.

What became of the world I once knew? Have my fellow apprentices survived the catastrophe that has befallen the Guild? The questions gnawed at him, but provided no answers.

Stric furrowed his brow, tapping a finger against his lip. Vrill had held the incantation steady while the tower came apart around him. Vrill had never failed. His exhale came slower, his grip on the Powerstaff loosened by a fraction. His jaw unclenched. His heartbeat steadied.

He scanned the dense forest around him. Trails wound through the underbrush like rivers, each disappearing into the thicket in different directions. Yet no clue presented itself. He rubbed his temples and exhaled sharply, scanning each trail once more for an elusive hint.

A shadow flickered at the corner of his vision. His gaze dropped to the log where he'd set the book. It lay open, pages fluttering like a frantic moth caught in an unseen breeze. The rustling stopped. Pages reversed course with deliberate intent. Blood drummed against his temples. Nothing in the forest moved. No wind stirred the leaves overhead, yet the pages turned.

The fluttering pages and their soft rustle came to a halt, and there, written in large, bold lettering, were two familiar words:

"STRIC DEAMARA."

His breath caught in his throat. "Of course, my name would be here." He picked up the leather-bound tome and set it on his lap, warmth spreading through his robe as if the book lived. The bold lettering shimmered for a moment before melting away like ink in water, replaced by a new line writing itself before his eyes.

"It is about time, young Stric!" His pulse jumped. The words melted away, new letters forming in their place.

"Greetings! I am Talnar," the script unfurled with theatrical flourish, "keeper of records, journal of the Grandmasters, repository of knowledge for the Magicians Guild, and presently a very patient book lying forgotten on a log!" The words drained from the page as the next formed. "I was beginning to think you'd wander off in a daze and leave me here flipping my pages until I faded into dust!"

Stric raised an eyebrow. A slow breath out. On top of everything that had happened since he woke, an impatient book that thought itself funny.

"If that was your idea of funny, I'm afraid your humour needs a bit of work," Talnar wrote, the words wiggling across the page.

His fingers trembled against the leather binding. *A talking book. A mind-reading, talking book.* His free hand pinched the bridge of his nose. Pain sparked, sharp and real. *Not dreaming, then.* His gaze dropped to the pages, where new words were already forming.

"Neither dreaming nor insane, young Stric," Talnar's words flowed with gentle certainty. "I know my existence seems impossible. Easy enough to explain, though."

"Well, then, explain it." Stric settled back against the log. "Because right now I'm lost in a forest with no idea where I am or where I'm supposed to go."

"Patience, young Stric. First, you must understand. Long ago, when magic was new and..." The words halted mid-sentence. Pages rustled irritably. "Actually, that history lesson can wait. You're rather anxious about being lost, aren't you?"

Stric's hands spread wide. "I don't know where we are, which direction to go, or what our destination even is."

"That," Talnar wrote, "is simple. We are going to find Prince Dreese."

"But how do we find him? We are lost in the middle of nowhere!"

"Vrill and I visited him as a newborn. His tiny hand touched me. I know his spirit, and through me, you know his spirit. Your magic will do the rest. You do know how to cast a simple compass spell? Don't you? Focus it on your Powerstaff, and it will pull toward him."

Stric stood, raising the Powerstaff. Its surface hummed under his touch, warmer than training sessions, more responsive, as if the wood itself recognised the urgency. His grip steadied. Whatever lay ahead, at least he wasn't truly alone.

"Wait," he paused before beginning the incantation. "I still don't understand why Vrill chose me for this. I'm just an apprentice. Others were more qualified."

His shoulders sagged as if carrying stones invisible to all but him. The Powerstaff wavered in his grip, requiring both hands to steady it. The crystal's surface reflected his drawn face.

"That," the letters materialising more slowly, "is a question that will answer itself in time. For now, trust that Grandmaster Vrill chose wisely. Trust in your abilities, even if you don't yet understand their full extent."

His grip on the Powerstaff steadied. His spine straightened. The wood had warmed in his hands. The crystal sat still.

"Now," rose the words, "cast your spell. But prepare yourself. The magic may feel different from expected."

Stric raised the Powerstaff higher, the crystal at its tip warming beneath his focus. He whispered the incantation, each word vibrating through his bones. As the spell took hold, the staff's warmth deepened. Something moved through the wood into his palms. Not the single clean thread his training had built. Something layered. Two things at once.

A sudden tug from the Powerstaff jerked him sideways, an invisible force guiding with determination. The magic hummed through him, not the single clear note from his training, but in layered vibrations echoing through his bones. Multiple frequencies harmonising. He'd never felt magic respond this way.

His knees buckled slightly. The spell drained him faster than it should have.

"Interesting," appeared as Stric glanced down at the pages. "Did you notice anything unusual about how the spell felt?"

"It flowed more easily than expected." He turned the staff in his hands, frowning. The weariness in his shoulders made no sense. A compass spell shouldn't have cost this much. "And something else, like an echo or..."

"A harmonic resonance."

The text completed itself before Stric had stopped speaking.

"What does that mean?"

"Perhaps nothing. Perhaps everything. Time will tell." The words faded, replaced by new text. "For now, follow the Powerstaff's guidance. Prince Dreese awaits, and there is much work to be done."

Talnar's pages rustled in the gentle forest breeze, as if the ancient tome was pleased with how things were progressing. The Powerstaff continued to urge him forward, though the magical drain made each moment require more deliberate effort. He placed the book in his breast pocket and followed the tugging staff, the pull insistent against his palm, its warmth deepening when he aligned with it.

The first day passed through a relentless green landscape. Stric pushed through underbrush that caught at his robes, following the Powerstaff's pull. Vines draped between ancient trunks. Roots twisted across his path. Golden light pierced the canopy in dusty shafts.

The forest breathed around him, rustling leaves, distant bird calls, chittering creatures that fell silent at his approach. But twice, the silence persisted after he passed. Twice, he felt eyes tracking his movements. When he stopped to listen, the undergrowth rustled fifty paces behind. When he moved, it stopped.

By evening, his legs burned with each step. He collapsed against a tree trunk, breath ragged, and pulled Talnar from his pocket. Bark pressed rough against his spine.

"How much farther?"

"Distance matters less than direction. Rest. Recover your strength."

Stric's fingers traced the leather binding. Warmth spread from the tome onto his lap. "You said you'd explain how you came to be." His stomach cramped with hunger, but his gaze stayed fixed on the pages. Something rustled in the darkness beyond the faint glow of the Powerstaff.

"Very well. Though you should know," the words paused, as if Talnar were gathering patience, "this explanation works better if you don't fall asleep halfway through. I've had students snore through my best material."

Images appeared on the page opposite the words. Drawings that moved and shifted like memories made visible. "Picture this. A time when the air buzzed with discovery. Magic was new and dangerous. Eager fools wielded power without understanding, always the same sequence: discovery, overreach, ruin."

Charcoal scenes unfolded in the gathering dusk. A boy cradling a crystal, wind exploding through the classroom, papers scattering, the teacher's face flushed with fury. A merchant's smirk as prices climbed at his stall while nearby spices withered under his gaze.

"Reckless manipulation led to tragic consequences," the text continued. The images darkened. A village reduced to ash and rubble, smoke spiralling skyward like ghostly tendrils. Stric could almost hear the echoes of laughter now suffocated beneath soot-stained silence.

An anguished face, eyes wide with terror, mouth agape mid-cry. Around the figure, chaotic magic swirled like storm clouds, trailing darkness that whispered of regret. The unknowing wielding power without grasping its consequences.

Another figure cloaked in shadows, eyes glimmering with malicious glee. Darker magic writhed around them like serpents, coiling around vibrant flowers that withered in their wake. Intent prevailed here, malevolence unleashed with full knowledge.

His eyelids dragged downward. The charcoal drawings faded as Talnar's pages stilled. Sleep came fitfully. Stomach cramping. Dreams bleeding together, empty chairs at Academy tables, Pelter's grin fading to ash, Eldena's laughter echoing through burning halls. He woke gasping, bark rough against his back, dawn still hours away.

In the darkness, something large moved through the undergrowth. Deliberate. Measured steps. A slow arc around his position, never closer, never farther. Circling. Patient. The sound whispered through ferns like a promise kept, a hunter confident enough to take its time. Stric's fingers found Talnar's binding. The ancient warmth settled against his palm, but his body had nothing left to give. His eyelids grew heavy again despite the threat. The rustling continued its patient orbit, but the sound grew distant, muffled, as if heard through deepening water. His breathing slowed. The world dimmed. Sleep dragged him under like an undertow he couldn't fight. The sound moved away through the forest, abandoning him in search of weaker prey.

Cold woke him. Dawn's light filtered through the leaves in shifting patterns, and with consciousness came thirst, fierce and immediate. The morning brought confirmation of what the night had held. Near his makeshift camp, massive paw prints pressed deep into the soft earth, leading in a deliberate circle around where he'd slept.

Moss clung to every surface, thick and vibrant, while ferns unfurled fronds the size of his arm. The air hung thick with moisture, carrying sweet decay and rotting vegetation, and underneath, a musk he didn't recognise. Territorial.

He found a muddy puddle collected in a tree hollow. The warm, gritty liquid slid down his throat. His hands shook as he lifted the second palmful to his lips. Fifty paces behind, the undergrowth cracked. He froze, water dripping between his fingers. Silence. Then, slow, deliberate movement. Circling.

He didn't wait to see what emerged. The compass spell pulled him forward, and he followed, stumbling over roots that seemed to reach for his ankles. The Powerstaff grew heavier in his grip, and the simple spell now required deliberate concentration.

Hours blurred together as he pushed deeper into the forest. The sun tracked invisible overhead, its passage marked only by the shifting quality of light filtering through the canopy. Morning's golden glow faded to the harsh brightness of the afternoon, then softened into the amber wash of late day. His legs moved more through habit than will, each step a negotiation with a body that threatened mutiny.

Thorny vines snagged his robes. The canopy thickened overhead, dimming the light to perpetual twilight. Strange fungi glowed faintly from tree trunks, phosphorescent blues and greens that would make him visible in the darkness. He pushed faster, ignoring protesting muscles.

In one hollow, a deer carcass lay undisturbed by scavengers, flesh withered and grey rather than rotting, as if something had drawn the life from it without touching the body. The wrongness made his skin crawl. He moved faster.

The afternoon wore on, shadows lengthening into dark pools between the ancient trees. The world swam before him. Twice, he caught himself mid-stumble, the Powerstaff the only thing keeping him upright. The forest sounds shifted when he moved, branches rustling where no wind blew, undergrowth settling after his passage as if something else had disturbed it moments before. Each time he stopped to catch his breath. Silence. Then, the whisper of movement just beyond sight.

When evening finally arrived, painting the forest in shades of grey and violet, Stric could go no further. His legs buckled beneath him, and he collapsed against a fallen log. He sat, chest heaving. Talnar remained in his pocket. His hands wouldn't move.

The forest settled around him. Twilight deepened between the trees, turning familiar shapes into strange and threatening ones. Somewhere distant, a bird called its last note before darkness claimed the canopy. Hunger seized his stomach, claws tearing at his insides, but even the thought of food made his throat tighten with nausea.

When he finally withdrew Talnar, the book's pages rustled with unusual insistence, as if it had been waiting impatiently for his attention. Words appeared immediately, bold and determined.

"You saw the chaos yesterday," Talnar's words formed slower, as if sensing Stric's flagging attention. "But from darkness came order. King Balthor dispatched his advisor Kanath to recruit the most experienced and virtuous magic practitioners across Veltak. Virtuous being the keyword, they'd seen enough damage from ambitious fools."

New images formed. A grand hall with a vaulted ceiling adorned with celestial motifs representing the duchies. King Balthor emerged from the charcoal strokes, his regal cloak billowing behind him as he proclaimed his decree, shadows curling around him like tendrils of fate.

Hundreds of distinct silhouettes filled an assembly room beneath flickering candlelight. Determination was etched into every face. Ambition and fear glinted in every eye.

A branch snapped in the darkness beyond the Powerstaff's faint glow. Close. Too close. Stric's hand found the staff, fingers wrapping around wood still warm from earlier magic. He held his breath, listening. The forest held its silence for three heartbeats, four, before the undergrowth whispered with a slow, retreating movement.

His grip loosened, though his pulse was still pounding against his ribs. The charcoal images on Talnar's pages waited patiently, as if the ancient book understood interruption was part of survival in these woods.

"One hundred and thirteen individuals convened in Talnaress," the text continued, "where King Balthor requested them to establish a council and academy dedicated to the instruction and study of magic."

Stric watched twelve sigils inscribed within a circle appear on the page, with a thirteenth at the centre. "They elected thirteen council members," Talnar wrote. "These thirteen then voted on the Grandmaster who was to lead. They chose Grandmaster Acher."

An ornate scroll unfurled in the drawing, its illuminated letters detailing Balthor's proclamation. The announcement of the academy's creation and the prohibition against magic wielded outside the Guild's walls.

Stric's vision blurred as the last images faded. His throat burned, parched beyond the muddy water's meagre relief. The gnawing in his belly had become something sharper, a constant ache hollowing him from within. Thirty paces distant, golden eyes reflected in the faint glow. Low to the ground. Unblinking. The undergrowth rustled, not one creature, but two. Three. A guttural sound rolled through the darkness. Not quite a growl. Not quite speech. Testing.

His fingers found the Powerstaff. The wood hummed, but his magic felt thin, stretched. One spell, perhaps. Maybe two. Then nothing.

Desperate magic erupted from the Powerstaff. Wild. Searing. Everything he had left blazed white, tearing through the darkness. The golden eyes vanished. Undergrowth crashed as the creatures retreated, fleeing from the brightness.

The light died. His hands shook violently. The Powerstaff's crystal dimmed to barely a glow. That single burst had drained him more than a day's worth of compass spells. His body sagged against the tree, consciousness flickering.

Talnar's warmth pulsed against his chest. Steady. The last anchor before darkness claimed him completely.

Grey pre-dawn light filtered through the trees when consciousness returned.

His body ached. Mouth tasted of dust and copper. For a heartbeat, he couldn't remember where he was. Hunger twisted his gut. The forest. The creatures. His dwindling magic.

The golden eyes were gone, but claw marks scored the tree ten paces from where he'd collapsed. Fresh. Deep. A message carved in wood: We could have reached you.

He moved before full consciousness returned. Grabbed the Powerstaff. Stumbled forward, following the compass spell's pull with single-minded desperation.

Shaking hands gripped low-hanging branches for support, the bark rough against his palms. Humid air pressed into his lungs, thick and warm, a weight his body hadn't trained for. He swiped at the sweat blurring his vision.

The forest changed, trees growing massive, trunks wide enough for three men standing shoulder to shoulder. Roots erupted in twisted archways. Lianas thick as his thigh draped from branches high above.

Behind him, the predators maintained a distance. Shadows pacing shadows. Patient. Letting exhaustion do their work.

The sun tracked its descent, light bleeding from the canopy until shadows merged into twilight. When he could no longer distinguish roots from shadows, when his legs refused another step, he stopped. A dead tree became his rest, bark cold against his spine. Talnar's pages rustled in his pocket with unusual insistence. He withdrew the book, and words appeared.

"You need to understand what I am," Talnar wrote. "Not just what I contain, but how I came to be."

The charcoal images showed thirteen magicians hunched over a circular table, their spectral fingers etching invisible patterns in the dusky air. Their eyes exchanged cryptic glances as they unravelled mysteries together.

"Grandmaster Acher determined that knowledge must outlive its Grandmasters," the text flowed. "He proposed that each council member contribute a part of themselves. Opening their minds and hearts to share all their experiences and gained knowledge. The council unanimously agreed."

Stric leaned closer, fatigue forgotten as the scene unfolded. The thirteen figures glowed, their combined magic swirling above the table in branching threads, each one distinct before folding into the next.

"The spell was cast within a month." This drawing showed thirteen magicians circling a radiant tome. Talnar himself. Light danced across jubilant faces. "And I was born. Seventy-four Grandmasters over a millennium; their knowledge, successes, failures, discoveries, all here. This is why Vrill entrusted me to you."

Stric's throat closed. Swallowing hurt. His fingers traced the book's worn cover. Seventy-four Grandmasters between worn leather and parchment. Every failure and discovery from Grandmaster Acher's Guild, warm against his trembling hands.

The words blurred. Fever burned behind his eyes, turning the forest into a wavering green inferno. Sleep pulled at him like an undertow as he tucked Talnar away.

His eyelids dragged downward, heavy as stones. For one breath, silence. The forest held still, waiting.

The undergrowth exploded.

Golden eyes burst from the darkness, massive shapes lunging from three sides at once. No more patience. No more circling. The pack had decided.

Stric rolled sideways, fingers finding the Powerstaff through pure instinct. Magic erupted. Wild. Desperate. Everything he had left. Light blazed white-hot, searing through the clearing. Tendrils of white light burst from the crystal, crawling across the ground in branching patterns. Seeking. They found the first creature and wrapped around its legs in crackling brilliance. The beast shrieked, convulsing as the energy coursed through it. The tendrils surged onward, hunting the others. Golden eyes scattered as the magic lashed out, serpentine and furious, driving the pack back with each searing touch. The creatures shrieked, recoiling from the assault, their coordinated attack breaking into a panicked retreat.

The light died.

The edges of the world softened to ash. The Powerstaff fell from his hands, crystal dark and cold. Empty. He'd burned through every reserve, every scrap of strength. His legs wouldn't hold him. The forest tilted sideways.

He hit the ground hard. Couldn't move. Couldn't lift his head. Talnar's weight rested against his chest through his robes, the only warmth left in his body.

Stric's vision narrowed to a tunnel, then a pinprick.

Then nothing.

Chapter 3

Trust Takes Root

Consciousness returned in fragments. Grey light. Damp earth beneath his cheek. The Powerstaff's crystal dim beside his outstretched hand. Stric's fingers found bark, rough against his palm as he hauled himself upright. Every muscle fought him. His shoulders refused to roll forward, spine locked at angles that drove hot needles through his lower back, hips grinding with each attempted shift. He was still alive.

The forest held its breath around him. Too quiet after the night's violence. No golden eyes watched from the shadows. No guttural sounds tested the darkness. The predators had fled, had to have fled. Nothing stayed near prey that fought back with that kind of desperation.

He gathered the Powerstaff, using it to lever himself fully upright. When his hand closed around the smooth wood, his breath was released. He hadn't known he was holding it. The staff's familiar weight. The crystal's dormant pulse. The grooves in the wood, familiar beneath his damaged palms. Talnar's weight pressed reassuringly against his chest through his robes. Four days without food. One night, fighting for his life. His body demanded rest, but the compass spell still pulled forward, insistent as the tide.

The pull became everything. It lived in his feet, not his thoughts. His feet found the path without consulting his mind. Trees passed like ghosts at the edge of vision. Green becoming grey becoming green again. The forest breathed. He breathed with it. Each step was a half-conscious surrender to the staff's urgency.

Time dissolved. The sun tracked overhead, unfelt. His hand whitened around the wood, the only anchor to waking thought. Forward. Always forward.

Images flickered through his mind like fever dreams. His body collapsed against a nameless tree, flesh becoming soil, bones becoming roots. The forest, patient as stone, waiting to claim what exhaustion delivered. Birds circling. His final resting place marked only by moss and silence.

The spell knew something his exhausted body had forgotten. Stopping meant never starting again.

His awareness finally sharpened when a rustling like a bird trapped in fabric came from his pocket, snapping him back to the present. He jolted as the rustling became frantic tapping against his chest. His fingers trembled as he reached into his pocket and pulled out Talnar.

The familiar weight settled into his grip, and the trembling in his fingers eased as the cover flew open, revealing large lettering across the page. "Stop that." The words dissolved, new letters forming. "Vrill didn't send you to rot in a forest. Look around."

His eyes swept over the dense underbrush that framed a narrow, beaten path. At first glance, the path resembled another game trail, bigger than most he had come across. But as he looked closer, distinct impressions of footprints came into view. The prints overlapped each other, heading in both directions. Soles had packed the path tight, leaves worn smooth and scattered as though brushed aside each day.

"Thank you, Talnar." He exhaled, and the corners of his mouth moved. Something tentative against four days of grim effort. "People. Both ways lead to people." He glanced down the paths, each promising mystery and discovery. He weighed them in silence. "So, I guess I'll pick one." He tucked Talnar back into his pocket, the book's warmth spreading through his fingers, and nodded. One more look down each path. He set off to the left in measured strides.

After travelling the well-worn path for a short time, staying alert for any sign of people, he caught the scent of cold water. Sharp. Mineral. The forest's warm damp cut away by it. Bird calls, distinct and close ahead. He emerged from behind a dense thicket. A small lake, its surface dancing with shards of sunlight, reflecting a sky painted in fathomless blues and pearl-white clouds.

He took a much-needed drink, splashing water over his face, neck, and hair. The clean liquid ran down his throat, refreshing him in a way the muddy puddles could not.

The water cleared his head. Across the lake's far shore, a branch hung at an unnatural angle. Recently snapped, the bark was pale where it had torn. Not wind damage. Too deliberate. Too fresh.

His hand found the Powerstaff without conscious thought. The forest breathed around him, but underneath the normal rustles, something else moved. Pacing. Parallel to his position. Maintaining distance but never losing the trail.

They hadn't fled. They'd simply waited. Patient as stones.

"Someone gets their water here. Back the other way, then." His pace shifted before thought caught up. Faster steps, eyes darting between trees for smoke, structures, any sign of habitation. Every shadow resolved into a potential doorway. Every sound sorted itself into categories: wind, animal, or the possibility of human voices. The scent of cooking meat haunted him, though his nose found only loam and growing things.

Stric made his way back along the narrow path, each step sending a sharp pang through his stomach, yet the promise of relief pushed him forward. Eventually, a modest shelter emerged among the towering trees. His steps faltered. Stopped. Sunlight filtering through the canopy cast patterns across the ground. A sanctuary woven from large interlocking branches formed the walls, and thick leather-like leaves draped across the roof. Against the towering trees, it was a small human thing. Branches lashed where they crossed. The roof leaves dark with age, layered dense against rain.

He paused, listening. The presence that had shadowed him for days had vanished. That patient pacing awareness. Gone.

The absence hit him harder than the pursuit had. Predators didn't abandon tracked prey. Not unless something worse had entered the territory. Something that made golden-eyed hunters flee rather than feed.

He moved towards the shelter, each step measured and silent. Ears and eyes strained for signs of welcome or warning. A gentle murmur drifted through the trees. A woman's voice, tinged with urgency and barely discernible. His steps slowed, but did not stop. His free hand moved to the Powerstaff.

He couldn't see the rear of the dwelling through the tangle of branches and sprawling bushes. The voice had come from behind it. He picked his way around. The sight of a young woman stopped him cold.

She stood in a small clearing, long golden hair flowing down her back. Her green eyes were darting continuously, mapping escape routes while her weight shifted to the balls of her feet. Every muscle in her frame coiled with readiness, the posture of someone who had learned to turn terror into strategy.

Every rustle in the undergrowth pressed against his chest. She focused on something beyond his view. Her feet planted wide, knees bent. Her breathing controlled.

As he edged closer, cold seeped through the damp at his collar, into the back of his neck. She shifted position. He took another step out from the cover provided by the bush. Towering above the young woman loomed a monstrous golem. An immense form composed of interwoven stone and dirt. The creature's body formed an intimidating amalgamation of jagged rocks and clumps of earth.

Its eyes glowed with an eerie green light. Pulsating with every movement. A colossal hand rose above her, its shadow swallowing the clearing, stone dragging the air down with it.

She dove sideways, rolling smoothly across the earth. A massive stone fist crushed the space where she'd stood. Dirt exploded in all directions, but she was already moving, coming up in a defensive crouch. Her eyes darted around the clearing. Searching for anything she could use as a weapon or an advantage.

The forest dissolved. Trees, woman, dwelling, all bleeding to grey at the edges of his vision. Only the golem remained sharp. Only the raised fist. Only the crystal atop his staff, warming beneath his white-knuckled grip as power built along his arm, and spreading beneath skin like lightning seeking ground.

With a swift arc of his arm, Stric brandished the Powerstaff. An incantation tumbled from his lips as he spoke ancient words known by heart. "Shield her!"

A shimmering barrier of blue light enveloped the young woman, casting a glow over her alert face. With a thunderous crash, the golem's massive fist struck the barrier. It shattered. Fragments rained down around her, glittering in the sunlight. The golem roared. A guttural sound that reverberated through the earth and left Stric's ears ringing. His knees wavered, unsteady beneath him, but he pushed forward.

Stric had no choice. Attack or die. His fingers found the staff's grain. His breath dropped deep. The magic came slowly, dragging through channels scraped raw, but it came. The staff's crystal glowed a brilliant white. Brighter. Brighter still. His energy drained with each pulse.

A searing beam erupted from the crystal. Blue-white light struck the golem's chest. The impact resonated through its massive frame. The creature lurched backward. Thin fractures spider-webbed across its rocky surface. Shards broke off with sharp cracks.

Stric's muscles locked. Sweat broke across his brow. He poured his last reserves into the spell. The beam intensified. Bright light flooded the clearing. The golem's eyes flickered like dying embers as the cracks deepened. Spreading further.

The Powerstaff thrummed in his grip, pulse resonating through his bones. The golem's eyes flickered. Once. Twice. Then went out. Cracks deepened across its chest, spreading like frost across window glass. The construct shuddered once. Then collapsed. Stone crashed to earth in segments, each piece losing cohesion, leaving only rubble and silence.

His knees buckled. Each breath scraped raw. His hands trembled. He pressed his free hand against a tree as the world tilted. The Powerstaff felt like deadweight in his trembling grasp.

The barrier faded, dissolving into the air. Through the settling dust, the woman stood, still on her feet. Still breathing. The Powerstaff suddenly weighed nothing in his hands. His knees threatened to unlock entirely, sending him to the ground in a heap, but he locked them. Forced himself forward.

Each step required conscious effort as he reached her side. She straightened. Her keen eyes assessed him with the same intensity she'd shown when facing the golem, as if calculating whether he posed a different threat.

"Are you alright?" Stric asked, checking her for wounds, his free hand pressing harder against the Powerstaff to keep himself upright.

"I'm fine." Her voice was clipped, edges sharp as flint. She took a deliberate step back, maintaining a distance between them as fingers sought the knife at her waist. "What do you want?"

"Want?" The word arrived ahead of its meaning. His jaw stalled. "I just... You were in danger. That thing would have..."

"I know what it would have done." She cut him off, jaw tight. "Barok Tana's Spellcasters don't risk themselves for strangers. What's your price? Information? Service? What do you want from me?" Her eyes narrowed. She studied his face with the systematic patience of someone cataloguing what she found. "Or do you expect gratitude to buy you something else?"

"There's no price... I saw someone in danger and..." His gaze dropped from her face to the Powerstaff in his trembling hands, then back to her watchful eyes. How could he explain that no price existed when she clearly lived in a world where everything cost something?

"And played the hero." Her stance changed. Her weight settled back on her heels. Ready to move but no longer coiled to strike. Her hand drifted from her blade's hilt, hovering instead near her belt. Still cautious, but the knife remained sheathed.

Her gaze fell to his hands, where they gripped the staff. Calloused palms and dirt beneath his nails. Her brow furrowed. Her gaze dropped to his hands again, then back to his face.

"How convenient that you were nearby. How fortunate for me!" Her voice held its scepticism, though the edge of it had dulled. "Spellcasters always have reasons. Always want something. So tell me what you want, or leave me alone."

Stric's shoulders drew back despite his exhaustion. His voice came steady, each word deliberate. "I am no Spellcaster of Barok Tana! I am Stric Deamara, an apprentice magician of the Magicians Guild." He raised the Powerstaff, holding it out for her inspection. His voice carried quiet pride, the kind born from belonging to something he believed mattered. "I received this Powerstaff from Grandmaster Vrill, who entrusted me to carry it."

She looked at the staff. Not at him. At the staff. Her chin came down a fraction. Her fingers, which had been moving near the knife at her belt, went still. The runes, the crystal, the particular quality of the light moving in its depths. Something in there held her eyes for a long moment. Her lips parted. Closed again. Her hands curled at her sides. The cost of what she saw moved across her face.

"The Grandmasters and the Magicians Guild were destroyed before I was even born." Her voice was quieter than before. The accusation still there, but smaller. "You must be an agent of Barok."

His jaw tightened at the name. Something moved through his face that hadn't been invited there. His knees wavered, and he caught himself against the Powerstaff with more force than intended.

"I am no agent of Barok. He will never be my master. I seek to oppose him!" His grip on the staff whitened between words. The tremor in his shoulders deepened. "The one who sent me was a teacher, an educator in the proper practice of magic."

She studied his stance, his expression, the way he held the Powerstaff with the careful respect of one taught to revere its power. Her breathing slowed as she considered his words.

He had destroyed the golem. Not captured it. He did not command it to stop while he questioned her. He destroyed it, at obvious cost to himself, before saying a single word to her.

"How long has it been since the Magicians' Guild was destroyed?" He placed each word with care. His grip tightened on the Powerstaff as he spoke them.

"Twenty years ago, just before I was born." Her brow furrowed, and she tilted her head. "Why do you ask?"

"So, I have been gone for twenty years. Everything has changed." The words came out hollow.

Twenty years. The number pressed into his chest. He stood in a world that had kept moving without him, and the weight of it settled the way a spent Powerstaff settled in the hand. Wrong. Heavy in the wrong place. Friends. The Academy. Pelter's gap-toothed grin. Twenty years of that, and none of it had waited.

"What do you mean you have been gone for twenty years? You were probably just a baby when it happened!" A thread of something else had entered her voice. Some of the certainty had left it.

He shrugged, focusing on a loose thread on his robe rather than meeting her penetrating gaze. "Forget it. Just my thoughts wandering."

The forest breathed around them. Leaves rustled overhead. Somewhere distant, a bird called tentatively, testing whether danger had passed. Dust still hung in the air where the golem had fallen, catching mid-morning light in golden motes.

"Alright." The word came out reluctantly, pulled from her against better judgment. "You did destroy that golem..." Her jaw tightened. Her eyes dropped from his face, then came back. "... and saved my life."

Her eyes held his. Still searching. Still testing.

"Thank you." The words emerged stiff and unpracticed.

"You are most welcome." Despite everything, something wry found its way into his voice. Brief. Gone before the next word. He tightened his grip on the Powerstaff as his legs reported the bill. "I understand. It baffles me. I can't expect you to make sense of it."

A pause settled between them. He could hear his own ragged breathing in it. She studied him: the sweat on his brow despite the forest's coolness, the shallow rise and fall of his chest, the tremor in his hands.

Her shoulders dropped, tension leaving them by degrees. The knife stayed sheathed. The space between them held.

"You don't look so good," she said. The accusation had drained from her voice. What remained was precise. Measuring.

Stric's attempt at a reassuring smile faltered as his vision blurred at the edges. "I will endure."

"You look like you're about to collapse." She tilted her head, studying him with fresh eyes. "When did you last eat?"

"Four days. Perhaps five." The admission cost him something, a vulnerability he hadn't intended to show. "I've been searching for... for the person I need to find. Haven't stopped much."

Her stance shifted. Her weight settled differently, shoulders dropping by degrees. "You're telling me you destroyed that golem on no food for four days?" She shook her head, and for the first time, something that wasn't suspicion or fear flickered across her face. "That was either very brave or very stupid."

"Perhaps both," Stric admitted.

She glanced over her shoulder at the dwelling she'd built, then back at him, clearly calculating risks and options with the speed of someone whose survival had always depended on such assessments.

"They will track the golem's last location and discover its fate," she said, her voice returning to that practical efficiency. "I must leave here. You should too before they arrive." She moved towards her dwelling with purposeful strides, but paused at the threshold, hand on the doorframe.

"In that case, may I trouble you for something small to eat?" Stric's voice trembled with fatigue, his shoulders slumped as the adrenaline wore off. The emptiness returned, made worse by his magical exhaustion.

She turned back to face him, and for a long moment stood there. She looked at him, swaying. The way his grip on the staff adjusted. The loose hang of his robes on a frame that had shed weight on the road. Her jaw eased. The line between her brows softened.

Her fingers tapped against the doorframe, a rapid calculation visible in the tension of her shoulders. Her gaze swept across the forest. Measuring distances, assessing cover, and counting the hours until dark.

When she looked at him again, the assessment in her eyes had turned. Still measuring. No longer looking for a threat. "Come inside. I won't be able to carry it all anyway. I'll give you a satchel, and you can take what's left over."

Stric paused at the threshold. The word came unbidden, rough in his parched throat. "Thank you."

The sharp-sweet tang of dried herbs reached him as he stepped into the dwelling. Bundled with intent. Feverfew beside willow-bark. Mint near the ginger root. A hunter's pharmacopoeia arranged for rapid selection in darkness or emergency.

Glass jars lined shelves in deliberate progression: grains descending from left to right, preserved fruits ordered by season, each sealed with beeswax that bore her thumbprint. Calculated stores. Each jar was positioned within arm's reach of where she'd need it: the cook pot, the preparation surface, and the door for quick packing.

Tools hung in sequence. Knife near whetstone. Flint beside kindling. He had seen enough hurried camps to recognise the pattern. What was kept close, what was sacrificed when time ran out. This arrangement had been refined. He didn't need to count how many escapes had gone into it.

The rich, mouth-watering aroma of a stew sitting on a rough-hewn log table curled towards him, prompting a rumble from his stomach.

The woman moved through the space with practised efficiency, stuffing provisions into two satchels. She knew exactly what to take for travel, which items were essential, and which could be left behind.

She paused occasionally, her eyes flickering to him where he stood just inside the threshold. Assessing. Always assessing. Ensuring that this calculated risk didn't escalate into a threat. Her hand never strayed far from the knife at her belt, even as she worked.

At the sound from his stomach and his eyes going to the pot, she gestured toward the table. "Go ahead, sit and eat what you can. But be quick."

Stric settled down with a weary sigh, resting his Powerstaff against the table beside him. He plunged a spoon into the hearty broth with eager hunger, each mouthful spreading warmth through his chest in rings. The way heat moves from banked coals. Incremental. Reaching places he'd stopped expecting to feel warm again. He devoured the meal in moments, scraping the last morsel from the bowl with a piece of bread.

The woman finished her preparations, her eyes darting to the empty bowl as she dropped a supply-filled satchel on the table. "Take this and move if you want to leave before anyone arrives."

His gut clenched. He doubled over as his body rejected what it had craved moments before. Cold sweat beaded his forehead while he tried to keep the meal down. The rich scents that had made his mouth water now overwhelmed him.

His stomach churned, threatening to send the meal back the way it came. Cold sweat dotted his brow as he struggled to steady his quivering hands. Stric knew he had to push forward. He picked up the satchel, retrieved the Powerstaff, and took measured breaths, trying to calm his rebelling gut and gather what little strength remained.

Each step required tremendous effort. His muscles shook as though the effort of standing had debts due on it. Minutes of easy movement traded for these staggering ones. He clenched his jaw, urging himself forward, his legs sending back information his mind didn't want.

"Now you look worse." She stepped closer, her hand settling on his arm with surprising gentleness. "Are you going to be alright?"

Her hand settled on his arm. Wood smoke and wild herbs. The nausea that had threatened to send the food back up eased. Quieter. His rib cage expanded fully. Air reached where it couldn't before. One complete breath, with room in it.

Strange. With one touch, the world steadied.

"I will go on." He leaned against the doorframe. The words rang flat.

Her fingers drummed a rapid pattern against her satchel strap. Her gaze swept the forest. Trees, shadows, the hours remaining until dark. When she looked at him again, the set of her mouth had changed. Something in her jaw had resolved from assessment to decision.

"You won't last an hour alone like this." Her voice carried the weight of someone who had already done the calculations. "I can't just let you leave." She straightened her shoulders. "I'll travel with you, at least until you're back on your feet." A tactical decision made by someone who understood the value of capable allies.

His knees unlocked. The doorframe caught him. It's rough wood pressed into his palm as he steadied himself. She would travel with him. He had asked nothing of her. Offered nothing in return. And she had said yes anyway.

"You would do that?" The question had barely passed his lips. "Travel with a stranger? When you don't even trust me?"

"I don't trust you," she confirmed, her eyes meeting his with unflinching honesty. "But you destroyed that golem at great cost to yourself. That counts for something." She secured her satchel over her shoulder with practised ease. "And maybe... maybe you're not what I thought you were. Time will tell."

The worn cauldron hanging in the hearth caught her attention. Her fingers traced the doorframe, reading the knots in the wood like old stories.

A last look at the dwelling that had kept her safe: the worn cauldron, the bundled herbs, the knife marks scoring the preparation surface. Shelter. The cold hearth's ash still on the air. Survival.

All of it left behind for a stranger with a staff too beautiful to be a lie.

She crossed the threshold. Her boot found forest soil. Cold through the sole, the damp immediate, the ground giving slightly under her weight. Pine resin hit her first, sharp through the cool air. Loam underneath. The faint rot of leaf litter. Two days of rain, maybe three.

"Come on then," she said, not looking back at him as she adjusted the weight of her pack. "If we're doing this, we should move. Distance between us and this place before they arrive."

The canopy above the path broke into scattered panels of light, thirty feet of visibility ahead before the trees closed it off. She could read the ground that far. No more. She moved with purpose, not looking back at what she'd built, what she'd protected, what she now abandoned.

Ahead lay paths she'd never walked. Dangers she couldn't predict. A companion she didn't trust but couldn't quite dismiss.

Behind them, the shelter stood empty. Smoke fading from a cold hearth. Herbs still hanging in careful bundles. A life she'd built alone, now left for the forest to reclaim.

She'd fled before. But never toward something. Never with someone.

She had spent years building something tighter than the dwelling's interlocked branches. One belief, tested against everything she'd lost, confirmed by all of it. All who wielded power were the same. She had never found a joint that failed.

One man was now putting pressure on a single crossing point.

She didn't know whether this choice would prove wise or foolish. She didn't know if Stric Deamara would prove himself worthy of walking beside her. But her feet kept moving. Her hand stayed away from the blade.

Her mother's old stories. The ones about magicians who protected rather than preyed. The ones she'd stopped believing in when she was eight.

The stories hadn't prepared her for the weight of a man barely standing, using his staff to stay upright rather than to command. They hadn't prepared her for a golem destroyed before a single word was spoken. They hadn't prepared her for being asked when he could have taken.

Stric stumbled slightly, catching himself on his staff. His knee dropped an inch before the wood held him. He kept moving. Exhausted, visibly and entirely, but still placing one foot ahead of the other, still following whatever mission drove him forward despite every reason to stop.

Her hand moved fractionally from her blade.

Not trust. Not yet.

But now there was the possibility of it.

Chapter 4

Lessons Learned

The dense canopy wrapped around them, pine scent thick in the humid air. Bird songs echoed through the distance, falling silent at irregular intervals as if sensing unseen watchers. Ahead, the woman moved with efficient purpose, her pace steady and uncompromising.

Stric's knuckles whitened around the Powerstaff. He drove it into the ground like a walking stick, using it to haul himself forward one step at a time. The shaft jarred against his palm with each impact. His lungs argued. His feet pushed forward anyway. Each one required conscious effort, but he kept his gaze on the woman's back as he struggled to match her pace. Every rustle in the underbrush snapped his gaze to shadows too deep, too dark.

The woman glanced back, eyes surveying the treeline behind them before resting on him. Her head tilted as if catching sounds he couldn't hear. When the birdsong fell silent, her hand drifted toward the knife at her waist. She waited, scanning the forest, then continued forward without comment.

Neither spoke. The woman's boots found solid ground with practised certainty while Stric's stumbled over roots and caught on undergrowth. His breath came ragged. Sweat plastered his robes to his back.

When his laboured breathing grew too loud to ignore, she slowed. Her stride shortened to match his.

The forest felt different from his first nights alone. No golden eyes tracked his movement from the undergrowth. No patient presence stalked just beyond their trail. His shoulders, which had spent days coiled with tension, eased. His grip on the Powerstaff relaxed from desperation to something steadier; his steps found a rhythm. By midday, when sunlight filtered through the canopy at its brightest, his voice emerged, cutting through the quiet forest air.

"I realise I never asked for your name. You've been so kind to me, and here I am, a stranger."

The woman slowed her pace. Her shoulders tensed before she turned to look back at him. She studied his face for a long moment, as though weighing something she couldn't quite name. Her fingers fidgeted with the edge of her sleeve. When she finally spoke, her voice carried a gentler cadence than before, quieter. "It's Teela. Teela Reyna."

The words hung in the air between them.

Stric nodded. "Thank you, Teela." He took a deep breath as he searched for the right words. "For everything."

Teela nodded. She tucked a strand of hair behind her ear, and after scanning the treeline, she turned her gaze back to the path ahead.

Stric's gaze drifted toward Teela. Sunlight caught in her long blonde hair as she turned at a distant sound, a bird leaving a branch. Her gaze tracked its source before sweeping the treeline, missing nothing. When she looked back at him, her expression held the same attentiveness.

Teela's hands guided branches aside rather than forcing them. She stepped around delicate ferns, choosing her footing without slowing her pace. She navigated obstacles that made Stric stumble as if following an invisible path.

Stric matched his breathing to her steady rhythm. For the first time since arriving in this forest, his chest eased, his steps surer.

The lake he had left earlier came into view, its surface alive with ripples, a cold smell rising off the water. Teela's pace slowed as they approached the water's edge. Birdsong moved through the canopy above. Stric's grip on the Powerstaff eased.

"Wait," Teela's voice cut through the serenity as she held up her hand. Her eyes moved across the shoreline, into the shadows beneath overhanging branches, and along the waterline where footprints might show. "We'll make this quick. We need to keep moving."

Her fingers brushed against the smooth leather lining as she rummaged through her satchel to retrieve two water-skins. She passed one to Stric. He accepted it, his grip settling around the leather, his gaze holding hers a beat past the exchange.

Teela knelt beside the lake and submerged her waterskin. Water gurgled in with gentle bubbling. Stric crouched next to her, fingers brushing smooth stones as he filled his borrowed waterskin. Ripples spread between them.

Stric's eyes flicked from Teela to the horizon, thumb tracing his waterskin's edge. His hands tightened around the leather. The vast forest stretched in every direction. Endless trees, endless isolation.

Teela's fingers sealed the waterskin without looking, cap and strap in two movements. Stric swallowed hard. The words formed and dissolved on his tongue three times before he found breath to speak them.

Stric hesitated, his gaze darting between her intent face and the horizon. He drew a breath, the words hovering unspoken until her steady gaze met his own.

"Teela." His throat closed on the word, his voice steady yet laced with urgency. "There's something I want to tell you about why I'm here in this forest." He paused, watching her reaction.

Teela's eyes flickered with something unreadable. Caution, perhaps, or the instinct to withdraw. Her shoulders drew back, and though she met his gaze, her expression had shuttered, becoming careful and guarded. She gave the barest nod, a gesture that granted permission but promised nothing.

The dense forest breathed around them, sunlight shifting through the canopy above.

"I have been tasked with a mission. I must find someone very important. Someone who holds the key to defeating Barok Tana."

Teela's hand stopped moving toward her waterskin. Her jaw tightened. She turned her face away, fixing her gaze on the lake's surface as if seeing something else reflected there. The muscles in her neck tensed. Her breathing grew shallow. Fingers curled tight around the waterskin until the leather creaked.

The birds fell silent.

She turned away, checking their surroundings. Scanning the treeline, cataloguing shadows, measuring distances to cover.

She blinked, and the present crashed back. His hand lifted, then stilled at his side. Teela forced herself to breathe, to unclench her fists, to press her palms flat against her thighs until the trembling steadied.

"Barok." Her voice emerged barely above a whisper. Caution threaded through her words, but underneath lay something forged in pain.

A shadow passed overhead. Too large for any bird, too swift for any cloud. Teela's head snapped up, tracking movement through the trees that was nothing more than leaves and sky.

"We should be careful in saying that name." She spoke in a barely audible voice. "Many say it has power. That he has ways of hearing it."

Stric nodded, his grip tightening on the Powerstaff. His shoulders bowed as he spoke. "Yes, his rule threatens all who dwell within Veltak. I must find this person and restore him to his rightful place, or all hope will vanish."

Teela studied Stric, her brow furrowed, deepening the shadows in her eyes as she weighed his words. This man. This stranger, who spoke of defeating the very monster who had torn everything from her, sat before her with his gaze level and his hands still on the Powerstaff.

"And you believe this person can stop him?" Her voice held an edge of doubt. Her fingers tapped against her side.

Stric's gaze held steady on hers, not dropping. "I have faith in the prophecy that guides me. The Powerstaff channels magic to lead me to him, and it will aid us against Barok."

Teela reached out, her fingers brushing over the engraved runes on the staff as if testing its truth. The Powerstaff hummed at her touch, sending warmth through the tips of her fingers. Magic. Real magic, responding to her touch. Her fingers pressed harder against the crystal, then went still.

"A spell?" Her fingers drew back from the crystal, slow.

Stric nodded. "Yes, it points me toward the person I'm seeking, leading me closer with each step." As he spoke, the Powerstaff gave a tug, as if showing Teela. "But I fear it's not a journey I can undertake alone..."

"This forest, and how to survive in it, is unknown to me. There are dangers I cannot face by myself." He hesitated, drawing in a breath as if steeling himself against his vulnerability.

"Teela," his voice softened. "Your knowledge of the forest and your unwavering strength could mean our salvation."

Teela folded her arms across her chest, her foot tapping against the crisp, rustling leaves carpeting the forest floor. Her eyes flickered between Stric's earnest gaze and the canopy above, then settled back on his.

Teela's eyes locked on Stric when she looked at him again. "I know that name." She studied Stric's face. The stillness in his hands. The set of his jaw. Her foot stopped tapping. Her arms loosened across her chest.

Teela turned her back on the forest rather than face potential threats. Her shoulders dropped a fraction. The habitual scan of the treeline did not come. She took a deep breath, letting the silence stretch between them before speaking. Her eyes held steady on his, though her jaw worked as if chewing words she couldn't quite swallow.

She glanced at him before her gaze dropped again. Her thumb brushed over a worn spot on the strap of her satchel. "I need you to understand something. That monster... He's the reason..." She paused, swallowing hard. "He took everything. Everyone. I've been out here alone because of him."

He shifted his weight forward, barely an inch.

"Which means," meeting his gaze directly, "this isn't just your quest anymore. I have my reasons for wanting him defeated." Her voice grew stronger, more certain. "I will join you. I have my own reasons."

Stric's grip on the Powerstaff loosened. His shoulders dropped. He sat back heavily, as if the waterskin in his hands had suddenly become too heavy to hold upright. "Thank you, Teela." He paused before continuing. "I cannot express how grateful I am for your support."

Her hand lifted toward his shoulder, fingers hovering in the space between them for a heartbeat before falling back to her side.

"I need to be away from here before dark."

She adjusted the strap of her pack and started walking toward the forest, where a cool breeze carried the earthy scent of fallen vegetation.

"Wait," Stric rose to his feet, brushing dirt from his trousers. "I need to check which direction we should go."

Teela paused several paces ahead, glancing back over her shoulder. A flicker of uncertainty crossed her features before she turned to face him more fully, though her fingers still fidgeted with the strap of her pack.

Stric lifted his Powerstaff and spoke the ancient incantation. The crystal brightened with each syllable, heat building in the wood against his palms. Energy shimmered around him. The air hummed with magic as a glow enveloped the crystal. The Powerstaff pulled northward, the tug distinct in his palms.

Teela's eyes widened at the display, her gaze fixed on the glowing crystal. When the light faded, she studied him for a moment longer, as if reassessing something, then gave a nod. "North, then." Her voice carried a hint of resolve, though her hand remained on her pack strap. A small anchor of caution, she wasn't quite ready to release.

The sun dipped toward the horizon, casting long shadows that stretched like dark fingers through the forest as the temperature dropped. Teela stepped into the clearing, her eyes scanning not just the area but the approaches. She walked the perimeter, pausing at each point where the forest met open space. Her gaze lingered on a boulder formation before she nodded to herself.

"We should find shelter here for the night." The word comfort died unspoken. "We will take turns watching. This clearing offers visibility, but it also makes us visible."

She moved to the centre of the clearing, testing the ground with her foot. "We will make a small fire. Enough to cook with, not enough to signal our location." Her gaze met Stric's. "If anything feels wrong, anything at all, we wake the other immediately."

"Grab some of these large leaves, and I will show you how to make some cover."

Stric wrestled with the leaves. Their tops cool and damp, dry warmth on the undersides. These familiar leaves he'd walked past for days could have been shelter. He'd shivered under open stars when the solution grew all around him.

Teela crouched down and began weaving, her fingers working with nimble precision. She showed him how to peel bark strips from nearby trees, twist them into cords, and layer the leaves like scales on a fish. With each branch Stric placed, the structure grew more solid. Leaves rustled as they draped them over the frame. A roof took shape above their heads.

Teela arranged the last layer, fingers moving with practised efficiency, each leaf overlapping the next.

Stric passed the leaves to Teela. Every movement precise, economical, effective. A smile tugged at the corner of his mouth. He passed her another leaf before she needed to ask.

"Now you can collect some wood for a fire while I prepare something for us to eat." She glanced in his direction. "Unless, of course, you prefer to cook?"

"No, I believe you will do a better job than I. Heating cold stew or beans reaches the extent of my cooking skills." Stric began searching for firewood. "Gathering firewood, however, offers something I have experience with."

Stric returned with another armful of wood and placed it on the pile he had gathered. Teela knelt by the cleared ground, her fingers stacking the kindling with practised precision, her brow furrowed with concentration.

A cool breeze rustled through the leaves as she positioned the last twig. Sitting back, she fixed her eyes on Stric, fingers drumming on her knee.

"Are you going to light this for me, or must I resort to rubbing two sticks together?" Her gaze lingered on Stric. "I collected what I thought I would need, but forgot to include my flint and steel."

"Neither do I. I left without warning and only have what was in my pockets."

"Are you saying that a man with a Powerstaff cannot start a simple fire?" Her arms crossed, the corner of her mouth tight with the effort of not smiling.

Stric's gaze dropped to the ground. His fingers fumbled with the Powerstaff, adjusting his grip twice before settling. Of course, he could start a fire. It ranked among his first learned spells. He squared his shoulders and steadied the staff.

His lips shaped the incantation, each word deliberate and low. The Powerstaff vibrated with magical energy, a low hum that resonated through his hands. The crystal atop it pulsed with a fiery glow, casting an ominous hue across his features. A licking tongue of flame leapt from it, twisting its way towards the kindling. Fire erupted from the wood with a whooshing roar. Heat slammed into them. Teela stumbled backward, arm thrown up to shield her face. Stric backpedalled, nearly tripping over his own robes. Leaves scattered in the blast of hot air. The kindling wasn't burning. It was incinerating.

"Thank you, Stric." Teela brushed leaves from her clothing, her fingers flicking away the remnants of Stric's mishap. Her grin broke sudden and wide, nothing cautious about it.

"You are welcome, Teela." His smile widened at the sound of his name.

"But next time, please try to keep my eyebrows intact." She pressed her lips together against what was almost a smile.

"We're lucky I didn't burn the whole forest down." Stric glanced at the charred remains of branches around them. He inhaled the smoky scent mingled with the crisp evening air, a reminder of his near disaster.

"True." Teela's shoulders shook. The chuckle escaped before she could stop it. "Your aim could use some practice."

"Practice makes perfect." Stric brushed ash from his hands, grinning. "At least we won't be cold tonight."

"I suppose that's one way to look at it. But perhaps next time just a little less... enthusiastic on the fire, okay?"

"I'll try to turn the power down a little." Stric flashed a mischievous grin. "No more singed eyebrows, I promise."

"Good," Teela nodded. She approached the crackling fire, still smiling, and gathered the ingredients for their meal.

While Teela prepared the meal, Stric sat with his back against a tree and removed Talnar from his inner pocket, as had become his habit the last few nights he had travelled alone. The rough bark of the ancient oak pressed cool against his back. He shifted to find a comfortable position. A gentle breeze rustled the leaves above while the aroma of Teela's cooking teased the surrounding air.

Stric glanced over his shoulder at Teela. The line of his shoulders eased. His fingers hesitated on the book's spine. Heat rose to his cheeks. Words weren't needed. Talnar understood his mind's whispers without them.

When Stric read from Talnar, knowledge flowed with startling speed. The words on its pages burned into his mind. The ancient tome revealed its stories and wisdom with eager generosity, seeping into his consciousness.

A routine took shape over the following days. Travel during daylight. Each night, as the fire crackled and Teela prepared their supper, Stric opened Talnar.

The book responded to his inquiries with images and sensations beyond mere words. The incantations he'd struggled to remember yesterday now came to his lips unbidden. His hands found the proper gestures before he consciously thought them through.

His left hand adjusted the staff's angle before he'd finished reading the passage that explained why it mattered. Questions he'd carried since his apprentice days found answers in Talnar's pages. Why certain gestures enhanced specific spells, how magical resonance flowed through crystalline structures. The Grandmasters lived within Talnar's pages, their certainty pressed against his palms through the leather, a weight of knowing that arrived before the words did. When he closed his eyes, the incantations arrived already shaped, already finished, as if recalled rather than learned.

Teela taught him how to survive in the forest during the day. In the evening, Talnar continued his magical teachings.

When Stric lit their next fire, he whispered the incantation instead of shouting it. A gentle flame emerged, licking the kindling with ease. The crystal's glow pulsed in time with his breath. No wild surge this time. Just a steady warmth spreading from the kindling's centre, catching each twig. Teela didn't need to dodge.

Stric still pulled Talnar from his pocket each evening, studying by firelight. But he no longer checked the darkness beyond the flames every few minutes. The golden eyes that had tracked his first nights alone never appeared. He could focus on the ancient text, both hands holding the book, his Powerstaff leaning against the tree beside him rather than clutched across his lap. When a branch cracked in the darkness, his hand moved toward the staff with confidence rather than panic. He could summon a barrier before standing now if needed.

The days blurred together. Each morning brought new terrain, each evening, the ritual of fire and food. Stric found himself watching Teela more. The economy of her movements, the way her eyes never stopped scanning, even when she laughed.

On their fifth night travelling together, darkness settled thick around their campfire. The forest pressed close, cold finding every gap the firelight left. Teela had been quieter than usual throughout the day, her gaze distant, fingers worrying at her knife with an absent rhythm.

While settling in after their evening meal, the firelight caught the tension in her jaw, the way her hands moved through familiar tasks, each motion arriving a beat late, her gaze somewhere past the fire. Stric tucked Talnar back into his pocket without opening it.

The last light painted the leaves copper and bronze. "I've been away," his voice caught like a rough stone in his throat. "What became of Veltak, the magicians, after Barok's attack? The Gui ld..." His words trailed off as he looked at her, searching for signs, perhaps an unspoken promise that not all was lost.

Her fingers tangled together. She bit her lip before speaking. "After the king passed, everything fell apart. Everyone was scared." She paused, eyes distant, then glanced at Stric. "My mum told me how they dragged Master Elrik from his tower. A flash of light cut off his cries." She drew a deep breath. "The apprentices were forced to obey or turn against each other."

A log in the fire collapsed inward with a sharp crack, sending a shower of sparks spiralling into the darkness above. Both of them flinched. Teela's hand moved toward her sword before the orange embers settled back into the flames.

Stric reached for his pack, drawing out his waterskin. He offered it wordlessly, holding it in the space between their blankets. Teela's gaze flickered to the offerings, her jaw tightening as though accepting anything from him might cost more than she could afford. She shook her head once, sharp and decisive.

He didn't withdraw his hand. The firelight played across his knuckles, patient and steady, until finally her fingers reached out and closed around the waterskin. She drank deeply, water trickling from the corner of her mouth before she swiped it away with the back of her hand.

"Mum said Barok's rule suffocates. Still does." Her voice emerged rougher, raw. "He built monuments in all the towns. Massive things, each one protected by Spellcasters." She paused, hands twisting the waterskin in her lap. "The Spellcasters enforce his laws. Anyone who opposes him faces punishment. They carry out raids to eliminate loyalists and rebels."

Stric shifted closer, the movement slow enough that she could track every inch. His hand lifted, hovering near her shoulder, fingers extended but not quite touching. The same hesitation she'd shown him beside the lake.

Teela jerked back, her shoulder pulling away before his fingers could make contact. Her breath came faster, eyes wide in the firelight. But then the tension in her jaw eased. The tight line of her mouth loosened. She held his gaze for three heartbeats, then slowly leaned back toward him until his palm settled against her shoulder.

Neither of them moved.

"Families live in constant fear. Even a whisper of defiance brings consequences. The Guild academy teaches twisted versions of the old practices."

She looked down at his hand on her shoulder, then back to the fire. "Survival is a daily struggle. Heavy taxes fund Barok's greed. Villages lie desolate. Fields untended. Markets empty." She paused. "But some still believe resistance flickers, waiting for the right moment."

The fire crackled between them, its warmth a fragile thing against the weight of all she'd spoken into the night.

Stric's hands trembled. The firelight cast shadows down the lines of his face, deepening each one. "May I ask how you came to be living out here alone?"

Teela shook her head, her eyes distant as if lost in a memory too painful to share. The muscles in her throat worked as she swallowed, and her shoulders curved inward, protecting something fragile within. She lay down, wrapping herself in a blanket they had taken from the soldiers. Stric lingered for a moment before lying down in his own blanket.

"Perhaps another time, Stric."

Her voice drifted to him, barely more than breath against the darkness.

Stric lingered in the silence after her words faded. The fire crackled, sending sparks spiralling into the darkness. His eyes dropped to the fire. "Before I met you, something hunted me. Every night. Golden eyes in the shadows, watching, waiting."

Teela's head tilted. "Forest cats. They're always around, looking for weak prey." She poked the fire with a stick, sending up fresh sparks. "You're not alone anymore. They know it."

"That simple?"

"That simple." She set the stick aside. "They're patient hunters, but not stupid ones. Two targets, one of whom knows how to fight?" She shrugged. "They'll find easier meals."

The casual dismissal of what had terrified him for days loosened a tension he hadn't known he was carrying. The predators had moved on. That mattered. But Teela beside him mattered more.

"I am here when you are ready, Teela. Good night."

Stric lay still. The fire crackled. The space between them filled with darkness. Then Teela's voice reached him, soft yet steady.

"Goodnight, Stric." The sound of it was low and unhurried. Then the fire, and the dark, and nothing else.

Sleep came slowly that night. Stric lay beneath his blanket, listening to the fire's crackling song and Teela's eventual steady breathing. Talnar's weight pressed against his chest through his robes.

The magnitude of what he'd been sent to accomplish pressed down through the dark. What Barok had done. What still needed undoing.

The forest whispered through the darkness. Somewhere beyond the firelight, an owl called. Stric's fingers found Talnar through the fabric, pressing his thumb into the spine's familiar crease. Tomorrow, they would continue north. Tomorrow, one step closer to finding the prince.

Tonight, he could rest.

Chapter 5

Ambitions of the Enemy

The Spellcaster Straves perched on a fallen log as dawn's first light pierced the dense canopy above. He tore off a piece of hardened bread and chewed on dried meat. Sweet birdsong mingled with the crisp fragrance of the awakening forest.

He snapped a twig without rising, the dry wood crumbling to dust in his grip. Dust that coated his fingers, grey and common. He wiped them against his robes with sharp movements. Shafts of golden light turned the morning mist luminous between ancient trunks, painting the woodland in ambers and greens. Here, amongst the rot and roots, he was just another animal chewing hard bread whilst his name gathered dust in the wooden halls of a farming village.

He stared at the endless branches. A shroud. If he died here, the moss would claim him within a week. In the capital, in those gleaming corridors where true power lived and breathed, no one would notice he was gone. That thought chilled him more than the morning mist pressing damp against his skin.

Behind him, the others made their preparations. Corporal Mek shifted his weight with each rustle, scarred fingers drumming against his thigh. Private Jen's grip rested on her sword hilt, sharp eyes cutting through the dimness. A werewolf prowled in tight circles, nostrils flaring at scents Straves had stopped tracking. He turned away from them, already calculating his triumph before Lord Barok. Him alone. The credit his.

The sharp scent of pine and loam pressed against his awareness, thick as the grey dust on his fingers. Rotting leaves squelched beneath his boots as he rose from the log, brushing crumbs from his robes with deliberate care.

He had chosen this expedition, commandeered these soldiers and the werewolf, and led them into the forest because success required witnesses to verify his triumph.

This capture had to be his ascension. It had to be. Ten years he'd spent in the lowly village as lesser mages climbed past him whilst he rotted in garrison duty. Ten years of bowing to a commander who couldn't light a candle with magic, of taking orders from small-town bureaucrats who wouldn't know a Powerstaff from kindling.

He gathered his Powerstaff, the familiar weight settling in his palm. The moment of leaving this wilderness filled his mind. A desperate hunger. The marble corridors. What waited in them? A single pair of eyes. Barok's eyes. He needed Barok to look at him, really look at him, and see that Straves wasn't just another disposable tool ground to dust in service. He needed to matter.

The memory of the handler swinging in the village square rose unbidden. The rope creaking, his boots twitching inches from the mud. Straves' throat tightened, a phantom rope itching at his skin. Even now, three days later, the sensation ghosted across his neck. Delays. Incompetence. The rope that waited for men who failed.

His fingers relaxed against the Powerstaff. The wood held steady beneath his palm. The handler had failed him, so the gallows had taken his life. Straves would not fail. He would feed another to that rope before he let it find his own neck.

Someone with magical abilities had destroyed that golem. A sorcerer bold enough to attack Barok's constructs. His breath quickened, pulse hammering against the phantom sensation still lingering at his throat. If he captured this adversary and presented him to Lord Barok. For acknowledgement. To be seen. To prove he existed as more than a name on a duty roster in some forgotten outpost.

He closed his eyes, summoning the image that sustained him past the rot and the birdsong and the roots that caught at every step. The throne room. Barok, looking down from that seat of absolute power, and for once, for one blessed moment, noticing the man who knelt before him.

He gathered Corporal Mek and Private Jen with a sharp whistle. They checked the gleaming obedience collar around the werewolf's neck. His fingers found the control crystal at his belt, thumb caressing the smooth surface.

In the village, Straves bowed to commanders, to councillors. And to bureaucrats who wielded influence he could only dream of possessing. But here, with this crystal warm against his palm, he was a god. He pressed his thumb harder against the surface. The beast's defiant stance crumbled. Shoulders dropping. Head lowering. Its gaze dropped to the mud at his feet.

He needed to see it. Needed something, anything, to yield to him. "Down," he whispered. Needed to hear the word leave his lips. Needed to see the creature sink lower at his will. "Remember who holds the leash."

The werewolf's muscles trembled as it crouched, and the tightness across Straves' ribs eased. Here, at least, his word mattered. Here, he wasn't invisible.

His jaw set in a hard line as he shouldered his pack, eyes fixed on the road ahead. He strode forward without waiting for his men to finish their preparations, forcing them to hurry after him toward the site of the golem's downfall.

At the golem's destruction site, shards of stone lay strewn across the forest floor. Straves knelt, hand hovering over a shattered fragment, tension creeping through his shoulders. A faint residue of warmth tingled against his palm, ancient magic echoing in the shard. The werewolf prowled, nose twitching. It stilled, ears flicking back, before a low, uncertain growl escaped its throat.

Each step was a battle against roots and tangled bracken. Damp earth released its mineral scent with every footfall, mingling with the green-rot smell of decaying leaves. Distant creatures called warnings through the canopy. Straves pushed on as the werewolf tracked their targets, the beast's strength guiding them through narrow, twisting paths between ancient trunks.

They splashed through icy streams and manoeuvred around thick underbrush that snagged at their clothes. Days stretched longer, each sunset finding muscles heavy and the cold biting deeper as they followed faint traces of their quarry.

For ten gruelling days, the pursuit continued. Cold ashes became warm embers, then smoke-scent in the morning air. Each discovery sharpened Straves' orders like blades on a whetstone. He roused them before sunrise, forced them onward past sunset, brooking no complaints.

The prospect of reassignment pulled him forward, but beneath the ambition, the phantom rope stirred. He'd gambled everything on this hunt. Commandeered soldiers without proper authorisation. Executed the handler without consulting his superiors. If he returned empty-handed, the gallows would swing with a familiar weight.

When fatigue threatened to break his resolve, he whispered an incantation over himself, and false energy sparked through exhausted muscles. The magic pushed back collapse for another few hours, but couldn't touch the phantom rope coiling tighter with each passing day. What if the quarry escaped? What if some other Spellcaster claimed them first? What if he returned to find his name already scratched from the roster, his quarters emptied, his fate sealed?

Conjured images sustained him when even magic faltered, but they'd changed. No longer triumph. Survival. Standing before Lord Barok's throne, yes, but not basking in glory. Proving he deserved to exist. Showing he was worth the air he breathed and the magic he'd been granted. The vision was different now. The throne room remained, and Barok's gaze. But beneath it, the handler's boots twitched above the mud. His own name scratched from a roster. The gallows, patient and empty.

Finally seen. Finally valued.

Or forgotten, and swinging from a rope.

The forest changed with each passing day. Three days of humid air that made robes stick and grips slip. Then, a brittle dryness that cracked lips and turned leaves to powder underfoot. Rain on the seventh day. Cold needles that weighed down clothing and turned the earth into treacherous mud. Straves slipped twice, the image of marble corridors growing more vivid with each squelching step. By the eighth day, rations required miserly precision, stomachs cramping around meagre portions.

The tenth day's dawn found them hollow-eyed and stumbling. Even Mek's nervous drumming had stilled. The werewolf's circles grew tighter, more agitated. Shortly after starting out, they discovered the remnants of their quarry's camp. Charred firewood lay in dark fragments, with a few scattered embers smouldering in the firepit, its warmth lingering in the cool morning air.

The birdsong stopped. Then the wind. Straves' fingers found the Powerstaff, knuckles bone-white around the wood. The faint aroma of smoke reached him. Recent, close. Too close. His nostrils flared as he tested the air, but beneath the hunter's focus, his pulse hammered an irregular rhythm. Ten days. Ten days of pursuit, and now the gallows or the throne room. Nothing between.

As the sun hovered high over the forest, the werewolf froze mid-stride, nostrils flaring as it caught a scent on the breeze. Ears flicked forward, attuned to every rustle and whisper among the trees. Through the dappled midday light, two figures moved through a clearing ahead, unaware of the pursuit.

His throat tightened. Two of them. What if Mek and Jen weren't enough? What if these weren't common vagrants stumbling through the woods, but trained sorcerers who'd destroyed the golem with ease? The phantom rope sensation returned, pressing against his windpipe.

Straves exchanged a glance with his men, jaw tight, throat working once. His fingers brushed against his Powerstaff. Trembling, he forced them still. "Remember. Take them alive," he said. The Powerstaff's crystal pulsed beneath his palm, responding to the gathering magic, but his hands felt slick with sweat.

His gaze fixed on the two figures ahead, measuring, calculating. Everything he'd gambled rode on this moment. Everything he'd sacrificed, every rule he'd bent, every risk he'd taken. If he failed here, the gallows awaited. If he succeeded...

He couldn't afford to think beyond survival.

The werewolf's ears flattened, then pricked forward. Nose testing the air again and again. A raw, mournful howl erupted from deep within its chest. The forest trembled in response; branches shivered as startled birds erupted into panicked flight. Ahead, the pair they had been tracking froze before spinning around, eyes wide. Hands went to weapons. Stances dropped.

Straves' eyes narrowed. His breath came quickly. The howl had given them away. His careful approach was ruined. The advantage was lost. His lips drew back to reveal clenched teeth as his eyes locked on the werewolf.

"Get them!" The words tore from his throat, too loud, too desperate. His fingers found the control crystal, pressing until the edges bit into his palm. The werewolf laid its ears back, hackles bristling, and for one terrible heartbeat, he thought it would refuse. The collar would fail. Everything would crumble right here, right now, with his targets within reach.

The creature hesitated, muscles tensing, and Straves' vision tunnelled. Not here, not now. Not after he'd come so far, sacrificed so much.

The werewolf crouched, ready to spring, and Straves could breathe again. But his hands shook on the Powerstaff as he raised it, gathering magic slippery and uncertain in his grasp.

This had to work. It had to.

The alternative was a rope and silence.

Mek and Jen drew their swords and charged as one. Their blades caught glimmers of scarce light. Straves hefted his gleaming Powerstaff, energy crackling along its length, as he aimed it at the two strangers poised for conflict.

All morning, the canopy had been silent. The usual chatter of forest life had vanished, replaced by a silence in which nothing sang, nothing moved. Stric's skin prickled. Teela's gaze darted among the shadowy trunks, her fingers often resting on the knife that hung at her waist.

The chilling howl of the werewolf split the air, sending birds flapping into the sky. They spun as one to face the unseen threat, Teela's hand finding her knife while Stric's fingers whitened around his Powerstaff, breath coming quick and shallow.

"Spellcaster!" Her knife was already forward.

Stric moved without hesitation, his hand darting up as he invoked his magic. Brilliant light erupted from his Powerstaff, flooding the clearing until the nearest trunks stood stark and pale against the dark wood beyond. It bathed the Spellcaster in a halo of colour before solidifying into an unyielding barrier that shimmered like tempered glass.

The barrier snuffed out the magic he had been building, suppressed by the shield encircling him. His Powerstaff went dark. Its glow extinguished. He gathered his power again, thrusting the staff forward. A bolt of concentrated energy erupted from the crystal tip. Rebounded. The spell slammed back into him with visible force. He staggered, doubling over as though struck. When he straightened, blood trickled from his nose, staining his lips. His eyes went wide, jaw slack. He tightened his grip on the staff, knuckles bone-white, and pounded it against the barrier. Each strike produced a dull thud that reverberated through the clearing, his arm jerking back with every impact.

Teela moved, unsheathing her knife, her eyes moving from one sword to the other. The male soldier charged at Stric, boots thundering against the ground, sword held back over his shoulder, ready to swing. Stric sidestepped, channelling raw energy through his Powerstaff that erupted into a dazzling arc, hurling the soldier back with a cry.

The female soldier swung her sword at Teela, trying to hit her with the flat of the blade. Teela moved low and fast, slipping under the swing before springing up, muscles coiled and ready to strike again. The fading light caught the edge of Teela's blade.

The woman lunged forward, eyes locked on Teela. Stric pivoted, attempting to block her path. While his movement diverted their attention, Teela darted forward. Her knife pierced fabric and flesh. With a sickening thud, her blade struck bone, driving deep into the soldier's shoulder. She stumbled back. Her face twisted in agony. Her fingers trembled and lost their grip. The sword clattered at Teela's feet.

The male soldier's eyes narrowed as he pushed himself upright, muscles straining as he lunged toward Stric once more. Stric steadied himself, lips whispering an incantation. The magical whip snapped through the air with a crackling hiss, sending fiery tendrils toward the soldier's face. He stumbled backward, shielding himself.

Stric held the soldier in his gaze. His stride broke mid-step, his gaze going to his comrade, who lay sprawled on the earth, grimacing with each agonising spasm, blood oozing through her fingers. He looked toward the barrier. The Spellcaster still battered his Powerstaff against its shimmer, each strike reverberating back with a hollow thud.

Stric clenched his jaw as magic built along his arms, energy sparking from his fingertips. He thrust his Powerstaff forward, wood gleaming in the dim light. A brilliant arc of crackling blue energy erupted outward, accompanied by a deep, resonant hum that vibrated through the air.

The energy struck the soldier squarely in the chest, lifting him off his feet. It flung him backward as if he were weightless, his limbs flailing. He slammed into the ground with a bone-jarring thud that echoed through the clearing. A guttural sound escaped his lips. His breaths were quick and shallow, eyes rolling back. The tension left his limbs.

Teela came to Stric's side, her chest heaving, hands trembling. She caught his gaze, her lips curving into a small smile. Stric responded with a silent nod but held his gaze steady.

The air shimmered around the Spellcaster under the crackling spell, its energy raising a low hum that pressed against the ears. The barrier's light threw hard shadows against the nearest trunks, pooling dark where the roots tangled.

Teela gnawed at her lip, casting glances at the Spellcaster trapped within, her fingers twitching at her side. "How long will the spell around him last?"

Stric's hand hovered near his chin before dropping back to his side. "I can strengthen it, give us maybe three days."

Her lips quivered as she spoke, her words escaping in a whisper. "Should we... should we kill them?"

Stric hesitated, a muscle tightening along his jaw, and shook his head. "I would prefer not to." His brow furrowed as he glanced up into the swaying canopy, his voice dropping to a murmur.

"If I confine these two as well. I am confident that two or three days will provide us with sufficient time to distance ourselves from this place."

Teela's eyes flickered toward the forest's edge, voice rising with urgency. "What about the werewolf?" she asked. "You can use your magic on it. Before it catches our scent!"

Stric raised a hand, halting her words. "No," he said, his voice steady like a firm anchor. "Werewolves are peaceful creatures," Stric said. His gaze settled on Straves, eyes narrowing on the control crystal pressed into his palm. "I believe this one has been coerced into working for this man," he said.

"We shall leave the poor creature be," Stric concluded, lowering his hand. Her shoulders dropped from their rigid line, the tension in her jaw easing. They exchanged nods.

Teela's eyes darted around the clearing, her brows drawing together sharply. "Very well!" she said. "But I want to put as much distance between us and this place before he is free." She gestured toward the trapped Spellcaster.

Pack-memory sang the truth. A familiar scent had drifted to the werewolf on the gentle breeze, emanating from the man they were tracking. Ancient knowledge stirred in blood and bone, whispers from elders long returned to earth. This scent trail matched that of a visitor to the den in puppy days, bearing the warmth of the old magic. The howl burst from its throat before wisdom could silence instinct, an acknowledgement-cry wrestling against the collar's commands.

The werewolf stood before the Spellcaster, the man's fiery gaze burning into its thoughts, leaving trails of dread prickling down its spine. Muscles seized with tension, quivering with the desperate urge to bolt. But the collar's grip held firm.

A faint hum resonated through its neck as the man's spell flared to life around the Spellcaster. The barrier swallowed all magic within its bounds. The collar's commands went silent. No more crystal-voice compelling obedience. No more pain-threads controlling movement. The moment the magical tether snapped, raw energy surged where the collar commands had pressed. Pressure lifted from its throat, gone between one breath and the next. Scent arrived without pain-thread; the world was sudden and full where the collar-commands had muffled it. It looked upon the world with unchained eyes.

Freedom-scent! Pack-call!

Charging into the dense thicket, the werewolf's powerful limbs propelled it forward as twigs and branches snagged at its fur. With each pounding step, dry leaves crackled beneath its paws while its breath escaped in harsh, ragged gasps. Delving deeper into a maze of brambles, it crouched low, eyes gleaming. Beyond steel-clang and spellwork-burn, blood-scent sharp on the air.

The werewolf's alert ears twitched as it leaned forward, its eyes narrowing at Stric's every movement. Power-wood-scent. Knowledge-keeper-scent. Same as den-visitor. Same as warmth-bringer. This one freed collar-chains. No command-words spoken. No thanks-seeking. Just freedom given. Pack-elder spoke of ones like this. Ones who walk with honour-scent.

Minutes passed before the werewolf slipped into the shadowy embrace of the forest, paws gliding over the underbrush as branches whispered in its wake. North. Pack-den. Elders waiting. Must tell. Power-wood walks again. Knowledge-keeper walks again. This one freed collar-brother. Must tell pack-elders. Must warn.

They secured the two soldiers and removed their weapons. Teela's fingers curled around the hilt of the sword. The weight comforted her grasp; she strapped the scabbard to her waist, the pull of it against her hip unfamiliar. The grip sat wider in her palm, the blade's weight redistributing with every step.

Stric turned. The barrier still held, its shimmer faint in the failing light, the Spellcaster a shadow at its centre. Two days. Three at most. His jaw tightened. He turned away and followed Teela into the trees.

She did not slow when the treeline swallowed the last of the light. Her stride held where Stric's shortened, and she said nothing about stopping. As they ventured into the darkness, Stric murmured an incantation over the Powerstaff. With a burst of light, the staff's tip ignited, its golden glow catching the hard set of Teela's jaw, the bruised hollows beneath Stric's eyes.

For the next three days, Teela set a relentless pace that left no room for complaint. They began each day at dawn, shadows elongating as they took their first steps. Quick bites punctuated their march through rustling leaves, hunger sidelined until night swallowed them whole.

Their words were scarce: a nod here, a grunt there. The forest closed in around them, changing with each mile travelled. Thick undergrowth gave way to more open woodland, then tightened again into dense thickets that forced them into single file. Teela's gaze flicked back every few minutes, as if she could feel the Spellcaster's eyes on her back despite the magical barrier and the growing distance. "No time to rest," she nudged them onward whenever exhaustion made Stric's steps falter.

Moss-covered stones became bare rock outcroppings. Birdsong shifted from melodic to sharp and warning. Even the quality of light seemed different, filtering through leaves that grew sparser and more windswept. Each environmental shift marked another league between them and the pursuit. Stric's grip on the Powerstaff did not ease.

When twilight finally forced them to halt, exhaustion hung between them like morning mist. Teela chose their ground, whilst Stric coaxed flame from tinder with whispered incantations that no longer required his full concentration. The fire caught, grew, pushed back the gathering dark.

Stric withdrew Talnar from his inner pocket, the leather worn smooth at the spine from too many pages turned. The rough bark pressed cool against his spine as he shifted, finding a hollow in the ancient oak.

Teela's knife rang softly against stone as she worked, the rhythm steady. The fire crackled between them, casting her face in bronze and shadow, whilst the dark beyond the firelight held still, the smell of damp bark and pine reaching them with each breath.

He opened the book, expecting another lesson on binding spells or the intricacies of elemental manipulation. Words appeared immediately across the page, written in Talnar's characteristically bold script, the letters larger than the last entry, the ink pressing deeper at every stroke.

"You've been wondering why Vrill chose you."

Stric's fingers tightened on the leather cover. He glanced towards Teela, but she remained focused on the fire, the blade in her hands catching light with each practised stroke. His thoughts whispered without a voice. How could I not wonder? I'm just an apprentice. No family, no lineage. Why me?

The pages rustled, and new words flowed across the parchment like ink bleeding through from another world.

"There's something you should know about Vrill's certainty. Something he never told you himself, but something I witnessed."

The pages turned themselves, revealing an intricate illustration that hadn't been there moments before. Charcoal images depicted a figure, Vrill, surrounded by swirling darkness and strange geometries that were painful to look at for too long.

"The night after you were found, the Oracle called to him."

The Oracle? I thought that was a legend.

"Most do," Talnar wrote, and somehow the words carried dry amusement even through ink on parchment. "The Oracle dwells in the between-worlds, a space existing outside our reality. A being, or perhaps a force, no one truly knows which. It called to Vrill in his dreams. Compelled him to seek it out."

The illustration shifted, showing Vrill standing before something vast and unknowable. The charcoal was thicker there, pressed deeper into the page; the shapes behind Vrill formless and enormous and wrong. The drawing made Stric's skin prickle.

"A journey like that requires magic most cannot imagine, and a cost most would not pay. But Vrill went. He travelled to the between worlds."

The image changed. A vision within a vision: Stric himself, standing beside a throne. Holding Vrill's Powerstaff, Talnar at his side. Upon the throne sat a young man with the king's sword across his lap.

"The Oracle does not speak," Talnar's words flowed beneath the image. "It only shows. This is what Vrill saw. You, as you are now. You, beside the throne of Veltak, with me and the Powerstaff. Standing beside the prince, grown to adulthood and restored to his throne."

Stric stared at the illustration until the charcoal lines doubled, tripled. Firelight wavered across the page, or perhaps his hands moved, tilting the book without conscious command. The throne. The sword. Himself.

And the cost? The question formed before Stric could stop it. What did the journey cost him?

The text appeared slowly this time, as though Talnar himself found the words difficult to form.

"Travelling to the between-worlds took some of Vrill's magic. Permanently. He was never quite as strong after that night, though he hid it well. I noticed. Spells that once flowed effortlessly now required concentration. Tasks that had taken seconds now demanded minutes. He never spoke of it. Never complained."

The pages turned again, showing a final illustration. Vrill standing before Barok's assault, the Timesling glowing behind him.

"That night when Barok's power overwhelmed him... Vrill might have stood longer had he not sacrificed part of himself for a vision of you. He gave up his strength to see your destiny. And when he finally understood what the vision meant, he spent everything he had left to send you here."

The words sat cold in his mind. Stric's fingers stilled on Talnar's pages, parchment rough beneath his touch. Across the fire, Teela's blade continued its rhythm against stone. Steady, certain, grounded. Everything he'd never been.

"When you were found as a boy of ten wandering the woods outside the Academy, the Council wanted to send you to an orphanage in Talnaress. A child with no memory, no family, no documented lineage? The Guild had never admitted such a student."

"Vrill fought for you," the text continued. "Argued before the Council that you be given a chance at the Academy. Half of the council thought him mad. But Vrill was... different after your arrival. Unnaturally certain, they whispered. He tested your magical resonance himself and declared it unlike anything he'd seen. Strong enough to convince them, eventually."

But why was he so certain? Stric's thought formed desperately.

"Vrill didn't understand it. Not for fifteen years. He knew only that you were crucial to something greater. That somehow you were tied to the throne, to Veltak's future. So he watched over you. Made certain you received the training you needed. Deflected the masters who thought you didn't belong. Ensured you had every chance of becoming what you were meant to be."

Fifteen years. Stric's thumb traced the edge of Talnar's binding, following the worn groove where Vrill's own fingers must have rested countless times. The Grandmaster defending him before the Council. Deflecting masters. Training him.

New words blazed across the page, larger, the strokes driven harder into the parchment.

"The Oracle showed Vrill your victory, Stric. Not your doubt. Not your failure. Your victory. That vision sustained him through fifteen years of questions and waiting. It gave him courage for that final, desperate plan. And now..."

The text underlined itself for emphasis.

"... Now you must have faith that the Oracle's vision was true. Vrill believed in you enough to sacrifice for you. Twice. Do you doubt my capabilities to remember this correctly?"

Breath huffed out through Stric's nose. The grip on Talnar's cover loosened.

No, he thought, wiping his sleeve across his face. I don't doubt you.

"Good," Talnar wrote. "Now stop dwelling on whether you're worthy and start becoming what Vrill saw. The Oracle doesn't show failures, young Stric. Only futures that matter."

The pages fell still. The illustration faded, leaving only blank parchment ready for new knowledge.

Stric closed the book carefully, holding its weight against his chest where it had rested for so many days now. The worn groove in the binding pressed against his palm. Fifteen years. All of it in that groove.

Across the fire, Teela glanced over, her blade stilling. "Everything all right?"

Stric met her eyes and found himself nodding. The Powerstaff lay beside him, warm wood humming beneath his palm when his free hand found it. Vrill's staff. The Oracle's vision. "Yes. I think... yes."

He tucked Talnar back into his inner pocket, the book's warmth settling into his sternum, into the space between one breath and the next. The Oracle had shown his victory. Vrill had believed enough to sacrifice everything.

His spine straightened against the bark.

The weight of Talnar rested against his heart, warm as banked coals. Tomorrow, they would continue north, the Powerstaff's pull warm and certain in his grip. Tomorrow, the hunt for the hidden prince would resume.

The Grandmaster had seen. Had sacrificed. Had known.

Across the fire, Teela's blade caught the moonlight as she worked. Her jaw held its familiar angle, attention bent to the stone, every movement the same as it had been before he'd opened the book.

The forest pressed close around their small circle of warmth. Above them, clouds crept across the moon like cautious fingers reaching for something precious, and deeper shadows moved with purpose through the trees.

Stric's hand found the Powerstaff lying beside him, Vrill's staff, the one the Oracle had shown him holding. The wood hummed beneath his palm with quiet power. Doubt didn't follow the touch.

But whatever came with the morning's light, the Powerstaff lay warm across his palm, and Talnar pressed steadily against his ribs.

The Oracle had shown his victory.

Stric intended to earn it.

Chapter 6

Escape

Teela shook Stric awake in the pre-dawn hush. Three days of hard travel since they'd left the Spellcaster bound in Stric's barrier. Three days of checking their back trail and finding nothing.

"Do you think he's following?" Her hand rested on her sword hilt, thumb tracing the pommel's familiar curves.

The Spellcaster's sharp features surfaced in his memory. That cold assessment in those eyes, measuring them.

Three days of empty trail lay behind them.

Stric rubbed his eyes, sitting up slowly. "We have a good lead on them by now."

She glanced towards the eastern sky, where dawn light was not yet painting the treetops gold. "We should still leave early. Keep the lead." Her fingers drummed once against the leather wrapping before falling still. "But I think we might actually be clear."

They walked the winding path as the morning mist burned away under the climbing sun. Stric's stomach rumbled. He pulled out a piece of stale bread, tearing off a chunk before offering the rest to Teela.

She took it without comment, but glanced back over her shoulder. Still checking their trail. Still vigilant.

"Do you really think we're clear?"

"Three days with no sign." She chewed the bread slowly, scanning the path behind them one more time before turning forward. "Doesn't mean I'll stop watching." A pause. "But yes. Probably clear."

The canopy thinned as they walked, ancient trees giving way to younger growth. Sunlight pierced through scattered leaves where the jungle gave way to open grassland. By early afternoon, the golden light had shifted to a harsh glare pressing down on the exposed field ahead.

The field stretched before them under a blazing sky. Teela paused at the treeline, her gaze sweeping across the open ground where wildflowers swayed in the breeze. No cover for the rest of the day's walk. Just amber grassland rolling towards distant peaks that shimmered in the afternoon heat.

She looked at the mountains, then at Stric. Her hand no longer jumped to her sword hilt at every question. "We're still heading there?"

"Yes." The Powerstaff's weight tipped northward in his hand. "It hasn't wavered."

Teela settled into the grass at the field's edge, pulling out her waterskin. "We've been walking for many days now, and I still don't really know where we're going." She took a long drink, then offered it to him. "Just north, and to find the prince." Her eyes held steady on his. "Where are we headed? What happens when we find him, Stric? What's the actual plan?"

Stric's fingers found Talnar's familiar weight through his robes.

"That way." He pointed to the mountains. "Beyond that, I honestly don't know." He paused. "But you deserve to know why."

His throat worked. The words sat heavy on his tongue. Time travel, prophecy. His hand trembled slightly against the fabric of his robes. What if she heard all this and realised she'd tied herself to someone chasing ghosts?

Vrill had trusted him. The Oracle had shown that victory was possible. And Teela had walked beside him for thirteen days without demanding answers.

Perhaps that same faith should guide him now.

He told her of the late-night summons from the Guild's council. His voice trembled as he described standing before Grandmaster Vrill, spine straight, hands clasped, the chamber's silence pressing down on him. He spoke of the Timesling, the device that had sent him spinning through time itself into this strange and terrible now.

Teela's brow furrowed deeper with each word. She glanced at his pocket where Talnar rested, then back at his face, searching. He spoke of events from before she was born. Her fingers stilled on the dried meat she'd been eating. One eyebrow rose slowly, a question forming in the arch. She leaned back slightly. Her eyes widened. Her breath caught. Her fingers loosened on the sword hilt. She was still now. Her eyes on his.

Stric paused often, gaze dropping to the grass between words, hands quiet at his sides.

When he finished, she shook her head. The corner of her mouth quirked upwards. "Well, that explains a few things." She gestured towards his pocket, where Talnar rested. "Like, why you sit reading from blank pages." She nudged him gently with her shoulder. The contact brief but solid. "I was starting to wonder if you'd lost your mind."

She chewed the last of her dried meat slowly, gaze drifting to the distant mountains. Her jaw worked longer than the food required. When she swallowed, the movement looked difficult.

She stretched, joints cracking, then rose to gaze down at him. "Time travel." The words came out flat, testing their weight. "A lost prince. A prophecy." Her hand found the hilt of her sword, her fingers tracing the worn leather. She met his eyes, searching for the lie she wouldn't find. "You're either the maddest man I've ever met, or..." She trailed off, shoulders rising in a breath. "We're already running from Spellcasters and their soldiers. Already hunted through forests and over mountains." A half-smile touched her lips. "At least now I know why."

Her eyes narrowed, mind working through logistics. "Say we find him. Say this prince is real and you can bring him back." Her weight shifted to a fighter's stance even whilst standing still. "What then? Does he have an army waiting? Allies who've been hiding, ready to rise?"

She paused, letting the question settle. "Or are we delivering one man, prince or not, to face a tyrant who's held a kingdom for over twenty years?"

The silence stretched. A bird called in the distance, lonely against the mountain wind. His throat worked. He opened his mouth, then closed it.

"I don't know." His gaze dropped to the grass between them. "Vrill sent me to find him. To bring him home."

The words sounded hollow. Incomplete. Plans built on faith and prophecy. "Beyond that..." He shook his head. "I have no answers. No army. No plan for what comes after."

He forced himself to meet her gaze. "Just a vision that says we'll succeed, and a Grandmaster's faith that somehow..." His voice caught. "Somehow, that will be enough."

A cool edge had crept into the wind off the mountains. Teela studied his face in the fading light. She offered her hand to pull him to his feet, her grip firm. "Come on, then." Her jaw tightened.

"I've followed you this far on faith. Might as well see where impossibility leads."

As they gathered their belongings, she cast one more glance at the mountains ahead. Her fingers curled around her sword hilt briefly before releasing it.

The grass had turned amber around them, the distant peaks pale against a deepening sky. Teela glanced at Stric, her eyes bright. She nodded. He nodded back as they approached the mountain range that called out to his Powerstaff.

Their path shifted from soft grass to jagged rocks. Each step now required careful placement. Pebbles clattered away from their boots, small sounds that echoed in the mountain stillness. A biting chill crept into the air, raising goosebumps along their arms.

The peaks loomed closer, dark silhouettes against the sky. The path grew steeper with each turn, testing their endurance. Vegetation thinned to hardy shrubs that huddled close to rocks for protection against mountain winds. Vibrant moss spread over the cold stone in defiant patches of life, whilst the crisp air carried distant scents of pine and snow.

Teela shielded her eyes with one hand, scanning the approaching darkness for shelter that might save them from a night in the open. Her shoulders dropped. A shadow between two boulders. A cave promising refuge from the encroaching night.

"Over there." She turned, arm extended, pointing at the shadow between the boulders. "We can shelter there."

Stric nodded, gaze resting on her profile a beat too long. They hurried toward the opening. Twisted vines curtained the entrance. They ducked inside, discovering a space, generous enough for comfortable refuge from the night.

Stric searched the barren slope for anything that might burn. Stunted shrubs clung to rock faces, their branches twisted by mountain winds and too green to catch flame. He settled for gathering dried lichen from boulder crevices and a handful of brittle twigs sheltered beneath an overhang. Sparse fuel that would offer more smoke than warmth. Each piece, brittle and dry between his fingers, was small against the cold bleeding up through the stone beneath his boots. Teela laid out their provisions and unfurled blankets over smooth rock, pressing each edge flat with the heel of her hand, working to create what comfort could be found on bare mountain stone.

On Teela's advice, Stric arranged the meagre fuel outside the cave's entrance where it could burn without choking them with smoke. The flame from his Powerstaff touched the dried lichen first. It caught reluctantly, smouldering more than burning, releasing thin wisps that the mountain wind snatched away. The few brittle twigs blackened and crumbled to ash almost immediately. What warmth the struggling fire offered barely reached their knees, the lichen smoke sharper and thinner than wood smoke, but the glow held the cave mouth in low amber and drew them both close.

"At least we won't have to worry about the Spellcaster finding us here," Teela said. As she sank against the cave wall, she allowed herself to breathe.

Stric nodded, eyes on the firelight catching the edge of her jaw, a faint smear of ash at her temple. "Yes, we'll be protected for the night."

They shared what remained of the provisions: bread broken between them, a waterskin passed without comment. Stric and Teela settled into blankets that held the day's warmth. Moonlight caught the twisted vines at the entrance, pulling each tendril into silver relief against the dark slope beyond. Cold stone through the blanket. The vines stirred once in the wind and stilled.

Stric woke in the pre-dawn grey and wrongness. Something had stirred outside the cave. A sound that didn't belong to the wind or stone. He lay still, listening. Only the breeze, and beneath it a stillness that shouldn't exist. The mountain ought to have been waking. His chest pulled tight.

The sound came again. Deliberate. The crunch of gravel underfoot.

His breath caught. He reached over to shake Teela awake, fingers finding her shoulder in the dim light.

"Teela," his whisper carried no further than her ear. "There's something outside."

Teela sat up, eyes wide, her gaze moving past him to the cave mouth before he'd drawn his next breath. "What is it?"

"Listen."

The crunching reverberated through the still morning air, unmistakable now as footsteps approaching with purpose.

Teela nodded. They moved towards the cave entrance with silent coordination born of shared danger. They peered through the screening vines. Three hulking figures in the pre-dawn grey.

Silver eyes caught the grey pre-dawn light. Muscles rippled under thick fur as they prowled near the entrance, each step placed without sound on the gravel. Their silhouettes cut against the approaching dawn.

Werewolves.

Stric's gaze met Teela's in the dimness. He pointed toward the cave entrance. She nodded. They knew werewolves were peaceful creatures by nature, hunting only to feed their pack. But the presence of these three so close to their refuge drove a contraction across Stric's sternum. The werewolf that had led the Spellcaster's hunt, collar gleaming at its throat, had escaped into the forest. Three days of an empty trail, yet that didn't guarantee freedom. Three shapes in the pre-dawn grey, and no way to know if enemies still hunted them through enslaved eyes.

They retreated into the cave depths, pressing back until stone met their shoulders and the entrance narrowed to a pale slit of grey. The cold of the rock pressed through the back of Stric's tunic.

Teela fastened her sword belt with movements sharp and sure. Her fingers found the hilt and stayed there, knuckles white against the leather. Her jaw clenched. She pressed her back against the stone.

Nowhere to run. Creatures outside whose intentions remained unknown.

Teela glanced at Stric. His brow furrowed deeper with each breath. His grip on the Powerstaff tightened until tendons stood out on the back of his hand. Dawn was pressing at the cave mouth. Teela's gaze moved between him and the entrance, hand on the hilt, waiting.

Cool air clung to their skin as they moved in the dim light. Each rustle of cloth returned off the low stone ceiling, sharp and doubled. Werewolf silhouettes lingered at the cave mouth, their heads cocked at angles that suggested they were listening.

Dawn light crept across the cave floor. Stric's fists clenched around the Powerstaff's shaft.

His jaw clenched. Teela's fingers tightened on her sword. Perhaps the pack would move on with their morning business on the mountain.

"No fear, magic-wielder." A voice came through the vines, pitched low, the vibration reaching Stric's chest before the words resolved into meaning. "Know me by scent-words if not by speech. Pack-memory carries your trail. We crossed paths befor e... when pack-bonds were broken."

Stric's eyes widened. His hand clenched tighter around his Powerstaff until his knuckles showed white through his skin. "What do you mean we've met? I'm sure I would remember meeting a werewolf."

"May I approach, pack-brother?" His ears twitched. The words came at the same low pitch. Stric's breath stayed shallow, held between his ribs. "Took man-shape for easier words between us. Less... less worry for magic-wielder and warrior-companion."

Damp air clung to Stric's skin. Help lay days away in any direction. If help even existed in this future. His brow furrowed as he glanced at Teela. She offered only a shrug, lips curving in something between a smile and a grimace. Trust, still. After everything.

Every choice carried her life alongside his own. His thumb pressed against the Powerstaff's crystal. Cold. Smooth.

"Pack-brothers, give us space?" Pricking his ears forward, listening. "Cave or open air? You choose."

Stric's weight shifted forward. He nodded to Teela. The decision was made. The vines at the entrance shifted in the morning air. "We will come out."

They emerged from the shadows into the dawn's growing light. The werewolf stood several steps away, his stance mirroring that of a man. Upright despite the obvious differences, broad shoulders level, each foot placed on the gravel without sound.

Stepping forward into full view, muscles rippled under coarse grey fur that caught the dawn light. Elongated canines, sharp and gleaming, pointed ears that twitched at sounds too soft for human hearing. Amber eyes, deep and glowing with a wild, lupine light. They found Stric and held. His grip tightened on the Powerstaff before he knew he'd moved.

"You honour Whhrll." His voice roughened, and he cleared his throat. "There are... things you must know. Pack -debts that need telling." His claws flexed against stone, leaving minor scratches that spoke of barely controlled tension.

The sun climbed above the mountain peaks, cold light falling sharply across the stone between them. Stric's gaze moved to Teela. The line between her brows had deepened. Her hand rested close to her sword's hilt.

"They took me, dark ones' Spellcasters." A muscle tightened in his jaw between each word. "Collar round my throat. Magic binding pack-bonds. Made me..." his voice broke, ears flat, "made me hunt pack-brothers. Dark hunt. Worst scent-words. Hunt-memory holds shame."

Whhrll's eyes narrowed to amber slits, the light in them gone hard and still. "I led that collar-master and his hunt-beasts to you. Pack-bonds were broken. No choice."

The creature straightened its shoulders with visible effort, releasing a breath that left a thread of vapour in the cold air. "During battle with collar-master, you cast magic." His ears were forward. "That broke false pack-bonds... pack-freedom returned."

Stric went still. "My spell?" His voice came out hollow. "It freed you?" The Oracle had shown Vrill his victory over Barok, but how many smaller victories had already been won without his knowing? How many others had been enslaved, forced to act against their nature? His chest tightened.

"Yes! Power shattered false-bonds! Followed your trail-scent for days. Caught old familiar scent-words... Talnar-memory! Could only sing warning-song when pack-memory recognised truth."

"After freedom returned, I fled. I watched the battle. Then I understood you were a magic-wielder of old, carrying power-scent from times before the darkness. Talnar, pack-memory remembered!"

Teela's brow furrowed. She said nothing for a moment, her gaze moving between Stric and Whhrll. "Talnar? You recognised the scent of a book that Stric carries?"

"Yes, and Grandmaster's staff." Whhrll's head dipped briefly, ears lowering a fraction. "Talnar is pack-brother to our kind. Pack-elders knew its bearers through long pack-memory." His ears flicked forward attentively. "Ran to my pack when scent-words came clear. Pack-elders sent me back. They would meet the new Grandmaster."

Stric jolted, the words hitting him. His grip came down on the Powerstaff's grooves before he moved. Grandmaster. Something settled heavily in his chest, too weighty for shoulders that had carried only apprentice burdens. The real Grandmaster had been Vrill. He was just an apprentice. He shook his head, backing away half a step. "I am no Grandmaster!"

"Talnar chooses its own magic-wielder." Ears forward. "Ancient power-scent knows worthy hands. Would burn false-hearts." Whhrll's claws were still against the stone. "Pack-memory holds truth. You are what old scent-words say you are."

"Come to Pack Den?" He gestured up the mountain. "Not far on safe trails. Pack elders wait for new words. Pack-protection surrounds all guests. Honour-scent grows strong with worthy visitors."

Stric looked to Teela for guidance, but she offered only a shrug. Trusting him to choose for them. The responsibility pressed against his chest. He stood with his weight shifting forward, then back. His gaze went to the mountain path, then to the Powerstaff's crystal, pale in the morning light. One story rose out of the rest. Travellers brought in from the winter dark, given furs and a fire. Then the other kind crowded close behind it, the ones that ended in high passes no one returned from. The Powerstaff pulled him towards these mountains, but magic could be fooled, manipulated by those with sufficient cunning. Was he choosing wisely, or was he a fool desperate to believe in allies when enemies surrounded them?

The Powerstaff tugged at his palm, a low, steady pull through the wrist towards the mountain path. The crystal brightened, faint but unmistakable, a warmth that ran up through the wood and into his forearm. Perhaps that was where the Powerstaff had been guiding them all along. Towards allies.

Stric locked eyes with Whhrll and gave a curt nod. His grip tightened on the staff. Voice steady, though something held hard across the back of his shoulders. "Give us a moment to gather our belongings."

Stric's hands moved through his pack. His gaze kept returning to the cave entrance, to the dawn beyond it. Accepting Whhrll's guidance would set them on a path far more complex than simple shelter. When they emerged from the cave, the werewolf stood facing the horizon, ears still, gaze fixed on the distance. Stric's pulse quickened.

"What do you witness?" Teela asked, following his gaze.

"Signs." He did not look back. "Pack-elders spoke of stirrings on the wind-scent through the mountains. Dark things, once sleeping, now awake."

The Powerstaff hummed in Stric's grip, responding to something ahead.

He glanced at Teela, then at Whhrll's patient silhouette against the dawn.

They were walking towards it.

Chapter 7

The Aid of Werewolves

They had climbed since dawn, following Whhrll's sure-footed path up the mountain as the sun tracked its arc overhead. Stric paused mid-step as another stone skittered into the shadows below, the sound swallowed by a depth he couldn't measure. "How much further?" The words emerged between measured breaths.

Whhrll's golden eyes swept the path ahead, ears forward, scent-checking the wind. "Pack-den lies close. Pack-elders know stranger-scent on the wind." The werewolves moved with liquid precision, each foot landing full and certain on surfaces Stric's boots barely gripped.

A valley opened below them, a thread of silver water catching the light through the treeline, the grass pale where it met the stone and dark where the valley floor levelled. The Powerstaff's weight shifted in Stric's grip, tip dropping toward the earth as his focus pulled to the green expanse. Teela's hand found his elbow.

Below them, water caught the golden afternoon sunlight in countless tiny mirrors, warmth lifting off its surface against the cold that had pressed in since dawn. Air filled his lungs. Air that carried the music of the flowing stream, the scent of water over rock. The gentle current bore fallen leaves downstream, some catching against stones before the current tugged them free. His fingers loosened on the Powerstaff.

Teela's gaze traced the natural barriers. The cliff walls, the single entrance, the water source. Her expression softened. Weight shifted to her forward foot, testing the ledge's stability. Her hand found her sword hilt, thumb tracing the pommel. Her eyes moved from the entrance to the water's edge.

The entrance to the werewolf's den lay hidden in plain sight. A shadowy crevice within jagged stone ledges, draped with vines and ivy. Inside sprawled a city unlike anything either had seen. Pathways wove through carved stone and earthen walls, converging on a grand plaza where sounds echoed and sunlight streamed through carved vents. Golden light played across Stric's face as he stood motionless. Teela's hand lay still at her side, the sword hilt untouched.

Groups leaned toward each other, hands cutting the air, whilst pups darted between clusters of friends playing games only they knew. Teela's gaze moved along worn pathways, carved channels routing water along the stone, a root as thick as her arm threading the joint between rock face and worked wall. "They have made something beautiful here! Wild and civilised at once."

In the centre of the den was a communal space where laughter echoed as some werewolves shared stories over steaming plates. Others fed in wolf form, shaggy heads dipping beside human-like hands.

Stric's fingers found Teela's hand. "Werewolves. Creatures our people fear. They built this."

"It feels like a peaceful village, somewhere I would have liked to grow up in." The words emerged quiet.

The werewolf pups tumbled through their games, laughter echoing around the cave, the high notes doubling back off the far stone before the lower ones had faded. A small one crashed into its sibling, and both hit the ground together, all limbs and open mouths, landing without thought of how they fell. They played within sight of their elders but never checked over their shoulders. Never calculated escape routes. Never tested whether the ground beneath them might vanish.

Whhrll gestured for them to follow as they wove through the lively village, dodging pups chasing each other through the den.

He paused at the threshold of a large dwelling, his posture tense, as a low rumble emanated from his throat. A similar sound came from inside. "Wait here, pack-brothers. Pack-elders speak old ritual words first. Honour-scent must be proper." He entered through the doorway. Inside, muted growls and soft snuffling echoed as if they exchanged low ritual words.

Returning with a single nod, he beckoned them, ears forward as he bowed. "Pack-elders welcome you now. May our scent-trails run together in good hunt." He held Stric's gaze a moment longer than necessary before sweeping away toward the tables.

Stric's eyes found Teela's. They stepped forward. As they entered the dwelling, three elders in their humanoid forms rose from their seats.

The pack elders' silver-grey fur caught the vent-light overhead, pale at the tips, absolutely still. Golden eyes that found Stric's face and held, without a flicker of checking, without moving to his hands or the staff.

"Pack-welcome, Grandmaster and companion," the elder said, voice pitched low, the cave air carrying it to the far stone without effort. "I am..." He turned his head, twitched his left ear, raised the right side of his lip, and protruded his tongue.

"Old wolf forgets. Humans carry different words. Pack-memory runs deep, but human speech comes hard to aged tongue." The elder on the right said with gentle amusement, placing a steadying paw on the other's shoulder. "I Grrwll, these pack-brothers Rrrll, and Rrggll. We carry old words of pack Grraall, sworn to hunt-bonds with Talnar-bearer."

"Pack-welcome, Elders of the pack... Grraall." His throat worked as the vowels dropped deeper than they wanted to. "I am Stric Deamara." He stepped back a half-pace, turning so the elder's gaze had room to include Teela. "My companion here is Teela Reyna."

Teela's chin dipped lower than a combat nod. Her hands rested open at her sides. "Pack-welcome, elders."

"I appreciate your respect, but I am only an apprentice magician." His hand found his pocket where Talnar rested, the book's familiar weight pressing through the fabric. The werewolf elders stood before him. Their weathered faces and golden eyes held centuries. His other hand shifted on the Powerstaff's shaft. Talnar pulsed against his chest with each heartbeat, its rhythm steadier than his own. The academy had taught him magical theory, formulae for barrier spells, and directional magic. None of his instructors had prepared him for standing before pack-elders who had not shifted once since he entered the room, whose stillness filled the space without effort.

"My pup Whhrll carries scent-words of your denial, magic-wielder. Yet power-scent speaks truth beyond humble words." Grrwll's golden gaze met Stric's, then flicked away.

Grrwll's ears flicked forward. "Dark-scent runs through these times, young magic-wielder. Dark-one hunts all packs, takes slaves, kills not to eat." His nostrils flared. His ears flicked back. "Yet if Talnar shares words with you, pack-memory will confirm the hunt-bonds between pack-elders and power-bearers." His voice filled the rock walls completely, the sounds of the settlement beyond the doorway quieting in its wake.

"Pack-bonds hold stronger than stone. Scent-words given are scent-words kept. This is pack-memory since first hunt-trails." Rrrll's claws tapped the rhythm of an oath on the stone beside him, each beat carrying in the cave's close air. "Pack-elders gave trust-scent to Grandmaster Vrill and all power-bearers before him. Old hunt-bonds run deep."

A subtle vibration thrummed against his chest, steady through the fabric, a warmth that did not belong to him. He drew Talnar from his pocket. Words already ran across the open page: "Werewolf noses can track a lie through three kingdoms and a thunderstorm, young Stric. Tell them everything. Their pack-memory extends back centuries. Attempting deception would be remarkably foolish, even for you. Besides, you need their help. Desperately, I might add."

Rrggll's nostrils flared as he approached, one ear rotating forward, his head tilting a precise degree to one side. "Your pack-scent carries more than human magic. There are... scents... I do not recognise."

"I'm just an apprentice magician." He repeated the words, sounding thin against walls that had heard the voices of true leaders.

"Perhaps," the elder said, golden gaze flicking away. "Yet Talnar-song rings different with you, magic-wielder. Not same scent as past power-bearers carried. Pack-memory holds old melodies; this one sings new."

He straightened, meeting the werewolf elders' eyes. "Very well, I will share everything, including why you will discover that I am not the Grandmaster!"

He drew a long breath. Let it out. He began speaking of how Talnar had come into his possession, recounting the fateful night he received his summons, the secret shared by Grandmaster Vrill, the Oracle's prophecy that promised victory beside a restored throne, the sacrifice Vrill had made to obtain that vision, and the journey that had led him to this point since then.

Grrwll's ear twitched left, then right. Rrrll leaned forward, his claws drumming once against the table. "This tale..." he began, then stopped, glancing at his fellow elders. "Talnar chose strangely this time."

Stric finished recounting the jungle battle that had freed their pack mate, his throat dry from speaking. Outside, the warm light had faded to purple shadows.

"Pack-memory tells Grandmaster Vrill's scent-words. He walked among all free-packs of Veltak before dark-scent rose over lands. He spoke of coming times when all packs would need alliance-bonds to survive." Grrwll's ears flattened. "He carried storm-scent about future-trails. Heavy with knowing that one. But he trusted Talnar-song would continue, asked pack-elders to honour its bearer when time came."

"You are Talnar-bearer, you are Talnar-chosen, you carry Grandmaster-scent, and pack-honour demands we assist your hunt." Rrggll's claws clicked against stone as he moved forward, each step placed a full beat apart. "Pack-memory holds little of prince-cub's escape-trail, but scent-words say tree-folk hide humans away from dark-one's reach." The elder's gaze met his pack-brothers, ears forward.

"My pup, Whhrll, will run trail-paths with you to land of tree-folk. Tonight you feast and rest with pack-warmth. Dawn-light will send you forward on good hunt-trails," Grrwll said, his voice carrying authority that held like stone.

As darkness filled the den's windows, the elders led them to a grand wooden table laden with the hunt's spoils. The scent reached them first. Roasted meat, rich and savoury. Stric's hand went to his middle. Teela stopped mid-step.

Platters bore the spoils of the pack's hunt: venison haunches glazed with honey and herbs, wild boar rubbed with mountain sage and something sharp that made the nose tingle, rabbit seasoned with rosemary. Steam rose from each dish. His stomach answered before he'd taken a step.

Grrwll swept his paw toward the feast, ears forward. "Early human-visitors showed pack-ancestors that fire-touched meat carries better flavour. Taught us herb-magic that makes good-hunt taste even richer. We remember this gift in pack-memory."

Stric lifted a tender morsel of venison to his lips, the meat melting in his mouth, herbs singing across his tongue in combinations he'd never tasted at the academy. Teela closed her eyes as she sampled the boar, the sage and spice unfolding in layers. Heat, then earthiness, then a sweetness that lingered.

Fresh bread accompanied the meats, still warm from the ovens, perfect for soaking up the herb-rich juices. The meal was paired with a robust wine that the werewolves had fermented themselves. Earthy notes that spoke of mountain springs and wild herbs. Words tumbled out between bites.

He clasped the hands of each pack member in turn. Full, they were led to their quarters.

The enormous bed filled most of the room. Teela stood in the doorway, her hands opening and closing at her sides. "It looks like we are sharing a blanket tonight, Stric." The words came out rougher than she'd intended.

Stric's hand found his pocket, Talnar's weight pressing through the fabric. Years at the academy, his own room, his own bed. Solitude so complete it became armour. "I could make do in the corner... if that would make you more comfortable." He didn't look away from her.

"No, it is all right. We are both adults, and the bed is more than big enough for us." Teela moved to the bed, running her hand over the fur covering. Soft. Thick enough to sink fingers into. The crystals set in the walls cast a warm light without flicker or smoke. Nothing like the camps they'd shared on the trail. She sat on the edge of the bed, testing the give. Her shoulders lowered from where they'd been riding high since entering the room. "We'll rest well tonight."

Teela's steady breathing filled the darkness beside him, the sound that kept his hands still resting on his chest, where Talnar usually pressed, but tonight the book lay on the bedside table. Close enough. Years at the academy. His corner of the library, his assigned seat in the dining hall, and his room with one chair because no one visited. He'd called it focus. Discipline. The breathing beside him suggested a different word entirely.

Soft tapping at the door wove into his dreams. He blinked awake to grey light through the carved vents overhead. Whhrll stood at the threshold, ears alert, checking the morning scent. "Trail-scent calls, pack-brothers. Sun rises on our hunt-path to tree-folk lands."

The aroma of fresh bread and ripe fruit greeted them at the tables. Herbal tea sent tendrils of steam into the crisp morning air.

The elders draped them in weatherproof cloaks and supplied them with travel provisions. The wool pressed heavily on cold shoulders.

As they packed the last of their gear, Whhrll turned to them with a nod that held a beat longer than courtesy required. "Long trail to tree-folk lands, pack-brothers. Thirteen sun-cycles if hunt-luck holds and danger-scent stays distant." His golden gaze met theirs.

Dawn mist clung to the path as they descended through layers of shadow and filtered sunlight. Each footfall released the earthy scent of decomposing leaves. Whhrll moved ahead of them without bending a single blade of grass, his golden eyes reading signs invisible to human perception. Bent grass that spoke of passing creatures. Scratches on bark that told of territorial disputes, air currents carrying scents of distant water and hidden dangers.

The mountain fought their descent. Loose shale sent pebbles clattering into unseen depths. Stric used the Powerstaff to probe each step, wood clicking against stone. When the path finally levelled, they entered the forest again. Rustling leaves, distant bird calls, shadows weaving patterns on their winding path.

On the second night in the forest, the fire burned low, the nearest trunks swinging amber and shadow with each shift of flame. A sharp crack pierced the stillness, as if the bones of the forest were snapping beneath something heavy. A creature loomed into view, a hulking silhouette swallowing the forest behind it. Two pale eyes held steady from the shadow, catching the fire's edge. Its short black fur stood on end, the hackles rising in a ridge from skull to tail.

Ribs pressed against skin beneath patchy fur. Drool hung in long strings from bared fangs, dropping to the earth in viscous threads. The creature's flanks heaved with each breath, muscles trembling with exhaustion or illness. Its eyes held only one thing. Desperate hunger that had driven it past caution, past fear of the fire, past the scent of three who might kill it.

It would risk everything for the chance of food.

Stric swept up his Powerstaff. Teela drew her sword. A low growl rumbled from Whhrll's chest. His gaze narrowed as his humanoid outline blurred, muscles rippling beneath his fur as he transformed into his wolf form. He launched before the creature had finished reading the firelight, snarl and strike arriving together. With a guttural growl, the creature lunged forward, fangs bared. But Whhrll was faster. A blur of fur and fury, colliding mid-air in a tangle of snapping jaws and thrashing limbs. The night air became a chorus of snarls and yelps, punctuated by the thud of the creature hitting the ground.

Stric's grip tightened on his Powerstaff, ready to cast protective spells. Beside him, Teela's knuckles whitened around her drawn sword hilt, should Whhrll need help. Both stood at the firelight's edge, useless, while Whhrll took the beast's full weight. The creature's head lowered, and the once stalwart growls wavered into uncertain whimpers. A rustle of leaves marked its rapid retreat, leaving its musk heavy in the air.

In the creature's wake, Whhrll's golden gaze swept the darkness beyond their firelight, ears alert to distant sounds. "No more hunt-beasts will come, pack-brothers." His nostrils flared. "Sick-scent on that one. Dark-one's corruption spreads beyond collar-slaves, touching even wild-beasts. Makes them hunger-mad, drives them past fear."

Days found their rhythm. Each dawn brought Whhrll's reconnaissance, his form dissolving into forest shadows to read night stories in disturbed earth and broken twigs. Each evening, he returned with provisions, and Teela transformed raw meat into meals that warmed icy hands and drove the damp from their clothes, their campfire throwing orange light across the bark of the nearest trees.

The forest shifted with their progress. Pine giving way to oak, stone to rich loam, familiar birdcalls yielding to fresh voices.

On the third day since leaving the pack den, the path widened enough for them to walk side by side. Stric's fingers traced the Powerstaff's worn surface.

"The Guild wasn't always what Barok made it." His voice broke the companionable silence. "When King Balthor founded it centuries ago, it was meant to bring order after the Time of Magical Chaos, when uncontrolled magic threatened to destroy Veltak."

"What kind of chaos?" Teela's hand rested near her sword hilt, the way it did when she tracked dangerous prey.

"Greedy magicians hoarding power for profit, reckless experimenters destroying entire villages, malevolent sorcerers revelling in decay and death. The kingdom was tearing itself apart."

They climbed a slight rise, her breathing steady despite the incline. "So Balthor created the Guild to stop them?"

"More than that." Stric stepped over a fallen log, offering his hand to help her across. "The original thirteen-member council had advisors from all the races. Elf, fairy, werewolf, and even vampyre. It served everyone, but not to control them. The Guild's original mission was cooperation."

Her mother had spoken of the time before Barok, when local leaders had still served their people rather than themselves. A muscle worked in Stric's jaw as he spoke. "So what changed?"

"Power." Stric looked back at the valley they'd left behind. "Over generations, the Guild became more insular, convinced of human magical superiority. By the time Barok joined, it had forgotten its original mission."

Whhrll halted on the trail ahead, ears swivelling to catch their human words. When they closed the distance, the young werewolf's gaze grew distant. "Old power-bearers walked among packs as hunt-brothers, not den-masters. They sought pack-wisdom, honoured our ways. Grandmaster Vrill carried strong wish to return to those good-trail times."

Her mother's stories hadn't been fantasies. The cooperation Stric envisioned once existed. "Your people worked with the original Guild?"

Whhrll's ears flicked forward with pride. "Aye, pack-sister. Pack-leader Balthor understood. Magic-scent belongs to all."

"That's what we need to rebuild." Talnar pulsed against Stric's chest. "Not the Guild as it became, but as it was meant to be. A force for unity, not division."

They walked in silence after that. The trunks had broadened, oak now replacing the narrow pines, their bark furrowed deep, and the leaf mould underfoot gave slightly with each step.

Whhrll paused at intervals, scent-checking invisible boundaries. "Old pack-markers here," he explained, gesturing to claw marks on ancient oak bark. "Pack Grraall's trail-claim ends at the fallen elder-tree ahead. Pack Rrrkal's territory begins where the river splits."

The fallen elder-tree stretched across their path, its massive trunk wider than three men standing side-by-side. Moss and ferns claimed its surface, transforming decay into new life.

"How many packs share these mountains?" Stric asked.

"Many packs. Pack Grraall is six hundred strong. Others smaller, some larger." Whhrll's ears flicked forward. "Pack-elders meet at moon-gathering. Share scent-words, settle boundary-disputes, honour alliance-bonds."

On the fifth day, ruins appeared through the morning mist. Stone foundations emerged from undergrowth, their faces grey-green with lichen, the mortar between them crumbled to nothing in long stretches; walls collapsed into geometric patterns. A well stood at the centre, its stones fitted with precision, now dry and choked with vines.

"Old human-den," Whhrll said, ears back. "From before dark-scent rose. Humans lived here in peace-times, traded with packs. Shared meat for metal-tools, herbs for woven-cloth." His claws rested on moss-covered stones. "When dark-one came, humans fled. Those who stayed became collar-slaves or died."

Teela moved through the ruins with the careful assessment of someone reading a battlefield. Her fingers traced doorframes built for families, hearths that had once held cooking fires. A child's toy wolf. Carved with loving detail. Half-buried in leaf mould. The silence pressed heavily.

Stric stood before what must have been a meeting hall, its entrance still partially intact. Stone benches lined the interior where councils had once gathered. The scale of Barok's reach stretched beyond the palace walls, beyond the capital. Village after village, community after community, scattered or enslaved. His grip on the Powerstaff tightened until the grooves pressed deep into his palm.

"Pack Rrrkal remembers these humans in pack-memory," Whhrll said, his syllables slowing, each word placed with care. "Good hunt-brothers. Honoured pack-ways. Their children played with our pups without fear." His ears forward. "Perhaps when dark-scent is driven from lands, humans will return. Old alliance-bonds could wake again."

They camped that night among the ruins, the standing walls providing shelter from the wind. The fire found the chisel marks in the stonework, old cut lines brightening and dimming as the flames rose and fell. Teela sat with her back against a doorframe, knees drawn up. Flames cast shadows where families had once gathered.

"My mother used to tell stories," Teela said, her voice quiet in the darkness. "Before she died. About the time before, when villages like this existed throughout the kingdom. When you could travel the roads without fear, when neighbours helped raise each other's children." Her fingers traced patterns in the dirt. "I thought they were just stories. Wishes for a world that never existed."

Stric's hand found hers in the darkness between them. "They were real. They can be real again."

The seventh day brought them to the site of a centuries-old battle. Weapons rusted into the soil, shields bearing unfamiliar heraldry half-buried beneath oak roots that had grown through them. A stone cairn stood at the clearing's centre, weathered by time but still deliberately maintained. Fresh flowers, mountain laurel, and wild sage had been placed with recent care.

"Pack-memory holds this place with honour," Whhrll said, approaching the cairn with head lowered, ears back. "Here, before Pack-leader Balthor's time, werewolves and humans stood together against raiders from across the sea. Many fell. Pack-brothers and human-friends. Victory came at high cost." He placed his own offering at the base of the cairn. A sprig of pine with needles still green. "Packs tend this cairn still. Human descendants once came, left flowers. No more."

Stric knelt beside the cairn. Names carved in stone, some in the common tongue, others in the flowing script of the old kingdom. Human and werewolf side by side, equal in sacrifice. This was what Vrill had wanted him to see: proof that alliances had worked before. That it could work again.

Days later, a gentler landscape opened before them. They followed a river whose course had carved a winding path through stone, flanked by willows and wild roses. Deer tracks lined the muddy bank. Fish broke the surface in the late afternoon light.

"Good-scent here," Whhrll said, breathing deep. "Water runs clean from snow-melt. Tree-folk lands begin where river meets the great forest. Two more sun-cycles, then we enter their territory."

That night, they camped beside the river, the cold of the snowmelt reaching their faces in the dark. Teela sat with her boots off, feet dangling in the cold water. Stars emerged one by one, constellations she had learned as a child.

Stric joined her at the water's edge. He sat close enough that their shoulders nearly touched, and neither moved to change it.

"When this is over," Teela said, her voice barely audible over the river's song, "what do you see?"

Moonlight broke and reformed on the current, the water carrying it downstream in fragments. "A council chamber with seats for all races. Decisions made together, not imposed by humans who think they know best. The Guild rebuilt around cooperation, not control." He paused. "And maybe... a place where neither of us has to be alone anymore."

Her hand found his in the darkness.

Where thick undergrowth had pressed close around narrow game trails, the forest opened into something more magnificent. Trees rose like castle pillars, their trunks wide enough to house an entire family. Branches woven between the high crowns in patterns so intricate that the spaces of sky between them came and went as they moved.

The air shimmered. Stric's skin tingled where it met the atmosphere. He stopped walking.

Teela's hand found his arm, her grip tight. "Is this real?"

The path broadened into a grand avenue, lined with towering tree trunks, their canopies so tightly woven that the light arrived already filtered, cool and green by the time it reached the path below. Rays threaded through the treetops, igniting leaves with a deep gold-green that had nowhere to go but down. A breeze lifted the hair from Stric's neck, and the shadows shivered across the root-knuckled ground.

Floral notes wove through the air. He breathed deep, and the scent carried something beyond perfume. Resin and deep earth, the kind that lives under old roots. A coolness at the back of his throat, unhurried. The crystal at the Powerstaff's head pulsed once against his grip, slow as a second heartbeat.

Teela stood motionless beside him, head tilted back, taking in the canopy that stretched higher than castle towers. Her hand remained on his arm. He covered it with his own.

They had travelled for thirteen days. From mountain stone, werewolf dens, ancient ruins, and river paths. Each step had brought them here, to this threshold where magic sang through every leaf and beam of light. The Powerstaff's crystal hummed against his fingers, so finely attuned it registered every root in the ground beneath him. Different strengths. Complementary.

Whhrll paused, scent-checking the sacred air, ears forward. "This tree-folk lands, pack-brothers. Though unseen, they are watching us." He led them to a hidden path.

As they followed, the sounds of the forest grew softer, the birdsong thinning until only a low resonance remained beneath it, felt more in Stric's chest than heard.

Chapter 8

The Usurper's Shadow

On the morning that Stric and Teela were to cross into Eldoria's embrace, far to the south and under entirely different eyes, Talnaress was waking.

A merchant hurried across Market Square, gaze fixed on the worn cobbles beneath his feet. Twenty years had taught him when to look away. The golem beside the fountain stood motionless. Its granite bulk casting shadows across the cobbles like collapsed bodies, rock fists still crusted with yesterday's brown stains.

Undead soldiers gathered around the gallows. Figures in rotting armour tracked every movement, fluid leaking from empty eye sockets. None of them breathed, and the silence where living soldiers would have murmured, shifted, coughed, sat against the ears like a hand pressed flat over them.

The fountain no longer ran. Its basin sat bone-dry, carved lip cracked in a fracture that followed the stone's grain. Fresh flowers wilted in the pre-dawn chill beside a child's ribbon, sun-faded to pale blue, tied around a broken ornament.

In the distance, where the Magicians' Council Hall once rose with proud towers, only blackened foundations remained. Ash and broken stones. Two decades of weeds claiming what the fire had taken, a reminder of what resistance earned.

The eastern districts fared worse. Windows shuttered tight even in daylight. Doors barred from the inside. Families that had once traded with smiles now kept to themselves, trusting no one, speaking only when necessary.

A golem stood at the intersection of Merchant's Row and King's Avenue, though no one called it King's Avenue anymore. Just "the wide street." Naming things drew on memory, and memory bred hope. Hope led to the fountain's edge or the executioner's axe.

The golem's head turned, glowing eyes tracking a rat that skittered between shadows. Its movement held terrible patience, waiting for someone to break curfew, to speak too loudly, to forget that Talnaress no longer belonged to its people.

It belonged to Barok Tana. And Barok Tana forgets nothing.

The city breathed in the rhythm of eyes that found the cobbles before a golem's gaze could reach them, of doors eased shut rather than closed. Twenty years of silent sentinels at every corner who never tired, never slept, never stopped watching. The faint sweetness of decay drifted through the streets. Even the wind couldn't carry it away. Twenty years, and the city still smelled of what he'd done to it.

In the highest tower of what had once been the royal palace, a different watch was kept.

Barok Tana stood before a table scattered with reports and maps. Tall and aristocratic in midnight-blue robes that fell in a scholar's drape. His white hair caught the light from the purple flames burning in their sconces, unchanged from the desperate young man who'd once stood before the Guild Council. But the reports before him represented something that shouldn't exist.

Two detections. His finger traced the first mark on the map. The northern forest, twenty-eight days past. A magical signature strong enough to trigger his surveillance network. Power wielded with exact economy. Output precise, calibrated, nothing wasted. Guild precision, unmistakable to anyone who understood what to look for.

Then nothing for days. Until the second detection, seventeen days ago, his finger moved northwest across the parchment to a point heading towards the foothills.

The same signature, he was certain, burning bright enough to register across leagues of wilderness. Stronger than before, as if the wielder had grown more confident. More reckless.

The direction was clear. A line drawn between the two points.

Guild precision. He recognised it because the knowledge to identify it had been stolen alongside everything else. The death-seed crystal pulsed warm against his Powerstaff's wood, and the seven voices fell silent.

Their silence was worse than their accusations. His fingers went still against the parchment.

The meditation chamber at Drakenholt. Bioluminescent fungi painting sacred walls in blue-green light. Geometric patterns glowing beneath seven bodies arranged in the posture of teaching, of trust, of absolute vulnerability.

His Powerstaff had erupted with stolen Guild magic. Binding energy flooded the chamber's own conduits, turning sacred geometry against itself. Paralysis distributed where enlightenment should have flowed.

Seven bodies locked in the same breath. Seven pairs of luminous eyes, still mobile, still tracking, still trying to understand what their minds already knew to be true. Teaching postures became a prison. Sacred space became a cage.

Sethara's claws had scraped stone. Five taps. Alarm. Terror. Then nothing.

The crystal's warmth faded to its usual low pulse. The voices returned, pressing against the edges of his awareness.

His finger resumed its path across the map.

The agent had dismissed the first signature in his own mind, writing it off as a minor anomaly unworthy of his master's attention. When the second signal arrived, the fool had tried to bury his earlier negligence along with the new intelligence. As if hiding failure from Barok Tana was ever an option. The golem's stone fists had made that lesson permanent for anyone else who might mistake incompetence for discretion.

In the flickering firelight, the light landed wrong on his hand. Caught the dark veins threading beneath skin too grey for any living man's. One breath, and the colour shifted back; the scholar's complexion was restored.

His eyes moved across the parchment. Dark eyes that reflected the flames without catching their light, as if something behind them swallowed illumination whole. He spread his hands across the map, long fingers flat against the parchment.

The signatures suggested someone with years of training. Two points on a map, eleven days between them, the trajectory unmistakable.

Eldoria.

His Powerstaff leaned against the table within arm's reach, always within reach. The master deathseed crystal crowned its length, pulsing with sickly crimson light that painted the tower stones in shades of old blood. Fused to the wood through a corrupted ritual, through stolen knowledge, through seven murders in sacred chambers.

The elves. He'd left them alone for twenty years because subduing their forest kingdom would cost more resources than their interference warranted. A strategic calculation that had served him well. They kept to their borders. He kept to his. An uneasy peace held.

But what if that peace had been a deception all along?

Had the elves been harbouring Guild survivors these past two decades? Hidden in their forests, protected by their borders, while he believed himself secure.

The Guild had maintained ties with Eldoria before it was destroyed. Before he'd burned the council hall, claimed the Academy, hunted every apprentice and Master to ground. Grandmaster Vrill, he had dealt with that old fool himself. Old alliances. Annual correspondence between Vrill and Eldoria's Mage Council. Records he'd since turned to ash.

If even one Guild magician had escaped to Eldoria twenty years ago, they could have continued the old traditions. Trained apprentices. Preserved the knowledge he'd worked to erase. And now, after two decades, one of them was moving through his kingdom with purpose, perhaps returning home after a mission, carrying intelligence about his defences. The first visible sign of a threat that had been growing in secret all this time.

His hand brushed against something in his inner pocket as he set down the reports. Paper, worn soft by decades. He drew it out, studying the crude lines with the same analytical attention he'd given the intelligence report.

A child's drawing. A magician with a staff shooting stars. At the bottom, in wobbling letters.

Barok, the best magic man in the whole world.

His sister's work. Seven years old when she'd drawn it, her small fingers sticky with breakfast honey when she passed it to him. He'd kept it through his apprenticeship, through his exile to Lormir Island, through everything after. The parchment had survived when so much else had burned.

This small hand had pressed it into his larger one.

She had stood waiting for him to look up, chin raised, her eyes on his face.

Years later, she tried to understand.

The village inn smelled of wood smoke and barley soup. Barok sat across from his sister, the weathered oak table between them.

She'd grown. Eighteen now, copper hair catching firelight the same way it had when she'd pressed that drawing into his hands. Eleven years since he'd left for his apprenticeship.

"You look different." Her hands wrapped around her mug, knuckles white.

"The island was..." He searched for words. Found none that wouldn't terrify her. "Difficult."

Her eyes studied his face, feature by feature, the way she'd once bent over parchment to draw him as a magician shooting stars. Looking for something. Her brother, perhaps.

His facial muscles arranged themselves into a smile. The expression held for exactly as long as he willed it, no longer.

"What happened to you?" The question emerged quiet and strained.

"I learned. The truth, or part of it. The Guild was wrong about many things. I found knowledge they tried to seal away."

"I still have the scars from Father's wood axe. You know that? You carried me to the healer and wouldn't let go of my hand until the stitching was done."

"The cut was deep. You needed four stitches."

Her jaw set. "Four stitches. That's what you remember? Not holding my hand. Four stitches." Her voice dropped. "Does any of it matter to you?"

"It matters. Your welfare is..."

"My welfare." The word came out bitter. "Like I'm a supply route. Like I'm some resource to be managed."

The fire crackled. Somewhere in the common room, a chair scraped against worn floorboards.

"Was it worth it?" Her voice cracked. "Worth whatever they did to you on that island? The kingdom you've laid to waste, the lives you've destroyed?" Tears tracked down her face, catching the firelight. "Worth becoming something that looks at me like I'm a stranger?"

"You're not a stranger." Sisters weren't strangers.

"I proved them all wrong," he leaned forward. "The Guild, everyone who said I'd amount to nothing. I showed them all. I rule now." He willed sincerity into his voice. "This should make you proud."

Her chair scraped against the worn floorboards. "You think that's what I wanted?" Her voice shook. "I wanted my brother. The one who helped me with sums. Who made me laugh. Who promised he'd come back and teach me real magic someday."

She wiped her hands on her apron. "That boy is dead. And I think you know it."

She picked up his untouched soup, carried it back to the kitchen, and returned to the common room to clear another table.

Barok sat alone at the weathered oak table, steady hands flat against the grain.

She might tell others what he'd become.

The thought arrived with the casual weight of wondering whether to order wine or ale. Strategic benefit versus exposure risk. Energy expenditure versus threat mitigation.

Nobody would listen to her. Their fear of his power would hold them in check. She had none. The risk was acceptable.

His fingers found the drawing in his pocket. The parchment crumpled in his fist before he registered the pressure. He smoothed it out. Wavering lines and a star placed slightly off-centre, preserved in wax and paper.

Barok, the best magic man in the whole world.

He folded the drawing. Returned it to his pocket. Rose and left without paying for the uneaten meal.

Tomorrow, he would return to Talnaress. Continue shaping his kingdom. The sister who'd believed in him had joined the brother she believed in. Gone, though neither had died.

Behind him, firelight still caught copper hair through the inn's window. He did not look back.

Barok stared at the drawing. Its colour now faded, but the lines were still clear. Someone had believed in him. A historical fact, filed alongside the founding of the Guild, the reign of King Balthor, and the faith of a seven-year-old girl.

All equally distant. All equally cold.

She loved you, Sethara's voice cut, cold as stone where nothing had breathed in a long time. *We see everything you see. Feel everything you cannot. Forever.*

Heat gathered behind his eyes. The seven pressed inward, voices sharpening from a murmur to something with edges. The drawing was still warm from being smoothed. The smell of the inn pulled backwards, barley soup giving way to stone. To the moment he had made her what she was.

Forbidden magic found Morvath's consciousness and took what it needed. Clean. Complete.

Light bloomed at the corners of the elder's eyes. Wrong light. Silver-bright veins spread across his skull like cracks in ice, pulsing beneath fur with each struggling heartbeat, carrying stolen knowledge towards the surface.

The second extraction came easier. Sethara's tactical brilliance laid bare. Her expertise, catalogued and taken to fuel the very corruption she had spent her life studying. Her final conscious thought had crystallised with bitter clarity before the spirit-binding claimed her.

I saw this. In his eyes. I should have acted sooner.

The voices quieted. They always returned.

He placed the drawing on the table beside the intelligence reports, covered both with a map, and returned his attention to the threat analysis.

The Guild magician. Eldoria. The possibility that his enemies had been preparing in secret while he believed them extinct.

Fresh parchment. The quill moved without hesitation, orders taking shape the way his hands always worked: certain, without pause.

Patrols reinforced along the Eldorian border. Surveillance expanded in coastal territories. Informant networks activated in every town between the detection point and the Elven forest. Someone with Guild training would stand out: questions asked, supplies purchased, patterns broken. All of it would flow back to this tower.

The net would close. It always closed.

If the elves had indeed been sheltering Guild survivors, twenty years of assumed extinction had been wrong. Twenty years of calculated peace based on a false assumption. The strategic balance he'd maintained would need revision.

More patrols watching the elves' forest, searching for the Eldorian border. A demonstration of reach. Pressure without force. They would see the patrols and draw their own conclusions. If they were guilty, if they were indeed hiding magicians, the pressure would force a response.

He would know the truth soon enough.

By the time he finished, dawn light had seeped through the tower windows. Three pages of orders lay before him, ready for dispatch.

The guard captain arrived within the hour. Greying at the temples, scarred across his jaw. A man who'd survived twenty years of service through competence and caution.

"You summoned me, my lord."

"Two magical signatures." Barok didn't turn from the window. "Moving northwest toward Eldoria."

A sharp intake of breath. "The Guild is destroyed, my lord. You destroyed them."

"So I believed." Now he turned. "It seems the elves may have been less neutral than they appeared."

The captain's jaw tightened. "You want the forest sealed."

"I want it watched. Every game trail, every mountain pass, every stream crossing. If a mouse moves between Eldoria and my kingdom, I want to know its name and destination."

"That will require..."

"Whatever it requires." Barok's eyes met his. "Do you have concerns, Captain?"

A long pause. "No concerns, my lord. Only solutions."

"Good. You have three days to double the forest presence. Dismissed."

The captain bowed and departed, his footsteps retreating faster than protocol demanded.

Barok stood alone in the tower room, maps spread beneath his hands. Purple flame-light caught the dark veins threading across his knuckles, the grey smudges on his fingertips that no amount of scrubbing could remove. Ash ground into the whorls of his skin. Permanent. Seven murders were written in stains that had outlasted twenty years of washing.

Seven piles of grey powder where guardians had knelt. Each pile held the exact shape of a meditation posture for one terrible moment before collapsing, scattering across stone that had been sacred until he profaned it.

Seven faces sinking into crystal darkness. Mouths open in accusation. Eyes wide with betrayal. Each image held for three heartbeats, preserved with perfect clarity, then swallowed into depths that would hold them forever.

The crystal had warmed in his palm, its pulse climbing steadily against his skin. He had said the words. His hands remained still. Where grief should have lived, there was nothing. Only the clean certainty of a plan completed. *I'm sorry*, he had said to Vyxara's ash. His throat produced the sound. Nothing followed. Not in his hands, not in his chest.

The crystal on his Powerstaff pulsed with seven heartbeats synchronised to his own, and he turned back to the maps.

The net was closing in.

His finger traced the line between the two detection points once more. Eastern forests to the foothills. Then northwest toward Eldoria. Purpose and direction. Perhaps someone returning to enemies who thought themselves hidden.

They would not remain hidden much longer.

Barok Tana gathered the reports and maps. The drawing disappeared beneath strategic assessments and deployment schedules.

Below the tower windows, the first patrol boots were already crossing the cobblestones, their rhythm rising through the stone into the soles of his feet. Somewhere beyond its walls, in forests he would soon scour clean, an unknown magician moved with purpose toward foes who believed they were concealed.

They had no idea what was coming.
Barok Tana was certain that he did.

Chapter 9

Among the Elves

Trees breathed. Stric pressed his fingers against bark that predated kingdoms. Ancient life pulsed beneath his touch. Patient and aware. Heat gathered beneath the bark and pushed up through his fingers in slow, deep pulses, each one climbing his wrist before the next began. His Powerstaff trembled against his palm like a tuning fork flicked by invisible fingers, its carved surface growing warm as magic thrummed through Eldoria's roots.

"They tower beyond memory," Teela's voice was barely audible above the forest's whispered songs.

Each trunk stretched wide enough to house families. Wind moved through the canopy in slow waves, carrying the deep smell of the upper forest down through the golden shafts of light. The air tasted of damp loam and wildflower sweetness. Unseen creatures murmured through shadow-dappled groves, their calls brief and low before the forest swallowed them again.

Hair prickled along Stric's arms, each strand rising as if pulled by invisible threads. The forest's whispers faltered, replaced by a silence that weighed against his eardrums like cupped hands. Shadows shifted within hollows, movements too deliberate for wind-stirred leaves, too purposeful for creatures seeking mere shelter.

Teela's hand moved to her sword hilt, her breathing shallow as she scanned the canopy above.

Every leaf stilled as if the forest had drawn one vast inhalation and refused to release it. Even the stream seemed to quiet its babbling. The forest was waiting. Watching.

The shadows exploded into motion. Elf sentries dropped from canopy heights, feet striking the earth without a sound, while arrows nocked to bowstrings in one fluid movement. Green and gold cloaks whirled as they surrounded the travellers, forming a protective circle that closed like flower petals, bows half-drawn but angled skyward in a gesture of greeting.

Silver hair caught dappled sunlight as the lead sentry stepped forward. His gaze moved across all three of them without haste, settling last on Stric with the completeness of a man whose assessment was already done. He held the gaze for three deliberate heartbeats, eyes level, before nodding. "Welcome to Eldoria, Grandmaster."

Stric's fingers traced his Powerstaff's grooves, the wood warming beneath his palm. The carved surface pulsed steadier than his own heartbeat. The elf's nod settled on him like a physical weight. His spine straightened before he'd consciously willed it, shoulders pulling back while his grip on the staff shifted.

"I am Elar. We have been watching your approach." The elf's gaze went distant for half a heartbeat before settling back into a formal welcome. "Your companion and Whhrll are welcome."

The title settled onto Stric's shoulders with less weight than before. "We are grateful for your welcome, Elar. I am Stric Deamara. This is Teela Reyna." His hand settled on Teela's shoulder as she inclined her head.

"I see Whhrll needs no introduction."

Elar's lips twitched into a reserved smile, his gaze flickering over Whhrll before settling back on Stric. "Whhrll and his pack-mates have left an impression on our lands." The elf's fingers drummed once against his bow.

Whhrll flashed a grin, revealing sharp canines gleaming in dappled light. His ears flicked forward, tail giving the barest wag as Elar's knowing glance met his. The elf's lips twitched in response.

Elar gestured toward the forest path. "Our queen awaits you in the forest's heart. Come."

Stric turned to speak, his words dissolved into empty air where Elar had stood. His pulse quickened as he scanned bark patterns that seemed to shift when viewed sideways, as if the forest itself had swallowed the elf whole.

Elar's voice drifted from the shadows. The elf had moved ten paces without disturbing a single leaf. Beside him, Teela stood perfectly still, facing the space where Elar had been. Her jaw set.

Stric's boots snapped twigs and crunched leaves with each step. Stark sounds. Clumsy against the elves' silence. He paused mid-stride, tilting his head, listening, watching for some technique he had missed. A careful step. Still, the soft crackle of dried vegetation. His gaze followed the elves' passage. Their feet found surfaces that welcomed them. The forest itself conspired in their grace.

Nestled within the giant trees, dwellings emerged from their hearts, the bark's natural grain running unbroken through wall and floor with no visible seam where living tree became living room.

Branches formed archways, while delicate vines curled around open doorways, rustling in the breeze.

Teela's breath caught in her chest, her gaze travelling upward through impossible architecture that made her neck crane. The wood spiralled beyond sight, defying every law of construction. She nudged Stric, pointing toward an elf brushing her fingers over a vine. The vine curled slowly around the elf's wrist, warm and unhurried, pausing there a single beat before slipping free.

Around him, vines answered Elven touches without hesitation, each one finding its way without reaching. Bark that yielded a fraction toward each palm. A vine following a withdrawing hand before it let go. When Stric reached for similar connections, his magic stuttered and sparked like a child's first words. His Powerstaff shifted between cool and warm against his palm. The wood pulsed. Intricate, layered. Deep.

Elves ascended spiralling staircases of living wood that wound around massive trunks. Crystalline sap windows refracted sunlight into dancing rainbows, casting shifting hues across passing faces.

Elar turned to them, his chin lifting as he gestured toward the tree. "This is the Great Tree of Eldoria; our Queen has been expecting you."

The Great Tree's presence struck them like walking into a mountain wind. Stric stopped mid-stride. An invisible weight settled across his shoulders. Undeniable. Measuring. Dry, still air met him at the threshold, carrying a mineral-cold smell of resin and undisturbed bark rising from the roots below. The staff responded, its carved surface warming. Beside him, Teela steadied herself against roots as thick as a castle wall. The air tasted of ancient bark.

Entering through an arched doorway fused with the tree's bark, Stric stumbled. When he caught himself against the living walls, harmonies thrummed through the wood like distant thunder, vibrating up his arm and settling deep in his bones where they echoed his own heartbeat.

Teela breathed deeply, wildflower perfume clearing the travel dust from her lungs, the line of her shoulders releasing a hold Stric hadn't noticed until it was gone.

At the far end, Queen Aeloria sat upon a wooden throne adorned with vines and blossoms. Bioluminescent blooms brightened around her, as if her very presence fed them.

Stric, Teela, and Whhrll bowed, with held breaths.

Golden waves of hair danced around Queen Aeloria's face and down her back as she rose. Each strand caught the bloom-light and gave it back golden. Her hazel eyes swept the room. Conversations died mid-word. An elf near the entrance straightened as her gaze passed over him, whilst another's hand stilled mid-gesture, fingers frozen against the carved armrest.

Emerald and moss swirled in the living weave of her gown. Each step sent ripples through the fabric like wind across a forest floor.

"Welcome, Grandmaster." Queen Aeloria's voice filled the room without rising, each word settling into the stillness that had formed ahead of it. "I am Aeloria. The forest whispered of your coming."

"Your Majesty. I am Stric Deamara. This is Teela Reyna."

Aeloria's gaze settled on him without searching, complete and still, the focus of someone who had arrived at her conclusions before he'd opened his mouth. "Tell me of your quest, though I believe I know what brings you here."

Stric stepped forward, forcing his breath even. "Your Majesty, Grandmaster Vrill sent me to find the whereabouts of Prince Dreese. He was taken from our world, and we believe the elves of Eldoria may know of his fate."

"As I suspected, you seek your prince," Aeloria spoke the words with the certainty of deep earth, as if the answer had been written in the turning of seasons. "He came with one of your own named Cearan and a palace guard named Kael."

Vrill's crystal ball. Two shadowy figures, one clutching an infant, fleeing through blaze-licked streets. The vision seared behind Stric's eyelids with such clarity he could taste smoke that wasn't there. His breath caught.

"We hid him in shadows so deep, even Barok Tana's reach would falter."

Stric's gaze snapped to Teela's. Her minute nod, she'd caught it too. Barok's name, finally spoken aloud.

The Queen's eyes grew distant with memory. "When whispers of Barok's pursuit reached our ears, we acted. We sent him through a wormhole to another world, far from the reach of he who sought him."

Air stuck in Teela's throat like swallowed thorns. "A wormhole? Another world? But how can we reach him?"

"The wormhole requires a celestial alignment. This will occur three moons from now. You must reach Darmoor Island when the portal is open."

Stric's knuckles whitened around his Powerstaff until the carved grooves bit into his palm. "Three moons. How can we know the prince remains safe?"

"Grandmaster Vrill once confided in me about his visit with the Oracle. I know now what his vision truly spoke of." Aeloria's expression softened. "Your prince travelled with sworn protectors whose oaths transcend the void between worlds. They will have kept him safe all this time. As the Oracle showed Vrill, three more moons are nothing."

Teela's gaze anchored itself to the Queen's ageless eyes like a sword driven deep into stone, her chin lifting. "We will do whatever it takes to bring him back."

The Queen's eyes softened as she nodded. "You stand as the great oaks stand against storms, Teela. The earth recognises those born to shield others. Your path shall bloom with thorns and victories, as all worthy paths must." Her gaze shifted to Stric. "You are most welcome to wait out the time until your journey can begin here in Eldoria. We will aid you in any way we can."

The Queen addressed Whhrll. "Noble guide, I have a task for you."

Whhrll's amber eyes caught the hall's golden light. He stood tall. "Whatever pack-bonds require, great one," he responded, his ears twitching forward with attention.

"Return to your pack and ask your elders to gather the warriors of all packs. We will need to unite if we are to make our stand." Her voice filled the hall, measured and unhurried, each word given its full weight. "Request that they gather here in Eldoria in four moons. This should be time enough for the Grandmaster to return with his prince." She paused. "Dine here and rest for the night so that you will be refreshed for your journey home."

Whhrll's ears flattened with respect as he bowed. "As pack-elders' wisdom guides, my lady. Trail-scent runs clear between your words and our den."

Elar stepped forward once more, ready to escort them to their quarters. As they followed, Stric straightened his shoulders, whilst Teela exchanged a nod with him.

The following days blurred. Before the first birds stirred, before the morning mist lifted from ancient roots, they were already moving.

Prince Dreese's rescue pulled Stric from sleep before dawn. Stars still pierced the canopy when he rolled from his pallet, Powerstaff humming in his grip. The training grounds. Teela would already be there, sword flashing through the grey pre-dawn light, breath misting white.

During the first week, Elar burst into Queen Aeloria's court as they shared an evening meal in the great hall. Sweat darkened his forest leathers, and his chest heaved from a hard run. "Your Majesty," he gasped, dropping to one knee. "Increased patrols of Barok's forces have been spotted along the forest's edge. Conducting systematic sweeps that bring them closer than ever to our borders."

The Queen's fingers stilled on her throne's wooden arm, her features tightening. "How close?"

"A day's march from our outer sentries, my lady. Young Spellcasters on patrol missions leading undead soldiers."

The words settled like frost across the hall. Silence stretched, broken only by the crackle of heart fire.

Stric's eyes traced the living walls. Organic curves he'd admired that morning. Paper-thin now. A shell of wood against the darkness beyond. The tree's heart light flickered. Or maybe his eyes had learned to see the truth.

That night, Queen Aeloria's voice came measured and low, each word spaced with care. "Your presence may be drawing attention. Forest whispers carry news of Barok's patrols growing more determined. They have long sought our city, but now they grow closer to finding us."

"Then our time here grows short." Stric's words came clipped and precise.

"Perhaps. But the wormhole's timing remains unchanged. We must prepare both of you for what lies ahead."

The forest's evening chorus faltered like a singer forgetting words mid-song. Night-birds that had called for centuries fell silent while others took up unfamiliar rhythms. Urgent, discordant. Stric's fingers moved to his Powerstaff instinctively.

Teela laid her palms against the rugged bark, deep grooves biting into her skin, the wood warm beneath her hands. Old bark and resin beneath her nostrils, and beneath that, something acrid that didn't belong to the forest. The elder trees leaned inward, their boughs creating shadows that swallowed the light.

A sentry named Aelith paused beside the training ground one morning, watching Teela work through sword forms. The warrior's gaze shifted, the sharp assessment in it easing by degrees, her shoulders settling. After several minutes of observation, she stepped forward.

"Your foundation is firm. But I see potential for more. Would you welcome training?"

Days later, the dawn's frost made Teela's breath visible as she worked through forms that had pulled against her shoulders the day before. Aelith waited with silent patience while Teela's strikes came too aggressively, too desperate.

"Your blade carries more than steel," Aelith observed. "Yesterday's pain teaches today's precision. Show me how your sword wants to move when it's not fighting your past."

Teela raised her weapon again. Her next strike went wider than the first, her guard dropping, stance opening where it should have tightened. Aelith's words had found their mark.

Steel rang against steel as Teela adapted, her movements gaining the fluid precision that marked Elven combat.

"Again," Aelith commanded. Teela's strike went wide, frustration making her movements sharp and uncontrolled.

"Your enemies will not fight with honour," Aelith continued, circling Teela like a patient predator. "You must always fight with honour, fight for those who cannot. Use that difference against your enemy."

Teela paused, the aggression leaving her grip by degrees. When she struck again, her blade caught the opening Aelith had left unguarded.

"Now you begin to understand," Aelith smiled. "Skill without heart is nothing more than violence. Heart without skill is a meaningless sacrifice. You are learning to balance both."

In the fifth week, Aelith produced a leather pouch that made the air itself recoil. Before opening it, she met Teela's eyes with grave intensity. "Barok's undead carry death's own stench. I have seen seasoned warriors vomit mid-battle, their skill useless against nausea."

The open pouch released an odour like summer-rotted meat mixed with grave earth. Wrong. Profane. Teela's stomach lurched, tears streaming as she fought the urge to flee. To run until the smell couldn't follow.

"Breathe through your mouth," Aelith instructed, her own eyes watering. "Find your centre despite the assault on your senses. In actual battle, this stench will be accompanied by the screams of the dying and the weight of your friends' lives in your hands."

Teela's sword trembled. Her grip tightened, leather wrapping slick beneath her palm. She blinked against the stinging but kept her blade steady. Muscle memory took over. Her breathing shifted. Short, controlled inhales through her mouth, already adapting to what would be far worse in actual combat.

Steel rang against steel. In the seventh week, Aelith feinted left, and Teela's body responded before her mind caught up, spinning right, sword arcing upward to catch the elf's true strike in a shower of sparks. For the first time, Aelith stepped backward. Her eyes widened, then her mouth curved.

Dawn training sessions became a ritual. Evening meals followed in silence, Aelith's presence no longer prompting Teela's hand to the sword hilt. She shared camp rations without first checking sightlines. Now, she turned her back to the forest while they spoke. A warrior's trust, given sparingly.

Stric wrestled with Talnar's secrets. Pages flipped faster than he could read. Symbols blazed under his touch, searing afterimages behind his eyelids whilst the book's consciousness pressed behind his eyes, dense with competing voices. His skull throbbed. When he traced a complex pattern, feedback crackled up his arm, leaving his fingers numb.

But Talnar's teachings carried structure, words, gestures, and focus. The elves offered something different entirely. Something that hummed beneath thought, that moved with breath.

Master Elarion's attention sharpened one afternoon, his gaze settling on Stric's locked wrists and the Powerstaff's fractured light, while Talnar's consciousness whispered competing instructions through his mind. The elder elf's weathered hand settled on

Stric's shoulder, interrupting the magical static that threatened to tear his concentration apart.

"Your tome teaches you to command magic," Elarion said quietly. "We can teach you to invite it. Come. Let me show you the difference."

Master Elarion gestured toward a centuries-old oak whose leaves exploded into violent motion. "Feel how the tree calls to the air."

Stric pushed his palm against the bark. Invisible currents surged through the wood. His Powerstaff screamed like a struck tuning fork. When he called to the wind, it answered with hurricane force, leaves swirling around them in a green tornado whilst his hair whipped across his face. The protective light that sparked around his shoulders flickered erratically, threatening to collapse under the magical storm.

"Control, not force!" Elarion shouted over the wind. "Feel the tree's rhythm!"

Stric closed his eyes, searching for the rhythm beneath both powers. He raised both hands. Fire sparked from his Powerstaff whilst earth-song flowed from his free hand. The energies clashed. Ground seared. Stone cracked. Sweat beaded on his forehead.

"Don't force them together," Master Elarion called over the thunder. "Let them find their own harmony."

There. A deeper pulse. His breath changed. When he opened his eyes, golden-green light danced between his palms in slow spirals, drawing warmth from his skin like a held coal.

One afternoon, as Stric practised weaving protective barriers around moving targets, the Master magician paused mid-instruction. His weathered face creased, the mid-instruction word dying in his throat, as the latest ward brightened and held its shape, running clear and even.

"Remarkable," he said, tilting his head. "In eight centuries of teaching, I have never encountered a human magician whose magic so resonates with our own. You hunger for our teachings in a way that defies explanation." He exchanged glances with his fellow instructors. "Most human magicians require months to achieve even the most basic of Elven techniques. Your magic reaches toward ours as if your very essence remembers something it shouldn't know."

Stric's knuckles paled around his Powerstaff. The carved wood grew warm, heat spreading up his forearms. Around him, the air shifted. Fine hairs rose along his arms. The Elven spellwork in the clearing brightened.

The elder elf nodded, his weathered fingers stroking his silver beard. "Perhaps there are truths about magic that even we have yet to comprehend." He paused, considering. "But remember this: such mastery will not go unnoticed by those who hunt magical practitioners. Barok's graduates know how to sense magical signatures. They will know the moment they encounter your power that you are no ordinary magician."

"Then I must be prepared for them."

"Tomorrow we train defence and offence together. Our reports suggest you'll face enemies who won't wait for you to prepare your next strike."

But always, even in these peaceful moments, their ears remained alert for sounds that didn't belong. The crack of a branch under an unfamiliar weight, the rustle of leaves without wind to stir them.

Tonight, Teela turned her head toward Stric. The moon cast silver light across the clearing, dappling their faces in radiance. "You once asked how I came to be alone in the forest where you found me." Her gaze flicked between Stric's face and the deeper shadows in the forest, her fingers drawing patterns in the grass. She drew a breath to speak, then stopped, the words hovering unformed. Her hand moved to rest against her thigh, where her sword usually hung, fingers curling around emptiness before settling back into the grass. "Would you still like to know?"

Stric nodded, his hand brushing against hers. "If you wish to tell me, of course, I would like to know."

Teela's voice emerged smaller than usual as she tucked a strand of hair behind her ear before returning her fingers to the grass. Each movement precise and controlled. "My father vanished during Barok's takeover, whilst my mother still carried me beneath her heart." The moonlight turned the moisture in her eyes into liquid silver.

The night breeze stirred the leaves above them, carrying sounds that made Teela's shoulders draw inward. Her fingers stilled in the grass, pushing down. "She would tell me of the night he stood against a storm to save a stranded neighbour, returning home soaked but smiling..." Each rustle in the canopy made her turn her head slightly, listening to ghosts that only she could hear, her breathing shallow and careful as if loud sounds might wake the dead.

"When Barok's forces stormed our village, my father stood tall, determined to face them." The unshed tears teetered on the brink of breaking. "He walked out the door that day and never returned. My mother's heart broke, yet she clung to hope, whispering prayers at night that he might still be out there, somewhere, alive."

Stric reached out, covering her trembling hands with his own.

She paused, gripping his hand. "After I was born, my mother was taken from our home and made a slave to the Spellcaster who had been put in charge of our village."

Teela took a deep breath. "She endured torment, forced to serve the very people who had destroyed our lives." A tear escaped despite her efforts. "When I was six years old, my mother seized an opportunity and escaped, fleeing into the woods with me."

"Before Barok's takeover, my parents had been hunters. They knew how to survive in the wilderness, and my mother taught me everything she knew. We lived off the land, moving from place to place, staying one step ahead of Barok's forces. She showed me how to track animals, find edible plants, and build shelters."

Teela's gaze fell to the ground as a tear slipped down her cheek. "But when I was fourteen, she fell ill." Her lips drew into a thin line.

She squeezed Stric's hand until her knuckles went white, her grip becoming almost painful as memories tightened around her chest. Her breathing grew shallow, each inhale a careful, measured thing. When she spoke again, her voice emerged smaller, younger.

"Despite my best efforts to care for her, she grew weaker with each passing day." Her voice wavered between past and present. "She passed away in her sleep. So quietly I thought she was only resting." Her vision blurred as tears rolled down her face.

Stric's breath caught. His fingers intertwined with hers, wrapping around them like lifelines. His throat closed. The words didn't come.

His grip on her hands tightened. His jaw set. Her mother's death. Her father's disappearance. The years spent alone, surviving on skills passed down before everything was taken away.

His throat worked, trying to force sound past the tightness. The forest sounds wrapped around them. Rustling leaves. Distant owl calls. The whisper of wind through ancient branches.

"You're not alone anymore." The words emerged rougher than he intended. "I am here for you, whatever you need."

But even as he spoke comfort, his next breath caught halfway. The words aligned themselves in his mind before he'd consciously spoken them.

She lifted her head, eyes finding his through the darkness. Moonlight reflected off the tears still clinging to her eyelashes. Something in his expression must have shifted because her breath caught. Her fingers tightened around his.

"Stric?" His name came low and careful.

He drew a breath. The forest air filled his lungs with wildflowers and deep earth. "I was ten years old when the Academy teachers found me." The words flowed quietly but steadily. Each one was a stone laid across a chasm he'd crossed alone until now. His fingers tightened around hers until his knuckles paled in the moonlight. "Wandering in the forest outside the Academy walls. Confused, lost." He paused, the next words harder than the first. "With no memory of where I'd come from or who I was."

Teela's grip tightened around his hand, her thumb tracing small circles against his palm. But she said nothing. Waiting. Witnessing. Her silence created space for truths he'd never spoken aloud.

"I don't remember my parents." Each admission felt like pulling thorns from flesh. "Don't know if I have siblings somewhere, wandering through life unaware I exist. My earliest memory is waking in those woods, alone, with nothing but..." He stopped, struggling with words that had no right to sound so absurd. "A certainty that wouldn't leave me. I was going to become a magician!"

The laugh that escaped carried more pain than humour, sharp and bitter as unripe fruit. "I must have said it a hundred times those first days. 'I'm going to be a magician.' A child's dream, except I had no idea why I believed it so strongly. Absolute conviction burning in my chest, with nothing behind it. No reason I could name. No memory to explain it. Just that."

The campfire crackled between them, casting a dancing light across her face. Shadows played in the hollows beneath her eyes, across the line of her jaw. Her gaze held steady on him, the kind that didn't shift or soften. His hands went still in the space between them.

"The Council didn't want to admit me." His throat tightened at the memory. Fifteen years. Still. "A child with no family, no history, no proof of magical lineage?" It violated every precedent. Broke rules that had stood for centuries. They debated for hours whilst he waited outside. Voices he couldn't hear, deciding his fate.

His gaze dropped to their joined hands. Her fingers had gone white at the knuckles, matching his own. "But Vrill..." His voice caught on the name. He stopped. "Vrill fought for me. Stood before the entire Council and argued that magic doesn't care about lineage or precedent. He tested my magical resonance himself, right there in the chamber. Made them watch as the testing crystal blazed brighter than it had for any student in living memory."

Teela's breath hitched, but she remained silent, letting him find his way through the story at his own pace.

"He convinced them to give me a chance. And for fifteen years, he watched over me. Ensured I received the necessary training. Protected me from council members who thought I didn't belong. Never explained why, and I... I never asked. Too afraid the answer might be that I wasn't worth the faith he placed in me. That one day he'd realise his mistake and send me away."

Teela's free hand shifted against his. "Stric..." Low and unhurried.

"You said you lost your mother, your family." He forced himself to meet her eyes fully now, letting her see the truth he'd carried in silence for years. The way his hands had learned to go still when someone asked where he came from. The hollow place where memories should live. "That Barok took everything from you. I never had a family to lose. Never knew what it felt like to belong anywhere but the Academy, and even there..." He shook his head, the movement sharp and frustrated. "Questions without answers. A past that doesn't exist. An identity built on nothing but determination and someone else's faith."

Fresh tears tracked silver down her cheeks, but her grip remained steady as stone, anchoring them both.

His throat worked. His voice roughened. "Your pain has names, faces, memories of laughter before the darkness came. You know who you lost, can visit your mother's grave and tell her about your day. Mine is just..." He gestured with his free hand, trying to shape absence into something she could understand.

"Emptiness. Questions that can't be answered. A void where a childhood should be."

The words kept coming, fifteen years of silence breaking. "Sometimes I wake in the night and try to remember. Force myself to dig past that first memory in the forest. But there's nothing. Not a face, not a voice, not even a sense of whether I was loved or abandoned. Did my parents die? Did they leave me deliberately? Was I stolen away, or did I run? I'll never know."

The next words lodged in his throat. He'd never spoken this thought aloud. Had barely allowed himself to think it in the darkness of those sleepless nights. "Sometimes I wonder if I was ever truly a child, or if I was born fully formed in those woods..."

The admission tasted like ash. "Already ten years old, already alone."

His breath caught. "But maybe that's why I understand. Loss is loss, even when it's the loss of something you never had. You grieve what was taken. I grieve for what was never given. Different wounds, same ache."

"You're wrong." Her voice cut fiercely despite the tears, cutting through his self-pity as a blade clears a path. She pulled her hand from his. His eyes dropped to the fire. But then both her hands came up to frame his face, forcing him to look at her. "We are the same. Both orphaned by circumstance, both alone until..." She paused, searching his face as a tracker reads uncertain ground. "Each of us is trying to find meaning in what remains. Both surviving when it would have been easier to surrender."

Her eyes shimmered with tears, but they weren't only for herself anymore. Her thumbs pressed into his cheeks. Steady.

"We're the same." The words found the back of his eyes. "Both alone, carrying wounds that shaped us. Both..."

"Not alone anymore." He caught her hands where they held his face, pressed them against his cheeks so she could feel the truth of his words. "Not if we choose each other. Family isn't always about blood or shared memories. Sometimes it's about who stands beside you when the world falls dark. Who sees your wounds and doesn't turn away."

She leaned forward until their foreheads touched, sharing breath and darkness. Her tears wet his face, or perhaps they were his own. He couldn't tell anymore.

"Then we're family," she whispered against his skin, the words a vow more binding than any spoken before councils or queens. "You and I. No matter what comes."

"You and I." His next breath came easier than the one before. Her hand in his, warm and real.

They fell silent, holding each other in the rising moonlight, fingers intertwined. A cool breeze rustled the surrounding leaves, carrying the ethereal, melodic strains of an Elven song from afar. The notes floated in the air, delicate and haunting.

A harmonic stayed in his sternum, unresolved. His shoulders dropped without his choosing. At the far edge of the clearing, a sentry turned to face the wards. Something beyond them, low and patient.

But tonight, they had this. A family forged from understanding, from seeing each other's wounds and choosing to stand together anyway.

His palms had changed. The calluses from the staff work sat deeper now. The whispers of Eldoria's ageless forests embraced them, though the embrace grew more protective than welcoming with each passing day. Each corner held secrets whispered in the rustling leaves, but now those whispers carried warnings alongside wonder. Under the silver glow of moonlight, they joined hands with the elves in dances, their feet moving in harmony with the ethereal notes of pipes. Laughter bubbled like a spring between joyous melodies, but even the celebrations carried an undercurrent of farewell.

The elves knew how to celebrate. His gaze cut to the tree line and back without his choosing.

Sentries held the forest's edge. Reports continued to arrive: Spellcaster patrols growing bolder, forest sweeps becoming systematic, and patrol routes drawing closer to Eldoria's protected borders.

During the seventh week, the Queen called Stric and Teela to council. Elar stood before the throne, dust from hard travel darkening his leathers. "The border patrols continue their grid patterns, your Majesty. Closer than before." He paused, something like grim satisfaction crossing his features. "But their Spellcasters are young. Newly trained. They pass within a stone's throw of our wards and sense nothing. Our concealment holds."

As the third moon edged nearer, Stric and Teela threw themselves into frantic preparation. Weapons needed sharpening, supplies required careful rationing, and their newly learned techniques demanded constant practice lest they forget everything under pressure.

Stric paced beside the campfire, unable to sit still while tension crawled under his skin. Every few minutes, he'd test his barriers, filling the air with a crackling energy that made nearby elves dive for cover. Beside him, Teela practised sword forms with manic intensity, her blade whistling through combinations that would have been impossible weeks ago.

Sweat gleamed on Teela's neck despite the cool evening air. "We're as ready as we'll ever be."

Stric's Powerstaff pulsed with accumulated power, its rhythm matching his racing heartbeat. "Are we, though? What if we fail? What if the prince..."

"Then we fail trying." Teela's grip tightened on her sword hilt. "But together we won't fail."

Stric sat by the campfire. Heat worked into his face. Sparks rose and died. Stone on steel beside him, steady, deliberate. The whetstone moved at the same angle it had held for an hour without deviation. Arcane energy crackled at his fingertips, power he'd never dreamed possible dancing between his palms.

Light moved in the crystal. Something at the base of his palm that hadn't been there a week ago. His fingers followed the staff's carved surface, feeling the power thrumming beneath. When his test came, would it be enough? His grip tightened until the grooves bit into his palm.

The night before their departure arrived. Elves moved through the clearing with quick, purposeful steps. Conversations died mid-sentence when Stric passed, replaced by nods that carried weight.

Silver light from the full moon cast long shadows over the forest. Under this luminous canopy, the elves gathered in a clearing where long tables groaned under carved wooden platters of something that smelled of pine smoke and honey, bread braided in patterns he didn't recognise, bowls of a dark preserve whose taste he had no name for. Laughter and the gentle hum of conversation mingled with the notes of pipes and elf voices raised in harmonious song. As they shared the feast, the elves toasted to friendships and bonds that had been built.

Even the Elven songs wove farewells into their melodies.

Dawn broke over Eldoria. The sky painted itself in rose and gold, filtering through the canopy in pale gold bars. Stric and Teela prepared for their departure while the smell of last night's fires still clung to his robes. A scrap of Elven melody kept returning, unbidden. The Queen assigned Aelith as their guide, her weight settled back on her heels, one hand loose at her sword, her gaze already fixed on the path ahead, as she stood ready to lead them to the boat that would take them to Darmoor Island, and the wormhole that would take them to Prince Dreese.

Queen Aeloria stood before the great tree, her regal robes billowing in the morning breeze as she addressed Stric, Teela, and Aelith. Her voice carried to every corner of the clearing. Movement around them stilled.

"The time has come," she said. Her gaze found Stric and didn't move. "The path to Prince Dreese will soon open. As you face the trials that lie ahead, carry what you have learnt here. The kingdom of Eldoria stands with you."

The Queen held Stric's gaze for a long moment before giving a final, deliberate nod, her lips curving. "But know this: our scouts report that Barok's forest patrols are growing systematic in their searching. They seek not random travellers, but to secure the forest borders from any threats. Trust your training, trust each other."

As they set off down the forest path, the morning light cast their shadows long behind them. The ancient trees watched them go, their branches rustling farewells in languages older than kingdoms. Safety dissolved with each step.

Ahead, the forest patiently waited.

PART TWO

The Lost Prince

Chapter 10

Leaving Eldoria

The forest swallowed them. Sunlight scattered through the canopy in coins of gold, warming moss while shadows held the chill. Aelith moved ahead, footfalls silent, pausing often to read signs invisible to human eyes.

Behind her, Teela's hand rested near her sword hilt, fingers drumming a rhythm against the leather. Stric shifted his pack's weight, the straps cutting into his shoulders, still adjusting to the demands of travel. Talnar's warmth pressed against his ribs through layers of cloth. Present. Patient.

"The patrol patterns have changed." Aelith crouched, weathered fingers tracing marks in the disturbed earth. Her voice placed each word at the same measured distance from the next. "These aren't random searches anymore."

Teela moved closer, eyes scanning the scuff marks. "Organised?"

Aelith's jaw tightened. "They're hunting for something they expect to find."

"Or someone." Stric's chest tightened.

"How close?" He pressed his palm against Talnar through his robes.

"Hours." Aelith stood, brushing earth from her hands. "Perhaps a day if we're fortunate. But they're contracting the search grid." Her eyes found his, measuring. "We are outside the boundaries of Eldoria's protection. Any magic use from here forward may be detected."

The weight of that settled over Stric like a lead cloak. The months of training. Unprecedented power flowing through him like golden-green rivers, and he couldn't use any of it without the possibility of alerting Barok's Spellcasters.

"Then we move fast," Teela said. Simple. Decisive. "Stay ahead of the grid."

Aelith nodded once. "Northeast. The coast waits, and with it, our escape."

They walked deeper into a forest that shifted character with each mile travelled.

For eight days, they pressed northeast through woodlands that transformed around them. The towering sentinels of the Eldorian borders gave way to smaller cousins, coastal pines with salt-weathered bark, twisted oaks that leaned away from ocean winds they couldn't yet see. The air changed, too. Pine resin gave way to a salt-tinged breeze. Bird calls shifted from deep-forest thrushes to gull cries that echoed from beyond the horizon.

Each evening, Aelith chose their camp with a scout's precision. Always with clear sightlines, multiple exits, and positioned where patrol paths wouldn't intersect their rest.

And every morning, the signs grew fresher. Broken branches at unnatural angles. Boot prints in mud that hadn't yet dried. The acrid scent of undead flesh lingering in hollows where something had passed hours before, not days.

On the eighth evening, as the salt tang grew strong enough to taste, Aelith broke her customary silence around their small fire.

"The Queen arranged for a boat." She fed a twig to the flames, watching it catch. "A fisherman from the coastal villages will have left it hidden north of the usual patrol routes."

Teela's gaze moved to Aelith across the fire. "How sure are you that it will be there?"

"The Queen believes him trustworthy." The sentence ended on a note lower than it had begun. Her fingers touched her sword hilt, a tell Stric had learned meant she was calculating odds. "The fisherman and his family have long been friends of my people. He knows the waters."

Stric's chest tightened. Talnar's warmth pulsed against his ribs. "And Darmoor Island? How far from shore?"

"A half-day of good sailing." Aelith met his eyes across the flames. "The wormhole opens with the celestial alignment. We cannot miss that window."

Cannot. Not must not. The word choice made Stric's shoulders climb toward his ears.

Teela's gaze moved between them, reading what neither said aloud. Her hand left her sword to rest briefly on Stric's forearm. Solid. Warm. "Then we'll reach it," she said. Simple. Certain.

The tightness around Aelith's eyes eased, the set of her jaw releasing by a fraction. "Your blade carries more than steel, Teela. Both of you do." She turned back to the fire. "Rest while you can," Aelith said. "Dawn comes quickly. We have four days to cover ground that should take six."

Four days. Until the coast and whatever waited there.

Stric closed his eyes but didn't sleep. Teela shifted beside him, her breathing never quite settling into sleep's rhythm. Across the hollow, Aelith remained motionless, watching the darkness with eyes that never seemed to need rest.

The forest continued to breathe around them.

The ninth day broke grey. No birdsong in it. The salt air had thickened overnight, carrying moisture that beaded on cloaks and turned breath into visible mist. Aelith's pace quickened. Her head turned more frequently, reading signs that made her jaw tighten.

By late afternoon, Stric's legs burned with each step. The pack straps had worn grooves into his shoulders that ached with every shift of weight. Beside him, Teela's breathing came harder than usual, controlled but audible. Only Aelith moved as though fresh, though sweat darkened the back of her tunic.

The forest opened up ahead. Sunlight pierced the thinning canopy in shafts that caught swirling dust motes. Their feet crunched over crisp fallen leaves and snapped twigs, the sound too loud in the afternoon stillness. The clearing beyond glowed golden in the setting sun's light, long shadows stretching across the ground.

Aelith's hand rose. They stopped.

The clearing spread before them, grass trampled in paths that spoke of frequent passage. Wildflowers dotted the edges. A rainbow of coloured blooms swayed in the breeze, carrying the wrongness, before the sight confirmed it.

The stench hit first. Rot and profaned flesh, sweet-sick corruption that made Stric's gorge rise. Teela's hand moved to cover her nose and mouth, breathing shallow through her fingers just as Aelith had taught her.

From the far treeline, figures emerged. Skeletal warriors in tattered armour, cloth clinging to patches of flesh that oozed darkly. Their bones glistened with moisture that caught the failing light like oil on water. Some had eyes, hollow voids staring with terrible patience. Others retained bits of decayed tissue, marbled veins threading dark against the pale tissue.

Behind them, a figure in Spellcaster robes stepped from the shadows. Young. Younger even than Teela. His grip shifted on the Powerstaff before he moved. Beautiful too, in the way of Academy scholars whose skin had never weathered and whose hands bore no marks of labour. Delicate features, pale skin. Her eyes moved between them in tight arcs, breath coming in short, controlled pulls. Her jaw clenched so tight that a muscle jumped beneath her ear. The corners of her mouth twisted upward with something hungrier than a smile. Her beauty somehow made the coldness of it worse. Innocence corrupted, like frost on delicate flowers.

Her Powerstaff trembled in her grip, her arm locking at the elbow as the shaking stilled.

"Seize them!" The command cracked across the clearing, pitched high with adrenaline, the young Spellcaster couldn't quite control. "Now!"

The undead soldiers surged forward, rusted blades scraping from their scabbards with the sound of nails on stone. Their movements carried mechanical precision, limbs jerking in unison, the movement of things whose joints no longer negotiated with each other. The stench rolled ahead of them, thick enough to taste.

Aelith's blade whispered from its sheath. She moved without hesitation, without wasted motion. Flowing between clumsy strikes like wind through branches. Each cut found its mark.

Her sword found the joint between the neck and shoulder of the first soldier. Bone separated with a crack that echoed. The corpse folded, and she was already past, spinning to drive her blade through another's spine. Vertebrae exploded into fragments that pattered against armour like hail.

"Aim for the joints!" Her voice cut through the chaos, reaching Teela even across the clanging steel. "Just as we practised!"

Teela moved into position beside Aelith, blade already drawn. Weight shifted, elbow finding its angle before thought could direct it. A wide stance. Flowing transitions. The way Elven warriors made each strike count.

The stench tried to overwhelm her. Her eyes watered. Bile rose in her throat. But Aelith had prepared her for this, too. She breathed shallow through her mouth, trusting the technique when her senses failed, letting training carry her through.

Her blade found the gap between ribs, withdrew, swept low to sever the knee joint that kept the next soldier standing. Her sword moved like an extension of her arm. Properly weighted. Perfectly balanced. Each strike echoed Aelith's teaching. Skill with heart. Precision with honour.

A soldier lunged. Its rusted axe aimed at her throat. She pivoted. Her blade drove upward through its jaw. The skull separated from the spine with a sound like green wood snapping.

Stric raised his Powerstaff, power surging through the crystal. His chest tightened. Every spell he cast painted a target on their location. But Aelith and Teela faced a dozen undead soldiers. His breath went out slow.

He channelled carefully, precisely, the way the months of Elven training had taught him. Breath slow, hands loose on the staff, the crystal brightening in response.

The crystal flared. Golden-green blazed from within, the colour that had made Master Elarion's breath catch. Light erupted from its tip. Something unprecedented, something that would be detected by anyone trained to watch for magical signatures.

The bolt leapt toward the undead cluster.

And splashed against an invisible barrier, scattering into harmless sparks.

Stric's heart hammered against his ribs. His fingers tightened around the Powerstaff until his knuckles showed white. The young Spellcaster stood behind her protective wall, lips moving through incantations that shimmered the air around the undead forces.

She was maintaining their shields. Standard Academy technique. He'd learned the counter during his apprentice studies. If he could complete the binding spell before she adapted her defence...

The air crackled as he began the next incantation. Words that Talnar had taught him flowed from his tongue with the weight of centuries. The ground pulsed beneath his feet. A rhythm that matched his heartbeat, power building until his forearms ached with the weight of it.

The young Spellcaster's eyes widened. Her chin lifted, lips going still mid-incantation. Trained precision, with a power greater than her own.

Her hand dove into her pocket, emerged clutching a small crystal that blazed with stored magic. Teleportation. Before Stric's binding could complete, before his spell could ensnare its target, she spoke the activation word.

Her form blurred, shadows folding inward like cloth pulled through a too-small opening. The crystal flashed.

And she was gone.

Stric's spell dissipated into empty air, power bleeding away unused. His chest seized. The Spellcaster would report within the hour. Every detail of their encounter, of his magical signature. Every advantage they'd had, gone.

The barrier dissolved with the Spellcaster's disappearance. The undead that had been protected stumbled forward, suddenly vulnerable, mechanical purpose undeterred by their commander's abandonment.

Stric channelled again, this time with the enemy unshielded. Blue-green light blazed. Warmth ran down through the staff into his grip, the blended power humming at a frequency that had no Academy name. The bolt struck the lead soldier's chest. Its ribcage exploded outward, bone shards embedding in the soldiers behind it like shrapnel.

He cast again. And again. Each spell carved through the undead ranks, leaving smoking craters where corrupted flesh had been. The air filled with the acrid smell of magic meeting necromantic corruption. Ozone and rot combined into something that made his eyes water.

But even as he fought, the knowledge sat cold in his gut. The hunt would intensify. And they still had days until they reached the coast.

Aelith fought with her shoulder angled for the next strike before her blade had finished the last, each step perfectly placed, each strike flowing from the last in seamless rhythm.

Her sword whistled through the air, each arc a blur that cleaved through their foes without mercy. Even outnumbered, even facing enemies that felt no pain and knew no fear, she made every strike count.

Beside her, Teela stepped inside an undead soldier's reach, blade driving up before it could correct, its sword arm swinging empty air. Her blade danced in the fading light.

The two women fought, but the soldiers were relentless. They would fall only to rise again, pressing the attack despite grievous wounds. One stumbled forward with ribs splayed open like broken cage bars, its sword arm swinging whilst blackened organs slid from the cavity with each lurch. Another dragged itself across the ground, legs shattered into bone fragments that clicked against stone, yet its clawed hands still reached for Teela's ankles.

Stric's magic arced through the battlefield. Each bolt found its mark, each spell precisely placed. The hybrid golden-green light painted the clearing in colours that shouldn't exist.

The last soldier collapsed into a pile of bones and rusted armour. Stric's ears rang from the absence of clanging steel. His arms trembled. His Powerstaff was heavy in his hands, slick with sweat. Around them, the undead lay in pieces, scattered like broken pottery.

Aelith sheathed her blade. Her eyes found the empty space where the Spellcaster had vanished.

"This isn't finished." Teela's voice came flat, controlled. Her gaze tracked the empty space. "That Spellcaster escaped to report our location."

"More than a location." Aelith's jaw tightened. Her weathered fingers wrapped around her sword hilt, her tell for calculating bad odds. "She witnessed a magician with great power."

"They'll dispatch larger squads," Stric said, the words tasting like ash. "They'll know what I am."

Teela's hand found his shoulder, fingers gripping hard enough to bruise. Her eyes met his. Fierce. Jaw set. Steady. "Then we move. Now. Fast as we can push."

Aelith nodded once. "The forest will slow their pursuit. But once we reach the plains..." she didn't finish. She didn't need to.

Open ground. Nowhere to hide. Days until the coast.

They started moving. Aelith leading them northeast at a long, punishing stride that ate ground and left no breath for speech.

The pursuit had begun.

They didn't stop until darkness forced them to. Even then, Aelith chose their camp with paranoid precision. A hollow beneath fallen trees that couldn't be seen from twenty paces in any direction. Cold camp. No cooking. Dried meat and hard bread were eaten in silence, broken only by the forest's night sounds.

Stric slumped against rough bark. His shoulders throbbed where pack straps had cut grooves. His thighs trembled when he tried to shift position. Beside him, Teela methodically cleaned her blade, movements automatic, eyes distant. Across the hollow, Aelith sat with her back to a trunk, apparently at ease, but her hand never left her sword hilt.

"How long?" Teela asked quietly, not looking up from her work. "Before they find us again?"

"Days. Hours." Aelith's voice carried the flat certainty of tactical assessment. "The Spellcaster will report upon her return. Commanders will organise a response and dispatch fresh, larger squads."

"But we're not there anymore," Stric said. His head throbbed. Using that much magic always left him hollowed out, echoing. "We're moving toward the coast."

"They will track us." Aelith's eyes found his in the darkness. "They will follow."

Teela's blade stilled mid-wipe. "The coast."

"The coast and open plains," Aelith said. "If they can position forces between us and the shoreline. They can funnel us toward a prepared ambush point." Her expression hardened. "Our advantage is speed. We know where we're going. They must guess."

"And once we reach the open?" Stric asked, though dread already supplied the answer.

"No cover. No concealment. They'll see us from leagues away." Aelith's fingers drummed against her sword hilt. "But we'll see them too. And the boat waits at the place the Queen provided."

If it's still there. If the patrols haven't found it. If the fisherman hadn't moved it. If. If. If.

Talnar warmed against his ribs. He pressed his hand to the book's outline through the cloth, the leather's warmth bleeding through the fabric into his palm.

"Rest now," Aelith said. "We will move out before dawn."

A brutal rhythm blurred the next three days. Wake before dawn, move until after dusk, collapse into an exhausted sleep that gave nothing back. The trees continued their transition toward the coast, pine giving way to stunted oak, the thick canopy opening to scattered coverage that let in more light and less shelter.

Aelith pushed them mercilessly. Every hour counted. Every mile mattered.

The twelfth day brought them to a stream that should have offered relief. Instead, Aelith froze at the bank, nostrils flaring. Her hand snapped up in the silent signal for danger.

Downstream, perhaps a quarter-mile distant, the stench carried on the water's current. Undead. Patrolling the waterways.

They crossed in tense silence, not daring to remove boots, soaking through leather to avoid leaving a scent. On the far bank, Teela wrung water from her cloak with shaking hands that had nothing to do with the cold.

By the thirteenth day, the forest had thinned to scattered groves. Ahead, through gaps in the remaining trees, they caught glimpses of open space. Golden grass swayed in the breeze that carried salt, cold, and the flat press of wind unbroken by trees.

The plains.

"Tomorrow," Aelith said, her cadence slowing on the word. "Tomorrow, we enter open ground. After that..." she didn't finish. After that, if pursuit found them, there would be nowhere to hide.

"How far to the coast once we're on the plains?" Stric asked.

Aelith's eyes found the horizon visible between the tree trunks. "A day. Perhaps less if we push."

"And the boat?"

"Where the Queen promised." But her hand found her sword hilt. "Hidden among rocks on an isolated beach, away from patrol routes. The fisherman will have placed it well."

That night, they camped in the last stand of trees, the plains visible as a dark expanse beyond. Stric stared into their small, carefully shielded fire and tried to calculate the odds. One day of exposure. One day, crossing open terrain. Undead pursuit behind them. Unknown forces ahead.

Beside him, Teela sat close enough that their shoulders touched. Her shoulder was warm against his through both sets of cloth. Across the fire, Aelith checked her blade's edge with slow, methodical movements that spoke of ritual more than necessity.

"Whatever comes tomorrow," Teela said quietly, her voice for him alone, "we'll face it together."

Stric's throat tightened. He managed a nod, not trusting his voice.

Aelith's eyes lifted from her blade, meeting theirs across the flames. Her expression softened in a way he'd rarely seen, the lines around her eyes easing, her hands stilling against the blade. "You've both grown strong these months," she said. "Stronger than you know. Trust in that strength. Trust each other." Her gaze held theirs. "Trust what Eldoria taught you."

The fire crackled. Wind moved through the last branches, high and thin where the canopy had opened. And beyond, the plains lay in darkness, emptied of any cover.

The morning broke clear and cold. Frost glittered on grass that stretched to the horizon. Gold and green rippling in the ocean wind. The last trees stood behind them like a wall they could no longer retreat into.

Stric's stomach clenched as he stepped into open ground. No canopy. No shadows. Nothing but sky and grass and distance. His robes fluttered in the constant breeze, blue fabric visible from leagues away. Beside him, Teela's fingers tightened around her sword hilt.

Aelith paused at the forest's edge. Her jaw tightened, her gaze sweeping the plains with a tactical assessment. "From here, we're visible to anything that looks in this direction. They'll see us. We'll see them. Speed becomes everything."

"How far?" Teela asked.

Aelith pointed northeast, where the plains eventually met the sky in a line so distant it might have been imagined. "The coast lies there. By dusk, we reach the boat."

If we reach it, and the plains don't swallow us whole.

Talnar pulsed warm against his ribs. Steadying. Present. Reminding him, he carried more than fear. He carried Talnar's warmth and a prince waiting beyond a wormhole they hadn't yet reached.

"So we keep moving," Teela said.

They walked into the open.

The grass came up to knee height, not enough to provide cover. Wildflowers dotted the landscape. Purple blooms that swayed in the constant wind, yellow clusters that caught the sunlight. Exposed when enemies were hunting.

The sun climbed. The plains stretched. And behind them, though they couldn't yet see it, pursuit followed.

The sun reached its zenith, heat beating down on exposed heads and shoulders. Sweat soaked Stric's robes beneath his pack, the salt air stinging his eyes. His legs burned with the relentless pace Aelith maintained.

Her stride broke rhythm for half a step, hand flying to shade her eyes against the glare. "Movement. Behind us. At the treeline."

Stric spun. The forest edge lay distant now, a dark wall against golden grass. For a heartbeat, nothing. The treeline held still. Then movement. Figures emerging from shadow into sunlight, too distant to count but unmistakable in their purpose.

Aelith's expression went cold, tactical. Her eyes tracked the pursuit, calculating with a warrior's precision. "Three squads at least." Her jaw tightened. "The reinforcements we expected."

"How long until they reach us?" Stric's voice came steadier than it had any right to.

"They can move fast, and the undead don't tire." Aelith's gaze swept forward, measuring the distance to the horizon.

"Can we outrun them?" Teela's hand found her sword, a tactical question seeking a tactical answer.

"To the coast? Perhaps. If we don't slow down." Aelith met their eyes, nothing shifting in her face. "It will be close."

"Then we run," Stric said, "and figure the rest when we get to the boat."

They ran.

Running through knee-high grass fought their every step. Stalks caught at legs, hidden roots threatened their ankles. Stric's breath came in ragged gasps, chest burning, legs screaming protest.

But Aelith didn't slow. If anything, she pushed faster.

Behind them, the undead ran with mechanical precision. No exhaustion. No need for rest. Their formation held across every dip and hollow in the ground, the distance closing stride by inevitable stride.

"They're gaining," Teela gasped, risking a glance backward. Sweat plastered her hair to her forehead. Her face had gone pale beneath the exertion's flush.

Stric glanced over his shoulder. They were close enough now to make out individual figures. The undead moved in formation with inhuman speed, tireless limbs eating ground with mechanical precision. Behind them, the Spellcaster struggled to keep pace, robes billowing, her staff glinting in the sunlight. The gap between her and her undead soldiers widened with each stride. Human flesh and bone couldn't match the relentless endurance of reanimated corpses.

"I know." Aelith's voice came tight with effort, even she couldn't quite conceal. "Keep moving."

The sun tracked westward. Shadows lengthened. The pursuit closed.

Stric's vision narrowed to Aelith's back ahead of him, to Teela's shoulder beside him, to the next step and the next and the next. His pack dragged at his shoulders, rubbed raw by straps. Talnar's weight pressed against ribs that heaved with each gasping breath.

Magic burned in his core, ready to be channelled, but using it would only drain him further.

"There!" Aelith's arm shot forward. "The coast!"

Stric lifted his head, vision swimming with exhaustion. Ahead, perhaps a mile distant, the golden grass ended in a darker line. The impossible blue of the ocean met the sky, a seam promising escape or ending.

Behind them, undead footfalls drummed against the earth. Closer. Closer. Close enough to hear the creak of rotting joints, the rustle of tattered cloth, the hiss of animated corpses that shouldn't walk but did.

"We won't make it before they catch us," Teela said, the words torn from her between gasping breaths.

"We will." Aelith's voice came without a waver, even as her breath laboured. "Because we must."

The grass thinned as they approached the coast. Sandy soil replaced rich earth. Seabirds wheeled overhead, their cries sharp and wild. The smell of salt and seaweed cut through the stench of pursuit.

The ground sloped downward. Grass gave way to sand. The ocean spread before them, vast and grey-blue, indifferent.

On the beach, tucked among tumbled rocks, a small boat sat waiting.

Exactly where the Queen had promised.

The boat rocked gently in the lapping waves, tethered to a weathered post driven deep into the sand above the tide line.

Weathered wood, patched sail, oars lashed inside. Real. Solid. Exactly where the fisherman had left it.

Stric's legs nearly buckled. They'd made it. They'd reached the coast.

Aelith reached the boat, and her footsteps faltered.

"What's wrong?" Teela asked, her voice already stripped of surprise.

"It's smaller than expected." Aelith's hand found the boat's gunwale and assessed its size. Her jaw worked. She looked from the boat to them, to the approaching undead. Back to the boat. Her hand went to her sword hilt. "The fisherman must have chosen what was available. What wouldn't be missed."

Stric stared at the boat. Small. Perhaps twelve feet bow to stern. Two rowers' benches. Cramped storage space beneath. Barely enough for...

"Two people," Teela said flatly. "It's built for two."

"Yes." Her hand tightened on the gunwale. "Three would overload it. Risk swamping it in open water."

Behind them, the thunder of undead footsteps grew louder. Stric turned. The pursuit force crested the last rise of grassland, silhouetted against the setting sun. Thirty soldiers in formation. All moving with mechanical purpose toward the beach.

Minutes. They had minutes.

"Get on board," Aelith commanded. Stric's next breath stopped half-drawn. "Quickly!"

"Wait..." His hand lifted toward her.

"Now!" Aelith's blade sighed as it left its scabbard. She turned to face the approaching force, positioning herself between the undead and the boat. Between death and her students. "We don't have time for discussion!"

Teela's hand found the hilt of her sword. Her eyes measured Aelith, the boat, and the distance to the pursuit. "No." The word tore from Teela's throat. "We can make it work. All three of us..."

"Cannot," Aelith's voice gentled even as the undead drew closer. "You know this, Teela. I taught you to see tactical reality clearly. Three in that boat means none reach the island. Two means you complete the mission."

The first undead soldier's feet touched sand.

Aelith met Teela's eyes across the short distance. Warrior to warrior. Teacher to student. Friend to friend.

Aelith's hand fell from her sword hilt. "Skill without heart is nothing more than violence. But a heart without skill is a meaningless sacrifice." Her grip tightened on her sword. "I have both. This is what they're for."

"Aelith..." Teela's voice broke.

"You asked me once why I fight." A tightness around Aelith's eyes that wasn't tactical. "This is why. To protect those who carry hope forward. To stand between darkness and light." She smiled, small, not reaching her eyes, certain. "To honour what honour demands."

The undead were near enough now to see the rotting features, hollow eyes, and raised weapons. Thirty soldiers. A force that should have overwhelmed three travellers days ago.

"Get in the boat. That's an order from your teacher, Teela. From the guide Queen Aeloria assigned to see you safely to Darmoor Island."

Teela's hand moved to her sword, but Aelith caught her wrist, stopping the draw.

"You fight for them now," Aelith said, nodding toward Stric. "For the prince beyond the wormhole. For the kingdom that needs saving." Her voice dropped to a fierce whisper meant for Teela alone. "Your blade is more than just steel. Use it wisely."

Stric's throat closed. Words failed. Insufficient, meaningless against what Aelith offered.

Talnar burned warm against his ribs, the book's presence a reminder that sacrifice had defined this quest from the beginning. Vrill had given everything. The werewolf pack had risked annihilation. Queen Aeloria had committed her kingdom. And now Aelith...

"We will carry your name forward," Stric managed, voice rough with grief he couldn't show and couldn't hide. "You will not be forgotten, Aelith. Not by us. Not by the kingdom we will restore."

Aelith's smile widened slightly. "Then, if I die, I die well." She released Teela's wrist, turning to face the approaching undead. "Now go."

Teela's fingers found Stric's shoulder, gripping tight enough to bruise. When he met her eyes, tears carved tracks through the dirt on her face, catching the dying sun's light. Her jaw set. Her hand moved from his shoulder to the oar. There would be time for grief later. Now there was only the mission.

"Thank you." The words emerged stiff, Teela's voice breaking through her characteristic reluctance with emotion. "For everything."

Aelith nodded once. Then she stepped forward, blade raised, positioning herself between them and death with the grace of someone who'd always known this moment would come.

"Go," she commanded. Not a request. An order. The ultimate gift from teacher to student.

Stric's hands found rough wood, splinters biting his palms as he and Teela shoved against the hull. The boat scraped sand, protesting, then found water. Cold spray soaked his robes as he climbed aboard, movements clumsy, belonging to the exhaustion in his limbs rather than any act of will. Teela followed, her sword still half-drawn, her instincts screaming to turn back, to fight, not to abandon her teacher. Her friend.

But Aelith had given them an order. And warriors followed orders, even when their hands shook while doing so.

The boat rocked beneath them. The ocean caught them, pulling them from the shore. Twenty feet. Thirty. The distance opened like a wound.

On the beach, the first undead soldiers reached Aelith. Her blade flickered in the failing light. One cut, two, three in rapid succession. Bone shattered. Limbs separated. She moved with the deadly grace of someone who'd spent centuries perfecting the art of Elven combat.

But thirty to one was more than even Aelith's skill could overcome forever.

Stric lifted his staff. Energy coursed through the crystal, sending vibrations through the air. His voice cut through the crash of waves and clang of steel, weaving a barrier spell. The spell that had saved them before. The spell that might give Aelith the space she needed to...

To what? Survive? Against so many? His chest tightened around the lie even as magic poured from the staff's crystal.

Iridescent cerulean light erupted, forming a shimmering wall between most of the undead and Aelith. The barrier separated the force, giving her fewer immediate opponents. Giving her a chance.

Through the barrier's glow, Aelith glanced back. Her eyes found them across the widening gap. Her chin dipped a fraction. Then she opened her mouth and released a battle cry that split the air, ancient and wild, the voice of Eldoria itself crying defiance.

The sound rolled across the water like thunder. It hit Stric in the sternum, drove the breath from him, and left his hands white-knuckled on the gunwale.

Aelith spun with lethal grace, her blade cleaving through the sword arm of one soldier, then pivoting to drive through the neck of the next. The remaining undead pressed forward, clumsy but relentless, undeterred by their opponent's skill.

She fought beautifully. Fought deadly. Fought with everything Eldoria had taught her across however many centuries she'd lived.

Her blade found another, driving through its spine with a cracking echo. As it collapsed into the sand, she spun and ran. Along the shoreline, away from where the boat had launched. The barrier still held the bulk of the undead trapped, their forms pressing against the shimmering wall like shadows behind coloured glass.

Aelith's cloak fluttered like a dark banner in the wind as she sprinted across the sand. Four sets of relentless footfalls followed in her wake.

The boat drifted farther. Fifty feet. A hundred. Aelith grew smaller with distance, still running.

Stric's knuckles whitened around his Powerstaff. Teela's lips moved in a wordless farewell. Elven words Aelith had taught her during their training. A warrior's prayer for the fallen. A promise that sacrifice would be remembered in the old tongue, the way her people had honoured their heroes for countless generations.

The barrier's light flickered behind them, still holding, still giving Aelith the time she'd fought to buy. A lone Elven warrior leading death away from those she'd chosen to protect.

She grew smaller. Smaller. Until she became one shadow among many in the failing light. And then, there was no shadow at all.

The wind turned cold. Salt spray stung Stric's eyes. He didn't try to tell the difference. Beside him, Teela made a sound. Raw. Broken.

Stric forced himself to stand, legs shaking, and set the sail with numb fingers. The canvas snapped in the wind, filling it and pulling them toward deeper water. Toward Darmoor Island, which waited invisible beyond the horizon. Toward the wormhole that promised Prince Dreese's rescue.

Behind them, the beach disappeared into the dusk.

Ahead, across water that reflected the first of the night's stars, their destination waited.

A kingdom's hope. A prince they would find and bring home.

No matter the cost.

Chapter 11

Dancing with the Enemy

Morning sunlight carved sharp shadows across the Academy courtyard, catching on intricate gate carvings where ancient battles were frozen in bronze. Victories Kallen would soon eclipse. The Spellcaster robes clung to her shoulders, stiff fabric that would soften with wear. Her fingers drummed against her thigh. Commander Tharne would see what the Academy's finest could accomplish.

The oath words still burned in her throat like swallowed fire.

"My magic, my life, my will, are bound to your command."

Barok Tana's eyes had gleamed like polished steel as she and her fellow graduates knelt, as their power shackled itself to him, the hall still in the held breath that followed the last word. The memory settled into her bones. A brand, a promise, a chain forged from her own ambition. Her stomach growled, breaking the reverie. Lunch first. Then Commander Tharne at the army barracks would learn what his newest Spellcaster could deliver.

The courtyard behind her held memories sharper than the steel at the gate guard's hip. Electric blue light sizzling through the morning air, tasting of frost and coming violence. That boy's face, his arrogance crumbling to terror as her energy ball found him. His eyes dropped to it mid-flight, the flinch half a second too late. His scream, then the laughter of those who understood the Academy's true lesson. Power demanded dominance, and mercy was weakness dressed in virtue's clothes. The Masters had worn disapproval like masks required by protocol, but their eyes had gleamed approval. She'd proven who deserved to stand at the top.

Her jaw loosened as she walked. That boy had screamed all the way to the gates.

Guards twisted heavy iron keys in weathered locks. The gates creaked open. The town of Treast sprawled beyond. Four years within Academy walls ending in a single step onto uneven cobblestones. The city's din replaced the rote count of drillmasters, the measured scrape of boots on stone. Cool air carried horse dung and cook-fire smoke and the iron tang of a smithy somewhere close.

They wove through the marketplace throng, past sizzling meat and fresh bread. At a small wooden table, Kallen shared a last meal with her fellow graduates in silence. The Academy had trained for competition, not for friendship. The bread was fresh, the meat still hot. She ate without looking up.

They exchanged a silent nod before she turned toward the army barracks. Markets gave way to military districts. Stone buildings grew more severe with each block.

The barracks gates rose before her, timber aged dark by decades of service. Kallen retrieved her posting scroll, parchment crisp with official seals, and presented it to the stern-faced guard. He examined the scroll, nodded once, and pointed toward a weathered administration building where her orders waited.

Stone archway, the scent of ink and old paper thick enough to taste. Dim lamplight flickered across peeling walls. Dust stirred by each passing footstep settled back onto warped floorboards. The corridor narrowed as Kallen walked, wooden doors marking minor functionaries until she reached the one marked "Commander Tharne." Her destination. Her proving ground.

An old man with a white beard and spectacles perched on his nose hunched over a cluttered desk outside the office. His eyes remained sharp behind the lenses as his fingers shuffled through the paper chaos. He spared her a single glance. "You the new Spellcaster?" The rasp in his voice suggested decades of dismissing young graduates who thought themselves important.

Kallen handed him her posting scroll, a parchment bearing official Academy seals. "I am to report to Commander Tharne."

The old man's glance lasted less than a heartbeat. "Hmmp-phh." He snatched the scroll and dropped it into an overflowing basket. It vanished among dozens of identical documents. His fingers rummaged through the clutter atop his desk and found fresh parchment. He began to scribble. The quill's scratch seemed louder than necessary.

"Announce me to Commander Tharne," Kallen's foot tapped against the wooden floor with a sharp rhythm that demanded attention. "Now."

The quill continued its scratch across the parchment. With deliberate slowness, the old man held out the finished document. "Here you go, Miss Importance." With a grin that suggested he'd used the title many times before. "Tharne was looking forward to greeting you. But he decided to give you an assignment that matched your level of importance." He cocked an eyebrow, waiting for her reaction.

The parchment crumpled in Kallen's grip. Scouting. Twelve undead soldiers through the forest on reconnaissance. Stinkers, the pen handlers called them.

Her jaw tightened. Orders were orders. Commander Tharne would see her competence even in commanding corpses.

The forest engulfed Kallen and her twelve stinking shadows. A dense thicket blocked the sky. Twigs snapped beneath her boots, bird calls echoed overhead, small creatures fled the undead's wrongness.

Days blurred. The compass spell pulled northeast. The Stinkers followed with mechanical precision. Tireless except for the creak of dried joints and the constant reek.

Kallen quickened her pace each morning, counting the miles toward mission completion. Four days of competent reconnaissance through this rugged terrain. Tomorrow, Tharne would note her efficiency. Her first assignment was completed without incident, and she covered her route faster than expected.

The clearing appeared on the afternoon of the fifth day. Just hours before, she could teleport back to Treast and announce her task completed early.

Her legs dragged when the clearing opened ahead. Sunlight pierced the canopy, creating patterns across the forest floor. Three figures stood at the clearing's far edge.

An elf, her silver hair catching the light, eyes scanning with a warrior's precision. Beside her, two humans. Wrong place, wrong time, wrong companions for innocent travellers.

Kallen's pulse hammered like war drums in her ears. Elves were rarely seen since Barok's rise. Withdrawn to their forest stronghold somewhere west of here, rumoured to exist deep in the northern wilderness but never found despite systematic patrols that had scoured every suspected valley. They avoided detection with an expertise that had frustrated Barok's commanders for years. Patrols returned with tracks that simply stopped mid-forest and nothing else to show for a week's march. But here she stood, silver hair catching the afternoon light like a banner of defiance, guiding humans through controlled territory as if Barok's authority meant nothing.

Kallen's hand found her Powerstaff, her fingers tightening around the wood, still smooth and unmarked. The crystal unstressed.

"Seize them!" Kallen's hand sliced forward. The undead snapped to attention, rusted blades scraping from scabbards. They advanced without hesitation, mechanical precision driving rotting limbs forward.

The elf's ancient steel whispered from its sheath. The man's eyes widened as the woman drew her blade, her stance suggesting military training.

Steel rang against steel. The elf spun through undead strikes, her weight never where a blade expected it to be. One strike, then a pivot. No wasted motion. The woman's blade found gaps with trained competence: guard positions, proper footwork, lethal thrusts.

These are not civilians. They are warriors.

Her spine tingled as the air vibrated. The man raised a Powerstaff, its crystal pulsing with a blue light that shouldn't exist outside Academy walls. Kallen's barrier incantation formed instinctively, her staff's crimson crystal flaring.

Blue energy crackled across the clearing. Golden-green threads woven through blue lightning, a signature no spellcaster should possess. The bolt struck her barrier and shattered across its surface, cascading into sparks.

Kallen's chest tightened, the staff pulsing hot against her palms where the bolt had struck her barrier.

The air vibrated again. Another spell building. This one would target her directly.

Her barrier wouldn't hold against a second strike.

I must report this.

Kallen's hand found the teleportation crystal in her pocket. Keyed to the barracks in Treast before leaving. Her Powerstaff lowered. Around her, steel clashed against bone as her stinkers fought. The man's staff glowed brighter.

She spoke the activation word.

Reality lurched. Combat sounds. Forest scent. Late afternoon light. All of it compressed into a single point and vanished. Treast's stone courtyard materialised beneath her boots, solid and safe.

Familiar cobblestones. The reek of the pens. Comforting after the forest air. Solid ground beneath her boots, stone walls around her.

Kallen burst through the archway. Her footsteps echoed down the corridor, each strike doubling back off the peeling walls before the sound could settle. The old clerk looked up from his desk as she strode past, his eyes widening.

"You should still be..." The old man's words died as Kallen strode past his desk without slowing.

"Announce me to Commander Tharne." Kallen's hand tightened on her Powerstaff. "Now."

He rose, positioning himself between her and Tharne's door. "Nothing you have to report bypasses..."

The Powerstaff's butt cracked against the wooden floor. The crystal flared crimson, casting a blood-red light across peeling walls. Shadows danced like flames. The air tasted of ozone, heat prickling across her knuckles where they gripped the staff.

The old man's fingers trembled. His voice dropped. "I'll inform him that you're here."

Commander Tharne's office: oak desk, stacked reports, wall map marking patrol zones. Leather and pipeweed smoke scented the air.

Tharne looked up from a document. Ice-chip eyes assessed her with the same precision he'd use on enemy formations. Silver beard, weathered face, hands scarred from decades of service. Not a man who tolerated interruptions.

"Speak." The single word cracked like a whip. "What urgent matter justifies your interrupting me?"

Kallen's spine straightened. The flush rising to her cheeks. "Sir. I encountered..."

"Forest encounter, northeast sector." Her shoulders dropped half an inch. "Three targets: one elf, two humans. All armed, combat-trained. The elf and the female human engaged my squad with professional competence."

Tharne's fingers stopped drumming. His full attention was focused on her.

"The male human wielded a Powerstaff. He cast offensive magic like I've never encountered before. His power exceeded mine..." Kallen's throat tightened, but she pushed forward. "With a signature I've never felt before. I blocked his first attack, but..." The admission burned. "I determined a tactical retreat appropriate to deliver this intelligence."

"A Powerstaff." Tharne leaned forward. All curiosity vanished into calculation. His eyes narrowed. "You're certain about this signature?"

"Yes, sir. The energy pattern was unlike any Academy training. Human magic with something older. Elven, perhaps, though I've never heard of such."

Tharne's fingers drummed once against his desk, then stilled. Decision made. "Barok himself ordered increased patrols in that sector. He's searching for something." His eyes fixed on her with renewed intensity. "You may have found it."

Kallen's breath quickened. "Sir, perhaps I should report directly to..."

"No." Her breath went out. "You report to me. I report to Barok when the intelligence is complete, not speculation from a graduate on her first assignment." Tharne leaned forward. "You'll return with reinforcements. Three additional squads, plus a tracking beast. Find them. Capture if possible. Kill if necessary. I want that Powerstaff and confirmation of a Guild member's survival. Then I'll have something worth presenting to Barok."

Kallen's stomach clenched. Return to the forest. Face that unknown magic again. Her fingers curled against her palm.

"Dismissed. Gather supplies. You leave at dawn."

She saluted and turned. Her quarters beckoned. A few hours' rest before dawn, and the hunt resumed. As she walked along the corridor, the memory of golden-green lightning played behind her eyes. That man's power. Her inadequate defence.

The clearing wore yesterday's battle like a scar. Scorched earth marked where her barrier had shattered. Twisted metal, remnants of rusted weapons. Skeletal remains scattered across trampled grass, some picked clean by carrion birds whose cawing punctuated the morning stillness. The acrid reek of decay hung heavy despite the breeze.

Kallen stepped past her failed first encounter. Three squads accompanied her now. Thirty-six undead soldiers, plus the pig-nosed troll currently snuffling at a femur.

The teleportation crystal had returned Kallen to the exact point of departure. The coordinates locked into its matrix. Three squads of Stinkers arranged in formation behind her. And the troll, sniffing.

The creature snorted, pig-snout low to the ground, nostrils flaring. Commander Tharne had these things captured and trained for tracking. Scent enough to follow a cold trail through two days of forest, and it required nothing but a pointed finger. Physical strength that matched three men. A troll's intelligence is barely above that of livestock. Simple commands only. No middle ground with trolls.

Kallen led the troll to where the trio had stood during the battle. "Track." She pointed to the ground.

The troll's nostrils flared. It snuffled the earth, processing scents with what passed for concentration. Lumbered across the clearing. It sat beside a headless skeleton, then looked at her with what might have been pride.

The troll had tracked the undead.

"No," Kallen grabbed its ear and hauled it back. "Track. Them." She gestured at the skeletons. "Not these."

Blank eyes. Ground snuffling. Another skeleton. This one missing its lower half. Sat. Waited for praise.

Four attempts before the creature finally caught a scent trail that led away from the clearing.

Two days through the dense forest, where the damp earth scent clung to clothes and skin like a second layer she couldn't shed. The troll maintained a relentless pace, snout to the ground, pausing only when scent concentrations promised proximity to prey that remained always just beyond reach. Behind them, the Stinkers followed with mechanical patience. Tireless hunters that neither ate nor slept nor questioned, knowing only the single command that drove them forward through endless trees.

That evening, as shadows lengthened into pools of gathering darkness, she came across a makeshift camp. The stone circle was arranged with practised efficiency. Cold ashes that had known flame within the last day. Crushed grass where bedrolls had pressed, three distinct depressions. Three targets who'd rested here. Kallen knelt and touched the ash. Cold, but not ancient. The texture spoke of recent burning, of warmth that had fled perhaps a day before. Perhaps less.

The troll confirmed with enthusiastic grunts that made her jaw tighten.

Kallen's legs ached from the two-day forced march, but stopping meant losing ground. The troll lacked the intelligence to stop until it finished tracking, and the stinkers could march through the night. So could she.

The incantation formed on tired lips. A stamina enhancement, apprentice-level but effective. Energy surged through her veins, artificial vigour pushing back exhaustion. The Powerstaff's crystal pulsed.

By the fourth day, the forest itself seemed to resist her passage. Kallen's legs moved through force of will alone, each step pulling against an exhaustion that magic could no longer fully mask. Four days of sustained marching, three nights without proper rest. Sweat soaked through her robes despite the morning chill. The stamina spell's cost compounded, the borrowed energy demanding repayment like a debt she couldn't escape. Bark scraped her shoulder where she'd listed sideways on a root, and the damp had worked through her collar to settle cold against the back of her neck.

The forest thinned. Sunlight pierced the canopy in broader shafts, illuminating the path ahead with cruel clarity. Around mid-morning, the scent of smoke cut through pine resin, sharp and immediate as a slap. A camp. Kallen's hand touched the fire circle. Warmth radiated from the stones. Recent. Very recent. The troll's excitement confirmed it.

Her Powerstaff trembled in her grip, vibrations spreading through exhausted muscles. Close. Finally close. Commander Tharne's approval within reach, despite the cost.

"Do not let it out of your sight!" Kallen's finger stabbed toward the troll, voice slicing through the clearing. She pushed the undead soldiers forward, their skeletal frames clattering as they moved. The troll, showing no sign of weariness, sniffed the ground and led them once more. Eyes fixed on the path ahead, she urged the group forward. The fatigue gnawing at her bones meant nothing. The prospect of catching up with the trio drove her closer.

As the sun climbed higher, the troll's stride lengthened, nose low to the ground, and the skeletal soldiers' clatter quickened behind it, the shadows of the trees casting long shapes across the path, motionless while the canopy shifted above them. Each breath a shallow whisper. Her grip shifted on the Powerstaff before she registered the change in the troll's pace.

Mid-afternoon. The forest ended abruptly at a grassland that stretched toward the horizon like an executioner's platform. Vast, exposed, offering nowhere to hide from watching eyes or consequences. Wind rippled through knee-high grass, a dry hiss where the forest had held silence. Kallen's shadow stretched long and exposed across the open ground. Nothing between her and the horizon.

Three figures moved across the open ground. Small against the vast plains, but visible. Finally, visible. But she was visible to them as well, to any observer with eyes to see her pursuit, her grip white-knuckled on the Powerstaff, her own form as exposed against the plain as theirs.

The elf's silver hair caught the failing light. The two humans flanked her. All three leaned into their stride toward the darker line where land met ocean, not one of them looking back.

"Pursue!" Kallen's hand stabbed toward the distant figures. The undead lurched forward, mechanical gait speeding up into something approaching a run. Tireless. Faster than any living soldier could sustain.

They pulled ahead. Kallen's exhausted legs couldn't keep up with their pace.

Commander Tharne's ice-chip eyes surfaced in memory, that evaluating stare. Academy graduation meant nothing if her first mission ended in excuses.

Push harder. Burn more magic. Risk collapse. The alternative: face Tharne with another failure.

Kallen drew a breath and whispered the stamina incantation again. The Powerstaff's crystal flickered, warning of depleted reserves, then flared amber. Borrowed time. Borrowed strength.

Her vision narrowed. Breath tore through Kallen's chest. Her legs moved, one step then another, because stopping meant failure. The stamina spell burned through her reserves. Her magic draining faster than blood from a wound. Each step cost more than the last.

The plains stretched endlessly. The distance between her and her squad widened with each passing minute. Three squads of Stinkers against three trained warriors. The tactical advantage remained hers even if she couldn't arrive in time to command them directly.

The sun descended toward the horizon, orange and pink bleeding across the sky. Kallen's sight blurred. Distant figures reached the coastline. Her squad close behind the trio. Too far to see details. Too far to command.

She pushed forward anyway, mind clinging to one thought: arrive before they escape.

Kallen's legs gave out. She crashed to her hands and knees in the grass, gasping for air that wouldn't satisfy her lungs. Too far. Still too far. But she could see. Barely.

The shore. A dark shape bobbing in shallow water.

A boat.

The humans pushed it into the waves, clambering aboard. The elf held position on the sand, sword drawn, facing down the advancing undead.

The elf lunged, a silver blur cutting through two soldiers. Behind her, the boat drifted into deeper water.

The air vibrated with the release of magic from the boat. The man's Powerstaff blazed clear even at this distance.

Cerulean light erupted across the beach, a shimmering barrier separating most of the undead from the elf. She'd cut through the formation before the spell completed, and several soldiers remained engaged with her while the barrier trapped the others on the wrong side.

The elf fought, blade dancing through undead strikes. Efficient. Lethal. Buying time.

As another of her stinkers fell, the elf sprinted along the shoreline, four undead in pursuit. The boat continued its drift into darkness, two figures visible in the failing light.

Kallen remained on hands and knees. The boat, a dark shape against darker water, vanished into the night. Her squad stood useless behind the barrier's light, animated corpses waiting for commands. The elf, a distant shadow along the shoreline, disappeared into the gloom.

Gone.

Her fingers dug into the grass. Commander Tharne's ice-chip eyes waited in Treast.

The troll lumbered over and sat beside her, its pig-snout snuffling at her face. That vacant grin, pleased with itself for tracking the trio all this way. Proud of its accomplishment. Its snout swung toward the waterline, still searching.

Kallen's hand found her Powerstaff. Its crystal pulsed red. Dangerously depleted, but enough for this. The incantation formed through gritted teeth, her knuckles whitening around the grip. The pig-snout pushed closer, warm breath hitting her cheek.

A blast filled the air with acrid smoke and ozone. Where the troll had sat, only scorched grass remained. A blackened scar on the plains that would fade with the next rainfall. As if failure could be erased as easily as ash washed from stone.

The blast's echo faded. Distant waves broke against wet sand, rhythmic and indifferent, and her own ragged breathing refused to steady.

Commander Tharne. She'd have to return. Report the escape. Face those ice-chip eyes with nothing but excuses. The Academy's top graduate, reduced to explaining how three travellers had outmaneuvered her twice.

Kallen pushed to her feet. Her legs shook but held. The trip back to Treast awaited.

Then whatever came after.

Chapter 12

Into Another World

Night had surrendered to the grey promise of dawn as Stric adjusted the sail one final time. His shoulders protested the movement, stiff from hours of gripping the tiller through the darkness. Salt crystals itched at the corners of his eyes. He rubbed them with the back of his hand before reaching for the Powerstaff wedged beside him. Heavier than when he'd last checked their heading. The pull remained constant, drawing them through the last stretch of open water toward the island's hidden shore.

Aelith's battle cry still echoed in the silence between them. Throughout the long night, neither had spoken her name, though her absence pressed against them like winter fog. Invisible but pervasive, chilling everything it touched. Teela's fingers repeatedly found her sword hilt, muscle memory finding the worn leather, the corrected grip Aelith's hands had shaped. But the leather pressed differently against her palm. Too familiar. Too quiet.

Each time Stric reached for the Powerstaff to check their heading, its weight pressed heavier in his grip. Aelith's blade raised, the word drifting through the air. Go. His throat tightened. The price of their mission, left on a beach they'd never see again.

The horizon blushed pink and orange, the colours bleeding across the rippling sea. In the distance, the jagged silhouette of an island rose from the water, its outline sharpening with the growing light. Teela stood at the bow, one hand on the mast, her gaze fixed on their destination. Neither had slept. Neither had suggested it.

Stric navigated toward a secluded cove where towering cliffs offered shelter, wildflowers clinging to cracks in ancient stone. The vessel's hull scraped against sand. Waves knocked softly at its sides, each one pulling the hull back toward open water. They gathered their packs, exchanging nods.

Stric slung his pack over his shoulder and drew a deep breath. The cool sea breeze did little to steady the tremor in his hands. He stepped from the boat onto unfamiliar land. His chest tightened, each heartbeat a drum.

He turned, offering Teela a hand. She met his gaze, exhaustion etched in the set of her jaw. A tightness at the corners of her eyes that hadn't been there before the beach. She took his hand. Her vault from the boat carried the precision Aelith had drilled into every movement. Efficient, controlled, honouring her teacher even in this small act. But as her boots touched sand, her free hand drifted to her sword hilt again, fingers tracing the worn leather where Aelith's hands had positioned hers.

"Your weapon is an extension of will, not a substitute for thought." The teaching echoed, sharp and clear, as if Aelith stood beside her still. The sea stretched behind them, pale and still under the morning light, each wave folding quietly onto the sand. Salt lingered in the air as Teela's feet touched sand, fine grains shifting beneath her boots.

They heaved the boat onto the warm sand, grit crunching beneath their boots as they studied the solitary path winding into the heart of the island. Golden rays stretched through the trees, dappling the path with shifting patches of warmth. Above them, gulls cried out in lazy arcs, their wings cutting through the morning air.

Stric looked at Teela. She answered with an imperceptible nod, her jaw hardening. Each footstep grew louder as fine grains gave way to coarse gravel. With every step, the outline of a structure emerged from the landscape. A white stone building rose ahead like a spectral beacon, stark against the shadow-pooled faces of jagged rocks.

An old man emerged from within, his long grey hair tousled by the breeze, his eyes crinkled beneath thick brows. His gaze fixed on the ground as he shuffled around the building's side, oblivious to Stric and Teela drawing near. His feet dragged through the gravel, guiding him toward a lush patch of green that clung to the building's edge.

Stric hesitated. The man's frail form swayed with each step. He called out, "Excuse m..."

The old man let out a cry. He leapt into the air, spinning around. His hands cut through the air in wild arcs. As he landed, his knees buckled beneath him, sending him sprawling onto his backside with a sharp thud that pulled a grunt of pain from his throat.

Stric and Teela rushed over. "Are you alright?" Teela asked, crouching beside him as Stric reached out a steadying hand.

"I am so sorry!" Stric's brow furrowed as he knelt beside him. "I never meant to frighten you."

"That's all right, son." The old man wheezed, catching his breath. "It's been so long since I've heard another voice. Yours just caught me off guard!"

"Are you hurt?" Teela asked, kneeling on his other side.

"I am much better now!" he answered with a growing smile. "Although I am wondering whether I died in that fall and am being visited by an angel."

"Aren't you just the sweetest man!" Teela said, a rosy hue creeping into her cheeks, her eyes bright despite the sleepless night.

Teela's shoulders dropped, tension easing from muscles held tight since the beach.

"Can you stand?" She asked, her voice tightening. "Should we help you inside?"

"That would be very nice, lovely Angel," the old man replied, his gaze lingering on Teela. "Let us get inside and be seated, then you can tell me what brings you to this lost and lonely island."

Taking an arm each, they helped the man into the building. The glow from the hearth cast shadows on rough wooden shelves, a single bed in one corner, its blanket folded flat across it, the floor swept bare. Teela moved to the hearth, lifted the kettle, and set it over the coals, her hands finding what they needed by touch.

They sat together around a small table; the chairs woven out of seaweed, their strands glistening like ocean reeds in the firelight.

Stric shifted in his seat, his fingers drumming against the seaweed chair. He parted his lips to speak, but the old man cut him off with an unexpected question.

"We have not made our introductions. My name is Marka," he said, his voice level and unhurried. "I am the caretaker here." For a moment, Marka's gaze drifted to the horizon, his expression distant, before he continued, "and guardian of the wormholes."

"I am Teela," she said with an open smile, "and this is Stric. It's very nice to meet you, Marka."

"The pleasure is mine, lovely lady Teela," Marka replied, his eyes crinkling at the corners as a wide grin spread over his face. His eyes found the Powerstaff before they found Stric's face, the grin settling into something sharper. "Vrill sent you? Didn't he? You are looking for the prince?"

Stric's eyes widened, his mouth falling open. "Yes, Grandmaster Vrill sent me... how could you possibly know that?"

"I recognise the Powerstaff you carry as his..." He stopped mid-sentence, his eyes lingering on the staff. "I've known him for a very long time." His face softened, and his voice dropped to a near whisper. "I have witnessed firsthand the power he could wield." His gaze drifted to where flames crackled in the hearth. "So I know you did not take it from him by force."

"Twenty years ago, several weeks after Talnaress burned, a boat appeared on my horizon." Marka turned toward the window, as if he could still see that distant sail. "I watched it struggle against the current. When they finally beached, I saw why."

He leaned forward, firelight carving deep shadows across his weathered face. "Master Cearan stumbled onto the sand first, an infant bundled against his chest. Then Kael, his armour dented, sword never leaving his hand. The Elves came last, eyes scanning the horizon as though Barok's forces might materialise from the sea spray itself."

Marka's fingers traced worn grooves in the arm of his chair. "Cearan carried Vrill's message along with the prince. The Grandmaster had instructed him during their escape from the burning palace. Take the baby to the elves; they would help to get him here, and I was to help get them beyond Barok Tana's reach."

Barok Tana. Marka's hands stilled on the chair, knuckles whitening. Cearan had told him what they'd fled. A city burning, loyal soldiers executed, anyone who'd served the royal family hunted like animals. Cearan's jaw had barely moved when he'd described it, his eyes on the floor, the words pressing out through his teeth. And now the one had finally come. He looked toward the window. In twenty years, no sail had come from Veltak.

"That first night, while I tended the infant and Kael stood watch, Cearan told me Vrill's plan." Marka's voice softened, his eyes dropping to his own hands. "The Grandmaster had told him another would come seeking the prince one day, long after they'd fled to safety. I would know Vrill had sent them because they'd carry his staff." He looked to the Powerstaff resting against Stric's leg, his head tilting as if confirming something he'd already known. "Though my old friend never mentioned his messenger would arrive accompanied by such beauty!"

"So you knew we were coming?" Stric's eyes narrowed with curiosity as he tilted his head.

"Yes," Marka nodded, his gaze flickering between them and the restless flames licking at the hearth. "I just didn't know when you would arrive."

"Is that why we gave you such a fright when we arrived?" Teela asked, tucking a loose strand of hair behind her ear as she leaned forward.

"I've been alone here for so long!" Marka's voice wavered. "It's been twenty years since anyone has managed to journey to this place." His gaze drifted to the dust-covered windows. He paused, his brows drawing inward, the line of his mouth tightening. "Though many unwelcome visitors have attempted to breach this sanctuary," he said. "But thanks to Vrill, they have not succeeded." He nodded towards Stric's Powerstaff.

"How did Vrill stop them?" Stric leaned forward, eyes narrowing.

Marka rose from his chair. Dust motes swirled in his wake as he moved to a shelf near the window. His fingers traced the spine of a leather-bound journal, its cover cracked with age. He pulled it down with both hands, keeping it level, the withdrawal slow and deliberate. "My grandfather began this work," he said, opening to pages filled with sketches of swirling patterns and careful notations. "Stumbled through one while surveying the island's mineral deposits. He emerged three days later. After escaping from a beach he couldn't identify, with stars he'd never seen before. Look here."

He turned the journal so that they could see it. A crude drawing showed a shimmering portal, with careful measurements and calculations surrounding it. "My grandfather made this sketch, his last entry before he disappeared." Marka's voice dropped. "He stepped into one of the thousands of wormholes scattered across this island and never returned. We never learned where he went, or if he survived the journey."

His finger traced the careful notations surrounding the drawing. "My father inherited his research, but also his danger. A group of merchants had been funding my grandfather's work. Their interest was profit. Only ever profit. They wanted to exploit the wormholes for trade routes, for military advantage, for control over every path between worlds." Marka's jaw tightened. "The lives that might be lost, the worlds that might be harmed. They cared for none of it."

Marka returned to his chair and set the journal on the table in front of Teela. "That's when Grandmaster Vrill arrived. My father had sent a desperate message to the Guild, begging for help against the merchants' corruption. Vrill came himself." A small smile softened his weathered features. "He was magnificent. Within days, he'd exposed the merchants' funding for what it was. Attempted theft of dangerous knowledge for profit. He helped my father break their contracts and send them away empty-handed."

"But Vrill didn't stop there." Marka gestured to the surrounding walls. Faint runes covered the stone, pale blue and faintly luminous. "Together, they built this sanctuary. Vrill's enchantments protect it. Only those with a good reason can find this island. He helped my father develop a system of teleportation crystals, a safe way to reach specific wormhole entrances without stumbling blindly into the wrong ones."

Marka's hands stilled on the journal cover. His gaze went somewhere past the room's walls. "When my father died, Vrill continued to visit. He became my family. He taught me to maintain the enchantments, to create new crystals, to study the wormholes safely." His voice strengthened. "And in the end, he trusted me with the most important task..." His gaze lingered on Vrill's Powerstaff, "protecting Prince Dreese's escape route, and waiting for the one who would bring him home."

His eyes found Stric's. "This sanctuary has stood as a bulwark against those who would misuse these doorways between worlds. Three generations of my family, aided by Vrill's wisdom and magic, have kept this knowledge safe."

His gaze drifted from the ancient journal to Teela, who studied the sketches with the same focused intensity she brought to sword practice. His grip on the staff relaxed, and the familiar weight settled against his palm.

Marka took a deep breath and rose. He moved toward a shelf lined with dusty tomes. His fingers grazed the spines until they paused on an old, tattered volume with a faded leather cover. He pulled it from its resting place, its pages yellowed with age, and leafed through them with care, turning each page from the corner, barely pressing the edges.

"Yes, here we are," he said, settling back into his worn chair with a creak. "Earth, as its inhabitants call it, can only be accessed for eleven days every two years." He glanced up from the book on the table, meeting Stric and Teela's eyes. "The portal alignment began at dawn today, so you can't stay there longer than ten days, or you'll have to wait another two years to return."

Stric nodded, his brow furrowed. "Thank you, Marka. We will need to leave as soon as we can. Time is crucial."

Teela leaned forward. "We should eat before leaving. I'll prepare something."

Marka rose halfway from his chair. "That would be wonderful, lovely Angel!" He rubbed his hands together.

They shared a hearty breakfast of fresh flatbread, honey, ripe fruit, and aromatic herbal tea. Steam curled from their cups, carrying the scent of dried herbs. Flatbread tore with a soft crack in the quiet morning. When the meal was finished, Teela and Stric cleared the table and cleaned up.

Marka thanked them with a nod and stood up. "Come." He guided them into a corridor where shadows stretched along the walls. Intricate carvings depicting ancient symbols adorned the passageway, and glowing runes cast a pale blue light across the stone surfaces, cold as moonlight on winter snow. They stopped before a grand door, its surface ornately carved with swirling patterns and more runes.

Marka flicked his wrist. The door opened with a whisper, its hinges gliding in well-oiled grooves, releasing a breath of air tinged with old dust. Beyond the threshold lay a room in chaos. Light poured from crystals embedded in the walls.

Crystals scattered across a wooden bench, some tiny as seeds, others formidable and jagged, their faces refracting light into sharp bursts that bounced across the walls and boxes. Boxes overflowed and stood in teetering stacks around the room, one careless movement away from collapsing into chaos should Marka disturb their balance.

His fingers moved over them with practised reverence. "These crystals transport you to the correct wormhole entrance. Step into the wrong one and you might emerge anywhere in creation... Or nowhere at all." He paused over a red crystal, testing its weight before setting it aside. "Each crystal is attuned to a specific wormhole, a specific destination world."

Marka picked up another crystal. He scrutinised it for a moment, then threw it aside. "No, not this one." He continued his search, his focus unwavering as he picked up and discarded several more crystals, each discarded crystal deepening the crease in his brow. "Where is it? I know I left it here. Without it..." His voice trailed off. Stric's hand tightened around the Powerstaff, the grooves pressing hard into his palm.

With each discarded crystal, Marka's movements grew more frantic, his hands plunging into the pile with increasing agitation.

He picked up a yellow crystal. It slipped from his grasp, shattering on the hard stone floor.

The explosion of light froze them all. Colours burst across the stone walls. Violent flashes that seared afterimages into Stric's vision. The fragments scattered, each piece pulsing with fading energy, and for one terrible heartbeat, Stric wondered if they'd just lost their only path to Dreese.

"Blast it." Marka dropped to his knees. His hands shook as he gathered the shards, each clink against stone loud in the sudden silence. "These crystals hold immense power. One wrong activation and..." He didn't finish, but his weathered hands trembled as he swept the pieces into a pile. "We cannot afford another mistake like that."

Stric's throat tightened. If the Earth crystal shattered like this one...

Marka rose, moving back to his search with renewed care, each crystal now handled as if it might detonate.

Stric turned his head toward Teela, his brow furrowing as he raised a questioning eyebrow. His thumb found the grooves of the Powerstaff. Thousands of wormholes meant thousands of destinations. And Marka needed to find the one specific crystal attuned to Earth's wormhole amidst this chaos.

Marka's eyes widened. He lifted a small blue crystal, light pulsing within its depths. The crystal's glow washed across his face in azure waves.

"Here it is." His pace quickened as he crossed toward them, the crystal extended ahead of him. "I'm sure this is the one that will get you to Earth." Marka's grip on the crystal tightened as he nodded. "Yes, I'm positive this is the one!"

"You must hold it together or be touching each other. Then tell it to take you to Earth, and it will teleport you to the wormhole entrance." The crystal glimmered in Marka's palm. "You'll need to step through the wormhole itself to reach Earth. To return, use the command home, and it will bring you back here. Misplace this," he said gravely, "and you'll find yourself marooned on an alien planet."

The lightness went out of Marka's face, his weathered fingers tightening around the crystal. "When you arrive at the wormhole, you must not stray from the direct path. Walk straight to it and step through immediately." His eyes held theirs. "The area around wormholes is... unstable. Those who wander have been lost in other dimensions. Never to return."

Marka's thumb stilled over the crystal. "And when you come back, this is equally important. You must not take more than five or six steps from where you arrive before activating the crystal to return here." His knuckles whitened around the blue crystal.

"There are other wormholes all around that area. It's too easy to step into another one and be lost forever."

Stric's brow knotted tight, his fingers drumming against his thigh. "Do those who travelled with the Prince not have one to return here?"

"No! I only have the one attuned to Earth's wormhole," Marka said, holding out the crystal. "I used my magic to teleport them to the wormhole entrance twenty years ago... I was stronger then, and could manage the spell. But I kept this crystal safe all these years, knowing someone would need to follow."

"I sent them without a return path, because this crystal was the only way back," Marka said, his gaze fixed on the blue crystal as though it might shatter under pressure. "It was necessary to allow you to follow."

Teela leaned forward, her eyes wide and bright. "You sent them? Do you possess magic yourself, Marka?"

Marka chuckled, his fingers playing over the gem's facets. "I've picked up a trick or two from Vrill," he said.

Teela's eyes softened, a nod passing between her and Stric. The crystal's multifaceted glow caught in their eyes, blue-white and shifting.

As Stric's fingers closed around the crystal Marka held out to him, a cool sensation ran through his fingertips.

Teela stepped forward, her touch firm yet gentle on Marka's shoulder. "Thank you for everything," she said.

Stric nodded in agreement, gripping Marka's hand with a firm, appreciative shake. "We owe you much."

"Safe travels, my friends," Marka said. "Remember, you have ten days, and do not misplace that crystal."

Stric's eyes narrowed as he met Teela's gaze. Stric held out the crystal, and Teela extended a hand towards it. Their fingers brushed against each other on the crystals cool surface, sending a shiver up their spines that mingled with the thrumming energy beneath.

Shoulder to shoulder, they inhaled. The crystal's pulse quickened beneath their joined grip, matching that of their breathing. Their voices cut through the air: "Take us to Earth."

The crystal dissolved the room into nothingness. For a heartbeat, weightless. Suspended between one breath and the next. Then, solid ground met his feet with jarring force.

They stood on a rocky plateau. Before them, perhaps five paces away, the wormhole hung in the air. A vertical tear in reality itself. Its edges moved like water disturbed by an unseen hand, pulsing with an otherworldly light that shifted between deep purple and electric blue. Beyond its threshold, darkness swirled with pinpoints that may have been stars, wheeling in patterns that made his eyes ache.

Marka's warning echoed in Stric's mind. Don't stray from the direct path.

Around them, the plateau stretched bare and featureless. A path leading straight to the wormhole. To either side, he glimpsed other distortions in the air, other tears in reality. How many wormholes surrounded them? Dozens? More? Each one a doorway to somewhere unknown. One wrong step, and they would be lost forever.

The wormhole pulsed. It pulled at them with gentle but insistent pressure, like a tide drawing them toward deep water. Stric's fingers tightened around Teela's hand. Her palm was warm against his, her grip steady.

"Straight path," she said, her eyes fixed on the tear before them. "No wandering."

Together, they stepped forward. One step. Two. Three. The pull grew stronger with each pace, the air itself seeming too thin. Stric's heart hammered against his ribs.

With another step, they reached the threshold. The moving edge of reality itself stood before them, so close that the hairs on his arms rose.

He met Teela's eyes. She nodded, jaw set with determination.

They stepped through together.

The sensation struck like falling and flying at once. Stric's stomach lurched. His legs weakened, or perhaps ceased to exist entirely. He couldn't tell. Reality bent around them, folding in ways his mind couldn't grasp. Stars wheeled past, or perhaps they wheeled through stars. The distinction held no meaning here.

For a fleeting instant, from the corner of his vision, Stric glimpsed two figures. A man and a woman, standing in the darkness as if they belonged there. Solid. Real. But when he tried to turn his head to focus on them. Nothing, only the sensation of falling through the void.

Reality folded. Reformed.

The rush ended. Teela gripped Stric's arm as they staggered, knees buckling as if the ground beneath them had turned to liquid. They stood firmly on solid ground once more.

Stric's breath came ragged, his mind still reeling from the transit. Had he glimpsed something in that void? Two figures watching? No. Impossible. Just his mind struggling to process the incomprehensible. And yet the memory lingered, refusing to fade as a dream should upon waking.

He tucked the crystal into an inner pocket, next to Talnar. Marka's warning surfaced through the disorientation. Misplace this, and you'll find yourself marooned on an alien planet.

They found themselves in a cave, jagged walls reverberating with the rhythm of their ragged breaths. Ahead, a shaft of sunlight painted a golden path across the rough stone floor.

Teela glanced at Stric. "Did we make it?" she said, her grip on his arm loosening, her breath catching as she stepped toward the light.

"Let's find out," Stric said.

Their shadows stretched along the stone floor behind them as they approached the sunlight. Each step measured, yet eager.

Stric squinted as his eyes met the stabbing brilliance of daylight, each beam a sharp lance against his vision as he and Teela exited the cave. The air tasted different here, heavier than Veltak's forests, carrying scents he couldn't name, foreign and faintly acrid.

A group of elves stood poised. Bows drawn. Arrows nocked and aimed at the newcomers.

The elves stood rigid like their drawn bowstrings, eyes narrowed and unyielding as they locked onto their targets. Teela's gaze swept the defensive line in a heartbeat. Six elves in a semicircle. One tall man on the left flank with a sword angled at his hip, blade edge already toward them. One magician on the right clutching a Powerstaff that flickered with arcs of blue energy. The rocky outcrop behind the defenders offered cover. The cave mouth behind them was the only viable escape if this turned hostile.

In one fluid motion, she drew her sword, positioning herself half a step in front of Stric. Her weight shifted to the balls of her feet. Aelith's training manifesting in muscle memory. *Defend your position, control the space.* The lesson came in Aelith's voice, not her own. For a heartbeat, her free hand moved toward where Aelith should have stood. Then she channelled it, as her mentor had taught her to channel fear. Aelith had died to buy them this moment. Teela would not waste it.

The defenders formed a tight semicircle, their bodies tense and alert, ready to protect the small village behind them. The village lay nestled in a valley, surrounded by towering trees whose leaves moved in the breeze. Sunlight filtered through the branches, casting dappled patterns on the ground, illuminating the thatched roofs of the cottages and the winding dirt paths that led to the heart of the community. The defenders' silhouettes stretched long and dark against the sunlit backdrop.

Stric adjusted his stance, the Powerstaff's weight settling into familiar alignment with his arm. Vrill had chosen him for this. To find the prince and restore what Barok had broken. Ten days to search an entire world.

The magician's breath caught, and his fingers trembled as his eyes locked onto Stric's Powerstaff. "That staff," he said, "it belongs to Grandmaster Vrill!" His eyes widened as they darted between Stric and the artefact. "How did you come to possess it? He would not have given it up willingly!"

Stric's shoulders pulled back, and his chin lifted, his eyes never wavering from the magician's. "Grandmaster Vrill entrusted his staff to me." Stric tightened his grip around the Powerstaff as he spoke. "We are here in search of someone, and we believe that he is here on this planet."

The magician narrowed his eyes, each word slow and deliberate as he scrutinised the strangers. "And who might you be seeking?" He relaxed his grip on his staff just a fraction, a curious tilt to his head betraying his interest.

Stric's gaze swept across the defenders, lingering on the magician and the warrior who stood at opposite ends of their formation. The magician's grip on his Powerstaff, the thumb pressed flat against the crystal housing. The warrior's feet planted at the distance of a man who'd drilled on palace stone. The magician's weathered features, the warrior's battle-worn stance. These must be the two who rescued Dreese from the palace.

"Prince Dreese of Veltak." Stric stepped forward, lowering his Powerstaff. His gaze steady, his tone firm, each word deliberate and unyielding. "We seek him under Grandmaster Vrill's guidance. Barok Tana has ruled for twenty years, but his tyranny deepens. He's tightening his control over everyone and everything. Veltak bleeds under his rule. We need its true king before there's nothing left to save."

Some defenders shifted uneasily, their whispers like rustling leaves. Others exchanged tense glances, fists tightening around their weapons. The magician's gaze found the warrior.

"I am Cearan," the magician said, lowering his staff. "And this is Kael, formerly of the Royal Guard of Veltak." He gestured to the warrior across from him. With a fluid motion, honed by years of drills, Kael slid his sword into its sheath, the click resonating with practised discipline.

"Grandmaster Vrill entrusted us with the prince's safety. He helped us escape the fallen city and guided us to the elves," Cearan now gestured to the surrounding group. The elves exchanged knowing glances, nods passing like ripples through their ranks.

His voice trembled, and his grip tightened on his staff as he spoke, measuring each word. "With them we fled through the wormhole, and have waited here since for the summons Grandmaster Vrill said would come."

Cearan lowered his staff entirely, exhaling. His furrowed brow smoothed out. "The summons has arrived," he said, his gaze falling to the ground. "Come." He motioned toward the village. "We have much to talk about."

The group trod along the winding path, towering trees to either side, their leaves catching the wind in a dry, rattling rush foreign to any forest he knew. Stric squinted at the village ahead. Its edges rippled like heat rising from sun-baked stone. He blinked and rubbed his eyes, unsure if it was a trick of light or something more.

Cearan turned toward him. "What you're seeing," he said, "is our protection. A complex illusion that hides us from the people of Earth." His voice became gravelly.

Cearan glanced at the horizon as if seeing it anew. "In our first days here," he said, "this world was so unfamiliar, so different from our own! The fear in the eyes of the few we came across made us understand the illusion was a necessity." He paused, lost in memory for a moment. "The natives of this world have no magic and are not ready for it. They fear what they don't understand."

As Cearan led them into a modest dwelling, the scent of aged parchment mingled with the earthy aroma of burning wood from the flickering hearth. Shadows moved across the walls, painting fleeting pictures.

Cearan pulled a chair from the wooden table and sat. His eyes lingered on their new guests before he gestured to the empty seats with an inviting nod. Stric settled into the offered chair, his fingers drumming an erratic rhythm on its rough-hewn arm. Teela sank into the chair beside him, her shoulders dropping as she exhaled. Kael leaned against the wall, arms crossed over his chest. His eyes darted across the room, never settling.

Cearan let out a heavy sigh, his shoulders slumping. "Dreese has always been captivated by the people and the culture of this world," he said, his voice low. "Dreese would trail behind Kael on every journey to collect supplies, peppering him with questions about the city and the strange people they encountered." Cearan glanced at Kael, whose eyes twinkled in agreement.

"A year ago," Cearan's face tightened, his eyes darkening as the memory surfaced, "that curiosity got the better of him. I remember him just before dusk, helping the elf Taran. Then he was nowhere to be found. He slipped through our illusion with a stealth we never anticipated..." Cearan forced himself to relax his clenched fists before continuing. "One moment he was there, helping, and in the next heartbeat... he was gone."

Stric and Teela locked eyes, her lips pressing into a thin line while his eyebrows knitted together. Stric leaned forward, his fingers tightening around the edge of the table. "You mean he's out there all by himself?" The words caught in his throat.

A tight smile crossed Kael's face and faltered at the edges. "Not entirely alone," he said, his voice steady but his eyes darting. "Dreese is resourceful. He has been taught by Cearan, the elves, and me since he could walk." His gaze cut to the window. "He knows how to survive."

"We believe he intended to return, but somehow... the shadows of their world wrapped around him." Cearan's shoulders slumped as he spoke, a heavy sigh escaping him. "We've searched as thoroughly as we could, but maintaining the illusion consumes all the magic I possess. The presence of elves would be too conspicuous, and Kael lacks experience in tracking someone through the chaos that exists out there." Cearan's voice steadied as he spoke again, his chin lifting. "But now, with your help, we might have a fighting chance."

"We must travel back to Veltak in ten days," Teela said. Her weight shifted to the front of her chair. "Ten days to track someone through unknown terrain and return him home."

Cearan nodded, rubbing his tired eyes before offering a faint, hopeful smile. "You'll get whatever you need," he said, "but the illusion can only be breached at dawn and dusk to avoid being seen." His nod was firm, his gaze level.

"Best if you wait until morning to depart." Kael's gaze flicked to the window, where dusk gathered in the corners. His jaw tightened. "Trust me on this."

Cearan nodded again, his jaw clenched, and his eyes narrowed. “Yes,” Cearan said, his voice firm yet warm. He flicked a hand toward Kael, who moved swiftly to swing the door open with a creak. “Time is short. You’ll need your strength.”

The elves glided into the room, their feet barely whispering against the floorboards, carrying an array of simple foods. Warm, fresh-baked bread with golden crusts, an assortment of ripe, colourful fruits, and a steaming pot of hearty stew. The warm scent of earthy spices wafted through the air, mingling with the sweetness of honeyed pastries. Stric’s stomach rumbled in anticipation. Kael slipped into a chair, exhaling, nodding to each elf as he reached for a steaming bowl of stew.

As they ate, his gaze moved to the empty chair beside Teela. In recent days, three of them had been sharing meals. Stric, Teela, Aelith. The chair sat at an angle no one had moved it to. Across the table, Teela’s eyes met his and held. Someone should sit in that space, commenting on the food and planning the next day’s training.

Neither spoke of it. They ate.

After the meal, Stric reached into the folds of his robe and withdrew Talnar. He placed it on the table. The whisper of turning pages filled the air. The others around the table leaned in.

Cearan’s breath caught. His fingers rose halfway toward the book before falling to his side, as if touching it without permission would be sacrilege. “Talnar.” The word emerged barely above a whisper. “Grandmaster Vrill truly has great trust in you, Stric.”

As if sensing the weight of Cearan’s words, the pages came to a halt. To everyone else, the pages were blank, devoid of any visible writing. Stric leaned closer, his gaze fixed on the text. Words formed on the parchment, ink pulsing with life. His voice steadied as he read aloud:

"A compass spell, young Stric? In a world without magic? Surely you question whether your abilities will function here!"

The text shimmered, reforming.

"Magic flows from the caster, yes. But it is drawn from Veltak's crystal vibrations. Have you forgotten what sits at the heart of the very staff you carry? The Powerstaff holds a Veltak crystal, a potent one. You bring your world's power with you. Your magic will work in this strange land, just as Cearan's does."

Another shimmer.

"The real question is whether you've learned to trust your own casting. Doubt not, young Stric. Or do and prove me wrong about entrusting you with both my pages and Vrill's staff."

He squared his shoulders. Around the table, the others exchanged glances. Cearan's expression shifted, the corner of his mouth pulling up, then settling. Kael's mouth curved at one corner.

They stirred long before light reached the stone sill, their shadows moving in the cool, bluish glow of early morning. Stric's fingers traced the Powerstaff's grooves, tightening and releasing, the pale grey light from the small window catching the crystal but leaving the runes in cold shadow. Teela caught his eye as he stuffed the last items into his satchel. The corners of her mouth lifted. His hand stilled at the buckle.

As they approached the edge of the illusion, the landscape rippled, the treeline warping at its edges before snapping back. Cold air settled into Stric's lungs with each breath. Kael's arms hung at his sides. Cearan's white robes held the early light. The elves waited, still a few paces back. Cearan's voice barely rose above a whisper. "May the stars guide you." In his outstretched hand, two small crystals glowed, casting fleeting rainbows onto his palm.

Teela picked one up, the light shifting in the crystal's depths as her fingers closed around it. "What are they?" she said.

Cearan's eyes twinkled with mystery. "Translator crystals," he said, nodding towards the hills ahead.

Stric clenched his Powerstaff, his jaw firm. "Thank you, Cearan. We will find him and return quickly," he said.

Stric and Teela stepped through the rippling barrier.

The fresh scent of the forest vanished, replaced by air that tasted of metal and something else. Something that clung to the back of the throat. Above them, the sky held a grey cast despite the morning sun.

A wall of jagged rock loomed behind them, the cold pouring off it in waves, its surface swallowing the early light without returning a trace. Stric's mouth fell open. He took a step back, his boot scraping against stone. The village was gone as if it had never existed.

Teela looked back to where they had come from. Solid rock. Nothing more. Her hands clasped and unclasped. A muscle worked in her jaw.

Ahead, a narrow, overgrown path sliced through sparse trees toward distant hills. Stric's eyes darted to Teela, his brow furrowed. She returned a tight-lipped nod. Together, they forged ahead. The Powerstaff pulsed with a faint glow in Stric's hand, its pull urging them forward.

With each step up the path, a strange, low vibration hummed through their feet. An acrid scent penetrated their pores, making their eyes water. The air grew heavy. It pressed down on their chests, quickening their breath and leaving a bitter tang in their mouths.

As they reached the summit, Stric stopped. His breath caught, held, and was released slowly. Beside him, Teela's hand found his arm, fingers tightening until her pulse pressed through the grip.

Below them, sound roared. Ceaseless, nothing natural in its rhythm. A thousand sources of noise that never paused for breath.

Stric's throat constricted. Somewhere in whatever sprawled beneath them, Prince Dreese waited.

They had ten days to find him.

Ten days to survive this.

Chapter 13

A World of Madness

Below them, black stone stretched wide, lined with towering poles. Sleek horseless carriages zipped past, their silver bodies blurring into shadows. The air here didn't breathe. It choked. Heat struck Stric's face in waves that carried something worse than warmth. Fumes seared down his throat, each inhalation dragging claws of burning oil and ash through his lungs. His tongue worked against a film that tasted of metal left to rot, thick enough that he wanted to spit but found his mouth already dry.

His jaw slackened. Teela's fingers bit through his sleeve.

Beyond the endless stream of carriages, towers of dull stone and glass rose into a sky that had forgotten blue. The dawn's light came filtered through layers of brown haze, turning the sun into a pale disc that struggled to illuminate the city below. Buildings wore their age in streaks of black grime running down cracked facades, in windows filmed with decades of grime, in gargoyles whose features had been eaten away by something like acid, leaving them to resemble melted wax more than stone.

The city sprawled in every direction, swallowing horizon and sky, a grey cancer that had long ago consumed whatever green earth had dared exist here. Everywhere, the carriages moved like an infantry column broken from its formation, weaving through the haze that hung heavy enough to smudge outlines into shadows. The city bustled with frenetic movement, yet stillness clung to it like grave cloth.

"What is this place?" Teela's lips pressed together, the words scraping out.

A high-pitched keening pierced the air. A jarring thud reverberated through the ground, rattling up through his bones. Stric's shoulders jerked. His breath caught, chest refusing to expand properly for three rapid heartbeats. Teela's nails dug deeper. Her gaze darted, pupils wide and dark.

Her hand trembled against his arm. Just once. Then, her spine straightened. She drew a deep breath into her belly, the way a Veltak footsoldier draws breath before a charge. A deliberate pull of air that transforms the body from startled to ready.

"Staying here is not an option." Stric's fist clenched white around his Powerstaff.

"I hate this." She swallowed hard, fighting down the acrid taste. "But you're right." Another breath, deeper. Her features hardened, sharpened at the corners of her eyes. Her breathing deepened, deliberate.

Stric placed his hand over hers. Their gazes held. The city pulsed. Tense. Vivid. Like rope singing on the brink of snapping.

They strode forward. The compass spell pulled through the Powerstaff, its energy a beacon cutting through a terrain that pressed back against the crystal's pull like a hand pushing against the flat of a blade. Each hour, the staff grew heavier in his grip, the price of sustained magic mounting. Beside them, the road unfurled, metallic and gleaming. Carriages wove through the city's sprawling edges in a ceaseless flow.

Earth engulfed them. Honking sounds. Hurried footsteps. A chaos they manoeuvred through, weaving between dull grey stone and steel. The distance grew between them and the serene village they had left behind. The green of it, the clean cold of the air, the silence between birdsong. All of it had belonged to another world. Fading. Distant.

Wide paved streets stretched ahead. Bodies surged past on all sides, shouldering the thick air. Teela stumbled on uneven pavement. A fluorescent sign above a doorway strobed red across her face. She flinched from it. Her gaze skipped to the next building and the next, finding no place to settle. Glass towers hummed, metal screamed, the air thick with something that had never known nature. Nine days. Nine days to find him and return.

People flowed past in rivers of hunched shoulders and down-turned faces, each illuminated by the blue-white glow of small boxes held before them like talismans against reality. They navigated the cracked pavement without looking up, stepping over puddles of iridescent liquid and piles of refuse with the precision of sleepwalkers. A woman nearly collided with Teela, her eyes never leaving the screen, her lips moving in conversation with someone who wasn't there. A man in a grey suit brushed past Stric's robes, glanced up just long enough to mutter, "cool cosplay," then returned his gaze downward without breaking stride. Someone behind them spoke sharp words about "calling someone" before their voice faded into the crowd's relentless forward surge. None of them truly looked, not at the dying sky above, not at the trash gathering in doorways, not at each other.

Stric and Teela pressed on. Their strides lengthened, purposeful, cutting a direct line through the aimless crowd that parted around them without ever truly seeing them.

With each step, the city roared around them. Grey dust coated their skin and clothes, working into every crease and fold, settling into the lines of their palms. Teela's spine went rigid. Her lips pressed into a thin line. Someone screamed over a blaring horn: "Get out of the way, you moron!"

Teela's green eyes swept from shadowy alleyways, where figures lurked in partial concealment, to towering buildings with windows resembling watchful eyes. Rancid garbage mingled with the carriage fumes and something sweet yet unfamiliar. Her hand found her sword's hilt, grip tightening until bone showed white beneath skin. Her weight shifted forward onto the balls of her feet, as it did when she read the ground before a fight.

Stric's fingers dug into the Powerstaff. Each step forward was guided by an unseen force whose gentle tugging urged them ever forward. His jaw tightened. Muscles coiled against the flutter nestling in his gut as they ventured deeper into this realm. Shadows danced and twisted against the cracked walls. In one alley mouth, a figure stood back from the light's edge, face angled away, the sole of one boot catching a yellow gleam before the crowd shifted and the space closed.

Shadows stretched long and thin across their path, casting patterns over their faces as they descended into the city's depths. The sun had made its journey across the sky and long ago begun its descent. Throughout the day, the compass spell's constant pull drained Stric. He shifted the Powerstaff to his other hand again. The weight that had been manageable at dawn now pulled at his shoulder with each step.

Their legs grew heavy. Each step was laborious. The city's air continued its assault with each breath. Stric's eyes watered from the combination of exhaust and something acrid that reminded him of burning pitch, but harsher. Beside him, Teela lifted her hand to cover her nose and mouth more than once, though it did little to filter the haze.

In the fading light, steel structures loomed above. Twisted forms cast grotesque shadows that fanned across the cracked stone like the spread ribs of a war banner torn from its pole. Large foreign signs flickered to life, casting garish hues across the street. Buzzing like the drone of tomb-flies circling above a battlefield grave. Staining the evening air with an eerie glow.

Teela's forehead creased at one sign depicting what appeared to be a naked lady outlined in flashing red. The words "The Cathouse XXX" blazed beneath her in garish letters. She paused at another sign, where a lady hung over a glass. Bold letters promising "Beer, Wine and Girls" as if it were an invitation. She moved on, lips pressed together, as though she could seal away the questions building behind them.

The Powerstaff vibrated with a rhythm that made Stric's breath catch and Teela's steps falter. Pulling them forward, almost against their will. It guided them to a building that loomed ahead. Sheer crumbling walls exhaling shadows cold enough to chill bone, stone so old the facing had begun to granulate. As they ascended, their feet scraped against stone steps worn smooth by centuries of footsteps. At the top, a door. Its paint peeling away in tendrils, revealing layers of rust.

Above the entrance, a sign bore the words

Marbourne Mental Health Facility.

Stric and Teela shared a glance. His brow drew together. Her head tilted slightly, questioning. Neither spoke as they studied the strange words. Stric reached out. His hand closed on the cold metal handle. He pulled. His muscles strained. The door did not move. He reset his grip, drove his shoulder into the effort, yanked again until his palm burned and his breath came short. The door did not move. They had come too far to be hindered by a locked door.

"You don't want to go in there." A voice emerged from the dark alley behind them.

They turned to find a man emerging from the shadows, his face mapped with grime that had settled into the creases around his eyes and mouth. The city's dust had become part of him, worked into the fabric of his tattered clothes and the lines of his skin. The wind carried the scent of unwashed body and garbage as he lingered just a few steps away, his eyes darting between them.

Stric's brow knitted together. "Why not?"

"It be where they put people nobody wants to look at anymore. Folk go in screaming, and if they come out, they come out silent." He rubbed his chin, casting them a sidelong look. "Tell you what... Got some money for food? Maybe I can help."

Stric's hand moved instinctively to the crystal beneath his robes. Its warmth pulsed against his palm. His own words emerged in the familiar cadence of his tongue, but the air around them shimmered faintly as the sounds shifted, transforming into something else entirely. Harsh, clipped syllables the man would understand. The beggar's lips formed strange shapes, sounds that should have been meaningless, yet each syllable arrived intact and distinct.

Teela's eyes widened. Her head jerked back as though struck, then her gaze snapped to Stric before returning to the beggar's face. Her eyes narrowed as her lips pressed into a line. She rummaged through her pack. "We don't have money." She extended her hand, posture tense, as she offered him a small loaf of bread and some dried fruit.

He hesitated. His gaze flickered between their faces and the provisions in Teela's hands. A wary smile cracked his lips as he took the offerings. "Alright then." He picked out a piece of dried fruit and popped it into his mouth. He chewed quickly, tucking the rest into a tattered pocket. "Why you wanna get in that place?"

Stric and Teela shared a look. His brows drew together at the incomprehensible symbols above the door. Her head tilted slightly, questioning. When Stric spoke, his voice came steady against the bitter chemical tang that clung to the back of his throat. "We're looking for someone. We think he's inside."

The man gave them a long, scrutinising stare. "People rarely go looking for folk in a joint like that," he said, munching on the bread. "All locked up tight. Might need someone to let you in."

The beggar glanced at the building, then back at the bread in his hands. "I got a place across the street, in the alley," he said. "Not much, but you can see this place, and you two don't look like you're from round here. You can stay long as you need. Maybe you got more a this?" He gestured to the food with a crooked grin.

Stric and Teela nodded. The beggar led them into the alley. The shouts and engine-clatter of the street thinned as they moved farther from it, the stink of exhaust giving way to something damper and older. They reached a narrow passage littered with thick paper boxes and debris. A faint stench of decay hung in the air.

A chuckle shook his chest. "Home sweet home," the beggar said, spreading a tattered blanket on the ground. "You can call me Vince. What's your names?"

"I'm Stric, and this is Teela,"

Vince tore off a hunk of bread and ate hungrily. "Don't get many visitors round ere," Vince said between bites, "least not the fancy type."

They settled in, Vince between them, where Aelith should have been. Teela's gaze lingered on the space for a heartbeat before she looked away, jaw tight. Neither spoke of it. Stric drew a slow breath through his nose and let it out.

The city's hum settled into the alley, a low vibration in the sternum. From their vantage point, the white building rose featureless, its walls unmarked by window or ornament, its blankness unchanged by the coming dark. The words "Marbourne Mental Health Facility" flickered as the last of the daylight faded, casting pale light across the pavement below.

Hours passed. The air grew cooler as the night deepened. Vince had dozed off, his hat pulled low over his eyes. Stric and Teela wrapped themselves in blankets from their packs. The building held its face to them, unchanged, its lit sign steady against the dark.

Stric's eyelids grew heavy when Teela's elbow nudged his ribs. "Look, someone is coming out."

A guard in a crisp uniform appeared, unlocking the door from the inside. He held it open, and a young man in white garments stepped out. The young man's hands dove into his pocket, emerging with a small packet. He extracted a white stick. Thin as a quill. And a metallic object Stric couldn't name. The movements turned swift and furtive, his eyes darting left and right as though hiding something. He placed the white stick between his lips, still glancing about. His shoulders hunched as he raised the metal object. It sparked to life with a tiny flame that made Stric's hand drift toward his Powerstaff before he caught himself. The young man touched flame to stick. Smoke curled upward in thin grey ribbons. A moment later, a scent like pipeweed drifted across the street to where they watched.

His voice came low, close to Teela's ear. "Do you think he might help us get in?"

Teela nodded, her eyes intent. "Let's go find out."

Vince stirred in his nest of blankets, mumbling before falling back to sleep.

They moved across the street. The cold city air bit at their faces, carrying the acrid scent of exhaust and something chemical that made Stric's eyes water.

The orderly stood beneath a flickering streetlight, his attention fixed on the white stick between his lips. He was young, with dark, shaggy hair and the slouched posture of someone who'd rather be anywhere else. Smoke curled upward as Stric and Teela approached, their footsteps echoing on the cracked pavement.

He didn't look until they were nearly upon him. "Excuse us." Teela's voice rose to a level that might have pleaded. "We need to get inside."

The orderly exhaled a long plume of grey smoke that mingled with the city's haze. His gaze slid over their medieval attire with the flat assessment of one who'd seen stranger things and cared about none of them. "Theatre troupe lose their bus?" He flicked ash toward the gutter. "Whatever you're selling, I'm not buying. And if you're here for charity, you picked the wrong place for that fantasy."

Stric took a step closer. "We're looking for someone. A young man. We think he might be inside."

"Yeah?" The orderly took another drag from his cigarette. "So, half the city is looking for somebody. That's what phones are for." He gestured with the white stick toward the door behind him. "Place is locked up tight. Nobody gets in."

"Please," Teela stepped closer. "It's important."

The orderly studied them for a long moment, his expression unchanging. His jaw shifted. His eyes stopped moving. He glanced at the door, then back at them, his voice dropping. "Look, I get it. Everybody's got their sob story. But doors don't open themselves for free around here, if you catch my meaning."

Stric's brows drew together. "We don't have any coins on us. Is there anything else we could offer?"

The orderly's gaze crawled over Teela, lingering. His tongue wet his lips as a slow grin spread across his face. "Oh, I can think of a few things." His hand made a crude gesture toward her.

Teela's spine went rigid. Her hand moved to her sword hilt, fingers wrapping around the grip with practised ease. When she spoke, her voice cut flat and cold. "If you value your life, drop that idea now. Touch me, and you'll be missing that hand. Keep talking, and I'll take your tongue."

The orderly's grin vanished. He took a step back, hands rising slightly, his jaw set flat. Like a merchant whose haggling had been rejected. "Alright, alright. Keep your hair on." He took another drag from his smoke stick, exhaling slowly as he recalculated. "I'm here until midnight. Take a smoke break every couple of hours. You come back with something valuable, something I can actually use, maybe I help you out."

He dropped the stick and ground it beneath his heel. "Cash. Jewellery. Something that spends." His eyes flicked to Teela's sword. "And leave the Renaissance Fair props at home. Security sees that, they'll have questions I don't get paid enough to answer."

Without waiting for a response, he turned and pulled open the door. The lock clicked behind him.

Stric and Teela stood in the empty street, the facility's walls rising above them, smooth-faced and unbroken. They exchanged a glance before turning together and making their way back toward the alley where Vince slept.

Stric and Teela found Vince sitting up. His eyes fixed on them, one corner of his mouth twitching upward. "That was quick," he said, pulling his hat lower over his eyes. "Didn't think you'd get in. Or out, for that matter."

Teela sat down beside Stric. Her mouth formed a hard line. "We have to find something valuable. That pig of a man wants payment to let us in."

"I'd help you if I could, but I ain got nothin of value, haven't for years," said Vince as he lay back down and prepared to go back to sleep.

Stric sighed. "We've got nothing that would interest him. Teela, any ideas?"

Teela met his gaze, a stillness settling on her face before she spoke. "You could ask Talnar."

Stric hesitated. "That's certainly worth a try."

Removing Talnar from his pocket, he opened the ancient tome. The pages remained blank for a moment, then ink spread across the surface in slow, even lines.

Words spread across the pages, bold then fading to flowing script. "Transmutation, young Stric. Surely you haven't forgotten that basic spell? Make them shine like the precious stones the greedy fool desires. You know the magic."

The answer broke through him like the cold splash off an upended bucket. Stric's spine straightened, the Powerstaff nearly slipping from his grip as realisation blazed across his features. His fingers tightened around the ancient wood, knuckles whitening with sudden purpose. "Of course!" His gaze snapped to Teela. "We need to find stones or pebbles."

Teela raised an eyebrow. "Stones, pebbles? That's not very helpful."

Vince raised his hat and sat back up, leaning forward, his gaze sharpening on Stric. "Stones, eh? Sounds like a plan," he said, raising an eyebrow and pointing towards the back of the alley. "You might find some in that pot, not that they will do you much good."

Stric and Teela made their way to the back of the alley, where shadows pooled thick between dumpsters. The pot Vince mentioned sat wedged behind a rusted drainpipe, half-filled with stagnant water that reeked of decay. Stric upended it. Water splashed across the cracked pavement, and ten pieces of rock tumbled out. Rough fragments of stone worn smooth on one side by whatever forces had brought them to this forgotten vessel.

They returned to where Vince sat, his hat pulled low. Stric knelt on his blanket and brushed aside some debris between it and Teela's blanket. "Here," he tapped the cleared space. "Put them together here."

Teela gathered the rock fragments, their surfaces gritty against her palms, and placed them where Stric indicated. The rough stones scraped together with a sound like grinding teeth.

Stric positioned his Powerstaff above the pile, its crystal catching what little light penetrated the alley. He drew a breath that tasted of ash and exhaust, then spoke the ancient words. His will pressed outward through the crystal, bending reality to older laws than those governing this corrupted city.

The runes along the Powerstaff's length flickered to life, pale blue light washing across the blanket. The rock fragments trembled. Rattled against each other. They rose, huddled together, hovering palm-height above the ground, tumbling against each other.

Stric's teeth ground together as he fed more energy into the working. The fragments moved faster, orbiting each other in tightening spirals. Their rough surfaces ground together with a sound like millstones working. Dust fell. A fine grey powder drifting down, piling in a growing circle. The air grew thick with it. Stric's eyes watered. Teela covered her nose and mouth.

The stones blurred into motion, their grinding surfaces creating a cloud that made Vince cough and wave his hand in front of his face. His jaw had gone slack, eyes wide and unblinking, breath held.

Then. Click. The spell released. Ten objects dropped onto Stric's blanket, bouncing once before settling. No longer rough rock fragments, but faceted stones of granite, each face cut with a geometric precision that caught the alley's dim light and threw it back in sharp-edged glints.

Stric lowered the Powerstaff. Sweat beaded across his temples despite the evening chill, and he wiped it away with the back of his hand. His breath came measured and deliberate, the way it always did after channelling magic. The Powerstaff's weight had increased; the familiar wood now pulling at his shoulder with each slight movement.

On the blanket lay ten stone pieces, each cut with facets that would shame a master jeweller's work.

Stric's hand shook slightly as he reached for the first stone. He steadied it, drawing breath deep into his belly the way he had been taught. The stone's facets bit into his palm.

"That was the easy part." He held the stone up to catch what light remained. "Now I have to make them into something they are not."

Teela leaned forward, her gaze dropping to his hands, her body gone still. Vince had gone quiet, his jaw closed, weight eased back, arms drawing in. Magic was one thing to witness in stories. Another entirely to watch unfold an arm's length away.

Stric brought the stone close to the Powerstaff's crystal. He spoke the words of deep transformation, his voice dropping into the formal cadence reserved for workings that reached beyond simple manipulation. Ancient syllables rolled from his tongue. The language of change, of unmaking and remaking. His will focused on a single burning point.

The Powerstaff's runes blazed brilliant blue, each symbol burning with an intensity that made Teela's breath catch. The crystal pulsed in rhythm with his words. Once, twice, three times. Heat radiated from its core, washing across Stric's face like standing too close to a forge.

The stone erupted with blood-red light. It vibrated in his palm. Humming with a frequency that rattled up through his bones and set his teeth on edge. The grey surface rippled like water disturbed by the wind. Colour bled outward, crimson as fresh wounds, as though the stone itself wept at its transformation.

The transformation was completed in a rush. Weight shifted in his palm. The rough warmth of stone became the cool, smooth density of something far more precious. The red glow faded, leaving behind a ruby that caught the alley's meagre light, shattering it in faceted brilliance.

Stric's fingers shook as he held it out to Teela.

She froze for a heartbeat. Her hand reached out, then carefully took the ruby from Stric's trembling fingers. "Stric, you did it!" The gem threw thin red lines across her palm, sharp against the grey of the alley stone. A smile broke across her face. The first genuine smile Stric had seen since Aelith fell.

"The spell itself is simple enough," he said, though his controlled breathing suggested otherwise. "But these gems lack something essential. They can never hold or channel magical energy. For spellwork, they're worthless." He gestured to the ruby in her hand. He glanced at the remaining stones waiting on the blanket. "But they'll shine and look pretty. They'll pass for the genuine article to anyone here."

Teela turned the ruby, watching light dance through its facets. "Then we have our payment." The smile left. Her jaw set, gaze moving to the stones. "How many more can you create?"

Stric's breath shortened as he grasped the second stone. He positioned the polished sphere beneath the crystal. "Shall we find out?" His will shaped the magic toward a different hue, a green cooler than the runes' blue, already pressing cold against the heel of his palm.

The runes flared once more, their light thinner against his palms, the crystal's pulse less sharp in his chest, the blue edge of each rune gone softer than it had burned a moment ago. The crystal pulsed its rhythm. This time, the stone took on a deep green glow reminiscent of sunlight filtering through Veltak's ancient canopy. The vibration intensified, rattling through his grip and up his arm until his shoulder ached with it.

The transformation rippled through the stone. Green spread like moss growing in accelerated time, swallowing grey until nothing remained but a stone through which the alley's dim light bent and fractured, deep and cold and impossibly green.

Stric released a breath, held longer than he'd intended, shakier than he'd have liked. His fingers slipped once before passing the emerald to Teela. The Powerstaff dipped in his grip before he caught it, adjusting his hold to compensate for the weight that shouldn't have increased but somehow had.

Stric drew a breath that did nothing to ease the weight settling into his shoulders. Each transformation would cost more than the last, his reserves diminishing with every working.

The third became a sapphire, blue as the deep ocean. His voice cracked midway through the ancient words, forcing him to steady it before continuing. The stone pulsed with azure light, its transformation swift but no less draining.

Seven remained. Stric's temples throbbed with each pulse of magic through the crystal. Sweat had soaked through his collar despite the evening chill settling over the alley. His arms trembled faintly.

The remaining transformations blurred together, each one grinding a little deeper into the space behind his sternum. Stone after stone surrendered its nature. Dull grey giving way to crimson, azure, and emerald. Each working cost more than the last, each ancient word scraping up through his chest as though the Powerstaff pulled them from cartilage and bone. The Powerstaff shook in his grip, runes guttering like candles in a dying wind. His voice cracked, steadied, cracked again. Vision swam at the edges, a grey narrowing pressing in from all sides.

By the time the last stone settled into gemstone clarity, Stric's arm had fallen to his side, muscles trembling from sustained exertion. He gasped, each breath scraping against battered ribs. Sweat dripped from his chin onto the blanket below, dark spots spreading across the fabric where wealth now lay scattered. The alley's shadows pressed closer, the smell of old wet stone and exhaust thickening as Stric's awareness contracted to the radius of his own arms.

Ten precious gems caught the alley's light, throwing out fractured rainbows. Rubies like captured blood, sapphires deep as ocean trenches, emeralds that held forest shadows, topazes golden as autumn's last warmth. Beautiful. False. But convincing enough to purchase what they needed.

Throughout the workings, Vince had remained motionless in his nest of blankets, his jaw slack then resetting, the lines around his eyes first smoothing then pulling tight, then smoothing again. He stood slowly, as though approaching something that might vanish if he moved too quick. His hand hovered over an emerald before picking it up, lifting it to catch the alley's dim light.

"I'll be damned." The words came low, Vince's head bent over the gem in his hand. "These look mighty fine." Vince's eyes moved to the sweat on Stric's face, the lines scored there that hadn't been there minutes before. "But I think I need to check myself into that place across the street. I'm seeing impossible things."

Stric managed a tired smile. "No, Vince. You're in your right mind, my friend." He selected a ruby and one of the sapphires, holding them out with hands that shook despite his efforts to steady them. "Here, these are for your kindness."

Vince's fingers closed around the gems one by one, slowly, his breath caught somewhere in his chest. He stared at them for a long moment before tucking them carefully into his deepest pocket. When he looked up, his eyes were bright with moisture that caught the neon glow from across the street.

"I don't have any idea how these came to be," he said, voice rough. "But me ma always said never look a gift horse in the mouth." He touched his pocket, as though confirming the gems remained real and not some fever dream conjured by hunger and hope. "You're good folk. Strange as hell, but good."

"Let's see if this is valuable enough for our not-so-much-of-a friend across the street," Stric said, though his voice lacked its usual strength.

Teela nodded, carefully gathering the remaining gems into a pouch at her belt. The pouch sat heavy at her hip, pulling the line of her belt. Eight transformed pieces of rock, each one representing a fraction of Stric's reserves spent and not yet recovered. "We'll wait for his next break. He won't refuse us this time."

They shivered against the evening chill as they left the alley. The sky darkened. The city was a blur of neon and headlights as they crossed the street. Stric and Teela huddled near the facility's door. Their breath misted in the night's chill air. Minutes dragged. The facility door reflected neon in long yellow smears. Traffic passed. Then the young orderly emerged.

He noticed them immediately. "Back for more, huh? Got something worthwhile this time?"

Teela stepped forward, her hand extended. One of the shimmering jewels lay nestled in her palm, its vibrant hues catching the harsh streetlight and throwing fractured colours across the pavement.

The orderly's eyes widened, but suspicion followed close behind the initial flash of greed. He plucked the gem from Teela's palm, holding it up to the flickering light above. His eyes narrowed as he slowly rotated it, the colours shifting and dancing inside the stone. He reached into his pocket and pulled out a set of keys, selecting one and dragging its edge across the jewel's surface with deliberate pressure. The gem held firm, unmarked.

His breath escaped in a low whistle. He brought the stone closer to his face, peering at it from different angles, searching for flaws or fakery. The weight seemed to satisfy him. His fingers tightened once, briefly, around the stone. Finally, he closed his fist around it, a satisfied grin spreading across his face.

"Alright," he said, pocketing the gem with a swift, furtive motion. "Who you looking for?" His tone shifted, accommodating now. Eager to please now that he held something worth the risk.

"A young man," Stric said, his eyes steady on the orderly. "His name is Dreese."

The orderly nodded. His head came up slightly at the name, a brief pause before he spoke. "Yeah, yeah, you mean Drew. He babbled that name when he first got here. I know him. Follow me, but keep it quiet." He held the door open just wide enough for them to slip through.

Inside, the air stopped moving. Dead. Air that had given up the pretence of life, trapped between walls that had forgotten sunlight. Strange glass tubes overhead buzzed with light that never flickered like proper flame, their harsh white glow making Stric's temples throb. The sound burrowed into his skull. A relentless hum that made thinking feel like wading through thick mud.

The corridor stretched ahead, painted in a pale, lifeless colour that resembled nothing in nature. Cold under a trailing finger, with no seam and no grain. Smooth. Too smooth. Like something had worn away every irregularity, every mark of human hands, leaving only this blank perfection that rejected warmth. The walls bore dark streaks at waist height. Handprints layered one atop another. Years of desperate grasping. And scratches that could only have been made by fingernails, scoring the surface in patterns that suggested words no one had been allowed to speak.

Everything smelled of pine trees that weren't pine trees. Something sharp and sweet attempting to mask sweat and an underlying scent that coated the back of his throat like bitter medicine. Beneath it all, another smell. Older. The reek of sweat and unwashed cloth left to ferment in sealed rooms, something biological beneath it, old and unaired.

This wasn't a place of healing.

The orderly led the way, his movements purposeful. As they rounded a corner, a guard looked up from his own glowing box. His hand rested on a black object clipped to his belt. The casual readiness in the man's posture told the rest.

The guard's expression showed no alarm, just the irritation of interruption. "Badge or bribe." The words came out flat, unhurried, the guard already looking elsewhere before the last syllable. "I don't care which."

The orderly hesitated, then turned to Stric and Teela with a demanding look. "Your friends here don't come cheap," he said, his voice low, nodding towards the guard.

Teela reached into her pouch with a sigh. Her fingers found a gem. She drew it out; the facets catching the harsh fluorescent light and throwing it back in amber glints. The guard's demeanour shifted instantly. His eyes dropped to the stone, tracking it the whole way to her open palm. He snatched it from her palm, his fist closing around it, knuckles blanching.

"Alright," the guard said, his voice now untroubled. "Just make it quick."

They continued deeper into the facility, a maze of sterile corridors and locked doors. The air grew heavier here, the chemical sweetness thickening until it tasted like copper on the back of his tongue.

The orderly led them to a new wing, pausing at a door with a small window set into the frame. "Here you go," he said, his voice lifting as he glanced at the door. "Drew's in there. Just don't take too long. If you get caught in there, you are on your own."

Stric and Teela exchanged a glance before stepping inside. The room was sparse. A bed that had cradled a hundred broken minds. A window that looked out onto the city's chaotic skyline, bars across it thin enough to see through, thick enough to remind. At a desk scarred with carved initials, desperate attempts at permanence, a young man sat hunched over a notebook. Pale in the fluorescent glare that cast harsh shadows across his angular features. His dark hair fell in dishevelled curls, partially obscuring hazel eyes that moved with intense focus across the pages.

Even from the doorway, the sketch took shape beneath his pencil. A tower with flowing banners, drawn with the careful precision of memory. The young man's shoulders curved inward as he worked. His fingers clutched the pencil with white-knuckled intensity, as though the drawing were the only thing keeping him anchored.

"Excuse me." Stric leaned forward slightly, words coming soft but quick. "Dreese?"

The young man's head snapped up. His hazel eyes locked on their medieval attire, unblinking. For a heartbeat, his gaze dropped to the drawing in his lap. The tower, the banners, before he slammed the notebook shut and pressed it against his chest. When he spoke, his voice was flat, each word spaced with equal weight.

Beneath the hospital gown, he wore worn sneakers with frayed laces and mud-stained soles. Shoes that had walked far before he ended up here. A folded bus schedule jutted from the notebook's pages like a bookmark. "My name is Drew. Dreese was just a creation of my imagination. A dissociative episode..."

His free hand had moved to cover the notebook's closed pages. Protecting what he'd drawn. Or hiding it. "Dr Collins helped me understand that delusions don't define reality. I've been cured and understand now."

The air left Stric's lungs. Stric took a step toward the young man. "Dreese." The name came quietly but certainly. "Your name is Dreese. Prince Dreese."

"No," Drew's knuckles whitened on the notebook. "That's not..."

"Cearan and Kael sent us." Teela's gaze held steady on his. "They're waiting for you."

A crease formed between Drew's brows, there and gone. His lips parted. Then, his jaw clenched shut. "I don't know those names."

But his grip wavered on the notebook.

Drew's shoulders hunched forward. His gaze darted between their faces. "I don't know them!" His pupils dilated, lingering on eyes, then mouths, then eyes again. "I'm not a prince." He swallowed hard, the words emerging clipped and precise. "I'm Drew, and I know what you are. You're some messed-up therapy experiment sent by Dr Collins. It won't work. My delusions are gone. I'm cured."

Teela exchanged a glance with Stric, then spoke. Her tone was firm but gentle. "We are not a test. It's real, Dreese. The elves sent you here with Cearan and Kael when Talnaress fell. We are here to bring you home."

Drew shook his head, the motion violent enough to make his hair fall across his eyes. He pushed it back with twitching fingers. His mouth opened, closed, opened again. Fear tightened his features, then something else flickered. Recognition. Longing. Then his jaw locked, and his shoulders came up. "Home? This is my home now. I've worked hard to get better, and you're not going to mess that up."

Stric's chest tightened as he watched Dreese turn back to the notebook. Drew's shoulders curved away, the notebook back in his lap. He opened his mouth to say more, but the sound of footsteps came from the corridor.

"Time's up." The orderly's voice cut sharply through the moment. "You need to get out of here."

Stric hesitated. His hand reached toward the young man, fingers curling back before making contact. "Dreese, please. You have to believe us."

"I don't know what you're trying to do, but it won't work. I'm sane now, and I'm staying that way." Drew's chin lifted, his gaze meeting theirs directly. But his chest rose and fell too quickly, and his weight shifted backward, away from them. For a heartbeat, his eyes softened, pupils widening as though struggling to focus on something just beyond their faces. Then his jaw clenched, and the moment passed.

The orderly nudged Stric and Teela towards the door. His heel struck the floor twice, and his hand was already on the frame.

As they were guided through the facility's maze of hallways, the walls closed in. Stifling and cold. Stric's chest tightened. The corridor lights passed overhead one by one, and with each step, the door behind them fell further away.

The guard from earlier gave them a knowing look as they passed, but the jewels in his pocket satisfied any actual concern. Behind them, the facility loomed as they stepped into the night air.

For a moment, the orderly lingered. A smug grin on his face. "Did you finish your convo?" he said, lighting another white stick. "Cause if not, I can get you in tomorrow night. Come earlier, just after sunset, and I can let you stay longer. But you know the drill. Bring something shiny." With that, he slammed the door shut.

Stric and Teela exchanged a glance. Her spine straightened. His fingers tightened around the Powerstaff, jaw setting. They had nine days left, but they would not give up, not after coming so far.

They made their way back to the alley. A horn blared somewhere behind them, then silence, then a train. Stric's fingers wouldn't settle at his sides. Vince was still at his makeshift camp, asleep in his blankets.

The next morning, Vince was gone. Stric and Teela spent their day watching the facility whilst waiting for the orderly to return. Stric's gaze kept returning to the far end of the alley, but around mid-afternoon, Vince appeared. With a grin on his face, he said, "Good, you're still ere. Come with me. The jewels you gave me got me a pretty penny! Got us a place to stay, too. Nicer than the alley, that's for sure."

He led them to a small, rundown motel a block away. "I paid up for five nights," Vince said, jingling a set of keys. "Room's small, but it's got a heater and some proper beds. Better than freezing out there."

Stric pulled off his outer layer and hung it on the chair. His shoulders dropped. The beds sagged in the middle, and when Stric sat, the mattress gave under him, and the heat from the radiator reached his back.

For the next five days, they spent their nights visiting Dreese. During the day, they rested in the shabby motel room. Teela would position herself near the door, with a clear line to the exit, exactly as Aelith had taught for unfamiliar spaces. Some lessons lived on, whether or not their teacher did. Outside, sirens wailed at irregular intervals, and footsteps in the corridor made them both tense until they faded.

Night after night, they returned to the facility. The orderly accepted his payment, holding the offered gem up to the flickering streetlight before opening the door for them. The guard's routine just as familiar: the flat assessment, the extended palm, the possessive grip around whatever stone Stric offered. Corruption worn smooth by repetition, a transaction as routine as any other in this dying city.

The second night, Drew sat with his back to the door when they entered, pencil scratching across paper with mechanical precision. "You're lying, and I'm not buying it." But his voice wavered.

"You must remember Kael and Cearan," Teela said softly. "They were with you when you first came here." Drew's pencil stilled mid-stroke. His eyes went wide and still before he shook his head. "No. I can't go back to that." The pencil resumed its scratching, faster now. Desperate.

Drew waited for them the third night, notebook closed on his lap, both hands flat against its cover. The chemical smell that had choked them on the first visit had dulled into something almost bearable.

Stric touched the crystal beneath his robes. "The magic you remember. It's still real, Dreese. We're using it right now to speak to the people here."

Drew's knuckles whitened. His throat worked. "That's not... that can't be..."

Teela's hand moved to the crystal in her pocket. "Cearan, Kael, and the elves are waiting for you. They never stopped protecting you."

The notebook trembled in Drew's grip. He said nothing. But he didn't look away.

He stood when they entered the fourth night, notebook clutched to his chest. His gaze kept drifting to the Powerstaff, then jerking away as if burned. The fluorescent lights buzzed overhead, filling the silence between them.

"Look at this." He held his Powerstaff aloft. The runes glowed softly, casting a warm light that pooled amber across the white walls and caught the underside of Drew's jaw. Drew's pencil clattered to the floor as his notebook rose from his grip, hovering before his eyes. Pages fluttering with no wind.

"Magic," Stric said, his voice even, each word unhurried. "It's real, Dreese. You're one of us."

Drew stared at the floating notebook. His lips moved, but no sound emerged. When the notebook drifted back into his hands, he pressed it against his chest, trembling. "I don't... I don't know." The words were barely above a whisper. His voice wavered, thinning at the end until the words dropped without landing.

The motel room's thin curtains filtered afternoon light, the colour of old bruises, across peeling wallpaper and water-stained ceiling tiles.

"We've used all the gems," Stric said, standing at the window. A narrow strip of earth lay behind the building. "We'll need more before Dreese is free."

A dead garden waited below in the courtyard, a rectangle of bare soil where even the weeds had surrendered to the city's poisoned air. They descended the motel's exterior stairs and found a dozen quartz stones hidden in the barren earth, milky-white and worn smooth by seasons of rain.

Back in the room, Stric arranged the stones on the bed's coverlet. The magic came harder this time. His will pressed through the crystal, meeting resistance as if pushing through mud rather than air. The quartz trembled, hesitated, then finally lifted into reluctant orbits. Sweat broke out across Stric's brow before the polishing was complete.

The transformations demanded everything, each stone fighting him, colours bleeding through white quartz in stutters that required him to drag ancient words up from reserves that protested their depletion. The Powerstaff shook. Runes guttered like dying embers. By the sixth transformation, his hands refused to steady, forcing him to grip the staff under his arm.

When the gem dropped onto the coverlet, Teela said, "No more," and it wasn't a request. She gathered the six gems and positioned herself in the chair near the door. "Rest. I'll wake you when evening comes. You need to conserve your strength; we may need it yet."

Before they left for the facility, Stric pressed two gems into Vince's weathered palm. The older man stared at the gems, their facets catching the neon glow from across the street.

"More?" Vince's gaze flicked to Stric's face. The shadows hadn't faded with rest. "You look like hell, son."

"We're close." Teela's voice softened. "Another night, perhaps two. Then it's done."

Vince's fingers closed around the gems with reverence. He tucked them into his pocket alongside the others, the weight of accumulated wealth making the fabric sag. "Strange folk," he said. "You keep this up, I'll be able to buy this motel and the block it sits on."

Dreese paced the small room. His movements restless and unsure. Hands gripping and releasing the notebook that had become his lifeline. "This... this can't be real," he said. His voice climbed and broke, the last syllable cutting short on an indrawn breath.

"It is." Teela's green eyes locked onto his with certainty. "You know it is, or you wouldn't be fighting it so hard."

Drew paused mid-stride. His breath quickening. "If it's true," he said, his voice dropping to a raw edge as his hands shook, "everything I've worked for... it's all for nothing?"

Stric stepped forward. "You saw the truth, Dreese. Their world prevents them from seeing it with you."

Drew sank onto the bed. His head falling into his hands as his shoulders shook. "I remember," he said. Tears formed in his eyes and spilled down his cheeks. "I remember the elves, and Kael, and Cearan."

His voice cracked. "For a year, I've felt so empty. They told me that I was being cured. That the hollowness meant I was finally well." He looked up at Stric and Teela, tears streaming down his face. "But it wasn't wellness. It was... forgetting who I was."

"It's time to come home," Stric said. A smile breaking across his face.

Dreese nodded. His posture beginning to straighten as prince and patient merged into one. "I want to go back."

The door swung open. The orderly standing there with a sly grin. "Time's up," he said, his voice grating flat in Stric's ear. "Get lost."

Back at the motel, Stric and Teela couldn't rest. They paced the small room, planning their next steps in low voices. They would go for Dreese the moment the orderly returned, and use whatever means necessary to sneak out with him.

The following night, they waited in front of the facility. Stric shifted his weight from foot to foot, the Powerstaff gripped tight in his palm. Teela stood motionless beside him, but her gaze tracked every movement on the street, every shadow that shifted. When the orderly's figure appeared in the distance, they both leaned forward. His steps were casual, but there was an edge to his voice. "You two really broke him," he said, lighting a white stick. "Told the doc you were magicians, and he was royalty, now he's in isolation."

Stric's chest tightened. A chill spread through his stomach. "Isolation?" The word cracked on the second syllable. His free hand clenched at his side.

He hooked his thumbs into his pockets. "Yeah. No visits, no contact, locked away beyond my reach. But make it worth my while, and I might tell you when they let him out again," he said.

Teela's spine straightened. Her jaw set. Her hand moved to her sword hilt. "We don't have time," she said. "We need to get him out now."

The orderly shrugged. Unconcerned. "Good luck with that," he said, flicking the white stick away. He disappeared into the building. The door slammed shut.

Stric's grip on the Powerstaff turned bloodless, the ancient wood trembling in his grasp. They'd come too far. Aelith had paid too much for a locked door to stop them now. The runes flickered to life, casting a blue light across his face. "We must find another way in."

Teela's hand fell from her sword hilt. Her eyes swept the building's facade, counting windows, measuring distances, cataloguing weaknesses. "The orderly mentioned isolation. That means a separate wing." Her gaze snapped to his. "We have to break him out."

Gravel shifted in the alley entrance behind them. "How?" Vince said. "That place is locked up tighter than a rich man's vault."

Stric turned. The Powerstaff's glow intensified, casting dancing shadows across the crumbling walls around them. "With something they don't believe exists." He met Teela's gaze. Her jaw was set, eyes steady on his. "Tonight."

The city's lights blazed around them. In two days, the portal would close.

He'd be free by morning.

Chapter 14

The Enemy Gathers

While Stric and Teela navigated the realm beyond the wormhole, dawn's pale light filtered through the palace's narrow window slits in Talnaress.

Two days had passed since the coastal encounter, two days since his network had detected another magical signature. His investigation into the previous detections had produced results. Three separate encounters with three incompetents. Two remained to answer for their failures.

Commander Tharne's execution had already concluded at dawn. A mere soldier dealt with swiftly and publicly. The two Spellcasters awaiting judgment in his dungeons were another matter. Straves and Kallen had been trained in magic and should have known better than some military commander.

Straves had pursued the targets for ten days before losing them. Kallen had encountered them twice. She reported the first to Commander Tharne, not to Barok. His investigation had turned up the sequence: Kallen's report received by Tharne and held. A second deployment was ordered. No word was dispatched to Barok after the coastal battle. None. Barok's investigation had uncovered the concealment. Now, the Spellcasters would answer for their failures.

In his private chambers stood a mirror. His reflection flickered. Grey skin emerged like mist through breaking clouds, dark veins threading across aristocratic features that had never been aristocratic. The transformation continued without adjustment, without care. No audience. No purpose.

A public facade required witnesses. Tall, refined, draped in midnight blue with white hair framing classical beauty. The scar from temple to jaw, earned in battle with Vrill, tracked white across grey flesh.

The master deathseed crystal pulsed atop his Powerstaff, its rhythm steady and inescapable. Fused permanently to his spirit in the corruption's final stage, it could no more be separated than his own heartbeat. Early in those first terrible days after the massacre, before understanding came, he'd attempted to release it. Wrongness crashed through him. Magic stuttering, vision blurring, everything wrong until clarity struck. The staff was as much a part of him now as the grey flesh and dark veins.

"Still pretending you're human." Morvath's voice came through his thoughts. *"Grey as tomb dust, yet you stand before that mirror."*

The corruption progressed constantly, veins darkening, skin taking on the pallor of old bone. His pulse remained steady. His breathing didn't change. No tightness in his chest, no catch in his throat. Nothing.

"Murdered us. Chambers meant for..." Sethara's voice cut through, fragmented and sharp. *"Twenty years wearing our knowledge like stolen robes."*

The seven voices murmured their eternal accusations, but he'd learned to work through their noise. They never stopped. They never would.

A muscle twitched in Barok's jaw. The only physical response his body still produced. The voices always came louder when consequences loomed.

The air in his chambers grew colder. Something that raised the fine hairs along his forearms and pressed into his eardrums like deep water. Barok's breath misted white despite the warmth. Frost crept across the mirror's edge, crystalline fingers reaching inward.

Twenty years, and it was still watching. The Shadow. Always watching.

"It's here," Morvath said. *"Come to observe its handiwork."*

The cold retreated. Not gone. Never gone. But withdrawing to wherever it waited between worlds. The frost on the mirror melted, leaving no trace. Barok drew a steady breath. His pulse beat its usual rhythm; his hands remained still where any man's would have trembled. His reflection showed no widened eyes, no tightened jaw. Just observation. Clinical. Distant. The way one might note ice spreading on a lake.

He turned away from the mirror. Three reports lay on his desk. The Spellcaster Straves's scouting log. Academy graduate Kallen's encounter report, and intelligence from border posts. The pattern had resolved.

A trained magician. Male. Young. Wielding a Powerstaff with a distinctive signature, his network had never registered before. Precision in spellwork, with a power that exceeded Academy standards. Magic that shouldn't exist anymore.

An elf companion with silver hair, warrior-trained, moving through his territory as if Eldoria's queen had sent her. Kallen's notes described their positioning: cover held without instruction, flanks adjusted without signal.

A human woman. Sword-trained. Moving as the magician's partner with the ease of shared purpose.

Together, heading northwest. Toward the coast.

His fingers stilled on the report. Northwest. Heading away from Eldoria's borders. Away from the elven kingdom that had remained carefully neutral for twenty years.

The question arrived unbidden: Could this have anything to do with the baby?

Twenty years of searching. Every lead was interrogated. Every rumour followed to a dead end. No body. No trace. The infant prince had died in the flames.

"Or Vrill found a way to hide him," Mythara said. *"somewhere you'd never look..."*

His jaw tightened. A trained magician with unprecedented power, moving with Elven allies. It could be a coincidence. Unrelated resistance activity.

Or it could be precisely what he'd dismissed as impossible for twenty years.

Scout Straves had pursued them for ten days through the wilderness before being defeated and losing them. Spellcaster Kallen had encountered them with an elven companion, then teleported to report to Commander Tharne instead of directly to Barok. And Tharne, that fool, had dismissed it as routine intelligence rather than the threat it represented.

The plaza's morning execution had drawn the mandatory crowd. Commander Tharne had knelt on the blood-stained platform just after dawn, his military bearing intact until the axe rose. The blade caught the first light as it fell. Steel met flesh with a wet crunch. Someone in the crowd retched. Others studied their boots with sudden intensity. His crime: concealing intelligence from his lord. He'd dispatched reinforcements. He'd done everything except the one thing Barok demanded: immediate reporting directly to him.

Barok's investigation had uncovered the concealment. The execution followed within the day.

Now Tharne's head decorated a spike above the plaza gates, eyes still open, expression frozen in the moment steel touched neck.

Barok crossed to the window. Talnaress sprawled beneath him, smoke rising from morning cook fires. In the plaza below, citizens hurried, heads down, eyes fixed on the cobblestones. A woman jerked her child closer as an undead squad passed. A blacksmith's hammer rang out, then stopped mid-strike when a patrol turned down his street. Silence rippled outward from the citadel like frost spreading across glass.

He'd never found the boy. Two decades of hunting through every lead. Nothing. The child had died in the flames.

Until now. A trained magician, moving northwest with elven allies.

Could it be connected? Could someone have been trained in Eldoria and sent to retrieve a prince who'd be of age now?

"They're coming... The heir you never killed... The throne you never..." Zorven's voice broke on the final syllable, a rasped catch before it gave out. *"We tried to warn..."*

The crystal pulsed at the apex of his Powerstaff. Seven rhythms, never quite synchronised. Twenty years and they'd never aligned with his heartbeat. Never would.

"Never be a part of you..." Sethara said. *"Imprisoned... only imprisoned by you..."*

The voices saw patterns everywhere, conspiracies in coincidence. More likely, this was ordinary resistance activity. Some remnant magicians gathering allies, planning some doomed assault.

But if they brought Dreese back... if the prince returned after twenty years... every noble family he'd crushed, every soldier he'd executed, every citizen who'd learned to fear. All of it could unravel around a royal bloodline he couldn't match.

He couldn't afford to assume. Couldn't risk being wrong.

He would send someone to succeed where others had failed. The crystal beat against his palm. If this were about Dreese, nothing less than absolute victory would suffice.

But first, he would make examples of those who'd disappointed him.

With a thought, Barok wove the familiar illusion around himself. The grey skin smoothed to an aristocratic pallor. The dark veins faded beneath elegant robes of midnight blue. White hair fell to his shoulders, framing features that spoke of intelligence and refinement. The scar remained. A calculated touch of humanity, of vulnerability that wasn't real. His green eyes took on their unnatural brilliance, the final touch completing an aristocratic facade of commanding precision.

The mask settled, a cool weight across his jaw, the pallor pressing smooth to the line of his scar. This is what they would see. This was what they always saw until the moment his attention sharpened, and the careful illusion faltered.

Barok descended from his chambers, the citadel's corridors opening before him like the throat of some vast beast. He moved heel to toe across the stone, each step deliberate, the Powerstaff's crystal casting faint illumination across the stone walls.

The guards had brought Straves nothing. His throat had gone to grit and his gut to hollow. His own ragged breathing filled the dark, and through it, the distant screams. His shoulders jerked. He forced them down. Another scream. Another flinch. He pressed his spine against the wall, willing his body to stop betraying him. His throat burned. Others had displeased Lord Tana before him. Their voices still echoed through the corridors. The footsteps stopped outside his door.

Three chambers away, Kallen's academy robes hung wrinkled across her rigid spine. The robes that should have marked triumph. Seventeen footsteps in the corridor. Pause. Seventeen back. A door closing three chambers down. Silence. Another door. Her fingers traced the same crack in the stone wall for the hundredth time. Copper flooded her mouth where she'd bitten her tongue. Her jaw ached from clenching. The footsteps stopped outside her door.

Straves's door groaned open first. He pushed himself upright, knees trembling as his weight shifted. A guard in polished black armour gestured with his sword. "Come." The word bounced off the damp walls. Straves's first step left a wet footprint. Sweat from his bare sole marking the stone.

Moments later, Kallen emerged from her own chamber, blinking in the torch-lit corridor. Her fingers released the wall, leaving wet imprints where her palms had pressed. Her eyes met Straves' across the narrow space. The muscles in his throat worked once. Neither spoke. Their ragged breathing said enough. The guards flanked them, armour clinking with each step as they began the long walk to Barok Tana's presence.

The corridor stretched ahead. Purple flames danced in iron sconces, shadows twisting independently of their sources. Alcoves gaped open, bones piled within. Ribs, skulls, fingers still clutching at nothing. Some chambers stood ajar, revealing instruments that gleamed in the purple light. Others remained sealed, but the stench of the condemned leaked through.

The temperature dropped. Frost formed on the walls despite the burning torches. The cold seeped through fabric and flesh alike, settling into their bones.

They reached a vast antechamber where the ceiling soared into shadow. Here, the guards stopped. One raised his gauntleted hand.

"Wait."

Straves's heartbeat thundered in his ears. Acrid sweat mixed with the citadel's pervasive odour of decay. Kallen stood still beside him, lips pressed thin, all colour drained from them.

Beyond the antechamber, massive doors loomed. Dark wood bound with iron, carved with runes that hurt to look at directly. The symbols shifted when observed. Between the runes, scenes of conquest had been etched. People kneeling before a towering figure, cities burning beneath dark skies.

The doors opened without sound or visible mechanism. They swung wide to reveal the throne chamber beyond. Cold air rolled out, thick with the sweetness of decay. Both prisoners staggered.

The purple flames reached the lower joints of the pillars and stopped. Above them, the vaulted ceiling was unbroken dark. Pillars of black marble stretched toward a vaulted ceiling lost in darkness. The floor was polished, reflecting the purple flames that burned in massive braziers. At the heart of the chamber sat the throne. Upon it sat Barok Tana.

The throne commanded the space: obsidian carved into curves that whispered of organic forms. Bone, sinew, something alive trapped in stone. Its high back rose like a skeletal rib cage. Purple light slid across its surface without catching, swallowed rather than reflected.

Then Barok's attention sharpened. The elegant aristocratic features rippled like water disturbed by a stone. Grey flesh surfaced through the maintained pallor. Dark veins threaded visible across his temple, pulsing with each heartbeat before the beautiful mask reasserted itself.

The elegant throne revealed its true nature: shadow-stuff writhing like smoke given terrible form. Dark mist coiled around its base and crawled up its sides. Within that mist, faces. Dozens of them, mouths stretched in silent screams, eyes stretched wide, the whites showing all around. The mist flowed, streaming toward the master deathseed crystal atop Barok's Powerstaff, then back again, in an endless cycle of tormented souls drawn into the crystal's pulsing heart before being expelled back into the mist's writhing darkness.

His skin took on a grey cast of old bone, threaded with veins of corruption that pulsed with stolen life. The scent of the grave rolled forth. Sweet and cloying. The grey flesh smoothed to an aristocratic pallor. Dark veins retreated beneath elegant skin. The writhing mist solidified into carved obsidian, faces within the smoke frozen into decorative patterns on the throne's surface. Both prisoners staggered, blinking rapidly. Had those been faces? Or merely shadows cast by purple flames?

"Approach," Barok commanded.

The word struck like a fishhook behind Straves's navel. His body lurched forward. One step, then another. Feet moved before thought could intervene. Beside him, Kallen jerked into motion as if yanked by an invisible rope, her breath catching on a strangled gasp. Their legs kept moving. The compulsion wrapped around their spines like iron bands. Walk. Obey. Approach.

They couldn't stop, even if they had wished to.

The braziers flared higher as they passed. The air grew heavier with each step. Something pressed into Straves's chest, thick and warm, clotting at the back of his throat.

Barok watched their approach with the patience of a predator. His green eyes tracked their movement with calculating interest. Unnaturally bright. He did not speak, did not gesture, simply let them come close enough that the tremor in Kallen's jaw was plain and the sweat had already darkened Straves's collar.

When they reached the base of the throne's dais, he raised a single finger. They stopped as if struck by lightning.

The silence stretched. Barok's gaze moved between them, weighing, measuring, finding them wanting.

"You both have encountered a magic user," he said at last, voice soft with lethal calm. "One wielding a Powerstaff." His eyes narrowed. "Yet neither saw fit to inform me directly. I find myself... curious as to why."

Straves shifted, his robes rustling. His lips parted, drawing breath to speak "...".

"Silence." Barok raised a single finger again, and Straves's voice died in his throat as if crushed by an invisible hand. "You will speak when I permit it, when I require it. Not before."

He rose from his throne with fluid grace, descending the dais steps without haste. Each foot placed with the same even pressure, arms loose at his sides.

He stopped before Kallen, towering over the young woman. Her knuckles had gone white where she gripped her robes. "You first. Tell me of this encounter. Every detail. Omit nothing."

Kallen swallowed twice before words would form. When they emerged, her voice cracked. "My Lord, I was leading a scouting party in the forest when we came upon three individuals. A man, a woman, and an elf. The man wielded a Powerstaff and attempted to cast a spell. I countered it and teleported immediately to report to Commander Tharne."

"Commander Tharne," Barok spoke the name as if it were a curse. He circled behind Kallen, each step deliberate. "Tell me, why you, a trained Spellcaster, chose to report this encounter to a mere soldier rather than to your proper superiors?"

"I... I assumed Commander Tharne would inform you, my lord."

Barok stopped circling. Kallen's breath stopped with him. The only sound was the low hiss of the nearest brazier.

"You assumed." The words dripped with contempt. "You encountered a magic user, one of significant power. And you assumed that someone else would handle the responsibility."

"She failed you..." Mythara whispered. *"You failed us."*

A muscle twitched in Barok's jaw.

"Commander Tharne met his end in public this morning. Stripped of his rank, stripped of dignity, stripped of life itself." His voice had not risen. Had not sharpened. "And you shall meet the same fate."

Kallen's face went white, then grey. Her knees threatened to buckle, but somehow she remained standing.

Barok turned to Straves. "And you? What pathetic excuse do you offer?"

Sweat beaded on Straves's forehead despite the chamber's chill. "My Lord, I apologise for my oversight. I was attempting to gather more intelligence before presenting my findings."

Barok's laugh rang through the chamber. The sound devoid of warmth. "How noble of you," he said, stepping closer. "To claim good intentions when your incompetence has forced me to waste time and resources."

This close, the aristocratic features wavered. Grey spread across Barok's jaw like ash bleeding through parchment. His green eyes deepened into hollow voids, twin wells of nothing, edged with crimson veins. The white hair darkened at the roots. The mask snapped back to the refined features, elegant bearing, the scar's calculated vulnerability.

"You want redemption?" Barok asked, voice soft and terrible.

The words tumbled over each other in Straves's eagerness. "Allow me to lead a more extensive hunt. I will mobilise more resources. This time, we shall neither underestimate our enemies nor falter."

Barok listened as patiently as a cat watching a mouse exhaust itself against the walls of a trap. When Straves finished speaking, the dark lord's expression had not changed by so much as a flicker.

"What makes you think," Barok said slowly, savouring each word, "that I would allow a self-serving fool a second chance?" He turned to include Kallen in his gaze. "Do you think either of you are worth anything to me? Worth the air you breathe?"

Neither prisoner breathed.

"I will recover this magic user," Straves pressed on, words tumbling faster. "I will bring him to you alive. I will..."

"You will do nothing." Barok waved his hand with a casual dismissal, and the shadows in the room shifted. "Nothing except serve as an example to others who might consider disappointing me."

He turned toward the guards. "Take them to the plaza. Have them beheaded. Publicly."

"My Lord! Please!" Straves cried, falling to his knees. "I had no understanding of the significance! I can still serve you!"

Kallen's chin dropped, the formal line of her shoulders gone. "My lord, I was following my training as best I understood it! Please!"

Barok looked down at them both with the dispassion of a man studying insects. "Forgiveness," he said, "is a privilege reserved for those worthy of it."

The guards grasped them by their shoulders, hauling them to their feet. As they were dragged from the throne room, Straves's voice rang off the obsidian walls: "No! Wait! Please, my lord, I beg you!"

The massive doors swung shut with a sound like a tomb sealing.

The guards escorted them through corridors that gradually widened. Natural light began to intrude through the arrow slits. The walls bore mosaic work: tiny tiles forming scenes of conquest. Cities burned in orange and red glass. Armies knelt on grey and black stone.

Other servants of the citadel passed them. Spellcasters in dark robes, soldiers in black armour. None met their eyes.

They emerged into the cold daylight. The plaza spread out before them. A vast space paved with crumbling stones. At its centre stood the execution platform, dark wood stained with the blood of previous victims. The crowd was already gathering: citizens who had learned that attendance was not optional.

As the guards dragged Kallen and Straves across the plaza, a figure watched from a balcony overlooking the scene. Valkan stood motionless, his jaw unmoving, his gaze fixed on the prisoners as they crossed the stones.

His eyes tracked the executioner's stance. Left foot too far forward, the man would need to compensate mid-swing. Twenty years of such observations filed themselves away in his mind with the same precision. Twenty years, and he'd never once required Barok's correction.

The crowd shifted. Someone retched. Valkan's gaze didn't waver from the platform, cataloguing the angle of the blade, the spacing between prisoners, and the guards' positions.

The executioner waited on the platform. A massive figure in black robes, a steel mask hiding any trace of humanity. Straves was forced to his knees first, then Kallen beside him.

The crowd pressed closer below, gazes fixed on cobblestones, shoulders hunched inward. When the axe rose, they studied their fingernails, counted stones, or found a sudden fascination in their bootlaces. Anything but the platform.

The executioner's axe caught grey light as it fell.

Moments after the executions, guards summoned Valkan to Barok's chamber. He moved through the citadel's corridors with a purposeful stride, past the stone walls and purple flames that had so terrified the dead prisoners. His chin stayed level, his hands loose at his sides. The citadel had become an extension of Barok's will, and Valkan had long ago aligned himself with that will.

He found his Master in the same throne chamber where Straves and Kallen had met their fate. Barok sat in apparent contemplation, one hand resting open on the arm of the throne. The illusion he maintained was perfect now. No flickers, no glimpses of the corruption beneath.

"My Lord," Valkan said, offering a precise bow. "You summoned me."

"Indeed." Barok's green eyes fixed on him and held. "The incompetence of your predecessors has created a situation requiring immediate attention. A magic user of significant power moves freely in my domain, protected by allies and armed with knowledge that could prove... problematic."

Valkan nodded. "I am at your disposal, my lord."

"You will lead the hunt," Barok said. "I will provide you with resources sufficient to ensure success where others have failed. I will not tolerate another disappointment."

"Consider it done, my lord." Valkan's fingers drummed once against his thigh.

"See that it is." Barok leaned back in his throne, his hands settling over the carved arms. "The trail begins where Kallen lost it. Follow it wherever it leads. Use whatever force is necessary. Bring this magic user back alive, bring me answers."

Valkan bowed again, deeper this time, waiting.

A cruel smile touched Barok's lips. "You will have everything you require. Golems, undead soldiers, trolls for tracking, and a group of Spellcasters to counter any magic they might employ. You will command a force capable of reducing a small city to rubble."

Valkan went still. Such resources had never been granted to a single mission before.

"When do I depart?" Valkan stepped forward, heels together, chin level.

"At dawn tomorrow. Use the remaining daylight to organise your forces and plan your approach. I want them moving before the sun clears the horizon."

"It will be done, my lord."

Valkan stood in the citadel's courtyard as dawn light bled across stone, the confiscated crystal from Kallen's failed pursuit warm in his palm. Behind him, his assembled force waited. Twelve golems crackling with necromantic binding, seventy-two undead in perfect formation, eight veteran Spellcasters with Powerstaffs already humming, and three trolls shifting their bulk at the rear.

He raised the Kallen's teleportation crystal. The spell matrices within it flared to life. The coordinates locked onto the coastal clearing where she had abandoned her squad after the target's escape.

"Brace yourselves," Valkan commanded. "Physical contact. Now."

Two Spellcasters stepped forward and placed their hands on his shoulders. Behind them, the chain began, undead grasping skeletal hands to armoured shoulders, trolls gripping Spellcaster robes, golems' stone fingers clamping onto undead spines. The entire force linked in a web of connection, every soldier and creature touching another, all paths leading back to Valkan at the centre.

The crystal blazed white-hot in his palm. Its spell matrices screamed as they expanded far beyond their intended capacity. One person travelled easily, a dozen strained the weave, but an army? Magic erupted outward, engulfing the massive force connected to him.

Reality tore.

They materialised on the coast in a thunderclap of displaced air that knocked seabirds from the sky. Sand sprayed outward in a perfect circle. Valkan's knees hit the beach. His hand spasmed open.

The crystal fell and shattered.

Fragments scattered across the sand, surfaces blackened and smoking, all magical resonance extinguished. The spell had consumed it entirely, then cracked it apart from the strain of transporting so many through such a narrow channel.

Behind him, three Spellcasters retched violently. The others fought for air. Even the trolls groaned, massive heads hanging low.

Valkan forced himself upright, vision swimming. Salt spray whipped across his face. His scorched palm throbbed with each heartbeat. But they had made it.

He drew a steadying breath, then another, willing the world to stop tilting.

"Form up," he commanded, his voice rough but carrying authority. "We have a trail to follow."

The ground was littered with the remnants of Kallen's failed pursuit. Cleaved bones scattered across the sand where soldiers had fallen during the elf's last stand. And standing motionless beyond the wreckage was what remained of Kallen's squad. Twenty-eight skeletal soldiers in perfect formation, still upright, weapons held in positions that had once been combat-ready. They stood like statues, oozing eye sockets staring at nothing, waiting for orders from a Spellcaster who would never return.

Without a master to command them, they remained patient, eternal, and purposeless.

Valkan surveyed the scene, ignoring the chill wind that whipped around him and his forces. He gestured to one of his Spellcasters. "Bind them to your control. We'll have use for them yet."

Their quarry had taken to the sea. A magician and a woman warrior fleeing on a boat. An elf holding off the undead single-handedly while the others escaped.

This was planned. Purposeful. Someone had sent them with resources and training. The question was where they'd gone and what they sought that was worth risking Barok's detection.

He clenched his jaw, but only briefly. A setback, nothing more.

"Search the area," Valkan commanded. "There must be another trail."

His forces spread across the beach. One Spellcaster called out from further down the shoreline. Valkan moved to investigate.

Four sets of skeletal tracks headed along the coast, pursuing. Dark drops of dried blood between light footprints leading in the same direction. Their spacing suggesting someone running despite an injury. The elf hadn't escaped unscathed.

The trolls sniffed the air, their grotesque faces contorting with effort as they picked up the scent. Blood and elf. Their eyes widened with sudden interest, and with grunts and snorts of excitement, they lumbered along the coast, following the tracks.

As Valkan studied the trail, his eyes narrowed. A slow breath left him through his nose.

"The elf," he said. "She fled along the beach. Injured." A gesture brought the Spellcasters and undead into formation. "After them. Her trail will lead us to the others."

Trolls led the way, their pace slow but sure. Light dropped to a half-dark as the canopy knit shut above, golems carving a path through trees with casual destruction.

Hours into the pursuit, skeletal remains appeared. Scattered across the forest floor, the bones cleaved cleanly. The elf's work, unmistakable.

A day later, a second one. This one showed signs of a more challenging fight. Shattered ribs, skull cracked. She was weakening, perhaps, or the soldier had gotten closer.

Days turned into nights. Spellcasters began stumbling, faces slack, gaits loose. The trolls' pace slowed. Even the tireless undead slowed in the deepening cold, their footfalls heavier, the gaps between each step stretching.

On the eighth day, a third skeletal soldier emerged from the leaves where the elf had made another stand. One pursuer remaining.

Forward. Each camp shorter. Each rest break grudging. The elf was alone now, injured, with only one tireless hunter still following. But she'd destroyed three soldiers while wounded and fleeing. Dangerous. And leading them somewhere.

They climbed steep inclines and navigated rocky outcrops. On the eleventh day, they found the last soldier. Bones scattered at the base of a steep ravine, as if it had pursued her over the edge and she'd finished it at the bottom.

The blood trail continued. Fainter now, but the trolls could still follow it.

After sixteen days of marching, the forest itself changed. The air shifted, warmth cutting through the chill, carrying scents of growing things and something deeper, older. Then the trees, their leaves taking on an ethereal luminescence that pulsed like distant stars.

The trolls stopped. Their massive heads swung left, then right, nostrils flaring. One took three steps east. Another turned west. The third stood motionless.

Behind them, a Spellcaster drifted off the path. Then another, wandering in slow circles as if searching for something just out of reach.

"Hold position," Valkan commanded, moving forward through the ranks.

The air thickened as he passed the trolls. Pressure built against his chest like invisible hands pressing inward. Hair stood on end along his arms. Skin prickled with the sensation of being watched by a thousand unseen eyes.

Another step. The trees ahead shimmered, shifted. For a moment, they were farther away than they'd been. No, closer? Direction wavered. South felt like it might be... east? West? Days of marching southwest with absolute certainty suddenly felt questionable.

He stopped. Jaw clenching. Southwest. He'd been travelling southwest. Always southwest. Yet the certainty wavered.

Elven magic. Layer upon layer, built over centuries.

Valkan took another step toward the boundary. The elf. They'd been tracking...

What had they been tracking?

His Powerstaff grew warm against his palm. The elf. The magic user. Sixteen days of pursuit. The thought solidified, edges sharpening.

He took one more step forward. His vision blurred at the edges. The forest ahead looked... wrong. Empty. Just more trees, nothing special, nothing worth investigating. Why had he come here? He should turn around. Head back. This wasn't the direction he'd meant to travel anyway...

No.

The air hummed with a watchful presence. His right foot had turned without instruction, heel raised, body already half-rotated towards the way they'd come.

Valkan stepped back from the boundary. The pressure eased immediately. His vision cleared. Direction solidified. Southwest, he'd been travelling southwest, of course, he had. The purpose of his mission came back into sharp focus: find the elf, find the magic user, report to Barok. How had he nearly forgotten?

He drew a steadying breath, jaw tight. That was how the elves had remained hidden. Twenty years of searchers turning away, convinced they'd made navigation errors.

"Eldoria." The word came out low. His right hand tightened on the Powerstaff shaft. The elf they'd been tracking. She'd come home.

Valkan's eyes narrowed as he studied the canopy ahead. His force was formidable. Against fortified human cities, they were overwhelming.

But Eldoria was different. The elves didn't fight like humans. They didn't mass their forces or hold ground. They flowed through their forest like water through roots, appearing from nowhere, striking from everywhere. Their archers could kill from distances his Spellcasters couldn't match. Their wards could tangle his golems and his undead. They could make his trolls useless with confusion.

They could make the forest itself a weapon.

Twelve golems weren't enough. One hundred undead weren't enough against thousands of elves fighting in their own territory, protected by a magic his Spellcasters barely understood.

Valkan turned to address the senior Spellcaster who served as his lieutenant. "You are in command until I return. Maintain position here. Establish surveillance on the boundary, but do not, under any circumstances, advance beyond this point or approach the wards. The elves are watching. I can feel their eyes on us. Do not give them a reason to strike first."

His lieutenant nodded sharply, asking no questions.

"I am returning to Lord Tana for reinforcements."

He took several blank crystals from his pouch and cast a teleportation spell, keying the location to them. After placing them carefully back in his pouch, he withdrew another, this one keyed to his chambers in Talnaress.

"Home," he said, and reality folded around him.

The world compressed, then released. The forest's warmth sheared from his skin, replaced in an instant by the stone walls of his chambers. Valkan materialised smoothly, boots landing solid on familiar floor.

He paused a moment, drew a deep breath, then another, allowing his magical pathways to settle. Just the hiss of displaced air, and he was home.

He straightened, adjusting his robes. Another jump remained before this day ended, and he would need to conserve what reserves he could.

His fingers closed around the crystal, then released it.

Valkan made his way through the halls toward Barok's private study, a smaller chamber where his Master often worked on matters requiring particular focus. The guards recognised his urgency and escorted him without delay.

He found Barok seated at a massive table of polished basalt, a detailed map of the kingdom spread before him. Markers showed troop positions, supply lines, and strategic objectives across the realm. The dark lord looked up with sharp anticipation as Valkan entered.

"My Lord," Valkan stepped forward. "I believe I have found Eldoria."

Barok went absolutely still. The only sound was the faint creak of the table's edge as his fingers pressed flat against the map.

"Explain," Barok commanded, his voice soft and dangerous.

"We tracked the path the elf took after her escape. I believe it led us directly to their border. Whether deliberately or in desperation, I cannot say." Valkan's expression hardened. "Their wards are unlike anything I've encountered. Deception magic, layered so subtly it feels like your own thoughts. I tested the boundary myself. The moment I crossed the threshold, the wards tried to convince me I was seeing an empty forest. Made me question my direction. I nearly forgot why I was there, what I'd been tracking."

He paused, letting that sink in. "I had to use magic to anchor my thoughts against the manipulation. Without it, I would have turned around and left, convinced I'd made a navigation error, never remembering I'd found Eldoria at all. That's how they've stayed hidden all these years. The scouts forgot that they had found anything."

"The magic user took refuge there. The elves have sheltered him, and I am certain they possess knowledge of his current location." Valkan chose his following words carefully. "My current force, while formidable, is insufficient to penetrate their homeland. The outer wards alone nearly turned me around. The deeper layers will be far worse. We would be destroyed before reaching their heartland."

Barok's chin lifted a fraction. His gaze settled on a point past Valkan's shoulder, then returned, sharpened.

"The elves," he said. "Twenty years they hid. And now they break their silence to shelter those who would oppose me. This confirms what I have long suspected. They harbour sympathies for the resistance, waiting for their moment."

He rose from his chair with fluid grace, and the crystal against Valkan's hip pulsed once and went cold. "You will return immediately. Scout their defences and maintain surveillance until reinforcements arrive."

Valkan bowed, his grip tightening once on the folds of his robe. "What reinforcements should I expect, my lord?"

The corners of Barok's mouth drew back before his lips settled into something that might have passed for a smile. "I will send a force that will leave no doubt of our capabilities. One that will reduce their ancient trees to ash if they continue to harbour my enemies. I will remind the elves of why their ancestors chose isolation over confrontation. When I am finished with Eldoria, it will serve as an example to any other race that might consider defying me."

Valkan produced the crystals from his pouch, ones he had used to mark their position. "These will lead your forces directly to our location. I keyed them myself. There should be enough power there to move sizable forces many times. I will be waiting to coordinate our advance."

Barok took the crystals, their surfaces pulsing with stored magical energy. "You are dismissed. Do not fail me, Valkan. The stakes of this pursuit have risen considerably."

"I understand, my lord. The elves will regret their decision to involve themselves in this matter."

Valkan withdrew from the study, a tightness working its way up through his chest. As soon as he exited, he withdrew another crystal he'd keyed to their position at Eldoria's border. Its surface pulsed faintly with the magical beacon he'd set. He raised the crystal and spoke the activation word.

Reality fractured.

The world compressed and released. Valkan's boots landed on solid ground. Eldoria's forest rushed into existence around him. But his Powerstaff felt heavier than it should. The crystal's usual hum had dulled to barely a whisper. His magical pathways registered hollow, scraped clean.

His lieutenant appeared at his side. "Sir? Are you..."

“I’m fine.” Valkan straightened, ignoring the way his fingers trembled against the staff. “Report!”

“No contact with elven forces, sir. We have detected magical observation, but they have made no aggressive moves.”

“Good. They are likely debating how to respond to our presence.” Valkan surveyed the trees of Eldoria’s border, fingers moving briefly across the staff’s surface. “Maintain current positions and establish a defensive perimeter, and create a clearing. Reinforcements will arrive soon, and when they do, we will remind the elves of the cost of defying Lord Tana.”

The air hummed with magical energy as his forces settled in to wait.

Chapter 15

The Rescue

Stric and Teela walked through the darkened streets, Vince keeping pace beside them. The facility's lights faded behind them as they turned corner after corner, the chill night air sharp in their lungs. Stric's fingers tightened on the Powerstaff with each step. Two days. The wormhole would close in two days, and Dreese would remain locked beyond their reach forever.

Vince unlocked the motel room door, its hinges protesting with a metallic whine. The space was small and dim, the single overhead bulb casting harsh shadows across peeling wallpaper and threadbare carpet. Stric set his Powerstaff against the wall. Teela moved to the window, checking sight lines to the street below.

They gathered around the small table, its surface scarred with cigarette burns and water stains. Vince dropped into the chair by the door. His gaze tracked their movements with watchful stillness.

"What about the guards?" Teela's boot tapped against the floor. "There must be more than the one we have met."

Stric leaned forward, elbows on the table, his fingers drumming against the scarred wood as an idea formed. "We can use a magical illusion. Make them see something that isn't there, draw them away." His mouth lifted at the corners. "Or chase them away."

Teela's eyes met his. The crease between her brows smoothed as understanding struck. "And you can conjure those magic shields to block their path if they give chase once we have Dreese." Her hand settled on her sword hilt, grip tightening. "It might work."

Stric's grin widened. "Something unbelievable. Creatures from legend on a world that doesn't believe in magic." He pulled the Powerstaff closer, his fingers tracing the carved runes that pulsed with faint warmth beneath his touch.

Vince's eyebrows climbed toward his hairline. "You can do that?"

"I can."

Teela's jaw set, determination carved into every line of her face. "We leave in one hour. That gives us time to rest and gather what we need."

They spent the remaining time in preparation. Stric consulted Talnar, the ancient tome spread open on the bed, its pages offering guidance on sustaining complex illusions. Teela checked her sword's edge, the blade spinning through her fingers in a flowing pattern before she tested the balance with three precise cuts through empty air. Vince shook his head.

Talnar lay closed on the bed, its pages pressed flat.

The evening air carried a bite that seeped through their clothes as they prepared to leave the motel. Stric tested his grip on the Powerstaff, the carved runes responding with warmth beneath his fingers. Its weight had changed over these past months. Less burden, more tool. More extension of will.

Teela checked the position of her sword at her side. The familiar motion. Her eyes swept the street beyond their window, measuring shadows, marking alleys, cataloguing every route away from what they were about to do.

"The facility will have changed shifts by now." Her voice came low. "Night staff will be smaller, but they'll still be alert."

Stric nodded. The reality of what they were about to attempt settled into his bones like winter cold. Breaking into a secured building with magical creatures that didn't exist in this world. Mad when spoken aloud. Yet the alternative was unthinkable. Leaving Dreese trapped.

They stepped into the night, leaving the motel's fragile safety behind.

The facility's exterior lighting cast harsh pools of white against grimy brick walls. Stric and Teela positioned themselves before the entrance.

"I'm going to make quite an entrance." Stric raised his Powerstaff with both hands. "Stay close. The Powerstaff will guide us to where Dreese is being held, but be prepared for chaos once we step inside."

Teela moved closer to Stric, her hand resting on her sword hilt, every muscle coiled and ready. "Whatever you have in mind, Stric, I'm ready."

The intricate runes etched along the Powerstaff's length glowed, soft at first, then built into an intense, pulsing light. Heat radiated from the magical energy, warming the chilly night air around them like a forge breathing to life. Stric drew a breath, centreing himself. He spoke the words of power. Clear and resonant, each syllable shaped with precision. His free hand traced patterns in the air, directing the flow of energy, channelling it through the crystal at the staff's tip.

Stric completed the last gesture, his voice rising on the last word of the incantation. Power surged through him, flowing from core to crystal.

With a resounding boom that shattered the silence, the door exploded off its hinges, soaring into the corridor beyond with a thunderous crash that split the plasterwork on the far wall and sent a ceiling tile spinning to the floor. Metal screamed, bricks cracked, and the concussive wave flexed the corridor's narrow windows in their frames.

An orderly lurched backward in the corridor beyond, his coffee cup spinning from his grip to shatter against the floor, his shoulder striking the wall.

"What th..." Then his voice died in his throat.

Before him, three small dragons materialised from wisps of smoke and crackling energy. Their scales glinted like molten metal in the harsh fluorescent light, each the size of a person but moving with predatory grace. The heat from their phantom breath created waves in the air, distorting the corridor behind them. An acrid scent of sulphur filled the space.

The foremost dragon lifted its serpentine head and unleashed an ear-piercing roar that reverberated through the hallway. A sound so fierce and primal. The orderly's knees buckled.

He fled, his screams bouncing off sterile walls.

"Dragons!" Teela's laughter bubbled up from her chest as they stepped through the ruined doorway. "Dragons aren't even real on Veltak. After tonight, everyone will think they belong in this place."

They advanced into the facility's sterile interior. The dragons charged ahead, their claws clicking against linoleum floors as the smallest one let out another high-pitched roar. Papers scattered and fluttered as doors banged open, flung wide by fleeing orderlies. A nurse dropped her clipboard and sprinted away, white shoes squeaking against the polished floor.

"Do you see that, Teela?" Stric asked. One dragon tilted its head, lips pulling back from crystalline teeth.

"Yes!" Teela's eyes bright, her blade half-drawn. "One of your illusions is smiling!"

Emergency lights began flashing, bathing everything in a hellish red. Alarm bells joined the tumult, their electronic wailing adding to the dragons' roars. Stric's temples throbbed; the constant concentration required to maintain three separate illusions pulled at his reserves. Sweat beaded on his forehead despite the cool air.

They moved deeper into the building, following the Powerstaff's insistent pull. The magical instrument grew warm in Stric's hands, its runes pulsing with each step toward their goal.

A security guard rounded the corner ahead, his hand reaching for the weapon at his side. His jaw set, his fingers spread open, and his weight shifted back as the lead dragon padded toward him with smoke curling from its nostrils. The heat shimmered around its form, making the air dance. He turned and fled without drawing his weapon, his boots pounding against linoleum in panicked retreat.

"How long can you maintain them?" Perspiration ran down Stric's temple.

"Long enough." His illusions required constant energy to maintain their realistic detail. The heat shimmer of their breath, the weight of their footfalls that made fluorescent lights swing on their chains, the acrid scent that burned in the nostrils.

A heavy security door blocked their path. Stric paused, gathering himself. He spoke another incantation, shorter this time, his voice rough with fatigue. His hand swept forward in a sharp gesture, directing the gathered energy. The spell struck the barrier with a metallic shriek, sending it flying off its hinges to crash down the hall in a cacophony of tortured metal.

Behind them, distant shouts suggested the facility staff were organising some form of response. But the dragons kept them at bay, the illusions spreading throughout the building, causing chaos in every corridor they entered. Staff fled before them, some screaming about monsters, others shouting for sedatives, convinced they were hallucinating.

"This way." Stric turned left at an intersection, the Powerstaff's pull intensifying. They were close now. His breath came shorter as the effort of maintaining the spell taxed him.

Another door, this one reinforced with additional locks. Stric's magic tore through it, though the spell took longer to form, the words of power coming slower. The metallic clang of the falling door added to the building's cacophony of alarms and distant screaming.

The Powerstaff's pull was unmistakable now, drawing them toward a reinforced door at the corridor's end. As they approached, the dragons began to fade. Stric's energy was reaching its limit. The illusions dissolved into wisps of smoke, leaving only the scent of sulphur and the fading roar in their wake.

Stric's hands trembled on the Powerstaff. He drew one more breath, summoned the last of his strength, and spoke the final incantation. The isolation room door tore from its frame with a shriek of protesting metal and crashed down the corridor.

Beyond lay a small, sterile cell, and pressed against its far wall stood Dreese.

The young man was pale, wide-eyed, and dressed in the facility's standard-issue clothing. A grey shirt and matching trousers that hung loosely on his frame. He stood with his spine straight, fear in his eyes.

"You came back." His voice wavered, caught between hope and disbelief. "I thought..." His words caught in his throat.

"We're getting you out of here." Teela stepped into the cell with urgent strides. Her hand extended toward him. "We have to hurry."

For a moment, Dreese hesitated. His fingers twitched toward the notebook on the narrow bed. His anchor, his proof of sanity.

His shoulders squared. His grip steadied as he reached for Teela's offered hand.

"I'm... I'm ready."

They raced back through the facility, Dreese gripping Teela's hand as his heart pounded in his chest. The corridors rang with distant alarms and the sound of staff regrouping, voices shouting orders, feet pounding in pursuit.

Stric raised his Powerstaff, speaking words of protection. Blue energy crackled to life behind them, a barrier forming across the corridor, its surface humming with power as it blocked their pursuers.

Dreese stopped dead. The shimmering wall of light. Blue. Impossible. Magic. His breath came in short gasps. "No. No, this isn't..." His fingers went to his temples, pressing hard. "They said the hallucinations would stop. Dr Collins said I was cured."

The barrier spell tore through what remained of Stric's reserves. The ceiling tilted. The Powerstaff slipped in his sweat-slicked grip. His knees buckled.

"Dreese, help me!" Teela caught Stric before he hit the floor, her arm hooking under his shoulder.

But Dreese stood frozen. At Stric's collapse. His hands shook. "Which part is real? The dragons? The magic? You?" His voice climbed, panic threading through every word. "How do I know any of this is real?"

"Because I'm real." Teela's free hand shot out and gripped the front of his institutional shirt, hauling him close enough that he could see every fleck of green in her eyes. "And he's dying if we don't move. Now choose, Dreese. Choose what you believe. But do it while running."

She released his shirt and grabbed his arm instead, pulling him forward. His feet stumbled into motion, half-dragging, half-supporting Stric between them.

The emergency lighting cast everything in red-tinged shadows as they staggered through the maze of corridors. Stric's feet dragged against the linoleum, legs refusing to support his weight. Each breath scraped his throat raw. The Powerstaff dragged at his wrist, bone-heavy, but his fingers wouldn't release it.

They burst through a side entrance into the night air that bit against their flushed faces. Stric's legs gave out entirely on the threshold. Teela and Dreese lowered him to the pavement, his back against the brick wall.

The dragons had vanished completely, but wisps of smoke still hung in the air around the building. The sound of distant sirens approached, growing louder.

They moved through the city streets, footsteps quick but measured, staying in the shadows where possible. Hearts raced. They reached the motel to find Vince standing outside, worry carved deep into his weathered features. His head snapped up at their approach.

"Where've you been? The place went nuts!" Vince said, eyes wide. "Sirens screaming, the whole nine yards!"

"Long story." Stric's grin came crooked, his weight sagging against the doorframe.

"Don't believe most of what I've seen or heard in the last few days." Vince shook his head. His gaze landed on Dreese. The institutional clothing, the lingering fear in his eyes. "So, this 'im?"

"Yes. This is Dreese. We must get him home, but first, we need to rest and sort things out."

Vince nodded and opened the door to their cramped room. "Well, you all better come in."

The room smelled of damp carpet and old cigarette smoke. Dreese sat on the edge of the bed, hands resting on his knees. The thin mattress sagged beneath his weight, springs creaking. His hands trembled. The dragons, the escape, these people who had risked so much for him.

"Thank you." The words barely rose above a whisper. "I didn't realise how much I missed... everything. How much I missed who I really am."

Teela stepped closer, her hand settling on his shoulder. Her warrior's grip softened, fingers gentle against his shoulder blade. Warmth passed between them, her thumb stilling against the cloth of his shirt. "We're just glad we found you."

Stric nodded, setting his Powerstaff against the peeling wallpaper with careful reverence. The runes still glowed faintly, slowly dimming as the magic dissipated. "We should rest tonight. Tomorrow, we'll return to the elven village. Kael and Cearan will be overjoyed to see you."

Vince, who had been watching the exchange with curious eyes, cleared his throat. "So, you're all heading back to wherever it is you came from?"

"Yes." Stric's fingers found the corner of the table, gripping it for support. "Our time here is limited. We must return to our world before the door closes. Two days. That's all we have left."

Stric's knuckles whitened against the table edge before Teela turned to Vince. "Would you like to come with us? You've been kind to us, and there might be a place for you in our world."

Vince's weathered face broke into a smile that transformed his entire appearance. But he shook his head. "That's mighty kind of you, but I think I'll stay put. Been talking to the owner of this place. Seems he's noticed I've come into some money recently." He winked at Stric. "Says he's looking to sell. I still got some of those gems you gave me. Not sure if they'll be enough to buy this place, but I think I'll try."

"You'd make a fine innkeeper." Dreese's spine straightened as he spoke, his gaze settling on Vince without wavering.

"Been down on my luck for years." Vince's chin came up. He set his palms flat on the table. "But now I got a chance to get back on my feet, make something of myself right 'ere. Always wanted a place of my own, somewhere folks could rest their heads. Somewhere people like you could find help when they need it."

Vince's eyes crinkled at the corners, his rough hand patting his pocket where the gems rested.

Stric leaned forward. "Then that is what you should do, and we will see to it that you can."

They spent the evening sharing stories. Dreese opened up about his year on Earth. The confusion that had eaten at his soul like acid, the mornings waking to a ceiling he didn't recognise, the days walking streets with a name he couldn't keep hold of. His words came haltingly at first, then faster, his eyes dropping to the table and staying there. Vince listened with rapt attention, shaking his head in wonder at tales that would have sounded like madness just days before. Now Vince sat with his elbows on his knees, his cold coffee untouched at his elbow.

As the night deepened outside their small window, they settled into peaceful sleep. The mattress dipped under Dreese's weight, the pillow rough against his cheek, the street noise below fading to a low murmur.

Pale light filtered through the thin curtains. Dreese was the first to rise, standing by the window and gazing out at the world he was about to leave behind forever. Cars passing below, people hurrying to work, a world that had no idea magic existed. Teela joined him, and together they ventured outside to the small, neglected garden that bordered the motel.

The morning air was crisp, carrying a bite of approaching winter. Dreese and Teela wandered through the small, unkempt garden behind the motel. Weeds pushed through cracked concrete with stubborn determination, and scattered among them were smooth pebbles of various sizes and colours. River stones, probably left over from some long-abandoned landscaping project.

"These should work." Teela knelt to gather a handful of the largest stones. Dreese joined her, his fingers selecting the most uniform pieces with the instinctive eye of someone born to assess value, even if he didn't quite remember why.

"It's strange. Leaving this world. For so long, it was all I knew. Or thought I knew."

Teela nodded. The crease between her brows smoothed, jaw unclenching. "It's never easy to leave a part of yourself behind. But you're not losing anything. You're reclaiming who you are."

They returned to the room with pockets full of pebbles. Stric was awake, his Powerstaff resting against his knee as he consulted

Talnar, the ancient tome spread open on the bed. Vince sat at the small table, nursing a cup of coffee that steamed in the morning air, its bitter scent filling the small space.

"We've brought you something." Dreese emptied his pockets onto the table. The pebbles clattered against the scarred wood, dull and ordinary. Grey, brown, speckled white.

Stric smiled, setting Talnar aside and taking his Powerstaff in both hands. "A parting gift." He looked at Vince. The older man's eyes widened.

Stric positioned himself at the table, selecting the largest pebble. He held it between his fingers, feeling its weight, its rough texture. Then he placed it on the table before him and raised the Powerstaff.

He drew a breath. The exhaustion from last night's working had lifted faster than he'd expected. The drain that would have kept him bedridden for a day after the forest battle now lifted in hours. Each spell cast, each working completed, expanded the reservoir he could draw from. Growing stronger through use, the way muscles hardened under a warrior's training. His reserves replenished faster now, though complex magic still demanded its price.

Stric spoke words of power, his voice resonant in the small space. His hand swept through the air in graceful gestures, directing energy through the Powerstaff's crystal. The runes blazed with a golden light that filled the room, making them all squint against the brilliance.

The pebble shimmered, its surface rippling like water. Rough edges smoothed into facets. The drab colour blossomed into rich brilliance. Diamond. Clear as mountain ice, catching the light and throwing rainbow patterns across the peeling walls.

By the time the transformation was complete, Stric had to brace his free hand against the table to stay upright. His arm trembled violently, muscles screaming from exertion. Each breath came ragged and shallow, his chest heaving like he'd run for miles. Sweat soaked through his collar despite the morning chill, dripping onto the scarred tabletop. The Powerstaff's weight had doubled, tripled, the wood biting into his palm as he fought to maintain his grip.

Teela was at his side before he swayed, her hand catching his elbow with the precision of someone who'd caught wounded companions before. "That's enough. No more."

Stric managed a weak nod. The exhaustion from last night's dragon working still echoed through his bones, and this final transmutation had pushed him to his limit. The room swam before his eyes. He let Teela guide him to sit before his legs gave out entirely.

One precious gem caught the morning light, throwing out fractured rainbows. Beautiful. False. But convincing enough to purchase what Vince needed.

Vince had remained motionless in his chair, his weathered face shifting from wonder to something approaching fear and back again. He stood slowly, as though approaching something that might vanish if he moved too quick. His hand hovered over the diamond before picking it up, lifting it to catch the light.

"I'll be damned." The words came as a whisper. "This looks mighty fine." His gaze flickered to Stric's face, taking in the sweat and exhaustion written there.

Teela reached for her belt pouch and withdrew the remaining gems from their supply. The ones they'd used sparingly to bribe their way to Dreese. She held them out to Vince. "Here. These are for your kindness. For everything you've done."

Vince's fingers closed around the gems with a reverence usually reserved for sacred things. He stared at them for a long moment before tucking them carefully into his deepest pocket. When he looked up, his eyes were bright with moisture that caught the light from the window.

"Still ain't got no idea how these come to be." His voice was rough. "But thank ya." He touched his pocket, as though confirming the gems remained real and not some fever dream conjured by hunger and hope. "You're good folk. Strange as hell, but good."

They gathered their few belongings. Stric's Powerstaff, Talnar, their translator crystals, and Teela's sword. Dreese took one last look around the room that had been his temporary haven between worlds, memorising details he knew he'd never see again.

"Are you ready?"

Dreese nodded. His spine straightened further, shoulders squaring. "I am."

Vince walked them to the door, the gems tucked safely away in his pocket. "Don't know what kind of magic you folks 'ave, but you've worked a miracle in my life."

They embraced Vince. Teela first, then Stric, then Dreese, each in turn. They stepped out into the dawn's light. Traffic ground past on the far corner. Somewhere ahead, a vendor called out prices to no one who listened. The pavement filled and emptied and filled again. With Dreese between them, they made their way through the urban maze, retracing the path that had led them to this strange dimension.

The journey back to the forest's edge took most of the day. No one from the facility pursued them. The city dwellers barely spared them a second glance. A man with a glowing rectangle pressed to his ear stepped around Stric's Powerstaff without looking up. Stric led the way, his Powerstaff guiding them toward the hidden village, toward the barrier between worlds.

"It's different now." Dreese slowed as they neared the forest boundary, his gaze lifting toward a strip of sky caught between the last two buildings. "Like I'm seeing everything for the first time. Or maybe remembering how to see."

Teela's jaw unclenched. Her eyes moved from the treeline to his face, slower than usual. "Because now you know who you are."

By midafternoon, they reached the outskirts of the forest, where the illusion shimmered at its edge. They found a secluded spot to rest and wait for sunset, when it would be safe to cross the barrier. The temperature had dropped, their breath misting in the cooling air.

Dreese stood at the forest's edge, looking back at the city skyline that rose in the distance. Somewhere in that urban sprawl was the facility, the only home he'd consciously known for a year.

"It wasn't all bad." His voice dropped. Teela moved to stand beside him, following his gaze. "I know it sounds mad, but... I learned things there. About survival. About holding onto yourself when everything tells you to let go." His fingers found the edge of his gown. "The person I was in that cell, the one who drew the towers and refused to forget... that person is part of who I am now."

Teela's hand rested on his shoulder. "You don't have to leave that behind. You carry it with you. All of it."

Dreese nodded slowly. The city lights flickered on as dusk approached, a million tiny stars blooming against the gathering dark. This world that had held him, shaped him, tried to break him, and failed.

He turned his back on it and walked toward the trees.

"Tell me about Veltak," Dreese asked as they shared the last of their provisions. Dried meat and bread that Vince had pressed into their hands. "What has become of it since I left?"

Stric's jaw set. His gaze dropped to the provisions between them, hands going still in his lap. "The nights grow longer and darker since Barok Tana took control. His rule spreads without mercy. Entire cities lie in ruins, their people suffering under his cruelty. The land itself languishes, the very air thick with despair and fear." He paused. The light in the trees had turned from gold to amber. "Dark magic fuels his power, and the deathless soldiers patrol the realm. Golems stride through once-thriving towns, their mere presence enough to break spirits."

Dreese's face paled, his hands clenching into fists. "Twenty years of this?"

"But it is not without hope." Stric's gaze came up. His spine had straightened without him seeming to notice. "Cearan and Kael have been holding faith for twenty years. There are others, people who kept their heads down and didn't forget. A kingdom doesn't forget its king, even after twenty years." He picked up a piece of bread and turned it in his hands. "It goes underground. It waits."

As the sun began its descent, casting long shadows through the trees, they approached the illusion. The air wavered and rippled like heat rising from sun-baked stone, distorting the forest beyond.

"Now." Stric's whisper carried through the clearing as the last rays of sunlight filtered through the leaves, painting everything gold and amber.

They stepped forward together. The world around them rippled, reality bending. Dreese's skin registered wrongness before his eyes could. A pressure without direction. A cold that had no source. His stomach turned over. Up became down, forward became sideways, and then snapped back into place.

Reality reformed around them.

The air. Clean. Pure. Pine and loam. Living wood, deep and green. The silence struck him next. Wind through ancient branches. The rustle of leaves. Birdsong threading through it all like music he'd forgotten existed. He stood still for a moment, waiting for the roar that didn't come.

He drew a breath that filled his lungs without burning. Then another. The tightness in his chest that had become so familiar he'd stopped noticing it eased.

A shout went up from the nearest structure. Cearan emerged and stopped. His eyes swept the clearing and found Dreese. The breath came out of him long and slow, his hands dropping open at his sides. Behind him came Kael, sword half-drawn, the draw stopping mid-motion. His hand went still on the grip.

"Dreese!" Cearan's voice broke. He crossed the clearing in four long strides. His arms came around Dreese with a pressure that drove the air out of him. He held. He did not let go. A breath, rough and slow, moved past Dreese's ear. "You've returned to us!"

Kael approached more slowly. His sword hand opened and closed twice before he reached them, as though uncertain whether to embrace or salute. His hand settled on Dreese's shoulder as Cearan finally released him. "My prince." The lines of his face shifted into something he probably hadn't worn since before the palace burned. "We never lost faith."

Dreese pulled back from Cearan's embrace, his hands still trembling. He searched the older man's face, cataloguing every line, every weathered feature. His throat worked twice before words emerged.

"When I was a child." The words barely rose above a whisper. "What did you tell me about my parents?"

Cearan's eyes held his. A nod, slow and certain. A verification. Proof this wasn't another delusion. "That your father was the bravest king Veltak had ever known, and your mother's laughter could light the darkest hall." His voice roughened. "That they died fighting to save you, and we swore on their memories we'd keep you safe until you could reclaim what was stolen."

Dreese's breath caught. His fingers tightened on Cearan's sleeve. "And you told me stories. Every night for years. About the palace, the throne room, and the gardens."

"The fountain with the silver fish." Kael's rough voice joined them. "Your favourite. You made us tell that story until you could recite it in your sleep."

"The rose garden where my mother walked every morning." Dreese's eyes grew bright. "The tower where my father held council. The great hall with banners." His voice broke. "I thought I'd made it all up. That Dr Collins was right, that I'd built a fantasy world to escape reality."

"You didn't build it." Cearan's hand settled on his shoulder. "You remembered it. We kept those memories alive because they were yours by right."

The breath went out of him. Tears tracked down his face, and this time he didn't fight them. "I'm home." Not a question. A statement. Truth settling into his bones like the solid earth beneath his feet. "I'm really home."

The elves gathered around them, their melodious voices raised in welcome and celebration that filled the clearing with music. Voices climbing in layers, each held note vibrating through the clearing until the sound settled against the ribs. His shoulders drew back. His chin lifted. The young man who'd hunched in his cell now stood with feet planted, accepting greetings as though he'd never stopped expecting them.

As night fell, they gathered at Cearan's dwelling. A fire burned in the hearth, its light moving across wooden walls in slow patterns.

The fire burned low as they shared stories into the night, voices building against the curved walls, each word still resonant after the speaker had moved on. Dreese's eyes grew heavy. He leaned against the wall, his features softened by the firelight.

"We should rest." Cearan rose, hands lifting from his knees before his feet had shifted. "Tomorrow we return to Veltak, and who knows what challenges await us there."

Teela nodded. She stared into the dying embers, her chin dropping, the firelight catching the line of her jaw. "We have only tomorrow left before the wormhole closes. We must be ready at dawn."

As the others retired, Stric remained by the fire, Talnar open in his lap. The ancient tome's pages glowed in the dim light, words forming and dissolving.

"I hope we're doing the right thing." Doubt crept into his whispered words like frost spreading across glass. "Bringing him back to a kingdom in ruins..."

Words appeared on the page, the script firm and certain: *The kingdom's hope lies in its rightful heir. Your path is true, Stric.*

With a sigh, Stric closed the book and sought his own rest. Dreams of Veltak filled his slumber. The white marble of the palace, the Academy's corridors.

Firelight had already been doused, and bedrolls bundled before the canopy brightened. The elves bustled with activity as supplies were gathered and preparations were made. They moved with practised hands, packing provisions and weapons. Straps pulled taut. A blade turned once in the morning light before it found its sheath.

Dreese stood in the centre of it all. His shoulders had lost yesterday's hunch. When an elf spoke to him, he met their eyes instead of looking away. His hands no longer twisted the hem of his shirt.

Kael approached, offering him a sword in a worn leather scabbard. The leather was dark with age and use, but well-maintained, the brass fittings polished to a soft gleam. "This was meant for you when you came of age. We've kept it safe all these years."

Dreese accepted the blade with both hands, the weight settling into his grip. He drew it from its sheath slowly. The metal gleamed in the light, ancient runes etched along its length, catching the sunlight and appearing to glow from within.

"Your father's sword," Cearan confirmed, approaching with a pack slung over his shoulder. Tears threatened at the corners of his eyes. "The sword of the kings of Veltak. It's time it returned to its rightful wielder."

Dreese's hands tightened on the hilt. He tested its balance and the way it moved. His elbow dropped, his stance widening half a step, the adjustment arriving before any intention to make it.

As the sun climbed higher, long light cutting through the canopy in angled columns, they gathered at the mouth of the cave.

Stric stood at the entrance, the blue crystal held in his palm. Its surface caught the morning light, glowing softly. "We'll walk to the cave entrance together. Once we're through the wormhole and arrive on the island, we must stay close. Very close." He met each gaze. "No more than five or six steps from where we arrive before we use the crystal again."

Cearan nodded, understanding dawning on his weathered features. "The other wormholes. Marka warned us twenty years ago. Stay together, stay close."

"And we enter one at a time," Kael added, his gaze already measuring the distance between the wormhole and the cave mouth.

"Take a few steps forward to make way for those behind; less chaos that way."

They moved as one through the forest, following the path that led deeper into the trees. The morning air carried birdsong and the scent of pine. Each step took them further from Earth's metallic tang, back toward the smell of pine resin and the give of moss underfoot.

The cave mouth appeared ahead, dark against the green. They entered its shadowed depths, boots scraping against stone. The temperature dropped. Their breath misted in the sudden chill.

The wormhole waited in the cave's heart. That same vertical tear they'd stepped through days ago, pulsing with purple and blue light.

Dreese stopped. His hand found the cave wall, fingers pressing against cold stone. "That's how I came here? Twenty years ago?"

"Carried by Cearan," Kael confirmed. His voice softened. "You slept through the whole thing. Didn't wake until we were on Earth, safe."

"I'll go first." Cearan stepped forward, his spine straightening. His hands found the strap of his pack and gripped once. All of it ending now. He turned back once, his eyes finding Dreese. The creases around his eyes deepened. His mouth pressed shut. "See you on the other side, my prince."

He walked to the threshold and stepped through. Gone.

Kael moved next. His hand rested on his sword's hilt for a moment. Then he released it and walked forward with a warrior's steady tread. The vertical tear's blue-purple light flared as he stepped through, then settled back to its slow pulse.

Dreese stood at the threshold now. His father's sword hung at his hip, his hand already finding the pommel without being asked. He looked back at the cave mouth, at Earth's light filtering through. A world that had held him, shaped him, tried to break him and failed.

Then he turned and walked into the wormhole.

Stric and Teela stood alone in the cave. The remaining elves had already departed, entering the wormhole in silent procession. Just the two of them now, as it had been at the start. The wormhole's pulse threw their shadows against the cave wall in slow blue light.

"Together?" Teela's hand found his.

"Together."

They approached the threshold. At the edge, reality itself stood torn open before them.

They stepped through.

Stars wheeled past. Reality bent and folded. Stric's stomach lurched as the familiar sensation of falling and flying gripped them both.

And there, clearer this time. Two figures standing in the swirling darkness. The man stood tall, one hand raised as though pointing toward something beyond sight. The woman beside him held something that glowed with a soft light. They watched, waiting.

Stric tried to focus on them. But the transit pulled him forward, and the figures stretched and frayed as the stars wheeled past, until they were gone.

Reality reformed.

Chapter 16

In Search of Allies

The rush ended.

Solid ground slammed into Stric's feet, the impact jarring up through his legs. Beside him, Teela staggered, her grip on his hand tightening until his fingers ached. They stood on the rocky plateau, the same smooth stone they'd left days ago.

The others were already there, gathered in a tight cluster near the wormhole's exit. Cearan stood with his staff planted firmly, having recovered from his own transit. Kael had one hand on Dreese's shoulder, steadying the young prince. Sweat beaded along Dreese's hairline despite the cool plateau air, and he swayed slightly when Kael's grip loosened. The elves stood in a protective semicircle, their attention fixed on the two late arrivals.

"Don't move far." Cearan's grip tightened on his staff, his body angling toward the wormhole.

The wormhole pulsed behind them, still hanging in the air. Close by, distortions rippled in the air. Other wormholes scattered across the plateau like traps waiting to spring.

"We're here." They moved forward to join the group.

Stric's fingers closed around the crystal in his inner pocket. "Gather together, let's get away from here quickly!" Marka's warning burned in his mind. Five or six steps, no more.

They pressed together, hands on shoulders and arms. Teela's hand settled on his shoulder. Cearan's arm brushed his. Dreese stood in their centre, surrounded by those who'd kept him safe, who'd waited twenty years for this moment.

"Hold tight." Stric raised the crystal, his voice clear and firm. "Take us to Marka's dwelling."

The plateau dissolved. That familiar sensation of weightlessness, of being nowhere and everywhere at once. Brief. Disorienting. Then, solid ground returned.

They stood in Marka's courtyard, the white stone building rising before them. Morning sunlight painted everything in shades of gold. The scent of salt and sea replaced the smell of bare stone on the plateau.

The building's entrance burst open. Marka stumbled out, his long grey hair wild, one hand gripping the doorframe. His eyes moved from face to face, mouth working silently as if counting. Behind him, a path had been worn into the dirt, a track that spoke of hours pacing.

"Thank the stars." His hand fell from the doorframe. He crossed the courtyard in unsteady strides, voice worn rough from sleepless muttering, scanning them from head to toe, lingering on scraped knuckles, torn fabric, a livid cut along the back of Stric's hand. "I've been watching since before dawn. The alignment holds for another day, but I worried..."

His gaze settled on Dreese, and the words died.

The young man stood between Cearan and Kael, his father's sword at his hip, his spine straight. Dreese met Marka's gaze directly, held it without wavering. No seeking approval. No uncertainty in his stance. He stood level with both guardians, feet planted with equal weight, and something in the way he carried himself made Marka's eyes widen as he raised his hand to his chest, fingers splaying against his heart. He sank fully to the stone, forehead lowering until it nearly touched the courtyard.

Behind Marka, the worn path in the dirt suddenly made sense to Stric. How many nights of pacing? How many times watching the stars, calculating alignments, waiting for this moment?

"Welcome home, Your Highness." Marka's hand trembled where it pressed against the stone. "You are much needed."

When he rose, the warmth had left his features. "I believe things are starting to move towards an end. The very air tastes different these past days." His gaze swept across their faces. "You feel it too."

"Yes, Marka, we all feel it." Teela's fingers drummed against her sword hilt, rhythm uneven, unpredictable. Cearan stared beyond the courtyard walls, weathered features drawn tight. Kael had already shifted his weight forward, feet planted wide. "We need to return to Eldoria. Now."

Cearan reached into his robe. A green crystal emerged, catching the light and throwing emerald sparks across the courtyard stones. "Eldoria." He held it up.

Dreese stared. "That will take us there? All of us?"

"It will." The weathered planes of Cearan's face softened. His fingers curled around the crystal. "This crystal has waited twenty years to bring you home."

Marka stepped back three paces, boots scraping against stone. His jaw loosened, the restless motion of his hands going still. "Send my regards to Queen Aeloria and..." He cleared his throat, looked away toward the worn path his pacing had carved. "Stay safe. All of you."

They formed a tight circle, shoulders nearly touching. Dreese straightened, chin lifting until his eyes met the horizon. "I'm ready."

Cearan held the crystal aloft, its surface warming beneath his palm. "Eldoria." For a heartbeat, the word hung before them.

The crystal flared. The world twisted. Marka's building fragmented into emerald light. Stric's stomach lurched. Reality reassembled in a breath. Cold became warm, salt became pine.

Stric hit the grass. Beside him, Cearan swayed, one hand pressed to his temple, still gripping the now-dim crystal. Sweat beaded along the old magician's brow despite the cool forest air.

The luminescence of the elven forest wrapped around them like a living thing, recognising its own. Golden light filtered through leaves that sang with accumulated magic, each tree humming in harmonics that welcomed and warned simultaneously. The air tasted of wildflower sweetness and moss-covered stone, but something beneath the familiar scents spoke of preparation. Oil on leather. Steel being sharpened. The acrid tang of defensive wards reinforced beyond normal strength.

Movement flickered between ancient trunks. Elves positioned at intervals that spoke of military readiness rather than casual patrols. Arrows rested nocked, but not drawn. Eyes tracked their arrival with the intensity of those who'd grown used to watching horizons for threats.

Even the forest itself felt different. Its ancient patience had shifted into something more alert. Branches positioned to provide clear sightlines. Undergrowth was cleared in strategic patterns.

Elves emerged from behind shimmering trees. No footfall. No rustle of disturbed undergrowth. Presence where there had been absence. Smiles formed, then faltered. Hands extended in welcome, then stilled, mid-gesture, the reach unfinished. The forest itself held its breath around them, birdsong stilled. A familiar figure moved through the gathering crowd.

"Aelith."

The name stuck in his throat. Days of assuming the worst made her solid form seem impossible, a trick of forest light and desperate hope.

Teela's hand flew to her mouth. "You made it." Her feet moved before conscious thought, closing the distance. "You're alive. Yo u're..."

Aelith's warrior stance softened when she caught sight of them, her own eyes bright. She covered the remaining distance with swift strides, arms already opening.

"I knew you would return." Her arms closed around Teela with a strength that trembled at its edges. Teela's shoulders shook as she returned the embrace, fingers digging into Aelith's back.

For a moment, neither moved. Neither spoke. Something in the way Teela's breath caught and held, in the way Aelith's eyes closed for just a fraction longer than a blink.

Then Teela pulled back, her eyes scanning Aelith's face. Cataloguing what had changed.

Aelith stood before them alive, but changed. A healing wound traced her jawline, scabbed over but still raw at the edges where steel had come too close. Shadows pooled in the hollows beneath her eyes, dark enough to seem bruised despite four days of recovery. Callused from sword work before, now bearing fresh marks. Blisters from gripping her blade too tight, too long. Scars from catching herself on rocks during the flight. Evidence of survival purchased with pain.

Teela's gaze moved from wound to scar to shadow, calculating how much remained in reserve.

Aelith's hand lifted, fingertips hovering near the jawline wound without quite touching. "Four undead?"

"Lighter now." Her chin lifted slightly as she spoke. "Six days without stopping. They were persistent." The words came clipped, factual, but her spine straightened with each syllable. Her hand drifted to her ribs without conscious thought, fingers pressing where steel had never reached. "But I'm still standing."

"Yes." Teela's hand dropped, but her fingers curled into a fist at her side. Her eyes blazed as they held Aelith's gaze. "Yes, you are."

Stric stepped forward. For a heartbeat, Aelith's eyes met his. Her chin dipped once, barely a nod, but enough.

The breath left him all at once. His hand found the Powerstaff for balance, and the wood warmed beneath his palm. She stood here. Alive!

Cearan turned toward the horizon, eyes narrowing at the tree line. The lines around his mouth deepened. "The wind carries an ill omen. We must prepare for what's coming."

The elves moved with practised grace, but before preparations could begin in earnest, Queen Aeloria raised one hand. The forest responded first. Leaves ceased their whisper, birds stilled mid-song, and the insect chorus cut off together. Then, her people, chins lifting, hands dropping to sword hilts without a downward glance. "There is news you must hear before you rest." Her violet eyes found Stric's. "Come."

They followed her through the ancient trees to a clearing where several elven scouts stood waiting, faces carrying the same weight Stric had seen in those who'd greeted them. A map of bark and woven grass lay spread across a stone table, marked with positions.

Elar stepped forward, his forest leathers still bearing dust from recent scouting. "Your Majesty, we have confirmation. A force follows Aelith's trail from the coast. From what our scouts observed, approximately one hundred undead, with at least a dozen stone golems among them. A group of spellcasters command the force."

He indicated positions on the bark map with careful precision. "Approaching from here. But it's the trolls that concern us most." His jaw tightened. "They're following Aelith's blood trail, tracking her path directly toward our borders."

Aeloria's fingers traced the line of approach, calculating. "How close?"

"Seven days' march from our borders at their current pace." Elar's jaw tightened. "Eight if they maintain caution."

"Will they discover us?" The queen's voice remained steady, but her shoulders settled into rigid alignment. Her gaze moved from the map to the forest edge and back, calculating.

"Yes, Your Majesty," Elar met her eyes. "Trolls won't lose her scent; they will follow the trail to our borders. They won't breach the wards directly, but they'll mark where the forest's scent changes, where the boundary sits. Once marked, their commander will probe until he finds the seams in our defences."

Elar's hand dropped from the map. Seven days. Perhaps eight. A methodical enemy with the tools to find what had remained hidden for two decades.

Stric's fingers tightened on the Powerstaff. "They followed Aelith's trail. This is because of us." Beside him, Teela's hand found her sword hilt, the automatic gesture of a warrior calculating odds.

"This is because of Barok's tyranny." Her voice came low. Unhurried. Around them, the elven scouts stilled, their movements halted. Even the ancient trees leaned closer, boughs settling. "You did not create this threat. You revealed what was always coming."

Kael stepped forward, studying the bark map with a tactician's eye. "Your Majesty, can your defences hold against a force of this size?"

Her voice came measured, each word spaced with deliberate care. "Our wards have hidden us all this time. But a methodical commander will find the seams in our magical concealment." She paused. "Once he does, he will call on Barok to send reinforcements. We cannot rely on remaining hidden. We must prepare for discovery."

"Then we need allies." Cearan stepped forward. "Numbers to match theirs. Magic to counter theirs."

"The werewolves are coming, and when Stric first arrived, I dispatched agents to seek out known pockets of human resistance." She turned to address the gathering. "They will begin arriving soon, but these alone, even with our forces, will not be enough to counter Barok's dark magic, and if he sends reinforcements..."

Dreese leaned over the map, his finger tracing the marked positions. "What about their supply lines? A force of that size needs constant provisioning. If we can..."

Aeloria's hand rose, palm out. "We cannot strike at supply lines from a defensive position. Not when we're trying to remain concealed. Any sortie risks revealing our location."

He nodded, the movement stiff. Still learning. Adapting.

"There is another option." Aeloria's words fell into the silence with the deliberation of one who had outlived kingdoms. The scouts' eyes tracked her without conscious thought, bodies angling toward her. "The Vampyre clan of Drakenholt Mountain."

Stric's Powerstaff grew heavy in his grip. "They withdrew long ago. What would bring them back now?"

The line of Aeloria's mouth tightened. Around them, the elven scouts stilled. Even those too young to have witnessed it. Jaws tightened. Eyes dropped, then lifted.

"Barok."

Teela's hand moved to her sword hilt. "He attacked them, too?"

"Worse than an attack." Her voice thickened. "Twenty-one years ago, he came to them as a scholar seeking ancient knowledge. They opened their libraries to him. Their councils. Their sanctuaries." Her fingers traced an absent pattern on the stone table. "When he left, their chambers stood empty. Lines of teaching that stretched back millennia... severed." She met Stric's eyes directly. "What he took from them may be the only key to his defeat."

Talnar pulsed against Stric's ribs. "They'll see me as..."

"As one of his kind. Yes."

Teela shifted beside him. "If they've already encountered Barok, wouldn't that make them less likely to trust another Guild Magician?"

"Perhaps." Aeloria's gaze moved between them, measuring, weighing. "Talnar will help prove otherwise. But Stric..." She leaned forward. "You'll need to earn what Barok destroyed. Their trust doesn't return easily."

She stepped closer, and the scent of wildflowers and ancient earth surrounded him. "The vampyres cherish their independence above all else. That alone puts them at odds with a tyrant." Her gaze moved from Eldoria's borders on the map to the distant mountains where Drakenholt lay.

"Show them our border isn't the only one at risk. Show them what we all face if we stand divided."

Kael cleared his throat. "Your Majesty, forgive my bluntness, but we have seven days. Eight at most. Drakenholt Mountain is..." He paused, calculating. "Five days' travel minimum. Add time for negotiations, for convincing them..."

"Which is why they must leave immediately." Each word came at the same flat pace, no room between them for another voice to find an opening.

Silence held for a heartbeat. Stric's knuckles whitened on his Powerstaff. Teela's free hand tightened into a fist. Both straightened.

"We will do what is necessary." Teela's voice held steady as the stone beneath their feet.

Aelith stepped forward, but Aeloria raised one hand. "Your skills are needed here, Aelith. Prince Dreese has days to become the warrior Veltak needs. Not months. No one else can prepare him in time."

Her fingers brushed her sword hilt, instinct reaching for what she knew. Steel, combat, the front line, where enemies could be faced directly. Then, away, fingers spreading wide before curling into a fist. "Your Majesty, I can..."

"I know what you can do." Aeloria's voice softened. "I also know what we need. Dreese requires your assistance. Eldoria requires your presence. Time is against us."

Aelith's gaze moved from Aeloria to Dreese, who stood straighter under the weight of her attention, then to the map spread across the stone table. Strategic positions. Defensive planning. The kind of preparation that required someone who understood how battles were won before first blood was drawn.

Teela's hand found Aelith's arm. "She's right. Dreese needs you more than we do. You've already taught me everything I need."

Aelith studied Teela's face. The stillness in her shoulders, the steadiness of her gaze on the forest's edge, the way her hand rested on her sword hilt with the ease of a tool she no longer needed to reach for. Just a few months ago, Teela had been skilled but alone. Now she stood as a warrior who would honour what she'd been taught.

Aelith's gaze returned to the map. Her fingers traced the defensive perimeter, pausing at three key positions where inexperience would cost lives. Dreese's eyes moved when hers moved, stopped when hers stopped. His spine had lengthened without him appearing to notice it.

A breath. Deep. Released slowly through her nose.

The fist uncurled. Fingers relaxed. "Then I will prepare your prince to stand beside you when the time comes." She turned to Stric, shoulders squaring as her spine straightened. "Talnar chose well. Trust your power, Grandmaster." A pause, then to Dreese: "We begin at first light. I hope you remember more from Kael's lessons than I expect."

Stric's gaze dropped for a beat, somewhere past the map. Unfocused. He blinked hard, then nodded.

"Stay vigilant." Aelith's steel-grey eyes found Teela's again. "The vampyres are our best hope against the undead. Make them see that Barok threatens us all."

"We shall." Teela's grip on Aelith's arm tightened, then released.

Aelith stepped back to join Cearan, Kael, and Dreese. The prince stood straighter in her presence.

As the elves dispersed to gather supplies, Dreese approached Stric, his eyes still caught on the distances between the map's positions, lips pressed flat the way they pressed when he'd already solved for something. He'd been studying the map even as the council concluded, his finger tracing routes, measuring distances.

"I should come with you." Not a plea. A tactical assessment. "If the vampyres question your authority, having the rightful heir present could..."

"Could put Veltak's entire future at risk if something goes wrong." Stric's hand settled on Dreese's shoulder, but his tone remained firm. "Think strategically, Dreese. What happens if we all go to Drakenholt and Barok's forces breach the wards while we're gone?"

Dreese's gaze left the map to find Stric, then back to the map. His finger traced a route toward Drakenholt, then stopped. His hand clenched, released, then moved instead to the defensive positions around Eldoria. Jaw tightening, eyes moving between the map and the council members, fingers curling and releasing at his sides.

Dreese turned back to the bark map. His hand moved from the Drakenholt route to hover over Eldoria's defensive perimeter. Paused there. "They'd find Eldoria under-defended. Leaderless."

His finger tapped three positions on the map. "Werewolves, human forces, elves. All arriving within days. Each fighting their own way." He traced the defensive perimeter. "Without coordin ation..."

"Chaos." Elves in trees, werewolves in packs, humans in formation. Three armies defending one position with no unified command. "They'd be fighting the same battle in different wars."

Dreese's eyes shifted from the map to Stric's and held. "I see it now. My place isn't on the mountain seeking allies. It's here, building the structure that makes those alliances matter."

His shoulders settled into alignment, the way Kael's did before issuing commands. "You bring the vampyres. I'll make sure there's an army worth leading when you return."

Stric nodded. The grip on his Powerstaff loosened by degrees.

Cearan stepped forward, placing his hand on Dreese's other shoulder. His weathered hand gripped with the familiarity of two decades of practice, steadying a child through nightmares, guiding a boy through lessons, and now supporting a king. "Together, we'll build a resistance that Barok cannot defeat."

Dreese's chin lifted. When he spoke, his voice carried the weight that moments before had belonged only to Cearan and Aeloria. "I will do everything within my power to unite us. We will be prepared."

He turned back to the map, already planning. Already leading.

Dreese traced defensive positions across the bark map, fingers moving without hesitation. He placed scouts at two critical junctions before Stric had even identified them as weak points. Aelith stepped closer, steel-grey eyes tracking each decision. When Dreese tapped the third position, she nodded.

"We need to ensure none who are coming encounter Barok's troops." Dreese's voice held no question, only calculation. "Which means we must position scouts here, and here." His finger tapped two junctions. "To intercept them before they cross warded territory."

Aelith stepped closer to the map, steel-grey eyes assessing. "A solid tactical foundation."

The elves melted back into the forest, movements soundless as shadow-shift. One moment, the clearing held dozens. The next, only Dreese remained bent over the map, shoulders loose, eyes steady and downward, finding no reason to search the treeline.

Stric turned toward the forest's edge, where the path to Drakenholt began. Seven days until Barok's forces arrived. Perhaps eight. Talnar pulsed against his ribs, its leather binding warm through his shirt, as though the book sensed the journey ahead.

Teela joined him, hand resting on her sword hilt. "Ready?"

"We leave at dawn." Stric's grip tightened on his Powerstaff. Behind them, Dreese's voice carried across the clearing. The same tone Kael used when issuing commands that wouldn't be questioned.

Stric glanced back. Dreese stood over the map with Aelith and Kael flanking him, three figures already deep in tactical planning. Eldoria would hold.

He and Teela had to deliver their part.

Chapter 17

The Shadow of Drakenholt

Metal rang against stone. Elven warriors strung bows and sharpened steel across the clearing, the sound of preparation as sharp as the coming cold. Stric coiled a rope with the same care Teela used when testing water skins for soundness. Tight, even. Their road led elsewhere. Toward colder peaks. Toward older betrayals.

Dreese's voice rose behind them, directing scouts to positions, questioning supply lines. The prince Stric had rescued, now commanding the defence he was leaving behind. Scouts moved before he finished speaking. No one waited for the second word.

Six days, perhaps seven, until Barok's forces arrived at Eldoria's borders. Not enough time. Never enough time.

Queen Aeloria approached, an amber crystal cradled in her palm. Its glow painted shadows across her face, its light deepening the lines beside her eyes. "For your journey to Drakenholt, and for your return."

Stric reached for it. Light spread through his fingers. Steady, golden, nothing like the electric hum of his staff's crystal. More like captured sunlight. "It will take us to the mountain?"

"Near its base," the clearing quieted as Aeloria spoke. "We have none keyed directly to the vampyre village. They guard their location too carefully. But this will save you days of travel."

Stric's fingers closed around the crystal. A way to the mountain, and a way back.

Aeloria nodded. Centuries lived in the set of her jaw and the measured weight of her gaze. "Your mission matters to all our races. Till we meet again, safe journey, my friends."

Stric and Teela stood in the clearing beneath the ancient trees of Eldoria, surrounded by those who would remain. Aelith stood with Dreese, one hand resting on the prince's shoulder. Cearan and Kael flanked them.

"Stay safe," Cearan's voice held steady, his hands still, fingers curled as though holding a spell he couldn't cast to keep them safe.

"May your courage guide you," Kael's gaze met Teela's. His hand moved to his sword's hilt. Hers mirrored the gesture. Both had failed to protect once. A muscle worked in Kael's jaw. Teela's free hand closed at her side.

The familiar faces blurred at the edges. Eldoria's canopy filtered golden light across the clearing, catching on armour and tearless cheeks.

Teela stood beside him, her weight already shifted forward. She nodded once. "It's time."

Pine and wildflowers filled Stric's lungs one last time. Warmth filtered through the canopy. The forest hummed with accumulated magic, its resonance settling low in his chest.

They stood together, hands clasped. The crystal blazed in Stric's palm, golden light racing up his arm. He met Teela's eyes. "To Drakenholt Mountain."

The crystal's magic poured through him as the forest dissolved. Green turned grey in a single blink. His stomach lurched as the ground shifted beneath him, solid earth trading for loose stone. The scent of pine vanished, replaced by dust and cold mineral air. Pressure built behind his eyes, a high whine in his ears, and the amber light cracked apart into splinters that reformed as mountain and sky.

Hard earth slammed against Stric's knee, the impact shooting up his spine. Ringing silence. Louder than any sound should be. The crystal's light faded, leaving his arm trembling and his fingers numb where they'd gripped it. Beside him, Teela caught his elbow as he swayed.

They stood before Drakenholt Mountain.

The mountain rose in jagged tiers, its summit lost in clouds that clung to the rock like smoke. Wind drove grit into his eyes until the ridges above became a serrated smear.

The air pressed thick in his chest. Each inhale stopped halfway, like breathing through wet wool. Beside him, Teela's hand pressed against her sternum, fingers spread wide as though holding her ribs together. The mountain swallowed every other sound. No birds, no wind through the grass. Just the crunch of their boots on gravel and the blood beating in Stric's ears, so loud the mountain must hear it too. Soil and scrub had drained to the same colourless shade, as though the mountain fed on all living things.

Carved runes pressed into his palm. The only warmth left. Drakenholt waited. Patient. Like it had swallowed things whole long before they came, and remembered none of them.

Teela's sword hilt bit into her palm, the leather grip leaving impressions in her skin. Her eyes scanned their surroundings, tracking every shadow and outcropping.

Stric raised the staff high. Its runes flickered to life, blue light pushing back against the mountain's crushing dullness.

The spell of direction surged through his chest and raced down his arms, pooling in his fingertips. "Take us to the Vampyres." The crystal tugged toward the winding path ahead, as if drawn by a lodestone. "This way."

They followed the spell's invisible thread, leading them upward. Rough terrain crunched underfoot. Loose rocks shifted with each step. Dust coated their tongues. Each footfall rang against the sheer cliffs like drumbeats announcing their arrival.

"You feel it too, don't you?" Teela drew her sword, steel sliding free. Her gaze swept the ridgeline, the outcrops, the places where shadows pooled too deep.

Stric nodded, focus fixed on the energy running through the shaft beneath his palm. "Like we're being watched."

She moved beside him, blade catching what little light filtered through the gloom.

High in the shadows, the path wound upward, steep and rocky, cloaked in a mist that carried the scent of old blood and cold granite. A bitter wind whipped around them, cutting through wool and skin, searching for the warmth at their cores. Fabric stiffened until their cloaks crackled with each movement.

Teela's grip shifted on her sword. The crags held too many shadows. The outcrops created blind approaches. Her gaze moved with the precision of someone who'd survived by assuming every blind spot hid danger.

"Stay sharp." Stric's voice cut through the wind. He drew closer as they navigated an outcropping that jutted from the cliff face, its edge crumbling under centuries.

They continued in silence, following the insistent tug from the crystal as it flickered with each twist and turn of their ascent. Pairs of glowing eyes flickered in the shadowy recesses. Amber points watched and disappeared.

After several arduous hours of climbing and navigating the treacherous ridges, they came upon a rocky outcrop overlooking a dark valley below. Columns rose thirty feet. Their tops vanished or crumbled. Whatever they'd supported had fallen generations past.

"What is this place?" Teela moved to the outcrop's edge, eyes scanning the valley floor. "Defensive position, with clear sight-lines." Her hand traced the air, mapping invisible walls. "Whatever lived down there knew how to choose its ground."

"An ancient settlement." The words barely carried across the space between them.

"One that was attacked?" She pointed to the columns. "They look as if someone broke them."

The columns stood like broken teeth. Sheared clean. The staff's crystal pulsed. Once. Twice. Responding to something in the ruined stone.

The crystal's pull guided them further down the path. Weathered stones jutted from patches of hardy grey grass, their surfaces worn smooth by time and neglect, carved with symbols too faded to read.

The taste of copper flooded Stric's mouth, sharp and metallic. Magic so old it had a flavour. The skin along the back of his neck prickled. His shoulders locked, the muscles pulling inward without his permission. Something in the stone already knew they were there. Voices from the stone pressed against his ears, too faint to understand but impossible to ignore. Teela's pulse quickened, the rhythm visible in the hollow of her throat.

The wood warmed against his fingers. His arm angled forward without deciding to, the crystal's hum rising from something he could ignore to something he couldn't. Husks of buildings spread before him, walls sheared to their foundations on one side, still standing full height on the other, stone so dark it swallowed the grey light rather than reflecting it, remnants of a bygone civilisation. Dark crevices carved into the rock, like scars.

"These look like cave entrances." One yawning void beckoned beneath a weathered archway, the darkness absolute beyond the threshold.

Shadows erupted from the cave's entrance, exploding outward with a force that displaced the air. Cold flooded through Stric's chest. Every hair on the creature's fur stood distinct. The dust motes between them hung frozen in the grey light. The shaft hummed beneath his palm, its crystal vibrating through the wood.

Four figures emerged. Muscular bodies moved across broken stone without disturbing a single loose rock, weight distributed with predatory calculation. Bat-like faces turned toward the intruders, their nostrils flaring.

Long pointed ears flicked back and forth, twitching with a sensitivity that captured even the faintest scrape of a boot on stone, the catch of breath in a throat.

Their amber eyes narrowed. Something sharper than animal cunning moved behind them.

Clawed hands flexed. Slow and controlled. Stric's grip tightened on the carved wood. His weight shifted forward onto the balls of his feet. Coiled.

"Stay back!" Teela's sword came up. She positioned herself between Stric and the creatures, body angled to shield him while maintaining her own defence.

Stric raised the staff, blue light crackling along its length. *Not yet.*

The creatures halted several paces away. Their pointed ears twitched. Silent communication passed through subtle shifts of posture, minute changes in stance.

One creature advanced, its sharp fangs glistening in what little light filtered through the clouds above. "Why are you here?" The voice trilled through the valley, driving into Stric's chest, settling in his bones.

Stric stepped forward. "I am Stric Deamara. This is Teela Reyna. We come from Eldoria seeking an alliance against a common enemy." The words emerged clearly despite the tremor in his legs.

He reached into his inner pocket. His fingers found the worn leather without searching, and the line of his shoulders dropped a single degree. "We are not all strangers." He pulled out the ancient book, raising it high. "Talnar has graced these halls before. Perhaps your elders remember."

The Vampyres exchanged glances, ears twitching. Then, the one who had spoken earlier said, "Remain here! I will return." It turned and vanished back into the cave with a speed that blurred its form, while the remaining three kept a vigilant watch.

One moment, three vampyres stood watch. The next, a fourth stood among them. Grey fur. Amber eyes. No footfall to mark its arrival.

The vampyre raised one clawed hand. The grey drained from the nearest stone first.

Colour returned. First, the grass beneath their feet, grey becoming green. Then the stone, harsh edges softening with moss. Flowers appeared in the cracks. Purple. Yellow. Vivid against the rocks.

Sunlight fell into the valley, striking the stone warm rather than cold, golden rather than leached.

The staff still hummed in his grip. Beside him, Teela's sword remained drawn, her hand pale around the hilt. His weight stayed forward on the balls of his feet, grip on the staff unchanged.

"Come," the vampyre beckoned, voice smooth where it had been sharp. "You have walked through our grief. The true path lies ahead."

The vampyre motioned towards the cave's mouth. They stepped inside. Cool darkness closed over them. The cave turned, revealing a cavern where cold light lined the walls, bioluminescent fungi casting the stone in blue-green colours that didn't exist above ground. The air tasted of minerals; the temperature never changed.

Without a glance back, the vampyre moved ahead. Deeper. Past alcoves where stone carvings showed battles fought before Stric's race had learned to write. Water dripped somewhere ahead, keeping time.

They arrived in an enormous chamber where three figures awaited. The elder Vampyres stood beside one another. Their eyes shone like polished stones. Stric stood straighter without thinking, vertebrae aligning as though their attention were a physical force.

"I am Stric Deamara. This is Teela Reyna. We thank you for granting us an audience."

The female Vampyre's gaze found Stric. His spine adjusted under it, the movement involuntary. Her luminous eyes were fierce. They settled on him and did not move again. The words he'd rehearsed during the climb drained out of him before he reached for them, thin against the weight of her stillness. His hands tightened on the staff. Talnar beat against his chest, the leather binding tapping against his ribs.

"We have allowed an audience only because you hold Talnar." Her voice filled the cavern, as though the mountain lent it strength. The dripping water stilled. Even the cavern's breath held, waiting.

She turned to Teela, acknowledging her with a slight nod. "Be welcome. I am called Lysara by humans and elves." The sound softened, almost musical. "Thrakul and Thrakmar, my kin." She gestured to the two male vampyres flanking her.

Thrakul's broad shoulders filled the space behind her, his angular features and robust build carrying a weight distributed low and already centred, hands open at his sides rather than curled. His ears flattened once. A warrior's greeting, spare of words.

Thrakmar stood with the stillness of deep water, delicate features framed by long silver hair, violet eyes that had already completed their evaluation before Stric had finished speaking. His head inclined a precise fraction, the scholar's acknowledgement.

Their expressions remained blank. Whatever thoughts moved behind those eyes remained locked away.

Stric gripped the staff tight. "We seek your help. Barok Tana's power continues to grow. His dark magic threatens us all. Queen Aeloria believes you may hold the key to breaking his hold over the undead and his golems."

Lysara's eyes held his. Stric did not release the breath sitting in his chest. The staff's weight pressed into his palm, while her silence settled. When she spoke, they narrowed. "You seek to break chains forged in our blood." Her voice dropped. "Knowledge stolen through torture and death. Power that was never meant to be his."

Thrakmar stepped forward. The fungi along the near wall dimmed as his attention sharpened, as though the cave's light bent toward his focus. "You speak of Barok Tana. Our records document his arrival well." His violet eyes fixed on Stric with analytical precision. "What precisely do you know of his time among us?"

The cavern's mineral air pressed closer. "Only that he stole something from you."

"He did more than steal from us." The spaces between Thrakmar's words lengthened, his voice dropping half a register. His gaze drifted to the empty chairs, then back. "He presented credentials from Grandmaster Vrill. Claimed to represent a revival of the treaties Balthor signed in the year of the Long Winter."

The word formed before anything else. Stric's jaw dropped a fraction. "I'm not..."

"We know." Lysara moved between them, no displaced air to mark the passage, her form simply there where it had not been. Her voice filled the gap between Stric's unfinished words and Thrakmar's waiting stillness. "Talnar proves your purpose." The sound sharpened. "But you must understand why we require proof."

The cavern air thickened against Stric's tongue, mineral-sharp. "What did he do?"

Thrakmar's silver hair fell forward over his face. He pushed it back with deliberate slowness. His violet eyes caught the crystal light, the refracted glow moving slowly across the irises. His gaze did not find Stric's face. It held on a point beyond him. "He spoke of Acher's original framework for cooperation between the races. Partnership, as our archives describe it." His jaw pressed closed between clauses, the scholar's composure fracturing along old fault lines. "He made it sound possible again."

Guild cooperation. The old partnerships. Talnar's pages had described these times as he read by firelight. "The Guild sent him?"

"So he claimed." Thrakmar's claws stilled against his belt.

"And you believed him." His hands stayed still on the table's edge. His chin level.

Thrakul's ears snapped flat. "We were curious. Wary." Each word landed like a fist. "Guild went dark." Scrape of claws on stone. "Then this one comes. Talking of renewal."

"How long was he with you?"

"Six moons." Thrakmar's shoulders drew tight against his frame. "Long enough to map our sleep cycles, to catalogue our meditation schedules." His jaw worked beneath grey fur. "To document every moment we lowered our guard."

The dripping water in the cavern stilled. Even the crystal light above them dimmed. Not a sound from the passages below.

Stric's arms hung heavy. His legs ached from the climb. He straightened anyway, meeting the elder's eyes. "The Guild wasn't always isolated. There was cooperation once. Real cooperation."

"Grandmaster Acher," Stric's hand tightened on the ancient tome. "Talnar speaks of him. The first to seek cooperation between the races."

Thrakmar's eyes widened a fraction. "You carry his legacy in your hands, and you know the name." His gaze dropped briefly to Talnar in Stric's hands, then returned. "He sat at this very table. Not demanding. Not stealing. Our earliest records speak of him with a respect we granted no other human before or since."

"Asking," Stric finished. Talnar had taught him this much.

"Balthor understood that power shared returns tenfold." Each syllable arrived slower, placed with deliberate pressure on the consonants. The sound settled across the back of Stric's neck. "His descendants learned a different lesson."

Thrakul's voice dropped to a growl. "Arrogance." Scrape of claw on stone. "Isolation." Another. His ears flattened against his skull. The fungi along the near wall dimmed, as though the cave itself flinched. "Broke everything." A pause. "Balthor knew better."

"So when Barok came speaking those same words..." The carved wood bit into Stric's palm. Somewhere overhead, a crystal dimmed.

"We believed the treaties might live again." Thrakmar's voice slowed between phrases, meeting the stone walls flat, carrying none of its usual resonance. "Our records now catalogue that belief as our gravest error."

Stric followed his gaze. The empty chairs caught his eye when they entered. He'd assumed ceremony. Seven chairs. Seven...

The stone floor tilted beneath him. "These aren't just for show."

Silence.

"No," Thrakmar's voice had lost its musical quality. "Seven of our elders sat here."

Another silence, longer this time. His jaw worked beneath the grey fur of his face. His fingers stilled against his belt.

"Hours," Thrakmar spoke to the empty chairs, not to Stric. "Days sometimes. Debating every decision." His silver hair fell across his eyes. "He sat among us as an observer."

"Learning our patterns." Thrakul's voice dropped.

"Far below." Lysara turned toward a passage that descended into darkness. "The sacred meditation chambers."

Stric waited. The cavern waited.

"He struck while they meditated." The musical quality of Lysara's voice cracked. Raw stone beneath silk. "While they were defenceless. Trusting."

"The ash is still there." Thrakmar's voice barely carried. "Seven piles. Seven alcoves we no longer use."

"You left it?" Teela's hand found the hilt of her sword.

"We will never sweep them away." His voice held. Immovable.

The acoustics carried his words through every shadow, every alcove. The final syllables reached the far end of the chamber after he had stopped speaking, the stone returning them in diminishing stages before silence reclaimed the space.

Lysara's eyes met Stric's. Cold. Empty. "In a single night. He ripped knowledge from dying consciousness. Left nothing but ash and screams."

"Seven," Teela's voice sliced through the cold. Sharp. Controlled. "Meditating. Defenceless. That's not a battle. That's beyond execution."

She met Lysara's eyes. "This was worse."

The cavern's temperature dropped. Stric's next breath misted white. "He didn't study his dark magic. He stole it, and with the blood of innocents, corrupted it."

"The same pattern." Teela's voice came low, directed at Thrakul. "My village. Barok installed a Spellcaster over us. My father stood against them and never came home. My mother spent six years enslaved before she could escape." Her jaw tightened. "He doesn't just conquer. He owns. The method never changes. Only the victims."

Thrakul's amber eyes locked onto hers.

"Yes," the word came hollow. The single syllable met the stone and died there. "The undead, the dark magic. All of it was built on murder and betrayal. Our magic gave him power over the dead." Her voice hardened. "But the golems. Those stone abominations." Her ears flattened. "That is not our work alone. He twisted what he had stolen and bound it to something else. Something we do not fully understand."

"What we do understand," Thrakmar said, "is the architecture of what he built." His violet eyes sharpened, gaze fixing on a point between himself and Stric. "Not merely soldiers. A network of influence."

"Spies in courts." Thrakul held up one clawed finger. "Officials bought." A second finger. "Broken." A third. His hand closed into a fist.

"The military force is only what you can see." Teela's sword hand tightened on the table edge. "The real threat is what you can't."

"He wants to remake the world." Lysara's voice cut through the chamber. "Every institution. Every race. Serving his will."

Talnar grew heavy against his chest despite its unchanged weight. The leather binding was cold where it should have been warm. "We have to stop him..." He straightened, meeting Lysara's eyes directly.

He drew a slow breath. His grip on Talnar shifted. "We do not come alone in this fight. Prince Dreese, the rightful heir to Veltak's throne, has returned from exile. He stands ready to reclaim his father's crown and restore the kingdom."

Lysara's eyes narrowed. When she spoke, the cavern's resonance layered each word so that it arrived from more than one direction simultaneously, the stone returning it a half-beat behind the source. "And why should this matter to us? Your kings are as the seasons. They all promise change." She turned away from him. The crystal light tracked her movement, shadows rearranging across the council table. "They all bring disappointment."

Her voice sharpened.

"Barok Tana wore the face of cooperation when he came to us." Each word deliberate as a chisel on stone. "Before him, how many of your rulers turned away from the old alliances? How many chose isolation over partnership?"

"Tell me, Stric Deamara." She held perfectly still. "What makes this prince different from those who came before him?"

The chamber's stillness pressed against Stric's ribs. Whether they believed in something better. That was the test.

"Because he chose to ask rather than demand." Stric met Lysara's eyes without flinching.

"Your scouts witnessed what Barok did twenty years ago. The slaughter. The coup. You know what happens when humans seize power through violence."

He reached into his inner pocket and drew Talnar free, lifting it slightly. "Dreese survived that night as an infant. He could have returned with an army, claiming his birthright by force. Instead, he came to Eldoria prepared to defend the elves' homeland, seeking an alliance. The same way I'm standing before you now."

Teela stepped forward. "He arrived at Eldoria with a sword, a magician, and a guard who'd dedicated twenty years to keeping him safe. He asked to see Eldoria's defences." She paused. "Not to inspect them. To understand them. To listen and to help." Her hand rested on her sword hilt. "That's what I saw."

Silence held for three heartbeats. Four. Lysara's ears stilled. Her gaze moved to the seven empty chairs, held for a breath, then returned to Stric.

"Words." Her voice held the syllables. She held Stric's eyes. "Barok Tana also had words. Beautiful words about unity and a restored partnership." Her pace slowed, each word arriving separately. "Show me proof that actions will follow these words."

Stric looked at the seven empty chairs. Then at the three remaining vampyres.

"Ten became three." The words came quietly. "Because Barok promised cooperation and delivered a massacre. Because he said he wanted to restore Balthor's vision, and then he..." The mineral air thickened in his throat. "He burned them alive for their knowledge."

He lifted Talnar. "This book was created when that cooperation was real, when Acher sat at this table and asked to learn, not steal. When humans understood that magic belongs to all races, not just us."

The carved wood of the staff bit into his other palm where he gripped it. "I can't undo what he did." The words came raw. "Can't bring back your elders. Can't fix what the Guild became." He forced the next breath through. "But I will rebuild it, as will Dreese. The way Balthor and Acher built it. A council where vampyre wisdom sits beside human. Where your knowledge is asked for, not ripped from the dying."

He met Lysara's eyes. His voice steadied. "If I break that oath, let Talnar's magic abandon me. Let me stand before you powerless. No better than Barok."

Talnar flared hot in his hand. A single, fierce beat in his palm, as though the book had heard and sealed it. The Powerstaff's crystal blazed, blue light flooding the chamber for one breath before fading to a glow that held steady. Stronger than before.

The dripping water stilled.

Lysara turned to Thrakul and Thrakmar. Their gazes locked and held.

Thrakul's jaw shifted. A slow, deliberate movement. Agreement.

Lysara held Stric's gaze. "We accept your oath." In the distance, the water resumed dripping.

She gestured toward wooden doors carved with intricate designs, symbols of their ancient heritage spiralling across their surfaces. "Come, let us gather in the feasting hall." She motioned for them to follow her.

Stric and Teela exchanged glances. The oath settled across his shoulders like stone. What would it cost to rebuild the Guild as Balthor and Acher had envisioned?

Teela's step toward the hall hesitated for half a heartbeat, her hand flexing once on her sword hilt before releasing. They fell in step behind the trio of Vampyres, boots silent against stone worn smooth by countless feet across countless years.

The hall was expansive, illuminated by crystals embedded in the stone walls, casting a soft blue glow. Long tables sat at its centre, draped in velvety material adorned with celestial patterns representing the night sky, stars and moons picked out in silver thread. The air carried polished wood, old smoke, and the savoury scent of thousands of underground meals.

"Please," Lysara gestured toward the table. "Rest here while we deliberate."

Stric settled into a seat. The chair creaked beneath his weight. Teela took the seat beside him.

Silence held for a moment. Then Teela's voice broke it, quiet beneath the stone above. "Your home is extraordinary." Her gaze moved over the carvings on the nearest wall, the silver thread tracing moons along each table's length, the crystal veins running unbroken through the stone from floor to ceiling.

Thrakul's voice dropped, catching in its lower register. "Thank you." His ears flattened. "Our homeland has endured great hardship because of Barok's treachery." The roughness in his voice entered the stone and did not return. The three Vampyres turned and departed, footsteps silent on the ancient floors despite their presence filling every shadow.

Servants moved between them without a sound, offering food. Pale tubers that grew in the deep earth, their flesh faintly luminescent even after roasting, tasted of minerals and something earthy-sweet. Fruit with skin like dark velvet that split under his teeth to reveal flesh the colour of amethyst. The mineral aftertaste lingered on his tongue, as though the fruit had drunk from underground springs rich with crystals.

"What are these?" Teela held up one of the tubers, studying its faint glow between her fingers.

A servant paused, bat-like features softening. "Deeproot. Grows only where the crystal veins run close to the surface." The trilling voice lifted at the close. "It is the mountain's gift."

"It's remarkable." Teela bit into the roasted flesh. Her eyebrows rose. "Like nothing I've tasted before."

The servant inclined her head and moved on. Stric chewed in silence. The amethyst flesh dissolved against his tongue, sweet and strange. Across the table, Teela rotated another piece of fruit in her fingers, studying the way the skin caught the blue glow. Neither spoke. The seven empty chairs pressed the air flat between them.

Through the stone walls, voices carried. Too distant for words, but the cadence rose and fell with the rhythm of debate.

Lysara's steps hit stone faster than before, jaw tight, the crystal light sharp in her eyes. "We have deliberated and come to our decision." Her voice arrived without inflection, each word at the same weight, the stone giving none of it back.

The crystal at the staff's tip brightened in rhythm with his heartbeat, faster than it should.

"The power Barok wields over the dead can be nullified." Each word struck with finality. "We can sever his hold. That is our domain." Her ears flattened. "But his golems. Those remain beyond us."

The stone floor shifted beneath Stric's feet. Half an answer. Better than none, but the golems would still tear through their lines.

"We will dispatch all the mages we possess to assist Eldoria, and the battles to come with Barok Tana." His breath held without him choosing it.

The crystal flared, or perhaps that was just his vision clearing after holding his breath through Lysara's pause. But he forced himself to listen, to hear all the conditions before celebrating.

Thrakul stepped forward, his powerful frame casting long shadows in the crystal light. "Warriors." He counted on clawed fingers. "To Eldoria." Another finger. "To support the elves." His massive frame straightened, shoulders filling the space between the crystal columns. "I lead them."

Thrakmar's voice threaded through the space like a counterpoint to his kin's bluntness. Patient. Measured. "I will lead the mages. Based on my assessment of our remaining practitioners, their training in the old arts should prove sufficient to disrupt the necromantic bonds Barok corrupted from our traditions."

Warriors. Mages. A real force. But the golems remained.

"Your mages can counter the undead." Teela leaned forward. "What about the golems?"

Lysara's expression tightened. "As I said. Beyond us."

"The golem I fought." The memory sharpened. Eyes flickering like dying candles. Stone losing cohesion. "Its eyes flickered out as if something had been released. Then it fell apart."

"The one we saw up close," Teela spoke to Thrakul. "It nearly killed me before Stric brought it down. Swords are useless against them. But it moved wrong, too fluid for stone. Like something alive trapped inside." She met his eyes. "Your warriors need to know what they're facing."

"A trapped spirit freed?" Lysara's ears pressed forward. "Our scouts have watched his golems from the ridges. Stone that moves with breath inside it. The binding is wrong. Forced." She turned to Thrakmar. "I believe he twisted our knowledge of spirit-binding and fused it to fairy earth-speaking. Two traditions forced together." Her voice hardened. "We cannot speak to stone. The earth does not answer vampyre voices. But it answers theirs."

"That may be the path." Thrakmar's voice threaded through the silence. "Two days' journey from here lies a fairy grove. Lysara has visited them in the years before Barok's corruption."

"And they would know?" Teela asked. "About creating or destroying golems?"

"The Fey operate as a collective." Thrakmar's hands pressed flat against the table, the careful, measured rhythm of his voice dropping a fraction. "Their groves share a consciousness. What one fairy observes, the entire collective possesses. If any single fairy has documented Barok's golem methodology, it will be known to all."

"We must go to them." Stric met Lysara's eyes.

"But the fey are cautious." Her voice dropped. "I believe Barok may have betrayed them, too. You will need to earn their trust before they will tell you anything."

"Two days' journey." Teela's voice. Calculating. "That leaves four days before Barok reaches Eldoria. If the fairies refuse to help, or if the information takes time to learn..."

"Then we fight without answers to the golems." Stric met her eyes. "But we have to try."

Teela nodded once.

A path forward.

Lysara's voice cut through the thick air of the council chamber. "You shall stay with us tonight. The night shadows approach, and the path to the fairy grove is treacherous. We will provide you with guidance in the morning."

The mineral tang had thinned. Stric exchanged glances with Teela. He drew a full breath, the first since the negotiations had begun. They wouldn't have to climb back down the mountain in the darkness. Wouldn't have to find shelter on exposed rock.

"Thank you. We are honoured by your hospitality."

Thrakul stepped forward, jaw set. "While you rest." He counted on his fingers again, a warrior planning logistics. "Thrakmar and I gather our forces." His hands pressed flat against the table. "Depart after midnight." His ears flattened. "Done waiting. Barok's time is due."

Thrakmar inclined his head. "I have lived long enough to know the shape of a waning moon." His violet eyes moved to the passage leading upward. "This one narrows with every hour."

Lysara's eyes rested on Thrakul as they began making strategic plans for their immediate departure. She turned back to Stric and Teela, gesturing toward a wooden door at the far end of the chamber. "Come with me. I'll show you to your quarters where you may rest until dawn."

As they followed Lysara through a winding corridor adorned with intricate carvings, Stric's grip on the staff loosened. For the first time since leaving Eldoria, his shoulders sat level instead of hunched.

A fireplace crackled at one end, orange flames casting shadows across the stone walls. Silken pillows scattered across plush rugs, soft after hours on hard stone.

"Rest well." Lysara stepped back into the hallway, footsteps fading to silence.

Through the stone walls, the sounds of preparation began. Boots on stone, rhythmic and purposeful. The distant clang of armour being assembled. Voices calling orders in the vampyre tongue, sharp consonants carrying through corridors. Thrakul and Thrakmar were rallying their forces.

Teela sank onto a cushion before the fireplace. Her shoulders dropped a full inch. "Can we actually defeat him?" Her gaze stayed on the fire.

"There are many uncertainties." Stric sat beside her, Talnar resting on his lap. Its rhythmic pulse matched his heartbeat. Slower now, steady. "But we have allies now. Powerful ones. If we can find a way to counter the golems, I believe we have a chance."

"One step closer."

Stric placed Talnar beside him and lay among the pillows. One step closer.

But Talnar's pages fluttered. Just once. So brief, Stric almost missed it.

Through the stone walls, boots marched in rhythm. Vampyre warriors departing. Fast.

Four days. The fairy grove was two days away.

Chapter 18

Off with the Fairies

The morning air outside tasted of minerals and cold stone, the last breath of Drakenholt's caves clinging to their lungs. They stepped into daylight, and the mountain stopped them both mid-stride. Green moss softened the rock face. Purple and yellow flowers pushed through cracks in the stone, their colours vivid against the grey. Warm sunlight touched surfaces that had been charcoal and lifeless on their arrival. They'd had no time to appreciate it then, climbing through the oppressive dark with ice forming on their cloaks. Now the mountain wore its true face.

"Follow this route with care," Lysara said from the doorway, her bat-like features framed by dawn's first rays. "The groves are protected by wards threaded through the essence of this land. But you may pass if you approach with respect."

The route beneath his fingers pulsed with warmth, as though the magic within it remembered the earth it mapped.

Her eyes flicked between them. "Not all fairies will welcome you. They sense intentions. Speak the truth and do so with honour."

Teela's fingers tightened on her sword hilt. "We'll do whatever it takes to get them on side."

Lysara stepped back from the threshold. "Prepare yourselves. With patience and perseverance, you might sway the fairies to aid us against Barok."

Stric glanced at Teela. She met his gaze and nodded once, her fingers flexing at her side the way they did before a fight. No hesitation. Whatever waited in the fairy grove, they would face it as they had faced everything since that first golem on the forest road.

Lysara stepped closer. "Go well." Her ears pressed forward, then flattened. She turned away before the gesture could be read.

Teela tilted her chin towards the sun, eyes closed. A breath. Then she opened them and nodded once.

The trail out of the valley cut across loose scree that shifted underfoot. Teela set the pace, boots finding purchase where Stric's slipped, and when the path narrowed to a ledge barely wider than his shoulders, she reached back without looking. He took her hand. Neither let go until the ground levelled.

They made camp on the ridge as the sun dropped behind the peaks. The stone beneath their bedrolls still held the day's warmth.

Thrakmar's map lay open across his knee, its lines bright against the low fire's glow. Something had changed since Drakenholt. The map's warmth no longer sat still beneath his fingers. It moved. A slow tide, ebbing and flowing, as though the parchment breathed in rhythm with the mountain beneath them.

The route ahead brightened under his finger. Where it lifted, the lines dimmed. The map knew the path ahead.

Teela stirred. "Still awake?"

"The map is different up here. More alive."

She propped herself on one elbow. The firelight catching the angles of her face. "Everything's more alive up here. Even the stone is warm." She laid her palm flat against the rock. "Like it's breathing."

By the second morning, the mountain stone had given way to soil, and the air had thickened with the scent of things growing. The trail wound beneath towering trees whose roots had cracked the rock apart, splitting the stone to dark earth, grinding grit across the path. Their leaves caught the light, turning it green and gold, filtering it through countless layers until the world beneath shone with borrowed light.

Ferns lined their path, fronds uncurling towards the map's warmth as though drawn to its glow. Flowers turned their faces as Stric and Teela passed, petals tracking movement like tiny sentinels. The air carried a fragrance unlike anything that grew from ordinary soil. Rich and green and humid, it thickened with every step, pressing into fabric and hair until breathing became tasting.

Dusk approached on the second day. The air changed, thickening. Magic pressed against them like humidity before a storm. The fine hairs on his forearms rose.

Teela stopped. One boot planted, the other hovering above a root. "Do you feel that?"

His knuckles ached where they gripped the Powestaff. "Something is near. The air has changed."

Shadows shifted between the trees. Teela's head turned toward each one, slow and precise. "We're getting closer," she said, her voice low beneath the silence that pressed around them.

From behind clusters of flowering bushes and bent branches came sounds. Whispers, faint giggles, the rustle of wings too delicate to belong to any bird. Figures flitted between the trees. Glimpses of gossamer wings caught the last rays of sunlight, tangling among wildflowers in colours more vivid than anything grown from soil.

"Fairies!" Teela's hand fell from her sword hilt. She stood perfectly still, the way she did when a fight demanded her full attention, except nothing here required a weapon.

The creatures peeked at them from hiding spots, tiny faces the colour of new fern fronds peering through colourful blooms. Their laughter rang across the twilit glade, sharp as quartz cracking underfoot.

"We seek counsel with you!" The words rang through the amber stillness, where the low sun caught every leaf, and the birdsong rang out.

"We come in peace!" Teela said, keeping her hands well away from her sword hilt.

The laughter hesitated, a single held breath, before continuing. But the notes had changed, sounding more playful than hostile now. A group of fairies emerged from their hiding spots, light green skin catching the last of the sun. Their wings caught the fading light, and clothing of flower petals in violet and gold rustled as they moved.

Their whispers tangled together, low and brief. They approached.

One fairy stepped forward. Silver hair framed a face of sharp, delicate features. Her skin, luminous as wet moss against the gathering darkness. Her eyes burned steady, bright as fireflies.

"Why are you in our sacred grove?" she asked. "You are not of our kin."

Heat spread through his chest. His shoulders dropped. "We are here seeking your wisdom," he said, meeting her gaze. "The dark sorcerer Barok Tana..."

The moment Barok Tana's name left his lips, the fairies drew back. A menacing hiss escaped them, a sound like wind through dead leaves. Their glow dimmed.

"If you have come here on his orders, leave immediately or suffer our fury," another fairy said, her tiny form rigid with threat.

"No!" Stric's voice cut through the clearing. "We are here seeking aid in his downfall. He is as much our enemy as he is yours!"

The fairies fluttered in a circle around them, their wings creating a soft chorus. Their vibrant colours flashed like living rainbows against the dimming light, swirling in patterns that made his eyes struggle to focus.

"Why should we trust you?" one fairy asked, her voice keening like wind through a crack. Another finished the thought without pause: "What proof do you offer?"

"We are not your enemies." Stric took a step forward. "I am Stric Deamara. This is Teela Reyna. Barok Tana is growing stronger every day. His reach extends beyond your groves. Every race in Veltak deserves the peace that existed before he seized power. We want only to stop him."

The circle held. The silver-haired fairy drifted closer, hovering before Stric. Luminescent eyes searched his, steady and unblinking. The moment stretched.

"Come," she said at last. Her light did not warm. "You will speak with all. The grove will decide what words cannot."

She turned, and the fairies followed, their wings fragmenting the dwindling light into a thousand spinning motes. The air pressed warm and close, the scent of blossoms tangling together as they navigated deeper into the heart of their sanctuary.

"Follow closely," the lead fairy said, her voice carrying command despite its delicate timbre. She glanced back over her shoulder, features framed by hair that held the ambient glow of a dozen nearby fairies, phosphorescent and cold. "You may call me Twill." She paused, turning to face them fully. "One mind, many bodies. One memory, many keepers."

Teela walked beside Stric, her gaze sweeping the treeline even as colour and light pressed in from all sides. Her hand brushed his arm once before falling to her side, fingers curling into a loose fist. The pathway twisted between trees that rose high above their heads, canopies interlocking in patterns that turned the sky into a puzzle of leaves and branches. Soft rays of light filtered down, broken and refracted by a hundred pairs of wings into shifting fragments across the forest floor.

More fairies joined them along the path, their laughter bouncing off ancient trunks and sparkling even in the shadows. They whispered among themselves, wings stirring with curiosity as they caught sight of the two humans.

Twill led them through winding paths adorned with flowers of every colour, petals varying from deep crimson to soft indigo blue. Nothing here had browned or wilted. No leaf bore spots of blight. The soil smelled of rain and growth.

The procession thickened. Wings stirred the air into warm currents that carried pollen and song. Where the first breath of the grove had been sweet, this deeper air tasted green and ancient, like sap rising through heartwood. Currents prickled against skin, a warmth that pressed inward into the meat of his hands and forearms. Thickened to something almost solid. As cloying as overripe fruit, pressing against the back of his throat.

The procession emerged into a clearing. An ancient oak tree stood at its centre, its trunk fissured into ridges the size of a man's forearm, the bark between them dark as old iron and thick with moss that held its own faint light. Branches spread overhead in dense, overlapping layers, so wide they replaced the sky entirely. Around its base, countless fairies gathered, their collective lustre flooding the clearing with light that shifted between soft blues and gentle golds.

"We have arrived," Twill said as her wings slowed, descending to a large mushroom cap that served as her seat. Light pooled around the oak's roots as hundreds more filled the space, their glow warming the bark. Many more settled into the branches above, their forms creating a living constellation among the ancient limbs.

Stric and Teela stood beneath the ancient oak's canopy. Hundreds of tiny eyes were fixed on them. Some leaned forward, wings angled wide. Others held back, glows barely a flicker, bodies half-turned toward the branches. The whispers had ceased. Wings stilled. The clearing's light steadied, unflickering.

"Speak your hearts," Twill commanded, her voice reaching the outermost fairies in the canopy without her raising it.

Stric stepped forward. He met Twill's earnest gaze, then glanced at the assembled fairies.

"Thank you for allowing us this audience," Stric said, his voice steady, though the Powerstaff hummed against his palm. "On the road to Eldoria, I destroyed a golem. Stone and dark magic given shape." His throat tightened. "Something screamed when it broke apart. Not stone. Not magic. A voice."

The elder fairy perched atop a nearby branch, leaned closer, her skin deepened to the colour of old moss, her wings still as folded parchment. "And why does this claim bring you here?" Her voice melodic yet sharp.

He met her gaze. "Lysara of Drakenholt told us the golem magic may have been stolen from you. Your earth-speaking, corrupted. Spirits bound where they shouldn't be." The Powestaff's hum deepened, matching something far below. "We march against an enemy we cannot defeat without help."

"We know of Lysara," Twill said, her glow warming. "Who came to us before the darkness did. She is remembered here with trust." Her gaze sharpened. "Who marches with you?"

"A prince ready to reclaim his throne. Vampyre warriors and mages are already on the road to Eldoria. Werewolf packs, gathering as we speak." He held Twill's gaze. "But none of them can touch the golems. Whatever dark magic holds those things together, no sword or spell we carry can break it."

Twill's gaze settled on Stric. "You speak a truth that strikes deep. Barok Tana's abominations are born from fairy knowledge, twisted by his malevolence."

His boots sank into soil that gave beneath him like something breathing. Around the clearing, fairies touched the ground as they settled, and wherever their fingers met earth, the moss thickened, tiny flowers unfurling in their wake.

Twill's wings hummed. "You see it. The Earth you stand on is alive. Every stone, every root, and crystal vein. All respond to those who know how to speak with them."

She approached a nearby stone, her lips shaping words too low for human ears. It trembled, then reshaped itself into a flower, detailed down to tiny petals and stamens.

Teela reached out to touch it, her fingers gentle. "It's beautiful."

"Beauty in harmony." Twill nodded. "We don't command. We converse. The earth gives to those who ask with respect. The singing roots carry our whispers from grove to grove."

Her glow flickered, dimming. "That was before Barok Tana came to our grove."

Around the clearing, several fairies drew close, wings overlapping, glows dimming to a shared blue.

Twill turned back to Stric. "A scholar once spoke to us of respect and curiosity. His words were beautiful. His intentions were poisonous."

She extended one tiny hand, palm up. "The earth knows what words conceal. Will you let it judge what we cannot?"

Teela stepped forward. In one smooth motion, she drew her sword and reversed it, offering the hilt to Twill. The blade's edge caught the fading light.

"If we lie," Teela said, "you hold my weapon. That's more than he ever gave you."

Twill studied the sword, then Teela's face. Her wings lifted a fraction, the tips parting where before they had been tight. Her glow pulled inward, losing its sharp outer edge.

She turned to Stric. "And you?"

His palm moved toward the earth before any plan formed behind it. He knelt, lowering the Powerstaff across his knees, and pressed his free palm flat against the moss.

The lattice humming far below rose to meet his touch, and something moved through the contact. A listening, patient, and thorough, passing through the bones of his hand and upward into his chest, the way sunlight passes through water.

The sound the golem had made when it broke, and where in his chest that sound still lived. The cold that had gripped his forearms since Twill's question first landed. Every hand already given its trust. Thrakmar's. Whhrll's. Held out in this moment alongside his own. None of it hidden. None of it false.

Then the deep paths found his magic, and the listening changed.

The Powerstaff answered without his asking. Golden-green light spilled from the crystal, warm where human magic ran cool, deep where fairy light ran pale, the two frequencies fusing into a third thing altogether. The light sank into the earth and raced outward through the crystal veins beneath the clearing, igniting the lattice in colours that had no name.

Every fairy in the grove went still.

Twill's wings stopped. She dropped an inch before catching herself, her eyes wide, her glow flaring until she lit the space between them like a captured star.

"How is this possible?" An elder fairy descended from her branch, a face the colour of old lichen, creased with confusion. "The earth answers you as if you were born from it. Yet your magic carries harmonies unknown to our kind."

The deep paths beneath the clearing pulsed in time with his heartbeat. A vast lattice spread outward through the earth, carrying the fairies' whisper-songs from grove to grove across Veltak. His power reached towards them as it did towards the elves. Open. Patient.

"What are you?" Twill asked, her voice faded to a breath.

"I don't know." His shoulders dropped a fraction. His grip on the Powerstaff eased. "With the elves, my magic listened. Here, the earth is listening back." The Powerstaff thrummed against his palm, each pulse matching a deeper vibration rising through his boots. "Something hums beneath us. Not just sound. An answer."

Twill hovered before him, her wings slowing until she nearly dropped. The elder pressed both hands flat against her branch, her head tilted as though listening to something beneath the bark. Around the clearing, fairies touched the earth, stone, and roots. One by one, their lights steadied, brightened, and turned towards Stric.

"The old songs speak of this," Twill said, more to herself than to him. "Before the traditions separated. Before each race claimed its own path." She looked up at him. Her eyes filled without spilling, wide and still, her wings folded against her back. "We thought those songs were only stories."

Tears rolled down her tiny, pale green cheeks. Her wings held still. Her glow didn't waver. Around the circle, moisture gathered in dozens of luminous eyes, their glow wavering like candle flames in the wind.

"You speak true, stranger. The earth itself confirms it." She spoke through her tears. "He has already done us great harm. You will understand why."

The light in her skin broke apart.

"He came to us as a scholar." The voice rose from the gathering, rough as bark. "Claiming to study the natural earth-speaking of Veltak." "The warming season he spent among us." Another voice, layered beneath the first, not waiting for it to finish. "Watching our ceremonies." A third: "Hearing our whisper-songs." The voices built on each other, each fairy adding a fragment, none needing the previous to end. One memory. Many mouths. "We thought him respectful and curious." Twill's voice cut through the rest, and every other fell silent. "We were fools."

The ancient oak shuddered. A shower of leaves spiralled down, and three fairies on a nearby branch pressed their faces into each other's shoulders. Twill's gaze tracked them. Her jaw set. Her wings drew close.

She did not continue with words. Instead, she placed her palms flat against the mushroom cap beneath her. Around the clearing, other fairies did the same, touching earth, bark, stone. A tremor passed through the grove, and the soil between the ancient oak's roots stirred.

The memory rose on its own. The earth itself showed what it had witnessed. Tiny figures of earth gathered in a circle around a larger form. The central figure's arms spread wide, each line rendered cleanly. Whole.

"At harvest's end," said the bark-skinned elder, her roughened hands flat against the earth, "when the earth yields its bounty, and our magic celebrates abundance, we gather for the Great Ceremony."

"Chir led us," another fairy added from a low branch, her wings folded tight. "The Keeper of the Trees. He sang the oldest whisper-songs."

"My closest friend." Twill's voice cracked on the word. Her wings trembled, their usual lustre dulled.

Around the clearing, the assembled fairies pressed closer to one another as Twill continued.

"The ceremony was beautiful that night. The earth sang with us, the earth beneath our grove humming with our joy. Chir stood at the centre of our circle, his voice threading the harvest blessing through the ancient oak's roots."

Around the clearing, the sweet, layered scent that had clung to them since entering the grove thinned to nothing.

Twill forced herself to continue.

"The air... it changed. Like ice forming on a summer stream. The human scholar we'd welcomed, the one we'd taught our whisper-songs, stood at the circle's edge. But he wasn't the same. The illusion we hadn't known existed... dropped."

She gestured, and the earth before them rose in response to her whisper-song. Soil and sand formed images, memory made visible through earth-speaking. Pale dirt shaped beautiful human features, then shifted to darker soil shot through with veins of black earth. Where eyes should be, tiny amethyst crystals embedded in the earthen face glowed with purple malevolence. The transformation sculpted itself from the ground.

"The Powerstaff he carried, which we'd thought was merely a scholar's tool with an ordinary crystal atop it. His illusion fell away from that, too. Beneath the false crystal, we saw it. The master deathseed crystal, fused to bone-white wood, pulsed with dark magic."

The ground beneath his boots had gone cold. A chill rising through root and stone, the earth's own flinch at the memory passing through it.

His Powerstaff flickered. A single pulse, there and gone, as if the crystal at its tip had caught an echo of that long-ago corruption through the grove's living memory.

"Before anyone could react, Barok raised his Powestaff. A shield erupted around him and..." Twill's voice broke. Several heartbeats passed before she could speak again. "Around Chir. The Keeper of the Trees was trapped inside that barrier with him. The rest of us crashed against it until our whisper-songs died on its surface. Nothing we did could penetrate it."

The fairy images showed dozens of tiny forms hurling themselves at an invisible wall, their magic useless against its surface.

"Chir tried to reason with him. Even then, even trapped, our leader sought peace. He asked why and offered forgiveness if Barok would leave and never return. He promised we wouldn't pursue vengeance."

The words landed like a fist beneath his ribs. A leader who offered forgiveness to his own killer.

Twill's hands clenched into tiny fists. "Barok didn't answer. Not with words."

"He raised his Powestaff, that bone-white abomination fused with the vampyre crystal, and aimed it at Chir. Then... he paused. For just a moment, his hand wavered. His eyes flickered, as if he were listening to someone none of us could hear. His lips moved, forming words we couldn't catch."

"Whatever was said, he rejected it." Twill's voice turned hard as stone. "His expression went stony. So cold. The wavering stopped. His hand steadied. And he began the spell."

Cold pressed through the soles of his boots, rising through clay and root. Threads of darkness, rendered in soil, reached from the staff towards the trapped fairy leader.

His breath caught. Extraction magic. Talnar had shown him the theory in dry, clinical passages, knowledge the Guild had sealed behind powerful wards, with good reason. His stomach dropped. The Powestaff's crystal pulsed once, sharp, against his palm. This is what it looked like when someone tore a mind apart.

"The extraction spell." Twill's voice dropped to something below speech. "We didn't know what it was called then."

The moss beneath his feet darkened, each blade curling inward as though the earth flinched from the memory passing through it. His teeth ached. A pressure behind his eyes, sharp and foreign.

The bark-skinned elder pressed her hands flat against her branch. Moss crept from her fingers into the wood. "The spell started as sound. A single note, wrong the way a bone set crooked is wrong. It found the deep paths and followed every connection outward."

From a low branch, a younger fairy spoke without lifting her head. "I was three groves distant. The note reached us between one breath and the next. Every whisper-song I knew went silent, replaced by a scream that had no voice."

"Every secret of earth-speaking." Twill's entire body shook. "Every technique passed through generations. Barok tore it all from Chir's mind."

Pain flared behind his eyes. Not his own. Something older, carried through the earth's memory and into the soles of his boots, through bone and marrow, settling at the base of his skull. Knowledge being ripped loose like pages from a book. He gasped. One hand braced against his knee.

Beneath him, the ground trembled. A thin line, hairline-fine, split the moss from the ancient oak's roots to where he stood.

Teela caught his arm. The crack sealed itself, moss knitting back together.

"Stric?"

"I'm all right." He wasn't. "Go on, Twill."

Twill's luminous eyes held his for a moment. Then she turned back to the memory-images, her light less than a candle flame.

"The pain..." Twill whispered. "Every fairy in the grove shared Chir's mind being torn apart."

The memory-images showed fairies throughout the grove convulsing mid-flight, dropping from the air like autumn leaves.

"Dozens died in the first moments. Those closest to Chir in friendship, in magical connection, in daily communion. They couldn't withstand the feedback. Their minds... stopped. They fell where they hovered, their lights going out like candles in a storm."

Somewhere in the canopy, a branch cracked, the sound moving through wood and sap from root to crown.

Around the oak's base, flowers curled shut, the movement spreading through root, petal, and fairy flesh.

The crystal at his Powestaff's tip dimmed. A flinch, as though the ancient crystal recognised what was being described and could not bear to illuminate it.

Teela's fingers pressed into his shoulder, hard enough to leave marks. Neither of them moved to break the contact.

Tears streamed down Twill's tiny cheeks, her glow pulsing erratically.

The bark-skinned elder's voice scraped through the silence. "We all endured it. Every grove is connected to ours through the deep paths. Some survived. Many didn't."

"All of us." Twill's tears caught what little light remained. "Every single fairy in Veltak."

The ancient oak groaned above them. A branch, thick as Stric's torso, sagged as though bearing a sudden weight. Leaves fell in a slow, spiralling rain that had nothing to do with wind or season.

Teela's hand slid from his shoulder into his. Her fingers tightened. He tightened back.

"When Chir finally... stopped... Barok lowered his staff. The surrounding barrier flickered but held. We were too weak to attack, too scattered by grief and pain. I was barely conscious, lying on the ground, my wings unable to keep me aloft."

The memory-images showed Barok surveying the carnage with those terrible glowing eyes. Fairy bodies littered the grove floor, their lights extinguished forever.

"Then he knelt." Every trace of brightness had left her body. "Beside Chir's body. He placed his hands on the earth. His lips moved, but instead of our gentle whisper-songs, he shouted. Commanded. Forced the earth to obey rather than asking it to cooperate."

The memory showed the ground erupting upward, stones and soil swirling together in an unnatural vortex. The fallen fairy's body lifted into the air, and something, a glowing essence, was torn from it.

"He bound Chir's spirit into the earth itself. Created a prison of stone and sand, animated by torment. The first dark thing rose before my failing eyes."

Her voice dropped to less than a whisper.

"Chir's spirit screamed as it was bound, unable to complete its natural journey. The Great Cycle was broken for him, and through him, every fairy alive knew the wrongness of it."

The shape was crude, more a shambling mound than a constructed form. It took one step, another, then... crumbled. The stones fell apart, sand scattered, and for a moment, the memory-image held: the fairies in the grove raising their heads toward the crumbled stones.

Somewhere in the grove, a fairy keened. A thin, high sound, cut short by another fairy's arms wrapping tight around her.

"He tried again, adjusting his stolen knowledge, corrupting our magic further. The second attempt held together longer. The abomination formed, stood, took three steps..." She paused. "I saw him hesitate. Just for a heartbeat. His hands stopped above the earth, fingers still, as if they'd forgotten the next instruction. Then his expression hardened, and the construct solidified. It stood there, waiting for his command, and the agony of the spirit trapped within burned through us all."

"The third..." Twill's voice was all but silent now. "The third came easily. Perfectly. Like he'd been creating them all his life. The magic that should only work through cooperation and respect, that requires harmony with the earth's willing participation. He'd turned it into a tool of domination."

Beside him, Teela's hand had found her sword hilt, her palm pressing flat against the pommel, the steel an anchor against something that moved through root and bone and had never once carried a body.

Twill took a shuddering breath.

"That's when the darkness took me. I collapsed, unconscious, more dead than alive. The connection to Chir had nearly killed me. I was one of those closest to him in every way. The feedback almost stopped my heart."

"But others stayed conscious." Twill's gaze moved to the bark-skinned elder, who sat rigid on her branch, moss-hair bristling.

"We saw." The old fairy's voice scraped like stone on stone. "We all remember."

"Barok didn't stop at three," Twill continued, her voice hollow and distant. "He moved through the grove, kneeling beside each fallen fairy. One by one, he tore their spirits from death's natural embrace and bound them into the earth. By the time he finished, thirty-three of his dark creations stood in our sacred grove. Each one screaming with a voice we could hear through the deep paths."

Thirty-three. His stomach turned.

Her wings stilled. Throughout the grove, every fairy had gone dark. They sat in true darkness for the first time since Stric and Teela had entered the sanctuary, the only light the fading memory-images sculpted from grieving earth.

"But the dying didn't end in our grove. The pain stopped hearts across every linked grove. Thirty more who never saw Barok's face." She looked down at her hands. "The circle has more silence in its song now. Voices that should have returned to the Great Cycle never will."

The number sat in his chest like a stone.

Twill was silent for a long moment, the memory-images fading from the air.

"When I awoke weeks later, those who survived looked to me for leadership, though I was anything but qualified. I had failed to protect them. Failed to see through Barok's deception. Failed to save Chir."

"But I was alive when so many weren't. And we had no choice but to carry on."

She looked up at Stric and Teela, her luminous eyes holding their gazes.

"That's what happened that night. That's what Barok Tana did to us. And that's why, when you speak his name, every fairy in Veltak remembers. We all carry it. Every single one of us."

Teela's hand had left her sword hilt. She stood with both arms at her sides, fingers slightly open, like a soldier who had reached for her weapon and found it would not help. "The golems."

Twill's light dipped. "Yes. Barok had mastered necromancy, we now know from where, and found a way to merge it with our earth-speaking. Our magic asks the earth to reshape itself. His magic tears the earth apart and binds tortured spirits within."

She gestured, and the soil formed the shape of a lumbering golem.

"Every creature that dies in Veltak, bird, beast, fairy, human. He captures their spirit before it can return to the Great Cycle. He binds these souls to his earthen constructs, creating soldiers that cannot die because they are already dead." Her voice broke. "We still hear their screams as the earth itself weeps at this violation."

"So there is no way to defeat them?" Teela's voice dropped low. "Must we watch as Veltak falls completely?"

Several fairies whispered among themselves, the sound like rustling leaves in a gentle breeze. Twill held up a tiny hand for silence.

"The tortured spirits cannot escape their earthen prisons." Twill's light steadied. "But if you can free the spirits..."

"We can destroy the golems." His grip loosened on the Powestaff.

Twill nodded, her light returning. "The master crystal on Barok's Powestaff. It's the heart of his corruption, amplifying his commands across Veltak. Shatter it, and the earth will remember itself. Then all the spirits can be freed."

Around the clearing, every fairy had bowed their head. Wings still. The lights dimmed to nothing.

Stric's grip on the Powerstaff had locked without his knowing. He forced his fingers to loosen, one at a time. Beside him, Teela stood rigid, her weight forward on the balls of her feet, every muscle locked against a threat no blade could answer.

Twill was the first to move. She pressed both palms flat against the mushroom cap beneath her, and light, faint as a dying ember, crept back into her skin. Around the clearing, other fairies followed. One by one, the way dawn reaches different leaves at different moments.

"It is decided," Twill said at last. "Every grove will send our finest earth whisperers to Eldoria to assist with the golems." At this, all the fairies in the grove stood and began fluttering their wings rapidly, the sound building into a layered hum that pressed against Stric's eardrums and sent a breeze throughout the grove.

"We may not be able to stop Barok from creating them, but we can liberate the spirits within individual golems on the battlefield." Her voice carried over the sound of winged applause.

Twill turned from her mushroom perch, the light returning to her skin. She spoke no command, but across the clearing, every fairy moved at once. Those nearest the oak's roots lifted in unison. Those at the grove's edge turned inward. A dozen hands reached for crystal shards at the same instant, without a word or signal passing between them.

Teela's gaze moved across the clearing, her grip on the sword hilt easing. "On a battlefield, that changes everything."

Twill's gaze sharpened. "Your commanders would still decide. But no unit would fight without knowing what approaches from every direction."

"By dawn's first light, we must be on our way. Rest here tonight. The grove will protect you."

The great oak at the centre of the clearing shifted. Its branches extended to create a natural shelter. Flowers bloomed around its base, their scent sweet. His jaw unclenched.

Stric bowed. The gesture came without thought. Beneath his boots, the moss brightened. A tremor passed through the clearing, and the thin crack that had split the earth during the memory sealed itself, fresh growth threading through where stone had fractured.

"We will get them home."

"May the earth remember your promise." Twill raised one tiny hand in blessing. "And may it guide your steps on the path ahead."

That night, Stric lay beneath the canopy. Stars burned through gaps in the leaves. Sleep was a long time in coming.

Birdsong had replaced the silence of the night. Somewhere above, wings caught the first light, throwing brief prisms across his closed eyelids. He sat up. The great oak's shelter had held through the hours, branches still curved overhead in their protective arch.

Teela stretched beside him, blonde hair catching the light as she blinked away sleep. "What time is it?"

"Dawn." Beyond the shelter's edge, the clearing had transformed. Dozens of tiny figures bent over patches of earth, hands the colour of spring leaves held in unison over moss-covered stones, whispered words passing between them. "They've been at it for hours, by the look of things."

Twill approached them, her skin bright as fresh growth in the morning light, wings catching the sun. "Today, we give you our answer in crystal and song."

She led them closer. The whisper-songs sharpened into individual voices. The crystals on the stones between them brightened with every phrase, sapphire and emerald hues deepening as though the gems were drinking the music.

Stric knelt beside the nearest group. One fairy held a crystal the size of his thumbnail over a stone, her lips shaping sounds below the range of human hearing. The gem brightened, then settled into a steady, warm glow. She placed it gently on top of the pile and reached for another.

"Each one remembers what was stolen," Twill said quietly. "When it touches a golem, it will remind the spirit inside what freedom felt like."

Hundreds of crystals lay amassed in neat piles by the time the work was done, Stric and Teela's hands sore from hours spent gathering alongside the fairies. The last of them secured their sparkling charges, wings beating so fast that the air hummed through the trees.

He caught Twill's gaze. "Thank you. We won't waste what you've given us."

Teela stepped forward alongside him and placed her fist against her chest. "On that, you have my sword, and our word."

Twill's eyes brightened. "You speak the truth. Your spirits are alight with purpose." She turned to the grove, where fairies readied themselves to fly, their delicate charges secured in tiny hands. "May the earth guide your steps. We will not be far behind."

As the last crystal settled into its bearer's hands, something moved inside its glow. A flicker. A presence, pressing against the facets like a face against frosted glass. The fairy holding it went still, her wings frozen mid-beat.

"They know." Her eyes didn't leave the crystal. "The trapped ones. They know we're coming."

The crystal dimmed. The fairy's wings resumed their beat, but her hands shook.

Stric met Teela's gaze. Cold settled at the back of his neck and did not leave.

"Until we reunite in Eldoria," Twill said, turning to her kin as they prepared for what lay ahead.

Stric and Teela stood together in the grove's warm light, preparing to teleport back to Eldoria. The crystals around them pulsed with light. Energy crackled against their skin, sharp as the static before a storm.

"We can't stay any longer." Crystal-laden fairies wound past them in a steady procession. Teela turned to Stric. "The crystals are prepared. Every hour here is an hour Eldoria doesn't have."

Teela stepped closer. Her hand found his, fingers curling around his palm with the same certainty she brought to a sword grip. The crystals nearest to them brightened at the contact.

The words of activation left his lips, and the grove shattered into light.

Pressure crushed inward. The sweet, layered scent of the fairy sanctuary vanished, replaced by nothing, a void where sensation should have been. His stomach lurched. His ears rang with a high whine that narrowed to a point behind his eyes.

Then air. Warm air, heavy with the scent of living wood. His boots found earth, and his legs buckled, one hand catching a tree trunk to stop himself from going down. Bark pulsed with life beneath his palm. The ancient tree's magic hummed through his fingers, a deep green resonance nothing like the fairy groves' bright harmonics. Beside him, Teela swayed, bracing against his shoulder until the trembling in her legs stilled.

The numbness in his fingers faded, and Eldoria's forest settled around them. Birdsong threaded through a canopy so high that the trunks disappeared into green and gold. The air carried bark and loam and a resinous depth that settled cool at the back of his throat. After the grove's urgent, crystalline sweetness, Eldoria's power felt like bedrock. Slower. Deeper. No less vast.

Teela scanned the treeline, her hand on her sword. "We're on the outskirts. We need to reach the city before anyone spots us."

Side by side, they made their way through the thick undergrowth, following a narrow path that wound its way to the elven city.

They emerged from the trees. Eldoria's architecture rose before them, buildings grown from the forest itself, their curves following the grain of living wood. Sunlight filtered through glasswork panels, throwing coloured light across the cobblestones.

A shout broke through the ring of voices and the knock of tools on living wood, a voice that pitched upward, cracking above the rest. "Stric! Teela!" Dreese came running towards them from among the elves, carrying carved timber. Colour rose in his cheeks as he closed the distance and swept them into an embrace.

"You're back so soon!" His chest still heaved from the run. "We feared you'd be gone longer!"

Teela returned his embrace. "It feels good to be back."

Cearan emerged next, alongside Kael. The magician's lined face eased when he saw them, and Kael's hand dropped from his sword hilt for the first time in what looked like hours.

Cearan stepped forward, placing a hand on Stric's shoulder. "You've done well to come back so soon."

"The queen needs to hear this." Stric's hand found Teela's, still warm from the grove. "Fairies are coming. Vampyres are already on the march. And we have a way to fight the golems."

Behind them, the forest stirred.

Chapter 19

Awakening the Alliance

Evening shadows stretched across Eldoria's clearing, long and dark beneath ancient boughs. Stric's fingers tightened on his Powerstaff as he joined the council circle at the great tree, its bark pulsing silver where Kael and Cearan already stood with Aelith and Dreese.

Air, thick with pine smoke, carried rendered tallow and sharpened steel, fresh sweat under leather, and pitch worked into new timber. Elves checking bowstrings with nimble fingers. Humans, loyalists who had begun arriving in the days before, tested blade edges against whetstones.

Aelith planted her feet wide, shoulders squared. "We must strengthen our defences whilst we await reinforcements." Authority in every syllable, the kind that required no volume.

Her gaze moved to the treeline. "Barok's troops move closer to our borders with each passing hour."

"Additional scouts will depart at dawn to monitor their movements." Dreese gave no pause for agreement, no glance toward Kael or Cearan to confirm the call was right. The scouts had already been named. The deployment routes already decided. He moved on to the next matter as though the first had never been a question at all.

"Supply inventories, weapon maintenance, defensive positions." Teela counted off on her fingers, her other hand dropping to check her sword hilt. "The vampyres, werewolves, and fairies bring their forces. More soldiers loyal to you are also expected."

"Though I have not stood upon a battlefield," Dreese's words came slowly, each placed with care. "I have spent all my short life studying with the greatest." His gaze moved from Kael to Cearan to Aelith and settled there. "Theory must serve where experience fails until experience can be won." Around him, elves and humans both had gone still, watching with eyes that held their target without sliding, shoulders angled toward Dreese where a week ago they might have looked to someone else.

Boots turned toward their tasks. The council broke apart, becoming an army.

Dawn came with the sound of hammers driving stakes into damp earth, the rhythm carrying through Eldoria before the mist had lifted. Stric moved through the camp, and the camp moved around him. Elven hands working fast along the outer ring, fresh timber rising where yesterday there had been open ground; above them, the forest itself lending its boughs as a second wall no tool had shaped. Sentries climbed before the light had fully arrived, taking their positions high in the canopy where distance would give warning. By the time full morning reached the settlement, the scouts were already gone, taken by the shadows of their paths without a sound or a farewell.

Three days passed in the rhythm of preparation. The whetstone's note ran under all of it. Fletched arrows mounted in bundles at every defensive position. Evenings brought the elven mages through the settlement, laying their enchantments into bark and stone until the air held a low hum just under hearing, the kind that settled in the bones before the mind could name it.

During these days, the loyalists continued to come, steadily, inevitably, until the fires pressed closer together at night, more boot prints darkened the earth, and more cook pots needed tending.

The first afternoon brought a woman whose posture said she had spent years learning to occupy less space, and a man who checked the exits twice before he crossed the clearing. Two younger faces, careful in the way of people who had survived by staying unnoticed. Their elven guide left them at the treeline and vanished back into the shadows of paths that Barok's scouts had never found.

By the next morning, the camp recognised the sound of their quiet, uneven footsteps, the particular weight of people who had spent years keeping their steps small.

As the third group of the day arrived, Kael burst from the treeline, chest heaving from a hard run. Sweat beaded his forehead despite the cool air, and his armour bore fresh scratches from hasty passage through dense undergrowth.

He wiped his brow with the back of one scarred hand. "Werewolves approach from the northern valley. A full pack, moving in formation around the enemy positions. They've circled wide to avoid Barok's scouts."

The assembled defenders straightened. Short words traded low and fast. Heads turned toward neighbours, the clearing filling with sound before the full meaning had moved through it. Their first allies had arrived.

The community poured into Eldoria's central clearing as Whhrll strode into view. His massive frame dominated the space, thick grey fur catching the golden shafts of sunlight filtering through the canopy. Behind him, dozens of werewolves moved with a predatory grace, each step placed with a precision that named the speed being held in check. Their amber eyes swept the clearing with calculating intensity, missing nothing.

Whhrll's voice dropped to a register that moved through bone rather than air. "Pack-call has been answered. Alpha-bond holds strong across territories. Packs that hunted apart now run as one beneath my lead. Many more follow, ready to drive the death-scent from these hunting grounds."

Cheers erupted from elves and humans alike. Aeloria stepped forward, extending her hand. "Eldoria welcomes you and your warriors."

Before the cheering had fully settled, Elar appeared at the council circle's edge, his expression measured in the way of someone delivering news he had been turning over since before dawn. "A report, Your Majesty." He addressed the queen with a slight inclination of his head, then turned to include the full council. "Our scouts tracking the approaching force have confirmed its arrival at our border."

He paused. The clearing held its quiet for three heartbeats. "The commander teleported ahead of his main column. Alone, then back again within the hour. They have held the position since. No advance, no engagement. They are waiting."

"Reinforcements," Kael said.

Elar's fingers stilled at his side. "Most likely. The question now is how long before the full weight of Barok's answer arrives."

Stric turned to Dreese. The set of Dreese's eyes shifted for a fraction of a second, then settled. "Then we work with what we have, as fast as we can." He turned back toward the council. "We knew they were coming."

They dispersed back to their tasks.

As the sun began its slow descent, they came.

The western light turned amber and deep gold, long shadows stretching between the ancient trunks, the air cooling against the back of his neck in the particular way of forests when the light drops faster than the warmth. Then the first of them crested the treeline. A single fairy, wings catching the dying light and fracturing it into ribbons of sapphire and copper. Many more, rising from the canopy behind her in a murmuration that brought the clearing to sudden stillness. Every head tilted back at once. The sound of voices cut off before it had fully formed.

The sky filled with colour. Wings that had been emerald in full daylight burned like stained glass against the sunset, trailing light that lingered in the air long after each fairy had passed. Tiny green faces turned downward toward Eldoria, mouths parted, the luminescent green of their skin brightening at the edges, their eyes holding the fixed, still quality of faces seeing something they had stopped expecting to find. They came from every direction at once, converging on the village's heart as the last sliver of sun touched the horizon, so that for one suspended moment, Eldoria blazed. Forest below, a living constellation above, the light of both joined at the treeline.

Twill soared ahead of her companions, silver hair streaming, her skin the luminous green of wet moss in dying light. "The groves have answered your call! Together we stand united against the scholar's shadow!" She spread her arms wide, her fellow fairies forming a glittering cloud around her, and the air itself vibrated with their presence as the first stars appeared above them.

Aeloria stepped forward from the assembled crowd, her bearing unhurried, her golden hair catching the last of the evening light. She inclined her head in a slow, deliberate bow. Twill's wings stilled for a moment. Then the fairy pressed both small hands together and returned the gesture, her glow brightening as she dipped forward in kind.

Stric's grip on the Powerstaff eased. Fairies filled the sky above, wings catching light the way his Powerstaff crystal caught a candle flame, each surface fracturing the same source into colours that had no names. They might actually survive this.

They came with the dawn, grey fur absorbing the low light, filling the paths between the trees without the sounds that a number of bodies should make. Thrakul led with Thrakmar at his side. The warrior's centuries were written in the breadth of his shoulders, his wingcleaver hanging easy at his hip.

The mage beside him, with the stillness of deep water, his violet eyes moving across the assembled forces with quiet, measured precision. Hundreds followed them, moving in a silence that displaced sound, as though the air itself stepped aside.

They held their breath, watching.

"We have waited many moons for this." Thrakul's voice struck the silence like a blade finding stone. "Blood does not forget."

The held breath came out slowly. Heads turned toward neighbours. A sound began in the chest and stalled before it reached the throat.

Over the remaining days, additional werewolf packs emerged from the woodland shadows. Fairy contingents continued to arrive from every corner of Veltak. Some carried precious stones that gleamed with inner light. Others brought enchanted herbs, carefully bundled in woven leaf-packets, plants that could strengthen warriors or heal battle wounds that would otherwise prove fatal.

In the spaces between these arrivals, the human loyalists continued to filter in. An older man with a soldier's posture and a youthful face, watching the ground at his feet. A woman who had kept her sword hidden beneath floorboards for twenty years, unearthing it only to hone its edge, waiting for the day she could finally draw it openly. They arrived in groups of twos and threes, took their place amongst the defenders without ceremony, and did not speak of what they had survived to be here.

An alliance formed. Warriors gripped weapons not yet drawn, bodies pressing forward before there was anything to press toward. Voices rose from every quarter, a cheer beginning in one corner and spreading outward before the reason for it had been spoken. Humans, elves, werewolves, fairies, and vampyres stood shoulder-to-shoulder beneath a common banner.

Around hastily constructed planning tables, different factions jostled for space. Elven tacticians gestured at maps while werewolf scouts growled objections; supply teams sorted through mismatched equipment with increasingly sharp exchanges. A man's eyes settled on the map and slid away from it. How could such disparate forces coordinate against an enemy who had ruled through terror for twenty years?

Disorder everywhere: voices overlapping, factions jostling at the same map. Dreese's shoulders squared. He stepped onto a log platform, raising his voice above the din.

"Listen to me!"

The noise subsided as hundreds of eyes turned towards him. The weight of their collective attention settled on his shoulders. Elven archers with fierce expressions, werewolf warriors whose powerful frames gleamed in the afternoon light, vampyres still where the elves and wolves shifted, wingcleavers resting flat against their thighs.

"We come from different worlds, each race bearing its own scars and stories." His voice broke on the last word and held there. Carrying the crack openly, the way a man carries a scar, he has stopped hiding. "But here, now, we face one enemy! An enemy who threatens everything we all hold dear."

Around him, the clearing grew still. Mouths shut on half-voiced arguments. Bodies stilled, turned toward him.

"We must stand ready," Dreese drew a steady breath. "Courage, we have proven. Strength we possess. What remains is to join courage to strength, so that our unity may break what his tyranny has created!"

Dreese let the silence hold for a moment, his gaze moving across the gathered faces as each one turned toward him. All watching, waiting.

"For the dead who deserve remembrance, and the living who deserve freedom. For all races, for all beings."

Cheers erupted.

The day after Dreese's words, as dusk drew close over Eldoria. Whhrll returned from his scouting mission.

"Barok's forces gather at the border." Ears flat against his skull. Hackles slightly raised. "They will attempt to breach at dawn."

The sun dropped below the horizon, leaving gold bleeding through Eldoria's trees and painting everything in shades of amber and blood. Evening shadows closed in around the gathered forces, weapons checked and rechecked without need. Leaders congregated beneath the great oak, its ancient branches serving as shelter.

Stric planted the Powerstaff's base against the earth and raised his voice to reach every listener, surveying the diverse crowd before him. Among them, quiet at the assembly's edge, stood the men and women who had kept faith underground for twenty years, come at last into the open.

"We gather as defenders of our homes," he began. "Tonight we prepare for battle, a battle that will determine our future and whether Veltak remains under Barok Tana's grip."

Dreese stepped beside him, firelight reflected in his eyes, the set of his jaw flat and hard beneath the skin. "Every race here carries scars from his reign. Each warrior stands with a purpose greater than themselves." His gaze paused on those quiet figures at the edge. "When we succeed in defending Eldoria, we won't stop there. We march on Talnaress to confront Barok directly. Will you aid us in this final push?"

Voices rose until the forest itself had found voice.

Dreese's spine straightened. His hand no longer shook on his sword hilt. "Too long has he inflicted pain upon all our peoples! The time has come to reclaim what was taken!"

Kael moved to join them. "Tactical preparations advance on schedule. Sentries double our perimeter watch; each unit rests near assigned positions. We remain vigilant. Barok will not catch us unprepared."

Across the gathering, Teela's eyes were already on Stric's. Neither spoke.

Thrakul approached with his cadre of vampyres flanking him. Firelight caught the edge of his wingcleaver and the sharp angles of his face. "Our warriors stand ready for your command." His deep voice struck the crowd like a war drum. "We have waited long for this."

"Tonight we stand firm," Twill's wings moved softly in the fading light as she hovered near the group. Around her, a small pocket of quiet persisted against the surrounding noise.

Stric planted the Powerstaff base against the earth. Its wood hummed beneath his palm in the rhythm he had come to measure his own pulse against. "We prepare for defence now, but when dawn brings victory, it will signal more than survival. It will herald our retribution against Barok Tana." He paused, letting the words settle. "Together we will reclaim what sank into his shadow. The land itself will remember us!"

Moonlight filtered through the great tree's dense canopy, casting intricate patterns across the mosaic ground beneath. This ancient sentinel had witnessed their unprecedented alliance, its silver-veined bark unchanged, the same as it had stood before any of them arrived.

Stric found Thrakmar seated alone at one of the large tables the elves had constructed, his silhouette stark against the starlit sky. Long silver hair shifted in the evening breeze. His pointed ears tracked sounds beyond human perception: the rush of wings high above, the scurry of some small creature in the undergrowth, the distant murmur of voices around campfires.

"You wanted to speak with me?" Stric approached the table, Powerstaff grounded against the earth.

The moment he set the staff on the table between them, its crystal went quiet.

It simply stopped its usual low pulse, the rhythm he had come to measure his own heartbeat against. Waiting.

Thrakmar's hand hadn't moved. He sat still, watching the crystal with eyes that had gone careful. His claws paused against the goblet. "It knows," he said. "It has known since I first laid eyes on it."

"Knows what?"

"What Barok built from our dead." He exhaled slowly, a sound like wind moving through deep passages where daylight never reached. "What the thing you will face truly is."

The temperature at the table shifted. His breath caught. His fingers moved toward the Powerstaff lying between them.

"Tell me."

"Our ancestors created deathseed crystals as meditation aids. Focus points for the study of life and death energies." His voice remained even, each word placed at its own deliberate interval, his hands unchanged against the goblet. "They can be altered. Corrupted. When violent death occurs near one. Suffering, blood spilled in terror or rage, transforms the crystal. Darkens it. Inverts its purpose."

In his pocket, Talnar stirred. A single flutter against his ribs. The crystal pulsed once: a single slow beat, like a heart registering a name it recognised.

"That's why your people guard this knowledge. To prevent such corruption from occurring again."

"We swore after the rise of the Blood-Cursed that we would never again let such power consume our kind or others." Thrakmar's claws stilled. His gaze dropped to the table's surface. One slow breath. "Then Barok came."

Thrakmar's claws clicked once against the goblet. "He did more than steal our secrets. On the very night he tortured and slaughtered our elders, he performed a ritual of unspeakable cruelty." His voice dropped to the space between breaths. "He harnessed their final moments, their agony, their terror, the last knowledge torn from minds still conscious enough to feel it go, to create something that should never exist."

Cold pressed against Stric's sternum. The cold didn't leave.

"He used their blood." It wasn't a question.

"Their blood was the medium. Their torment, the catalyst."

Thrakmar set down his goblet. The wine caught the moonlight and held it. Somewhere above them, an owl called once and fell silent.

"A Master Deathseed Crystal. One he grew from their suffering." Thrakmar's voice tightened, each consonant clipped, his hands flat on the table, a breath that didn't quite release between words. "He channelled their death agonies into a crystalline matrix, forcing their spiritual energy to coalesce into physical form."

"The crystal stores spirits, powering his dark magic. It funnels them into his golems and controls his army of the undead."

"The fairies believe their crystals can disrupt his control of earth elements." Stric's eyes moved to the staff. "That they can free the spirits trapped within..."

"They are correct to a point." Thrakmar's gaze moved to the Powerstaff resting on the table. His ears snapped forward, sharp with sudden interest. "Fairy crystals can't interact with the spirits trapped inside. They can only release them. The spirits will then return to the Master Deathseed Crystal, ready to be used against us once more."

He leaned forward, nostrils flaring. "Your Powerstaff. I've been observing it since our first meeting. The crystal it holds possesses unique properties." His violet eyes locked onto Stric's. "But there's something else. Something about you."

Before Stric could answer, Talnar lurched against his side with considerably less patience than the previous flutter. Leather snapped against his chest in rapid insistence.

Stric pressed a hand to his coat. "A moment." He drew Talnar out. The book dropped open on the table before he set it down, text appearing in bold lettering across the page. He read it aloud.

"I have been attempting to raise this matter since Thrakmar first fixed his eyes on your crystal. If the two of you could perhaps move a little faster, I would be most grateful."

One ear tilted forward. Thrakmar's expression settled, both ears angling forward now, with a slight cant to his head. His gaze fell to Talnar, resting on the table beside Stric's Powerstaff. "The crystal and Talnar. They have known each other for many centuries."

It was not a question. Talnar's cover lifted once, pages fanning in brief acknowledgement, and settled again.

His voice dropped to a quieter, more careful tone. "May I examine both you and the staff more closely?"

After a moment's hesitation, Stric handed it over. Thrakmar held the staff in both hands, fingertips adjusting fractionally once his palms settled, his grip easing as though too much force might disturb what the crystal held, eyes fixed on the crystal at its head. But as his claws contacted the surface, his entire body went rigid.

"As I suspected," his hands stilled on the staff.

Stric leaned forward. "What is it?"

Thrakmar's violet eyes locked onto Stric's. "Your staff's crystal. It's hungry for our magic. But more importantly..." His voice dropped to a whisper. "So are you."

"I don't understand."

Thrakmar set the staff down on the table with trembling hands. "In three centuries of life, I have heard legends of bridge-mages, individuals who can channel multiple magical disciplines. I believed them to be myths told to young vampyres about the time before the Great Separation."

"Most beings can only wield their racial magic. Some can use basic techniques of other races. The pathways in our minds, our very souls, are attuned to specific frequencies." He rose from his chair. "A vampyre cannot truly harness fairy magic. The systems are incompatible."

"Then how could I ..."

"Because your signature isn't singular." He rose and paced, slow and deliberate, each step at the same measured interval, turning at the table's edge without looking down, hands clasped behind him. "Your magical signature is complex, layered, like a chorus where there should be a single note."

The staff on the table. Thrakmar's intent gaze. Both waiting.

"Twill noticed something similar. She said the earth answered me as though I were born from it. That my magic carried harmonies her kind had never heard."

Thrakmar stopped pacing. "The fairy noticed it too?" His eyes widened. "Then it's true. You could harness vampyre magic as naturally as your own. The magic of all races is yours to wield."

"That sounds impossible."

"Bridge-mages are born perhaps once every several hundred years. The rarest of the rare, individuals whose souls can harmonise with multiple magical frequencies at once." Each word landed with measured deliberateness, the cadence of a man who had turned this knowledge over for three centuries. "Legend says they appear in times of greatest need, when barriers between peoples must be torn down."

Stric turned his hands over. The same hands as this morning. Nothing visible had changed. "Is that why Vrill said the oracle chose me? Not because I was convenient, but because..."

"Because it knows what you are." Thrakmar nodded.

Talnar's pages turned on their own, rapid and deliberate, cycling through dozens of pages before stopping hard. The text formed slowly across a fresh page, each word placed with care.

Stric read them out loud,

"*Vethra Tar.*"

Thrakmar went still.

Stric read on. "*The term is in an ancient language, from a time long before King Balthor's reign. The early Grandmasters learned the word from the elves. It means: born to all.*"

A pause in the text, then a final line, lighter than the rest. "*I suspected what you were from the forest, but said nothing until I was certain. I say this now so that you understand the full weight of the gift, not merely the brightness.*"

Thrakmar's ears pressed flat. The posture of a man receiving confirmation of something he had not dared to name aloud.

New text formed beneath. Stric read it aloud.

"*A Vethra Tar carries no natural resistance to magical corruption. The same pathways that allow attunement with all frequencies leave those pathways open in ways single-discipline mages are not. The rarer the gift, the greater the risk.*"

Stric sat back, pushing Talnar away from him. "You're saying I'm more vulnerable than other mages."

Talnar's answer came without hesitation. *"In some ways, yes. The multiple pathways that allow you to draw from every discipline also mean corruption has more doors to try. A single-discipline mage has one door to bar. You have many."*

Stric pulled the book back toward him. More text waited.

"The Grandmasters recorded this warning for a reason. The last Vethra Tar in living memory did not fall to an enemy. She fell to the corruption that found her open doors easier to walk through than most. The war that followed her fall lasted eleven years."

Thrakmar was already moving. "We must test this theory, we must enhance your abilities now."

"Test how?"

Thrakmar reached into his robes and withdrew a small vial filled with a silvery liquid that moved of its own accord. "This is why I requested this private conversation. What I am about to do must not be widely known. Barok has spies everywhere, perhaps even among our allies."

With practised precision, Thrakmar unstoppered the vial. "The crystal will accept our blood. Of that, I have been certain since I first sensed it." He paused, weighing his next words. "What happens beyond that depends on whether you are truly a bridge-mage. If you are not, the staff becomes a weapon against Barok's. If you are..." He let the thought settle. "Then something far greater."

"And if you're wrong about me?"

"Either way, you have a weapon to match Barok." Thrakmar held the vial ready. "But if I'm right, Stric, more than this war can be ended."

Stric picked up his Powerstaff. The crystal pulsed once at the contact, a vibration that travelled from the staff into his palm and held. "Do it."

Before Stric could have second thoughts, Thrakmar tilted the vial and allowed a single drop of silvery blood to fall onto the crystal atop the Powerstaff.

The effect detonated through his senses before conscious thought could catch up. The crystal didn't pulse. It exploded with a silver radiance that drove needles of icy fire up both arms. He gasped, tasting metal and something older, something that hummed in frequencies his bones recognised though his mind could not name. Threads of liquid starlight spread through the crystal's heart like veins of frozen lightning. They didn't stop at the crystal's surface but flowed down into the staff itself, transforming the ancient wood from dark oak to silver. The carved runes blazed with newfound power, each symbol igniting in sequence like heat climbing through metal.

The threads didn't stop at the staff. They crossed into his hands, his wrists, tracing pathways he hadn't known existed until they blazed silver. For one breathless moment, his veins ran cold with light. They drove upward through his arms and into his chest, moving through muscle and bone like icy fire finding its channels. He arched back, a sharp involuntary breath, his vision flooding silver at the edges before clearing. The cold fire found its bottom, settling into his sternum like a second heartbeat, steady and new. The silver threads held beneath his skin, running at the same depth as his own pulse. Like discovering a limb he'd always possessed but never known how to move.

Talnar's pages moved in a short, fast wave, flowing from spine to edge, then the cover slammed shut. Against the table, the leather binding shivered. Recognition, perhaps, or something stirred by ancient history.

Thrakmar flinched. Stric could not speak. Neither moved.

After a long moment, the cover lifted on its own, settling open to a blank page. No text came. Whatever Talnar made of the elder blood entering a crystal that had once helped create him, he kept between himself and the night.

"By the ancient blood," Thrakmar broke the silence. "It's true. You're a natural conduit for it."

"What have you done?" The transformation settled into a subtle but persistent radiance. The staff glowed from within, silver light pulsing in time with his heartbeat.

"I have given your staff the ability to resist Barok's necromancy and weaken his strength," Thrakmar resealed the vial with care and returned it to his robes. "I have imbued it with the power to destroy his Master Deathseed Crystal. But the transformation proves you're truly a bridge-mage."

New energy hummed through Stric and the Powerstaff like a second pulse. "How does empowering my staff weaken Barok?"

Thrakmar's claws curled against the table. His jaw set. "Because after years of handling the corrupted crystal, of drawing power from it, Barok has begun to transform. The crystal is a part of him, and he is part of it."

"He's becoming like the Blood-Cursed of your legends,"

"Worse. The Blood-Cursed were still, in some ways, bound by the natural laws of our kind. What Barok is becoming has no precedent." Thrakmar's claws extended as he spoke. "He will have abilities beyond what you've seen: unnatural strength, resistance to normal weapons."

Each syllable slowed around the thing he named, as if the word itself had mass. "But we are not finished. If you can truly wield vampyre magic, then perhaps..."

"Perhaps what?"

"We must find Twill now."

Stric stood. Warmth came from the silver wood into his palms, steady against the cold fire that had made it. "Why?"

"If you truly are a bridge-mage, you will be able to accept fairy magic as well. Your staff could become the first truly multidisciplinary focus in recorded history." Thrakmar's eyes gleamed, gaze moving sharply between the staff and Stric's face. "We could forge a weapon capable of countering every aspect of Barok's power."

They found Twill in the clearing where she had been organising her forces, Stric carrying Talnar at his side.

Twill's wings stilled. First at the book, then at the staff. "The old keeper." Her glow shifted toward white. "The groves have felt it since you arrived. Your focus. It's changed. What did you let into it?"

"Twill," Thrakmar said, "I believe Stric is what our legends call a bridge-mage. Someone capable of channelling multiple magical disciplines."

The fairy's eyes went wide, her glow brightening until she lit the clearing like a captured star. "Vethra Tar." Not a question. Her wings stilled entirely. "We thought it was gone from the world."

Thrakmar's ears flicked once. "We thought so too, but here one stands."

Twill hovered before Stric, her head tilting, her glow concentrating toward his hands. "Your hand...," she held out her own palm up.

Stric extended his palm, and the moment Twill's tiny hand touched his finger, light erupted between them, warm and deep gold, pressing against his skin like a held flame without the burn, spreading up through his wrist and into his arm. His knees softened. The ground beneath his boots pressed harder against his soles, denser, as though the soil had shifted its full weight upward. Earth magic moved through him like roots spreading through rich earth, like seeds quickening in spring soil, carrying a cool, slow pressure that rose through his arm in steady pulses. His free hand pressed flat against his thigh. He stood still. The staff sat differently in his grip. Balanced in a way he had not registered was missing.

Talnar lurched open in Stric's hand, pages spreading wide, and he lost his grip. The book hit the ground and fell open, its pages rippling outward in a slow wave before settling into stillness. No text came at first. Then, on a page near the centre, a single line appeared, smaller than Talnar usually wrote, without flourish or preamble.

"There it is."

"By the roots," Twill whispered, and her glow went so bright Thrakmar turned away. "The earth knew. Before any of us."

Twill pressed both tiny hands against the crystal atop Stric's staff. "Hold still. The roots know what to do." The silver radiance that marked the vampyre blood gained threads of deep green, earth magic interweaving with death magic in patterns that should have been impossible. Two forces crossed inside the crystal. The fairy magic, cool and slow, and the vampyre magic, deep and dense, pressing against each other at the join before locking.

Stric's Powerstaff now hummed with three distinct magical frequencies. Human, vampyre, and fairy, all locked together within the ancient crystal's matrix.

"Three roots, one tree." Twill floated back, turning the staff in the light. "It shouldn't hold. But it does."

Talnar's pages turned once before text formed across a fresh page. Stric read as Twill hovered closer.

"A millennium of collective memories, and not one of us witnessed this. I would have appreciated some warning before becoming part of a three-discipline magical instrument, but I confess the result is rather extraordinary."

Twill's glow brightened by a degree.

Stric read on. *"The Grandmasters who created me each contributed what was most essential in themselves. Those who were elven added their understanding of living things. Those who were human added their particular gift for reaching across what should not be reachable. They created me in the hope that one day someone would carry the disciplines of all races. Not because they knew it was possible. Because they believed it should be."* He paused at the last line. *"Vrill, of course, suspected it might be you. He had excellent instincts, if occasionally inconvenient ones."*

"What you hold now is more than a weapon. It is the only thing in existence capable of unravelling what Barok has built." Thrakmar studied the staff, his eyes moving over the silver wood and the multi-hued light shifting at its crystal's heart. "But it cannot be done from a distance. The elder blood within your crystal must make direct contact with Barok's. Crystal to crystal. They must touch."

Stric looked down at the staff in his hands. "Then how am I to get close enough to destroy his crystal?"

"That is up to you, Grandmaster Stric." Thrakmar's lips creased in what might have been a grim smile. "When we confront him in Talnaress, whilst the fairy crystals disrupt his control of earth elements and our warriors engage his forces, it may distract him and create an opening for you."

Thrakmar gestured to the staff. "When the moment comes, strike his staff with yours. The elder blood within your crystal will recognise the corrupted essence in Barok's creation and unravel it from within." One ear angled back. "But be warned: the resulting discharge of spiritual energy will be violent. Every soul Barok has bound into that crystal. Every spirit taken from village raids and battlefield dead will be released at once. You must be prepared for what that feels like."

"Before this moment, be aware. Barok will learn. He always does. When he understands what you are..." Twill's wings went still.

"Bridge-mages represent everything Barok despises. Our elders chose to give their blood. Twill chose to give what Chir gave his life protecting. He has never understood the freely given." Thrakmar said.

"I understand the trust you place in me. I won't fail your people."

"There is one last thing." Thrakmar's voice dropped. "After this is over, whether we succeed or fail, you must never speak of what I've told you about our magic. Not to your companions, not to anyone. The knowledge given must return to the mountains of Drakenholt once more."

"You have my word. These secrets die with me."

Before Thrakmar could respond, runes formed on Talnar's page. Script older than anything Stric had seen the book produce: angular, deliberate, each glyph pressed into the page as though carved rather than written. Stric retrieved the book.

The vampyre's eyes dropped to the script. His ears snapped forward. "This is written in the old tongue." His ears dropped a fraction. The ridge along his jaw relaxed. "The language of my people, before the Great Separation. I have not seen it outside our most ancient records." His claws drew back from the goblet. "I believe this is meant for me to read."

Stric stared at the page, then at Thrakmar. "You can read it?" He turned Talnar toward Thrakmar.

"I can." Thrakmar studied the glyphs in silence, his ears drawing back by slow degrees, his gaze dropping to rest on the glyphs.

"What does it say?" Stric asked.

"It says," Thrakmar's voice dropped to something careful.

"The knowledge entrusted this night passes no further. Bound by the collective oath of seventy-four Grandmasters. What was spoken here, we hold."

He held the book at arm's length, his gaze moving from the ancient script to its cover and back again before settling. "I did not anticipate the book bearing witness."

New text formed beneath, in Talnar's usual script. Stric read it aloud.

"I did not anticipate being present for it either. And yet, here we are. I find I rarely have much say in these matters."

Thrakmar placed a clawed hand on Stric's shoulder. "Strange, is it not? That it would take the threat of one like Barok to bring elves, humans, fairies, werewolves, and vampyres together after centuries of separation."

"Perhaps that's the one good thing to come from all this," Stric replied. "A reminder that Veltak belongs to all its people."

"And perhaps," Thrakmar's violet eyes dropped to the middle distance between them, holding there for three slow breaths, "with a Vethra Tar to unite us, it truly can."

Thrakmar and Twill moved back toward the fires, their voices dropping to the murmur of final preparations. Stric stood where they had left him, the staff in one hand and Talnar open in the other. Around him, the fires crackled low. The voices at other camps had dropped to murmurs. The crystal in the staff hummed faintly against his palm, steady and new.

He turned to the book.

Text formed without preamble or performance.

"You are attempting to decide how you feel. Allow yourself the time to do so. What occurred tonight is not a small thing, and you are not required to carry it calmly simply because others are watching."

"No one is watching now."

"No. They are not." The page held still for a moment. *"In the forest, very early in your journey, you cast a spell and told me it had felt like an echo. I want you to know. I said nothing because suspicion is not knowledge, and you had enough to carry without mysterious theories about your own nature."*

The crystal atop the staff, silver wood and three-coloured light, solid and strange in equal measure. "You could have told me."

"I could have told you that you might be the rarest form of mage in eight centuries of recorded history, uniquely capable and uniquely vulnerable, carrying a weight that broke the last person who bore it. Yes. That would have been tremendously helpful at that point."

Despite everything, the corner of his mouth moved. "Fair point."

"I am frequently right. You should know this by now." The page held still. The next words formed without the usual gathering of phrases. *"You are afraid. That is correct. Anyone not afraid tonight would be a fool, and whatever else you are, young Stric, you are not that."*

He stood with that for a moment.

"There is something else." The text came more slowly. *"The powers that now reside in your staff are not the limit of what I believe you can reach. Something more runs beneath it all."*

Stric leaned closer. The next words formed on the page, and he read them in silence.

He was still there when the fires burned low. When he rose, the settlement had gone quiet around him. He pocketed the book and walked back through the trees towards the small chamber the elves had assigned to him, pine scent mingling with earth under a sky thick with stars.

He paused near the entrance.

Teela stood in the doorway, her silhouette framed against the soft moonlight, arms crossed, watching him approach with an expression he'd learned over months of shared danger to read: jaw held level, mouth set, eyes giving nothing.

"I thought you'd be resting," he said.

"We have one last night before we face Barok's forces." She stepped forward, eyes holding steady on his. The green of them caught what light there was. "And I need to know something. If tomorrow is as dire as we fear, and we may not see the day after, I must know if your feelings for me are more than those of just comrades."

The breath he'd been drawing stopped mid-fill. He'd carried the answer to that question for a long time without letting himself name it, always telling himself there would be a better moment.

There was no better moment. There was only this one.

"Teela," he stopped an arm's length from her. "You mean far more to me than a comrade or ally." The words came simple and complete. "I love you. From that first moment in the forest, every battle we've shared has strengthened my love for you. You've been the reason I keep fighting. Not just for Veltak. For the chance to see tomorrow's sunrise with you."

Her breath caught. The tight hold of her jaw released. Her eyes widened and didn't close back to the flatness she usually kept.

"I want you by my side. Whatever lies ahead." The moonlight caught the silver threads still glowing in his Powerstaff, casting moving shadows across her face.

Tears caught the light in Teela's eyes. Her hand lifted, tentative and certain at once, and her palm pressed warm against his cheek. Her thumb traced the line of his jaw as though memorising the shape of him. "Then let us hold on to that tonight."

He pulled her close, and she let him. They settled into the small chamber together, the gentle glow from crystalline fixtures casting everything in warm amber light, the soft elven textiles thick and warm, the weave holding their heat.

Her breathing deepened. Her fingers entwined with his.

She lifted her head and found his eyes in the amber light. He reached out and tucked a strand of hair back from her face, and she caught his hand and held it there.

No words passed between them.

Later, he held her, her head against his chest. Her hand in his, the weight and warmth of each finger against his palm.

Outside, the settlement had gone quiet, only the distant movement of sentries on their rounds, the occasional low voice, the forest breathing in the dark.

"We're going to win tomorrow," Teela said.

He pressed his lips to her hair. "We're going to try."

She was quiet for a moment. Her thumb moved once across his knuckles. "That's enough."

Her thumb had already stilled. Eldoria's clearing held hundreds of warriors tonight, every fire burning low, weapons close to hand. Tomorrow, the golems would come. The undead. Whatever Barok had in store. And Stric would have to walk into the heart of it, carrying a transformed staff of silver wood and three-coloured crystal.

Her breathing slowed. Her fingers loosened in his, but did not let go.

Through the narrow window, stars burned above the canopy, unchanged, fixed in their positions over the sleeping camp. The transformed Powerstaff rested against the wall, its quiet pulse steady as a second heartbeat.

His eyes settled on them and stayed.

Eventually, sleep came.

PART THREE

The Vethra Tar's Bridge

Chapter 20

The Defence of Eldoria

The sound that woke them hit before it had meaning.

Stric came upright onto the cold floor. Teela was already at the window, her hand pulling the drape back hard enough to let in a bar of pale dawn. Her face changed.

Her eyes swept the treeline in a quick pass, jaw set, the line of her mouth flat and still.

"They're here."

Another horn sounded from the eastern post, low and two-not-ed. A third horn took it up further south.

Every muscle protested the cold and the sudden demand of dressing. In a corner, his Powerstaff pulsed, waiting.

His hands found Teela's face, calloused fingers against skin still warm from their shared heat. His thumbs traced her cheekbones, confirming she was still here. Still real.

She didn't pull away. Her hand covered his, pressing it flat against her cheek. Then she reached out and adjusted the purple sash at his waist. A small thing. Deliberate.

He nodded once. She stepped back.

Outside, the forest was already awake. An elven soldier ran past Stric, between the guest huts with an armful of arrows still bundled, unlaced and rattling. Two humans in half-buckled armour worked at each other's clasps without breaking stride, the oak roots underfoot making no concession to their hurry. Above, the canopy moved with fairies: a crystal-bearer dropped from a high branch and was flying south before her shadow crossed the moss.

No one shouted orders. The preparation had already happened. This was the execution of it.

Along the human line forming ahead of Stric, an older fighter. A woman whose armour bore the scratched-out sigil of some pre-Barok regiment pulled a cloth from inside her breastplate. Faded red-and-gold. She looked at it for the length of a long blink, then tucked it back without speaking. The soldier beside her had seen it. He said nothing either.

The hairs on Stric's forearms lifted as they joined the gathering warriors outside. Aelith stood at the forefront alongside Kael, her steel-grey gaze searching for weakness in their formation. She spotted Stric and Teela approaching and gave them a nod. Her chin lifted fractionally as her eyes tracked the way they moved: paired, each attuned to the other's position without looking. The scar on her jawline had been a raw wound when they'd last departed. Healed now to a pale thread that caught the early light. Her bearing showed nothing of it.

They turned as one, their paths diverging the way a river splits where the bedrock rises and will not move. No choice in it. The cold of the morning air pressed against his face. Teela moved toward Kael. Stric moved toward Dreese.

Dreese, with Cearan at his side, stood atop a watchtower that had been coaxed from a living oak. His hands gripped the railing as he surveyed the defensive preparations below, his gaze moving from position to position with the deliberate attention of a man taking inventory. The morning breeze lifted his dark hair.

At each commander's shoulder, a fairy had taken position. One settled at Stric's left shoulder, light as a dragonfly, wings barely moving. Another perched at Aelith's, a third at Kael's. Teela, moving to take her own position at the flank of the human line, acquired her companion as she walked: a tiny figure who dropped from the canopy and kept pace at her shoulder without a word exchanged. Higher up, Twill hovered at Dreese's side on the watchtower platform, the grove-mind's anchor in place.

Stric approached the watchtower. The elves, led by Aelith, checked their bowstrings with nimble fingers, the snap of tested tension punctuating the dawn. Arrows slid into quivers. Each archer's hand made one motion at the bowstring.

The humans under Kael's command adjusted their armour; the scrape of metal against leather was a counterpoint to their low conversations. Teela came to Kael's side, her eyes sharp as she inspected each warrior's readiness. She paused at a young soldier's pauldron, tightened a strap with practised efficiency, and held his gaze, the white line at his knuckle-joints, the pulse jumping at his throat, until his breathing slowed and his chin came up.

In the shadows beneath the trees, Thrakul's vampyres honed their wingcleavers. The asymmetrical blades caught sparse sunlight that penetrated the canopy, throwing star-shaped patterns across dark fur. Their amber eyes tracked movement, predator-patient.

Above, the crystal-bearers had already shifted south, drifting in formation toward the forest's narrowest approach. The earth-whisperers tightened into a coordinated cluster above the chokepoint, wing pairs angling in unison, following a command with no visible point of origin. What one knew, all knew. The grove-mind was already at work, reading the battlefield as one organism reads its own fingers.

Stric reached the watchtower base, the oak rough and cool under his hand. Power crackled in the air around him, barely contained energy that made the hair on nearby warriors' arms stand on end. In his right hand, he clutched his Powerstaff, the carved runes beginning to glow. The crystal pulsed with a rhythm almost like a heartbeat, warmth tracking upward through his palm.

The soft padding of paws on forest loam announced Whhrll's approach before the werewolf chieftain emerged from the tree line. Each stride covered ground enough for two of Stric's; the weight rolling loose through the joints. Mud and leaves clung to his coat, evidence of his circuit through the underbrush, and his breath misted white in the cool morning air. A fairy kept pace at his shoulder, drifting to match his gait, wings angled against the morning air.

His ears were flat against his skull, pressed down by what his nose had already told him. "Stone-walkers," his nostrils flared, "death-scent from the northwestern ravine. Undead. Circling." They'd tried to come around unseen.

He nodded, his gaze still ranging the treeline. Whhrll's muzzle wrinkled, exposing sharp fangs. "It carries on the wind, a rot-smell that offends the forest-bones themselves."

Dreese turned to the assembled commanders as Thrakmar approached. The vampyre elder moved with the stillness of deep water, his long silver hair catching the light, his violet eyes flat and still in the early light, the lines at their corners deeper than the morning warranted. Indigo robes whispered over the platform boards, and his claws clicked once against the railing as he gripped it.

Thrakmar's gaze found Stric and held there for a moment. "Their Spellcasters are layering shields. Grouped tightly behind

the golems." His fingers tightened on the railing, pale against the wood. "They expect any strike to come from us, not from above."
One breath. Thrakmar's eyes moved back to the treeline.

"My people are in position." Twill's wings stilled for a fraction of a heartbeat. "Ready to free the trapped spirits." She glanced at the fairies beside the gathered commanders. "Your orders will reach all the moment you speak."
Dreese's chin lifted a fraction. "Good."

He drew himself to his full height, shoulders back, and addressed his unlikely coalition. "Remember the plan. Draw them in, divide them, destroy them." He paused, letting the words settle into bone and blood. "Eldoria has stood for thousands of years against darkness. Today, we ensure it stands for thousands more."

The assembled leaders dispersed to their positions. Dreese remained on the watchtower, his eyes ranging the tree line above the northwestern ravine.

"May the forest guide us."

The first sign of the enemy was the sound of a horn, followed by a tremor in the earth, the heavy, synchronised footfalls of golems crushing undergrowth beneath stone feet. The forest itself recoiled from their approach. Birds fell silent. Shadows lengthened beneath the canopy. The very air grew heavier, weighed down by the cold seeping from the constructs as they came.

From behind a weathered oak, the first golem lumbered into view. The construct stood nearly twice a man's height, arms like fallen tree trunks, ending in crude stone hands. Each footfall sent tremors through the ground. From within it came something that had once known language. Fragments rolling across the open ground, a syllable repeating itself. From another, a name, half-formed, that broke apart before it was finished.

Whhrll's werewolves melted into the undergrowth, becoming one with shadow and root. Their fur shifted colour to match the dappled forest floor. Amber eyes, the only betrayal of their positions, gleamed from ferns and fallen logs.

A voice reached them from behind the stone ranks. Even unhurried.

"I have no interest in your forest or your alliance. The magician belongs to my lord. When you are ready to discuss terms, you will find me patient."

The magician. The words landed between Stric's ribs and wouldn't move.

A whisper of movement came through the canopy above. The hiss of wingcleavers parting air, then the crack of blades finding purchase in stone. Dark shapes descended upon the outer ranks of golems, vanishing back into the trees before the eye could follow.

Thrakul himself led the assault. The vampyre chieftain landed on the shoulder of a massive golem, driving his enchanted wingcleaver into the junction where stone neck met stone shoulder. The construct roared, a sound like grinding boulders, as it reached up. Thrakul had already gone.

At the same moment, a whistle like a curlew's call echoed from three directions. Branches parted for a heartbeat. Silver fletching flashed. Then the forest swallowed the archers again. Aelith's elves revealed themselves only in the briefest moments needed to loose their shafts before shifting positions. Their targets were the Spellcasters behind them. Through breaks in the foliage, the mages stumbled and halted, elven arrows finding gaps in magical shields and chinks in hastily raised barricades of force. The enemy's advance stalled.

The fairy at Stric's shoulder stirred.

High above the treeline, the fairy formation shifted without warning. Twill had not moved, had not spoken. Yet Dreese's voice carried from the watchtower. "Redirect the archers. Press the Spellcasters." In the same breath, the fairy at his shoulder whispered it back to him in a tone that matched Dreese's perfectly. He glanced up, and the crystal-bearers had already divided into two wings, one peeling east and one west, adjusting their coverage of the flanks as the elven archers pressed forward.

"Twill now." Twill did not relay the prince's order; it was meant for her alone. But it passed through the grove-mind like a root-pulse through wet earth, and the fairies descended from above like glittering rain, not one wing out of time. They hummed a single chord as they dropped their precious cargo onto the golems below.

Where the crystals struck, they adhered to the stone surfaces. Webs of pure white light spread across the constructs, seeking the imprisoned spirits within. The earth magic in the crystals called to the trapped souls, and the constructs shuddered where the light had taken hold.

Then, one by one, the constructs' cores flared with blinding light before imploding. Tortured spirits released. Prisons reduced to rubble. The freed spirits rose like mist into the canopy, their forms briefly visible. Farmers, craftspeople. Children.

Beyond the constructs, at the far edge of the treeline where the undergrowth had pulled back as though unwilling to touch him, a figure stood apart from the Spellcasters. Gaunt. Still. Dark robes with no insignia Stric could read at this distance. With a gesture from his Powerstaff, the crystal atop it flared with malevolent energy, sending a wave of heated energy surging outward.

Working from behind the main battle line, Stric let the flow of combat come to him. The burst came fast. He planted his feet and raised the staff, feeling the crystal pull at him, brightening as he drew his power up to meet it. Cold moved through his hands first, patient and precise, finding the channel the enemy had left open. Then warmth from below, a steady pressure travelling up through the wood from the earth beneath his boots, steadied his grip from a direction he hadn't expected. His own technique did what it always did under pressure: found the gap and drove through it.

The dark energy split around the defenders like water around a stone.

The commanders' magic had a distinct quality. Human, yes, but something had been added to it that made it grate at the edges. Overwhelming in volume. Ragged where precision should have been. A flooded river carving new channels through old soil.

Another burst came forth. His other Spellcasters joined him, combining their powers. The counterspell buckled under the assault, and much of the dark energy broke through. Where it touched the forest, plants withered and blackened, their leaves curling to ash.

Three fairies caught mid-flight plummeted to the forest floor, their wings gone to nothing. They lay where they had fallen, three small broken things among the roots and the leaf litter, their wings folded flat against the earth, leaves already settling around them.

Twill's anguished cry rang out above, a sound like breaking glass.

Every wing in the canopy faltered for a single, terrible beat, a collective flinch, their bodies registering the same loss at the same instant. Then they steadied together and pulled back to a safer altitude without a word.

Stric's chest constricted. He had spoken with one of those fairies in the grove. She had cradled a crystal in her palms while she explained how it would sing to the trapped spirits, her bell-like laughter ringing out at each question he asked. Now she lay broken on the forest floor, and the grief of their people pressed against his own chest like a fist.

The magic within his staff brightened.

"Fall back to the second position." The fairy at Stric's shoulder spoke the words from Dreese's voice, his order carried as if the grove-mind itself had breath.

Around the battlefield, every fairy beside every commander whispered it at once. Stric was already moving before the echo faded. Above, every fairy lifted and banked simultaneously, re-forming above the second defensive position before the words had fully died in the air.

The defenders pulled back in a deliberate tightening, drawing the enemy forces toward ground that favoured them. The figure at the treeline was no longer at the treeline. A shadow had risen from the forest floor, a conjured thing, flat and dark, hovering twenty feet above the undergrowth. The commander stood on it without looking down, his Powerstaff at his side, watching the shape of the battle the way a man watches a fire he has set and is content to let burn.

Vampyres vanished into the canopy, dropped, struck, and were gone again before the constructs could turn. Aelith's elves gave ground in stages. Loose three arrows, shift, silence, loose again. The forest swallowed them between volleys.

Stric deflected. Fell back. Another burst came. He deflected again.

The sun moved in its arc, the golems' shadows shortening, then lengthening, across the scorched earth.

At some point, the sap smell left the air. The absence registered before its cause. The forest's own blood, burned out by hours of discharged sorcery. By then, his hands had stopped shaking from cold and started shaking from the ache of channels pushed past recovery, the deep tremor of sustained deflection settled into his wrists.

The light through the canopy had shifted from dawn-grey to a flat, colourless overhead glare that bleached colour from everything. The sorcery had done something to the air. Every metal surface now carried a grey film, fine as ash, as though the moisture had simply been burned away.

Somewhere in the forest, Whhrll's packs were still moving. Stric knew it the way he knew the warmth of fairy magic through his boots. The undergrowth to the east held nothing. No amber eyes. No displaced shadow. They had gone deep, and they had not come back.

Before they had separated, Whhrll had said it plainly
When their rear is committed and cannot turn, we come. Not before. The alpha-bond would hold the packs until that moment, however long it took.

Stric held that silence, the way a man holds a breath he cannot yet release.

Beside Kael, Teela's sword flashed in the dappled light as she darted between the slower golems with lethal precision. While Kael relied on strength to break the enemy, Teela used speed and knowledge of the enemy's weak points.

"Left knee joint on the big one!" She angled toward a trio of human fighters struggling against a massive golem. They adjusted their attack. Two created a distraction while the third attacked the joint, bringing it crashing down.

"We cannot hold much longer!" Kael's voice carried to Stric over the sound of the closing battle.

Dreese stood tall on the watchtower as the pressure mounted. For weeks, every uncertain moment had pulled the prince's eyes to Cearan or Kael. Not now. The line held and broke and held again. His face was still.

With the enemy drawn in and fragmented as planned, their numbers were still greater than expected. The enemy commander's power grew rather than diminished as the battle progressed. The crystal atop his Powerstaff brightened, drawing energy from the chaos and death around it.

A thunderous crack split the air as one of the largest golems broke through Kael's line. Teela's shout reached Stric before the sight did. Her body was already moving, cutting toward the position she could not reach in time. The massive fist swept three human warriors aside. Their armoured bodies flew through the air, landing broken among the tree roots.

"Close the gap!"

Too late. Through the gap the massive construct had created, undead soldiers poured. Their vacant eyes and rotting flesh moved among the defenders.

A human warrior fell beside her, an ancient rusted blade protruding from her chest. Teela parried a blow meant for her own neck, countered with a strike that separated an undead soldier's head from its shoulders, then found herself pushed back as more enemies poured through the widening gap.

"Fall back to the next position!" Teela's command echoed through the fairy at Stric's shoulder.

Behind the human line, vampyre mages worked to counter the magic animating the approaching undead soldiers. Silver light moved between their clawed fingers as they traced intricate patterns over their crystals. Where their counterspells took effect, undead warriors collapsed, the blue light fading from their eyes as their souls found release.

For every spell they broke, the enemy Spellcasters cast two more. The undead continued to advance, pushing through gaps in the defensive line where golems had crushed the human defenders. Their weapons, blades green with verdigris or notched axes, cut down those who stood against them with mechanical efficiency.

"Prince Dreese!"

The voice reached him before the figure did. Aelith, moving through the press with the quiet efficiency of water finding a channel. She came to Dreese's side on the watchtower, silver armour dark with ichor across the chest, white-gold hair matted with sweat and forest debris. A long cut ran from her left temple to her jaw, intersecting with the older, healed scar, the two marks now layered one over the other. The fairy that had hovered at her shoulder was now gone.

"The eastern flank is collapsing." Her melodic voice was tight, the words precise. "Thrakul is wounded, and his vampyres cannot hold much longer."

Thrakul was across the battlefield: the vampyre leader clutching his side where a golem's blow had caught him, dark blood seeping between his fingers. His remaining followers fought around him in a defensive circle, their wingcleavers pulling back to guard rather than pressing forward, arcs shortening as the circle contracted.

Stric's grip locked on his Powerstaff. His gaze moved to the eastern undergrowth. Nothing. Then, from the depths of the forest behind them, came an unearthly howl, a sound that raised the hair on the back of Stric's neck despite knowing its source.

The circuit was complete. The enemy was committed. They could not turn, nor could they retreat. Whhrll had kept his word to the second.

Whhrll and his packs crashed into the enemy's rear in a storm of fur and fang. Multiple packs ran as one beneath his alpha-bond, a force vaster than a single clan, and the chieftain's path was read by the ruin he left behind. Undead flesh torn, Spellcasters scattered, the tight formation of the enemy's rear guard dissolving into confusion. One moment, they moved as massive wolves. The next, as hybrid forms, a man's reach and grip added to the wolf's weight and speed. Claws found gaps that no armour covered.

The assault threw the enemy's rear into chaos. Spellcasters turned to defend themselves, breaking their concentration and lowering their defences. Undead soldiers, receiving conflicting commands from their masters, milled about or attacked each other. The elves' arrows rained down on the Spellcasters, driving through the gaps that the werewolves' assault had torn in their formation.

"Rally to Kael!" Aelith's head turned a fraction of a second before Dreese completed the sentence.

The fairy at Stric's shoulder added nothing. His role required no relay. But the fairy at Thrakul's shoulder across the field whispered the same order in the same instant: close the line, and Dreese would reinforce Thrakul himself.

The elven commander moved, gathering her scattered archers with silent hand signals as she went. Dreese drew his own sword. His ancestors' blade, grip worn smooth by hands he would never know. He descended from the watchtower toward where Thrakul fought for his life.

The renewed line held firm. Kael's humans, reinforced by Aelith's elves, had stabilised the centre. Dreese himself had led a charge that relieved the pressure on Thrakul's beleaguered vampyres.

But their commander still stood, wreathed in crackling dark energy, untouched by the battle raging around him. And his staff was still gathering power.

The crystal atop it pulsed with something darker, denser, drawing colour from the air around it the way a wound draws blood. The trees nearest to him had gone still. A stillness of things that had stopped growing.

The enemy descended from his platform. Something moving across his skin like cold air finding gaps in armour. His Powerstaff had already shifted in his grip, the crystal's pulse quickening before he could name what it was reacting to.

The battle noise fell into a kind of distance. The tall figure moved through the chaos below, untouched by it. Dark energy wreathed him in crackling ribbons. The crystal atop his Powerstaff pulsed with each death the field delivered, drawing strength from the suffering around it.

Where he walked, the forest recoiled. Grass withered beneath those feet, leaves shrivelling on branches as he passed beneath them. His face, skin stretched tight over sharp cheekbones, eyes sunken and burning, turned toward the centre of the defenders' line.

"He comes for you," Cearan said quietly, moving to Stric's side. The older magician's face was drawn with exhaustion, his own staff dimmer than it had been at dawn.

Stric nodded, jaw tight. "He has been testing my defences throughout the battle. He's strong. Stronger than any of the others."

"Then let me stand with you," Cearan said, gripping his staff tighter.

"No," Stric placed a hand on his colleague's shoulder. "You're needed here. The wounded require your healing. And should I fall..." He left the sentence unfinished. Should Stric fall, someone would need to continue the magical defence of Eldoria.

Caelen's gaze stayed on Stric a beat past the nod. He turned away to attend to a group of injured elven archers.

Stric took a breath, gripped his Powerstaff, and stepped out from behind the ancient oak that had shielded him. The crystal at the peak of his staff glowed with pure, steady light, sharp against the approaching darkness.

He moved into a small clearing where the boundary between the two forces had blurred in the chaos, and there he waited.

Chapter 21

The First Weaving

Horns reached Valkan before he crested the final ridge, the signal running back through his column that the city lay ahead.

Eldoria's ancient forest spread to every horizon. Old growth, the kind that had been old before the Guild was first founded. No way to know how deep it ran or what moved in it. The Powerstaff in his hand hummed, the corrupted crystal atop it swirling with internal shadows. "The elven city lies just beyond the clearing." His voice carried without effort; dark magic amplified it. "Their defences will be formidable, but insufficient."

"The golems are responding slowly." Marek, the most skilled with golems of his Spellcasters, kept his eyes on the treeline. "The proximity to so much natural magic interferes with our control."

Valkan's lip curled. "Barok Tana's creations need not be elegant. Only unstoppable." He gestured with the Powerstaff, sending a pulse of energy through the nearest golem. The construct shuddered. The imprisoned spirit within wailed as it was forced to channel more power into its stone prison. "They will serve their purpose."

Behind the Spellcasters, the undead stood without fidgeting, without the small, unconscious movements of living soldiers waiting for orders. That stillness was the wrongness of them.

“Begin the advance.” Valkan’s gaze swept over his commanders. “Remember, our master demands that the magician be kept alive. Kill everyone else.”

His voice carried through the trees. “I have no interest in your forest or your alliance. The magician belongs to my lord. When you are ready to discuss terms, you will find me patient.”

Vampyres struck first, targeting the golems. Dark shapes dropped from the canopy in silence. The attack lasted seconds. A golem to Valkan’s right roared as something landed on it; the head separated in an explosion of rock fragments, and the bound spirit within escaped with a wail. Three more constructs staggered and went still. Then the shapes were gone, back into the shadow of the canopy before his Spellcasters could redirect a single ward.

Valkan turned on his heel, redirecting the remaining golems to close the gaps in the protective formation. It bought seconds.

The archers came next. Arrows rained down on his Spellcasters. Silver fletching flashed from three directions at once, each gap in the canopy closing before his eye could fix the source. Wherever a branch parted for a heartbeat, a shaft followed. The moonsilver tips burned through wards.

Marek staggered as an arrow pierced his shoulder. Around him, other Spellcasters had fallen, their bodies crumpling and the complex enchantments they had been maintaining unravelled. The golems under their control lurched to a halt, directionless.

“They’re in the trees.” Marek clutched his wounded shoulder as he turned to Valkan. “The arrows come from everywhere at once.”

Valkan’s face remained impassive, the crystal atop his Powerstaff flaring once. “Maintain the advance. I’ll handle their archers.” He raised his staff, channelling energy through the corrupted crystal, gathering power for a sweeping spell that would flush the elves from their hiding places.

Movement above, before the spell had built to full strength. Tiny figures dropped from the canopy. Fairies. Each released a crystal that adhered to the stone the moment it made contact. Webs of white light spread across the nearest golems, seeking inward.

Below, the crystals finished their work. A flare from within each construct, blinding and sudden. Then implosion. Where golems had stood, rubble remained. The spirits that had been trapped inside rose through the dust, visible for a moment, the shapes of people.

They had freed what was inside them. The shells had simply ceased to hold.

He filed it. It would require a counter he did not currently have.

He redirected his attack, a burst aimed at the fairies.

A counterspell met his attack before it could build to full strength and scattered it into harmless sparks. The technique was Guild. He knew the form, had used it himself. The force behind it was not.

"They're more coordinated than we anticipated." Marek continued to work his spells one-handed, his voice tight with pain. "This forest was supposed to be home to isolationist elves, not an alliance of..."

"Maintain your focus." Valkan's tone cut the sentence clean.

He raised his Powerstaff again, gesturing for his Spellcasters to join the working. Their combined attack went out as a wave, broader than the first, aimed above the defenders' line where the fairies had regrouped.

The counterspell rose to meet it. Strong. Stronger than one man should have been able to produce. Most of the wave broke apart and fell away. But not all of it. Three of the tiny figures in the canopy caught the edge of what got through and fell.

The defenders moved as a single body. No horns. No signals. The fairies at each commander's shoulder, one word from the centre, and the order arrived everywhere at once. A problem without a current solution.

His fingers drummed once against his thigh.

"Numbers alone will ensure our victory."

The defenders had been drawn back to a natural choke point, where humans and elves fought with unexpected coordination, holding his forces at bay despite being outnumbered. Valkan conjured a platform of shadow and now hovered twenty feet above the forest floor.

"Their resistance is impressive." Lenora, a skull-faced Spellcaster who had joined him at his observation post.

The human defenders were slowing. Stances held too long, weight shifting back instead of forward. "Direct the largest golems to focus on their centre." Valkan shifted his weight. "Have the undead follow immediately behind to exploit any breach."

Below, the undead shifted their advance, their line narrowing as they converged on the human section of the defensive line. Three massive golems, each twice the height of those around them, lumbered forward with increasing speed. Stone fists raised to crush the defenders who stood in their path.

"Their flanks adjusted before any signal could reach them." Lenora turned to Valkan. "How?"

"The line will break," he said. "Numbers are sufficient."

Below, the largest golem found the gap it had been pressing toward. Stone fists swung. Three human warriors left the ground and did not rise. Undead poured through the breach before the defenders could close it, rusted blades rising and falling in the same arc against those who remained standing.

The gap widened as the defenders scrambled to contain it and failed. The human section of the line folded inward, compressed between the undead driving through the centre and the golems hammering the flanks.

"Press the centre. Do not let them regroup."

The order went down the chain. His forces surged.

The line bent. One more sustained push, and it would not recover.

The screams came without warning. No sound from outside the perimeter, no disturbance at the treeline. The rear simply opened, and something fast was already through it, already among the mages before any ward could be raised. Striking the Spellcasters with a precision that suggested the target had been selected long before the attack began.

Lenora's voice cracked, "Werewolves!" She took a step back as a massive grey beast tore through three Spellcasters as if they were made of parchment. "They're destroying our rear guard!"

Already, many had fallen, their undead charges collapsing as the controlling magic dissipated. "Redirect the eastern golems. Crush these beasts before they reach the main force."

The order came too late. The werewolves moved with supernatural speed, darting between the slower golems, focusing their attacks on the vulnerable human Spellcasters. Their pack leader leapt fifteen feet into the air to tackle Lenora from Valkan's floating observation platform. Both figures disappeared into the chaos below.

Valkan steadied the tilting platform with a thought.

He took stock of what remained. The rear was gone. The flanks were folding. Most of his Spellcasters were down. Undead were standing motionless. The fairy coordination remained unexplained. The werewolf assault had been timed with a precision that suggested preparation, planned before the first horn sounded.

Twenty years of field command, and a broken engagement looked the same every time. What awaited him if he returned to Barok Tana without the magician looked the same, too. He had known this since the fairy assault shattered the first golem formations. Defeat was execution.

He had catalogued his opponent throughout the engagement: the pattern of his counterspells, the efficiency of his shielding, the way he conserved power where another mage would waste it on displays. The form was Guild. What moved beneath it was not. He had no name for the discrepancy.

Valkan lowered the platform and stepped into the smoke and chaos, dark energy wreathing around him, thickening as he walked.

He called to the remaining golems. Three massive constructs shuddered in their separate engagements and shambled toward the open ground ahead.

If he could not deliver the magician, he would settle for killing him.

Valkan walked into the clearing.

The human magician was already there. Waiting.

"My lord wants you alive. I, however, no longer care."

The words settled into the clearing. Around them, the forest had gone quiet, only the distant sounds of a battle that had not yet heard it was over. Stric did not answer. He adjusted his grip on the Powerstaff. The three golems waited at the edge of the clearing.

The enemy Spellcaster read his stance and struck without warning. A bolt of pure black energy lanced toward Stric's heart.

The barrier materialised. A shield of golden energy absorbed the attack with a sound like thunder. The force pushed Stric back several inches, his boots leaving furrows in the forest soil. The barrier held.

Their magic collided, crackling in the air between them. Light drove outward, hard-edged and white, bleaching colour from the bark of the nearest oaks. Grass under Stric's feet curled away from the heat. The force of each exchange pressed through the soles of his boots and up through the bones of his legs, a vibration that built with every blocked strike.

For every burst of dark energy, Stric produced a shield of golden light. For every binding curse, a counterspell of release. The crystal atop his staff brightened with each exchange, while the Spellcaster's pulsed erratically, drawing more from the bound spirits of the army he commanded.

Movement at the clearing's edge. Massive stone forms converging.

Retreat would allow the enemy time to gather. Calling for help would strip defenders from the main line, where they were desperately needed. His grip shifted on the Powerstaff, fingers finding the grooves. The braided current Thrakmar and Twill had helped him discover pressed back against his palm. Bridge-magic hummed within his staff, human, vampyre, and fairy energies waiting. But beyond them, at the very edge of his awareness, something else stirred. A single slow pulse moved through the ground beneath him, deeper than the mountain, coming from far below his boots.

The enemy Spellcaster snarled and redoubled his attack. A stream of purple-black energy struck Stric's barrier with such force that he slid backward several paces.

Stric drew on the braided current running through his staff and drove it outward in three directions at once. He would do what the fairy crystals had already shown him. He would speak to what was inside the stone. The three streams pressed through him simultaneously, a chord resolving in his bones rather than his ears. The golems did not fall. They came apart, stone dropping away as the spirits within rose.

Atop the enemy's Powerstaff, the crystal flared. The spirits Stric had just freed slowed, reversed. Colour and warmth slowly contracted inward, and the air around them dimmed as they were drawn downward to be consumed by the crystal. The next attack came fast and hard, almost strong enough to break through his barrier.

The backlash drove Stric to one knee. The braided current in his staff recoiled, three different rhythms suddenly out of sequence, pulling against each other through the same channels. His jaw locked. The pressure behind his eyes was absolute. Something gave way; a warmth spread across his upper lip, the copper taste of it reaching the back of his throat. His grip on the Powerstaff held by instinct rather than will, the wood burning against his palm, its light flickering.

"STRIC!"

Teela's voice. From across the battlefield, pitched raw and cracking, cutting through everything. His name in her mouth, the vowel stretched thin and splitting at its edges. It hit him behind the sternum. His knees pressed harder into the soil. He held it.

The Spellcaster advanced a step toward his kneeling opponent and gathered his power for a final attack. The crystal atop his Powerstaff emitted a high-pitched whine.

Against his ribs, Talnar pressed, warm and steady. A slow pulse, certain in the way embers hold heat long after the fire has gone out.

Stric did not need to open it. He had done that the night before, in the quiet after the fires burned low. What the pages had said then. A possibility. *"Something more runs beneath it all... It has never been asked. It may refuse. But it is there..."*

Stric reached out with his mind. To ask.

It began with a single breath.

He inhaled, and the forest inhaled with him.

His exhale carried something older than the Guild, older than the vampyres' sacred traditions, older than the fairies' earth-songs. It tasted of dark soil and slow water.

Warmth rose through the ground, through his boots and into his bones. Weight. The patient underground weight of things that had been growing since before memory.

Grass that had blackened from the combat bloomed green, spreading outward from where he stood.

The earth answered. Crystals responded. Every crystal in the forest floor, in the mountain rock beyond the treeline, in the deep lattice of veins the fairies had spoken of. They woke together, the way a chord resolves, each note distinct, all of them one. It moved through bone rather than air.

His Powerstaff pulsed in answer. Its crystal, already holding vampyre silver and fairy green, added a third rhythm, slower and deeper than either, the unhurried beat of the world itself. Stric's hands tightened around the staff without willing them to. The wood hummed against his palms, warm and steady, as though it had been waiting for this exact weight to settle into it.

The power pressed through every channel in his body at once. His teeth clenched against it. For one suspended instant, his vision narrowed to white at the edges as the world poured itself through a mortal frame that had not been built to hold this much. His jaw locked. Something burned in every joint simultaneously, the cost of asking too much of bone and blood. Then the channels held. They opened further than he knew they could.

Light bloomed from his skin, steady and warm: the heat of stone after a long day's sun, the dense weight of old roots, the slow warmth of stone that had not shifted since the mountains rose. His Powerstaff transformed in his hands. The wood turned silver white, as deep as the vampyre blood already threaded through its grain. The crystal, already enhanced with vampyre and fairy magic, pulsed now with that third rhythm, the heartbeat of the world itself.

Stric rose to his feet. The earth itself raised him.

The magician stood before him, transformed. No longer kneeling and bloodied. Risen. The hairs lifted along Valkan's forearms before his mind registered why. His Powerstaff had changed entirely, its crystal pulsing with a light that stripped away shadows.

Valkan had faced mages, sorcerers, hedge-witches, and the occasional self-taught prodigy across twenty years of service. He catalogued threats by type and weight, assigned probabilities to outcomes, and acted accordingly.

He had no category for this.

"What is this?" he said.

He launched another attack. Pure force, no elegance, because elegance required certainty about what he was facing.

The magician's hands had not moved on his Powerstaff. The crystal had not wavered once.

Valkan fought, abandoning finesse for raw power. He sacrificed more golems, drawing their bound spirits into his staff in a last attempt to match his opponent's strength. The crystal cracked under the strain, thin lines spreading across its surface like a web.

Pain lanced through Valkan's arm as the corrupted power began to backlash through his own body. Dark veins spread beneath his skin. He pushed harder.

"You should not exist." His voice had the flat precision of a man completing a report.

He summoned a mass of writhing shadows that lunged forward like hungry serpents, their forms opening to reveal the trapped, tormented faces of the spirits he had consumed.

The magician brought his hands together around his Powerstaff. Within its crystal, magic locked into a single note of perfect clarity.

Gentle. Inexorable. The way morning reaches into corners that have been dark for years.

It rolled across the clearing in a wave of pure light.

The writhing shadows touched it and ceased to be. Transformed. The tormented faces within them relaxed into peace as the spirits were freed. They rose like morning mist, dissipating into the natural cycle they had been torn from.

The wave struck him in the chest.

Beneath his skin, the dark veins pulled taut, then drew outward toward the surface, as though the light were extracting them. The extraction came from deep inside his chest, where the spirit-binding had settled deepest, and ran along channels behind his sternum, tracking the length of each arm to the fingertips. Each thread of dark power he had built over decades tore free at its root.

His Powerstaff's corrupted crystal shattered, the pieces dropping away and turning to mist before they reached the ground. The release of energy coursed through his body. The spirits he had consumed broke free, their essences tearing through the magical pathways he had constructed within himself over decades of spirit-binding.

And through it all, surfacing with strange insistence through the dissolution, a memory he had not visited in forty years: a hillside, somewhere in his youth, before ambition had ground out the boy who could stand there and take his mother's certainty for granted. Summer grass. The smell of it after the rain. His mother's voice calling from a distance, unhurried, certain he would come. He could not see her face. He remembered the sound of her certainty, young enough then to take it for granted.

Valkan crumpled.

His Powerstaff shattered as he fell, releasing the last imprisoned spirits it had contained. He aged decades in moments; the dark power that had sustained him was now gone. The hand that had gripped the staff lay open beside its shattered pieces, the skin loose across unfamiliar knuckles.

The memory of his mother's face would never come.

Far to the west, beyond the mountains that bordered the ancient forest, Barok Tana stood atop a tower in the stolen palace of Talnaress. Before him floated a sphere of shadow-stuff in which the last moments of Valkan's defeat played out in silence. In the sphere, Stric's purifying wave obliterated his servant. Barok Tana's hands did not move from the sphere's rim. His eyes tracked the last image before the mist cleared.

"So," he said to the empty air, his voice like silk over stone. "They are stronger than anticipated. They act as one body. That I had not accounted for."

"He comes for you," several voices whispered in his mind at once.

He waved a hand, dismissing the vision and the voice with a casual gesture. The shadow-sphere collapsed in on itself. The wisp of darkness that remained drew tight and vanished, and the cold it had carried pressed briefly against his hand before the room settled back to stillness.

Valkan served his purpose. Now I know what awaits me.

He turned from the tower's edge. His hands, as they left the stone rail, showed their edges imprecisely, the fingertips less defined against the dark air below, the corruption wearing at what it claimed.

Below, in the courtyard that had once welcomed the kingdom's merchants and petitioners, a company of his forces stood in their usual silence. Two dozen Spellcasters in dark academy robes, their Powerstaffs held at rest, breath visible in the cold air. Three golems occupied the courtyard's far end, motionless as carved stone except for the slow tracking of their glowing eyes. Between them, a column of undead stood ranked with the patient stillness of those who no longer experienced the passage of time.

A remnant, a holding garrison. Barok regarded them as a cartographer regards a single point on a map: useful less for what it was than for what it indicated about the larger terrain.

He descended from the tower.

His study occupied the highest interior chamber, its walls lined with maps and reports that his commanders sent by courier and crystal alike. The desk was empty except for a lamp, an inkwell, and a sheaf of blank parchment. He sat, drew a fresh sheet forward, and aligned its edge to the desk's corner. They were marching toward him. They believed they had won something today. He had spent twenty years ensuring that Talnaress held advantages no forest victory could negate, and now he would draw every remaining piece to this board before they arrived.

He took up the quill.

The orders were precise. Every commander holding a post beyond Talnaress's walls was to abandon it immediately and return to the capital. Every Spellcaster, every golem, every soldier walking or shambling or standing in formation throughout the kingdom was to be recalled at once. He wrote six copies, one for each sector commander. The language was uniform: directive, deadline. They would obey. They had no mechanism for anything else.

One thing he had not yet resolved pressed at the edge of his attention. The magician who had destroyed Valkan possessed power unlike anything Barok Tana had encountered before, power that had crossed the clearing without force, without assembly, as though the world had simply exhaled it. Power that bore no resemblance to anything he had prepared for.

He dismissed the thought and sealed each letter with a press of his ring into dark wax. Then returned to the tower balcony to look out over his city. There he waited for the guard captain's footsteps on the stairs, while planning his victory.

The alliance marching toward him had proven capable of the unexpected, had demonstrated unity where he had anticipated division, strength where he had expected weakness. He would not make the mistake of underestimating them, as Valkan had. That path led to becoming ashes scattered on a forest floor.

Let them come. There is only defeat for them here.

Chapter 22

The Price of Victory

The remaining golems stilled. Stone simply stopped being held together, and it fell. Above them, something moved upward out of the dust. Undead dropped where they stood, weapons falling to the ground. At the treeline, the last Spellcasters were already gone, robes swallowed by the undergrowth, not one of them looking back.

The borrowed light left Stric all at once. His knees found the ground before he understood he was falling, and his hands caught him a moment after that, shaking against the forest floor. Near the watchtower, two figures stood frozen. Cearan, his staff dim with exhaustion, jaw slack, and beyond him, Thrakmar, silver hair bright against the dark treeline, violet eyes fixed on the transformed Powerstaff where it had fallen beside Stric. Neither of them spoke. Neither moved.

The corruption that had touched the soil was already fading; fresh growth was pushing through the earth that magic had blighted moments before.

Boots on soil. Running. Stric turned his head toward the sound. His neck pulled tight with the effort, and the world tilted. Teela's wordless voice carried through the aftermath. She dropped to her knees beside him, her hands moving to his face, his chest, his arms. His chest rose and fell. Her fingers found his, and her thumb traced slow circles against his palm.

"Did we win?" The words came out hoarse.

She brought his palm to her lips. Held it there.

"We did."

The sounds of battle had left the forest. The warriors moved among the fallen, helping the wounded. A fairy dropped from the canopy ahead, landed on a human soldier's shoulder, and said one word. The soldier turned. His hand found the arm of the man beside him. Across the clearing, a ripple moved through the ranks. Heads lifted. Shoulders dropped. Somewhere above them, a bird called once into the silence. Then another. The canopy answered itself, note by note, as though the forest had been waiting to find out if it still could.

Dreese approached through the aftermath, and for a moment, he was still. A werewolf in a half-crouch, still breathing hard from the fight, lifted his muzzle as Dreese passed. He did not speak. He lowered his head once, deliberate and slow. Dreese held its gaze for a moment, nodded, then moved on.

Near the eastern line, an elven archer was binding a gash on a human's forearm with efficient, practised hands; the man held the limb steady. At the far end of the line, a werewolf in human form was sitting in the dirt, his back against an oak root, a fairy barely the height of his knee hovering at his shoulder, applying a salve.

"Eldoria stands," Dreese said, crouching down and clasping Stric's shoulder.

The light had turned amber. Wood-smoke, deep and settled now, had replaced the smell of ash. Voices had dropped to the register of people who no longer needed to shout.

They stayed where they were for a time. Dreese had crouched beside them long enough to read whatever he needed to read in his face, then rose and moved toward the wounded without a word. Others came. A nod, a touch briefly on Stric's shoulder. Most did not linger. Insects returned to the undergrowth, and Teela kept her hand in his, and neither of them moved until the light had shifted and the sounds of the camp had dropped to low voices.

She got him upright by degrees, her shoulder taking his weight without comment. He leaned into her, and they moved.

The camp came to him in fragments. Elvish voices blended with human ballads, the melodies trying to find each other: traditional elven minor keys probing at human major cadences, each adjusting, neither quite resolving. A human soldier paused mid-note, listening. The elf across the fire held the last phrase a breath longer than her tradition required, leaving space. The two of them looked at each other across the flames. Neither spoke. Vampyre tales of ancient battles drew listeners from across the fires, voices low and intent in the dark between the trees. The werewolves had reverted to human form, their voices lower in the loose circles they made, their laughter infrequent but, when it came, genuine. Thrakul lay on a stretcher of woven branches as they passed, his side bound tight, the bandaging already darkening at the edges; his eyes stayed open, fixed on the canopy with the patience of a warrior who had learned to treat pain as weather.

At one fire's edge, apart from the rest, Twill had drawn her knees up and folded her wings close. She did not look at the gaps left in the canopy. Around her, the fairies in the trees held the same posture. A chord with fewer notes than it should have had.

Ahead, near the next fire, a werewolf warrior crouched to lift a fallen soldier's hands and cross them, palms up, fingers spread across her chest. In the way wolves position a pack mate before the howl. A human was already on his feet, jaw forward, and the werewolf turned, and the sound from his chest brought three others nearby to their feet.

Stric's feet slowed.

"Kael has got it." Teela's fingers tightened on his arm, and they kept moving.

He glanced back. Kael stood between the two men, one hand raised, body angled into the space. The human's jaw dropped a fraction. The werewolf's chest stilled. Teela steered Stric forward, and he did not look back again.

She brought him down beside the largest healing circle with the same economy she had used to lift him. Folded cloaks behind his back, positioned against an oak's trunk without asking. The Powerstaff she laid beside him, close enough to touch. Its crystal had returned to its dormant state. The silver-white wood caught the firelight, pale and unchanged against the darkening ground. The ground pressed up through the cloaks beneath him. Voices came from distances that were too large for how close they were.

Teela did not speak for a long time after she had found him. Her hands had done the speaking. Her grip was a soldier's grip.

The fire between them breathed.

"You went to one knee." She was looking at the fire, not at him. "Bleeding."

"I got up."

Her jaw tightened.

"I saw." She turned her face away from him, toward the fire. "I couldn't reach you."

Stric turned his head. Her profile caught the firelight, jaw forward, eyes fixed on the fire without tracking it; the reflection steady in them, but nothing moving behind it. His thumb moved along the back of her hand, found the ridge of a knuckle, and stayed there.

"Next time," he said, "I'll try to fall closer to you."

A quick breath escaped her, bitten off before it reached anything else.

He squeezed her hand. She squeezed back harder and did not let go.

"Promise me." Still looking at the fire.

"I promise."

He lay still for a long moment after that, Teela's fingers wrapped in his, the firelight warm against his closed eyelids.

He was almost asleep when it came. Talnar stirred. A slow warmth, and the faintest press of pages turning, deliberate rather than frantic, the way someone knocks who is not sure if you are sleeping.

Stric reached inside his robes and drew the book out. He opened it. Text formed in the firelight, unhurried, as if the book too was exhausted.

I find I do not know what to say. That is, I should note, unprecedented. The Grandmasters recorded what they knew of the Vethra Tar. What they knew, it turns out, was the smaller part.

A pause. More lines appeared.

What lies ahead is a different matter. The man this Spellcaster served, I can only guess at. What he has become I cannot.

The writing stilled. Then, after a moment:

Rest. You have earned it. So, for the record, have I.

Stric closed the book and set it beside the Powerstaff.

Queen Aeloria stood at the edge of the healing circle. She wore no crown, only the forest-green of her travelling robes, her hands loose at her sides, her weight settled and still. She waited until Stric met her gaze and held it. Then she sat across from him on an upturned root, close enough for private words.

A moment later, a second figure emerged from the dark. Massive, grey-furred, and moving with the deliberate quiet of a predator choosing to be heard. Whhrll settled at the fire's edge and was still for a breath, nostrils working, reading the smoke, the blood, the sour sweat in the air, before his amber eyes fixed on Stric. He did not speak. He simply waited, as Aeloria had waited.

Aeloria acknowledged him with a slight inclination of her head. Whhrll's ears tilted forward once in answer.

"You frightened us." She waited. The clearing held the fire and the silence between them. Her gaze dropped to the Powerstaff where it lay in the grass beside him, held there for a breath, then returned to his face.

"We thought we had lost you." Across the fire, Whhrll made a low sound in his chest, a resonance that pressed against Stric's ribs rather than reaching his ears.

Aeloria straightened. When she spoke again, it was a sovereign's decree.

"You did not need us today." Stric started to speak. She raised one hand.

"But there may come a day when you do. If that day comes, if there is ever a moment when you need the full power of Eldoria at your back, it will be given freely. Without conditions. Without price. This is a promise between equals."

Whhrll's claws flexed once against the forest floor, then stilled. When he spoke, his voice was low, directed at Stric across the fire.

"Pack-memory held your trail when you fell." His amber eyes were steady. "Pack does not forget." A breath, deliberate and slow.

"Fang and claw were enough today." His gaze did not waver. "If you call, pack-magic too will answer. That word has not gone outside the den. It is not said lightly."

They did not wait for his reply. Aeloria rose first, and Whhrll rose with her, and they walked back into the dark in separate directions.

Teela had not stirred through any of it.

Stric sat for a long time after that, Teela warm against his shoulder, the Powerstaff a cool weight against his thigh.

He closed his eyes.

Pine resin sweetened the morning air that had been smoke and ash the day before. The first sound to return to the canopy was a fairy's single, soft note. She flew high overhead, her wings catching the early light as she moved between the torn branches. Others followed, drifting back to the gaps the battle had left, their presence a slow repair the grove-mind was already beginning. Below, small blue flowers pushed through soil that had been blackened the day before, their petals bright against dark earth. The mineral scent of disturbed soil came up through the wildflower pollen, and the breeze that carried it no longer reeked of Barok's corruption.

The alliance leaders gathered in Eldoria's heart. Maps and strategic documents lay spread across the flat-topped table.

Stric, still weak but present, sat beneath the great oak, Teela at his side, her hand never far from his. Talnar rested against his ribs, tucked inside his robe. A slow, steady heat radiated from the binding into his side. Not urgent. Patient.

"Our scouts report the enemy's remaining forces are withdrawing toward Talnaress." Elar stood at the far edge of the council, a bandage wrapped tight around his waist beneath his battle-stained tunic. His voice carried its usual authority, though the skin beneath his eyes had gone grey-white and tight. "They will reach the capital before us."

Whhrll's rumble carried through the clearing, his massive frame dominating his section of the oak's roots. "They flee with pack-tails down, but carry word to the den-master."

"Which means Barok Tana will prepare for our assault," Dreese studied the maps spread before him, his finger tracing routes through the capital's fortifications. "Whatever defences he had before, they will be strengthened now. He knows what's coming."

Leaders leaned forward. Eyes dropped to the maps. The debate moved to walls, to gates, to the disposition of whatever forces Barok had left to him.

Stric listened and said nothing. None of it answered the question that had been sitting at the back of his mind since he had gone to one knee in the clearing. The siege would bring the alliance to the walls. Dreese's commanders would manage that. But Barok was inside the palace, and the palace was not the walls. Whatever happened at the gates, someone still had to reach the man himself. Stric was the only one in the clearing who carried the magic to end it, and no tactical debate about fortifications was going to walk him through the palace door.

His hand moved to Talnar before he had decided to reach for it. The warmth through the binding had shifted. Steadier now. Attentive. Expecting the question.

He drew the book out and opened it across his lap. The others continued talking. Text formed on the page, word by word, unhurried, each letter already certain of what came after it:

Ah, there it is. Not "how do we breach the walls", that is Dreese's problem. Yours is rather more specific. King Aldric the Third was, by every account I contain, a man of impressive and well-documented paranoia. His engineers built it into the palace's foundations: passages that surface outside the walls. Aldric considered dying in his own throne room a personal failing he intended to architect his way around.

Cearan and Kael have traversed one of these passages, though I suspect neither of them gave much thought to its broader implications. I suggest you mention this before the council spends another half hour on the gates.

He closed the book and placed it on the table in front of him. He waited for a gap in the conversation. It came when Dreese straightened from the map, jaw set.

"There is something that needs saying." Stric's voice came rough but carried. The council turned. "The walls are Dreese's mission. Mine is getting to Barok. There are tunnels beneath the palace. Passages that surface in the city." He let that settle. "You press the gates. While Barok's attention is on the walls, I go through the tunnel."

Kael had gone still across the table. He looked at Cearan once, and for a breath neither of them moved. Then he turned back to the map.

"We used one." His voice was flat and precise. "The night the palace fell. A concealed entrance in the lower corridors, leading out through the city to the warehouse district." He paused. "We did not stop to map it. But I could walk it again."

Cearan's eyes had not left the map. "I suspect it was not the only one."

Dreese held Kael's gaze for a moment. Then he turned back to the map. "Show me."

Kael traced the route with his finger across the parchment, correcting once where his memory of the warehouse district exit placed the tunnel's angle differently than the survey recorded.

Dreese's gaze moved from the parchment to Stric. "You almost fell yesterday."

"I got up."

"Barok Tana is not the magician you faced. He is the power behind them all." Dreese did not look away. "I need to know you can still stand when it is him in front of you."

Beside him, Teela had not looked up from the map.

"And if you can't?" she said.

She lifted her eyes. Stric met them.

"There is no one else who carries what I carry." He said it because it was true, and they all knew it, and someone had to say it plainly. "That has not changed."

Dreese held his gaze for a breath. Then he turned back to the map.

Teela's fingers found Stric's once, brief and hard. Then she released him.

The sun moved. Maps were redrawn, routes argued and abandoned, fingers tracing approaches until the parchment softened at the folds. Voices rose and fell across the council stone: Whhrll's rumble against Aelith's precision, Kael's flat assessments cutting through conjecture, Twill's contributions arriving in clusters as the grove-mind fed her intelligence from the canopy above. Fairy lights came on with no one calling for them, the clearing darkening around the council while the work continued.

Queen Aeloria's voice carried quiet authority across the council stone when the tunnel strategy had settled into something the commanders could agree on. "I am no warrior," she said, her gaze moving across the gathered faces. "My place is here, with those too wounded to march. Eldoria will stand as a sanctuary for the fallen and the healing." She inclined her head to the assembly. "But my people's finest will march with you. Aelith will speak for Eldoria on the battlefield."

Kael's hand lifted from the edge of the stone. Aelith held Dreese's gaze for a breath, then released it. Whhrll's broad frame settled, the tension across his shoulders releasing by degrees.

"We break camp at dawn." Dreese straightened from the council stone. "The order goes out tonight: rations distributed, wounded assessed for transport or care. Those who can march, march. We carry our fallen to proper ground when Talnaress is ours." His voice carried flat and certain across the stone. "They handed us a retreat. We press it."

The council dispersed without ceremony, each leader moving back through the clearing with immediate purpose. Warriors rolled the maps. The fairy lights dimmed as Twill and her companions rose from the stone and scattered into the canopy above. Twill paused at the stone's edge, pressed her palm to the ground, eyes closed. She rose after a moment and was gone. The great oak stood quiet at Eldoria's heart, its roots still warm with the day's long battle beneath its branches.

Beyond the circle of fairy lights, an owl called twice and fell silent.

The forest held the deep black of the hours before grey came. Most of the alliance had found sleep, warriors resting in whatever comfort the forest could provide, but many had not.

The power Stric had channelled still moved through his body like the memory of lightning, as if his skin fit differently than it had before. Beside him, Teela dozed, her fingers clasping his even in sleep.

He extracted his hand with careful precision and moved through the camp. The cold settled in his bones. Fire after fire, warriors at rest. At the werewolf circle, massive forms sat around a small fire whose light caught in amber eyes and reflected from bared teeth when points were made forcefully. Their conversation carried on in growls and rumbles, punctuated by sharp barks. One word broke through into common speech, carrying over the fire: "pack-brother." His feet slowed without his choosing to slow them. A scarred muzzle in the firelight turned toward him for a moment, then back to the circle. He moved on.

Near the largest fire, where representatives from all races had gathered to share food, Kael sat in conversation with an elven warrior. Stric settled at the fire's edge where Cearan sat alone, the older magician's eyes on the embers, the light shifting in them as the coals settled. Stric sat beside him without speaking.

"I can feel the change in you," Cearan said, his voice shaped for Stric's ears alone. "The magic you touched has left its mark."

Stric nodded. His fingers flexed; small sparks drifted between them, residual and faint. The magical currents ran through everything now: the trees, the earth, the stones beneath his boots. All of it humming, where before it had been silent. A breath he had not known he was holding, finally drawn.

Cearan poked the fire with a stick, sending sparks spiralling into the lightening sky.

Stric sat with Cearan as the fire burned lower until the sky above the canopy had shifted from black to the deep blue that preceded grey. Then he rose, made his way back to where Teela slept, and lay down beside her. She stirred without waking, her fingers lacing through his.

He closed his eyes, and for a little while, sleep came.

The camp moved to readiness before full light; scouts ahead, craftspeople at the equipment, healers on their rounds. Stric stood at the base of the great oak, Teela beside him, watching the alliance prepare.

Above them, on a platform, two figures looked out over the same movement: Dreese, and beside him, Aelith. The early light caught the white-gold of her hair and the two marks on the left side of her face. The scar along her jawline, healed to a reddened thread from the ambush she had fled, and the newer wound running from temple to jaw, still raw from the previous day's fighting, two lines crossing each other like a signature the battle had left. She stood with a warrior's economy, each small shift of weight deliberate, nothing wasted.

Dreese's voice carried down. "A short time ago, those men had never been in the same place."

Below them, a werewolf and a human soldier carried a water barrel together. The conversation between them indistinct but audible in tone. A vampyre mage sat cross-legged beside a human soldier, both studying the same tactical map. Three elven healers moved between human and werewolf wounded with equal attention, pausing for neither. They moved with each other.

The barrel reached its destination; the werewolf set down his end, the human nodded once, and they separated without ceremony.

"We march within the hour." Dreese's command carried to every corner of the camp. "Talnaress will not wait for us."

Below, the camp shifted from rest to readiness without noise, without grumbling, the smooth movement of an army.

The weight of what was won and what was coming settled across Stric's shoulders.

Chapter 23

Return to Talnaress

By mid-morning, the army stood assembled beneath the ancient trees. Stric moved into the column. The surrounding faces all told the same story. Split lips. Bruised cheeks. Bandaged forearms. The thousand small marks that survival leaves on a body.

"We march to reclaim Talnaress from the usurper's grasp." Around him, hands tightened on hilts and bows. Eyes fixed on the road south. "I grew up knowing the city as a story. Other people's memories. Other people's grief." His voice did not waver. "Today, we start our journey back, and we take the story with us. We do not leave until it belongs to them again."

Cheers tangled with werewolf howls that rang off tree trunks. Fairy wings beat the air until the wind touched every face. Vampyre wingcleavers clashed.

The march began.

The first reinforcements arrived near the end of the day.

Werewolves emerged from fern-shadow and ridge-line mist as golden light filtered through the trees. Distant packs who had heard Whhrll's call and pushed hard to answer it. They had missed the battle by a day.

"Pack-leaders bring honour-scent!" Whhrll's ears stood forward, tail carried high. "We crushed the dead-things that walk. Together we crush what darkness-bringer sends next!"

The newcomers folded into formation with the ease of pack memory that reached back for generations. Some raced ahead on paws that left no mark on the leaf-litter, threading communication lines through the forest between groups spread too far for a voice to carry.

Elar's scouts moved ahead of them all, mapping the villages and roads that lay between the column and Talnaress, their reports on supplies and safe approach routes arriving at the column's head in quiet words passed hand to hand

---

Dawn came as a smear of grey behind the same black tree-shapes, again and again, until the accumulated weight of them pressed down on boot soles and shoulders. Light arrived late through the canopy and left early. Mist in the hollows before dawn. The same wet-bark smell in every breath, wildflowers gone to a dull sweetness once the nose stopped noticing. Ground that softened and firmed and softened again as the land rolled beneath them.

The canopy ended. Before them, the road opened. Flat country, pale with the early light, the sky suddenly vast after days of green shadow pressing close on every side.

An elven scout was already there, waiting at the forest's edge. Beside her, a small company of knights. Their armour bore scratches where hasty flight had scraped metal against stone. Their banners still carried the crown and oak symbol of Dreese's line before. The elf said nothing when they emerged. Simply turned and pointed toward the column's head.

The knights fell in behind Dreese. Their crown and oak banners snapped in the morning air. He went still for a breath, then squared his shoulders and kept walking.

These people had served a king who had a kind smile and a booming laugh. Cearan had said that once, at a dying fire, his voice careful with the weight of it. Had known his face. Had walked palace halls when the marble gleamed white instead of wearing soot like shame.

A tightness moved through Stric's chest. The road stretched ahead, pale and flat. His boots found the rhythm before his thoughts did.

That night, the fire had burned down to coals that pulsed red in the hollow between stones. Stric stood a few paces beyond the circle of light with his Powerstaff braced against his palm, drawing a narrow skein of power up from the earth. The first nights, the effort had left his hands shaking and his vision grainy at the edges. Tonight, the current rose cleaner. Quicker.

Green fireflies drifted low over the grass, blinking in time with his breath. Power moved through him in a thin, steady line instead of the stuttering bursts Eldoria had left behind. The ache in his bones answered, but it no longer tried to drag him to his knees.

"You're pushing too hard."

Teela's voice came from the dark as she stepped into the firelight, her arms folded, cloak loose around her shoulders. The shimmer along the staff's length had changed since she'd last seen him practice. It was steadier, brighter.

"This is lighter than what I'll need in Talnaress," he said. "If it breaks me now, it'll kill me there."

Her jaw worked once. "Seven days ago, you could barely stand without me under your arm." She closed the distance until she could have taken the staff from his hand. She didn't. "You're drawing more now than you did before the forest."

Power hummed against his skin. "Bridge-magic wants connection," he said. "Maybe that means it finds its way back faster when it has something to come back for."

Her hand settled briefly on his forearm, where muscle met bone. Firm. Assessing. "Then don't waste it falling over in a practice ring," she said. "You'll need all of it when we face Barok."

Wheel ruts cut deep into the mud at the village road's edge. The only sign of the small garrison that had left nothing but the people it had never considered worth taking.

The villagers stood in doorways with the careful stillness of those who had learned that armies, whatever banner they carried, meant cost.

Nobody cheered. Nobody ran. An elderly woman near the well held a child against her hip and watched the column pass with eyes that had forgotten how to read a face that posed no threat. She did not move until Dreese passed. Then something shifted in her spine, fractional, involuntary, as though a posture her body had carried for twenty years had briefly remembered an older instruction.

By the time the column cleared the village, three men had fallen in at its tail.

Boot leather had found every blister, pack straps had pressed their shapes into shoulders, and at the end of each day, the column had grown. Magicians who had kept their abilities buried for twenty years and now emerged, Powerstaffs drawn from hidden places, hands uncertain of the grip. Human farmers whose calloused hands remembered different work but gripped weapons, knuckles pale against unfamiliar wood. Surviving soldiers whose joints complained but whose knowledge of formation tactics remained sharp. They folded into the column the way the others had. Without ceremony. As though the road had always expected them.

The third week's cold found every gap in his cloak. Stric sat on a low rock at the edge of camp while the sky thought about light and then changed its mind, leaving the world in that thin grey. Frost rimed the grass.

His Powerstaff lay across his knees. A thread of magic ran its length, testing. The current answered with a strength that hadn't been there even a few days before. No stutter. No drag. Just a steady, rising pressure that asked to be shaped.

"When I was your age, I'd have called that impossible."

Cearan lowered himself onto the next rock with the weary care of a man whose joints had opinions. His own staff leaned against his shoulder, crystal dim but awake. Lines of fatigue cut deep around his eyes.

"You've been watching," Stric said.

"Since Eldoria," Cearan's gaze stayed on the faint glow along Stric's staff. "After what you did there, you should still be half-dead. Most magicians who burn that hot never make it back at all. The rest crawl." A slow breath steamed in front of him. "You're not crawling."

The earth's pulse moved up through Stric's boots, through bone. "Talnar said bridge-magic changed how the Guild's rules apply to me."

"Talnar's spent eight centuries cataloguing what's possible," Cearan said. "You're already off his shelves." His mouth twitched. Not quite a smile. "Whatever you've become, it's recovering faster than anything I've seen."

Stric's grip tightened, then eased. "Does that make you feel better about what I'm walking into?"

Cearan's fingers brushed the carved grooves of his own staff. "No," he said. "But it makes it harder to bet against you."

They crossed a valley where mist pooled in the hollows and made every breath taste of moss and old water. Climbed a highland where wind scoured exposed rock and the old fortifications stood as ragged stumps, stones split as though something had forced its way through them from beneath. On the far side, the trees opened.

Pine became oak, oak became birch, then fields and low hedgerows, and the mixed woods of Talnaress's outer territories, spreading ahead of them into the distance.

The word of their victory moved faster than they did.

By the time the column reached the larger settlements, people were already at the road's edge. Bread wrapped in cloth. Water skins. A farmer who pressed a bundle of dried meat into the nearest soldier's hands and stepped back before thanks could reach him, as though receiving gratitude was a thing he had lost the practice of.

Not everyone came out. Some windows remained shuttered. Twenty years of Barok's rule had taught people what hope cost, and not all of them were willing to pay it again. But by the end of the day, the column was longer than it had been at dawn. Farmers who had never held a weapon. People who had something to recover and had decided today was the day to begin.

With each passing day, the alliance grew. It changed.

An elven archer crouched beside a werewolf scout at the column's edge, neither speaking. The werewolf's nose dropped toward the grass. One bent stem. A displaced pebble. A scent-mark that no human nose would find. The elf's gaze followed the same line, reading what the eyes could interpret once the nose had pointed the way. A slow nod passed between them.

Werewolf patience, earned by inches. Fairy and vampyre, trading the language of life and death.

They camped on high ground. Talnaress lay a day's march ahead, distant lights against the dark, cold and sparse where a city that size should have blazed. The same silver light that had seen them leave Eldoria now found them here, the army vast beneath it. Five races converging on the same point on the horizon, moonbeams catching on steel and crystal and bared fangs.

The following day, as the sun descended behind them. The coalition crested the hill. Below, Talnaress lay open.

Where the Guild's Council Hall had once risen with proud towers, only blackened foundations remained. Ash and broken stones. Two decades of weeds claiming what fire had taken. Towers listing where foundations had crumbled. Gates hanging from broken hinges.

Stric and Teela stopped. Darkness pooled in courtyards where lanterns should have cast a welcoming glow. Shadows moved beneath collapsed archways, slow and purposeful where nothing living walked. At the city's perimeter, golems. Massive sentinels, still at this distance. Behind them, the undead stood in ranks. The smell of them drifted on the breeze. Rot and old iron and something beneath both, sweet in a way that had nothing to do with sweetness.

His Powerstaff hummed beneath his palm. The current that answered was nothing the earth had sent. Something pushed back. Something that didn't want to be drawn.

Inside Stric's pocket, Talnar flickered. He did not open it.

Teela came to stand beside him. Neither of them spoke. The city sat there and let itself be looked at. Beside him, Teela was still.

Dawn would bring battle.

Warriors of different races stood shoulder to shoulder, moonlight bleaching steel and crystal to the same white. Armour rustled. Quiet conversations moved between cooking fires, whose smoke rose straight in the still air. Cold found the gaps between the armour plates. Every word spoken. Every weapon checked. Every prayer whispered to gods both familiar and foreign.

Stric found Dreese at the fire nearest the command post, belt unbuckled, working the leather where four weeks of marching had rubbed his hip raw. Fingers found the pommel. Gripped. Released. Gripped again.

"I keep thinking about who we might lose tomorrow." Dreese glanced sideways at Teela. "Not just as soldiers. As people. Names I know."

Teela turned. Green eyes caught the firelight. "Then lead them well enough that fewer names are lost." Her voice was low and level. No room in it for argument.

Dreese's chest expanded. The fear would be there at dawn. He let the breath out slowly.

He buckled his belt. Straightened. "Bring the map."

Kael had it unrolled before Dreese had crossed to the flat ground beside the fire. The commanders gathered without being summoned.

Aelith emerged from the circle's edge, silver hair catching moonlight. The two scars crossed her face as they always did now. Her finger found the choke-points on the map without hesitation, the places where streets narrowed between buildings, and pressed down.

"Here and here, we hold these. We slow his reinforcements."

Kael's eyes followed Aelith's marks. A single nod. "She's right, unless they've changed."

Cearan's finger covered the paths. "Traps. Every street you'd expect them, expect more." His gaze turned toward the fire.

"Our mages will attempt to counter them." Thrakmar stepped into the firelight. Where he stepped, the warmth pulled back. Silver hair. Violet eyes that held centuries of dark knowledge behind them. He did not look at Cearan when he spoke. He looked at the map, and his finger came to rest on the hilltop east of the market district. Didn't tap. Just rested. "The odds disfavour this." Each word was placed with the precision of a man who had never found it necessary to repeat himself. "I want that acknowledged before I commit my people."

Silence. One beat. Two.

"Acknowledged," Dreese said.

"We will forge ahead." Thrakmar's finger lifted from the map. "Our mages join with yours. We target the Spellcasters. Draw their eyes upward and away from what moves beneath."

Whhrll had been still since the planning began, which for Whhrll meant the ears had not stopped moving and the weight had shifted forward onto the balls of his feet. Now he pressed closer. "While magic-makers pull their eyes skyward." A low sound in his chest that wasn't quite a growl. "Pack-hunters take the spell-weavers." He looked at Aelith. "Pack runs better when it chooses its prey."

Aelith didn't look up from the map. "Choose wisely."

"Twill." Stric turned. "The golems."

Twill's delicate features were level. She had not spoken since the planning began. Gold light pulsed from her wings in a measured rhythm. Then her wings slowed. "We will know them," she said.

Dreese studied the map. His hand had stopped on the pommel of his sword. "A conventional assault alone won't break his defences," he said. "Magic as powerful as his demands a magical response."

Stric's hand found the edge of the map. Inked walls. Streets that would soon be full of steel and fire. Beneath it all, the tunnel route they had agreed on at Eldoria, a line through stone that belonged to him alone.

"The walls stay yours," his finger rested on the palace mark. "I enter here. While our army holds his attention from the outside."

Teela's eyes found his across the map and stayed there a moment longer than the plan required. Her hand had closed tight around her sword hilt. Then she let it open and looked back at the map.

"Barok has had twenty years to ward what we ran through." Cearan's gaze didn't leave the map. "He'll know those passages exist. He may not know the branch. But he'll know the route we used."

Silence held for several heartbeats. The same passages that had carried Dreese out as an infant might yet return him as a king.

"Then I'll be careful." Stric straightened. "But this is our only path."

Nods moved through the gathered commanders. Firelight caught every jaw set tight. Old scars on every face in the circle.

The map. The firelight. These faces.

Dreese looked at the route Stric's finger had traced. "Same way out," he said. "Different direction."

They dispersed. Each carried what the morning would ask of them. The fires burned low.

Stric stayed by the map after the others stepped back, the coals painting the parchment in dull red. His gaze followed the dark line that ran beneath the palace. The hill fell away in that direction, down to the city he would enter from below. His hand tightened once on the Powerstaff's grip, then eased. That was for tomorrow. Tonight, there was still firelight, and Teela, and the thin edge of quiet they might not have again.

Teela's sword hand had been opening and closing since before the first light crested the hills in shades of amber and cold grey.

The allied forces assembled before the broken city of Talnaress. No cheering. Weapons already in hand. Mouths shut. Eyes on the gates.

Teela stood at Dreese's left shoulder. Kael at his right. Stric beside her, close enough that she could track the steadiness of his breathing without looking at him.

"People of Veltak," Dreese's voice wavered on the first syllable. Each word after it came stronger. "We walked past many doors that stayed shut on the way here. People who learned what hope costs. I don't blame them." He let that sit. "But you're here. You chose this ground. Each one of you knows what that cost was. We have chosen to stay together. This will make the difference."

He let the silence stretch.

"Talnaress waits. Let's return home."

Weapons struck shields in rhythmic thunder. Werewolf howls erupted from transformed throats. Wings beat the air until the wind touched every face. The sound built on itself. It hit Teela in the sternum, came up through her boot soles, leaving no room for anything else.

Teela did not look toward the city. Her gaze was set on Stric.

His jaw was set. His hand rested against the Powerstaff. Relaxed in a way that meant the decision was already behind him.

He turned and met her eyes.

His face softened. The tightness left his jaw, and the corner of his mouth moved the small way it did when there was no one else watching.

His fingers brushed hers, a single pass, and released.

Stric nodded. She returned it. The exchange took only a breath. No words. The plan had not changed.

Then he was gone, and Teela turned to the walls.

"On me." The fairy at her own shoulder carried it outward before the words had fully left her mouth.

The ground gave them their first warning.

A rhythm pressed up through boot soles before the golems arrived at the gates. Birds that had been silent since dawn had gone from every rooftop and ledge. Shadows shifted in the archways where nothing moved in the ordinary way.

Then the gates opened.

Twice a man's height. Arms like fallen trees. Eyes burning with captured light that had once belonged to someone. They crossed the open ground at a pace that suggested patience rather than urgency. The wailing of the spirits inside pressed up through the cobblestones, into the soles of Teela's feet, and through her bones, before it reached her ears.

She drove forward. Her sword came up, and she was in the vanguard before the golems had crossed half the distance.

"Find the cracks!" Her blade rang off stone and threw sparks across the cobbles. "Where spirit meets stone, that's where they will break!"

The Allied lines engaged.

Thrakul signalled without speaking; the old wounds along his side were still visible. His warriors moved through the chaos in the fluid way of people who had spent centuries reading darkness rather than light. Wingcleavers found the undead soldiers pressing in behind the golems. Those shuffling forms with rusted blades and the terrible patience of the already-dead. Dismantled them with clean, deliberate precision.

Across the field, Twill crouched where the old city wall met the cobblestones and pressed her palm flat to the stone. Still for two full breaths. Then she rose. The fairies stationed at each commander's shoulder shifted as a single thought. Those on the left flank broke toward the archway before the golems there had cleared it. Crystals left fairy hands and found the seams between corrupted stone and the spirits trapped within, collective and precise. Golems shuddered, went still, and collapsed. The spirits inside had been released for the moment.

More lumbered through to replace them, the line flexing under the weight and then closing again, shields and blades and bodies knitting tight where the gaps tried to open.

"Hold the line." The fairy carried the order, and the line held.

The battle turned darker before it turned at all.

Civilians emerged from doorways and alleys. Faces empty. Eyes present but absent behind them. They moved alongside Barok's forces the way a current carries debris. No direction chosen. Simply going where the water went.

Its wrongness landed before the tactical problem did. These were Talnaress's people. Twenty years of occupation had taken something from them that didn't show until their bodies moved. The wrong looseness of people whose will had been lifted out.

"Stop!" The fairy carried it outward in the same breath, and the order arrived everywhere at once. "They're not our enemies. They're under his control."

It shifted what she needed it to shift. Blades pulled back. The work became harder and slower: restraint rather than force, containing rather than killing. Two fronts at once. One against the golems and undead pressing forward, one against every instinct trained into her that said to strike at what was threatening her.

Each restrained blow left an opening she couldn't close. She paid for it. While making sure the surrounding soldiers paid it too.

The line held its principles and bled for them.

On the hilltop east of the city, magic arced downward in twin columns. Cearan's mages on the left, Thrakmar's vampyres on the right, working in tandem. Above the market district, light tore the air. Barok's Spellcasters' formation buckled and staggered back, a gap opening before they could reform.

Whhrll hit the gap before it could close.

"Pack-brothers follow."

They came out of the foliage on the lower hillside in a wave that had been absolutely still two breaths before. Forms blurring between shapes. Claws and speed and the deep sound of a pack that had already decided the outcome. They drove into the distracted Spellcasters with the precision of generations of practice.

Aelith's archers worked the edges, arrows finding Spellcasters without finding werewolves, the two movements fitting together the way they had drilled it until the seams disappeared. The scars along Aelith's jaw caught the light as she moved. She directed her archers without raising her voice. A hand signal here. A tilt of the chin there.

Barok's left flank broke apart.

"Forward!" The fairy carried it across the field, and the allied forces advanced. Cobblestones under boots. Magic crackling above the market district. The city receiving them, step by contested step.

The second wave of golems arrived.

These moved differently. Smaller, faster, and with the cold intelligence of something that had observed the first wave fail and adjusted. They targeted the fairies directly. Rocks and other objects thrown with crushing force tracked the smaller fighters.

Most of the rocks Twill's people knew before they arrived. The grove-mind read the arc and the intent, and bodies shifted before the stone reached them.

One stone arrived before the warning did. The fairy hit the ground. The pain of those the grove-mind couldn't reach fast enough moved through all at once before they had finished falling. A moment of arrested motion, then continuous. Wings that faltered and beat again. Hands that reset the grip before the next stone came.

"Fall back to secondary positions!" Kael's voice, from somewhere behind the reformed centre. His shield arm had the careful stillness of a limb being managed rather than rested. "Regroup!"

The line pulled back deliberately, opening space, reforming further in. Aelith's elves covered the withdrawal, arrows buying the seconds it required.

Teela stood in the reformed line. They had taken the outer streets, paid for every stolen yard in bodies and broken stone. The fairies had collapsed golem after golem throughout the morning; werewolves had torn through the Spellcasters' lines. The undead infantry had taken losses they could not feel. They did not slow. All of that, and still the weight pressed back.

And now there were more golems, Spellcasters, and undead emerging from the palace district than there had been at dawn.

A golem broke through the line before she had finished assessing. It scattered soldiers the way a boot scatters leaves. A fairy's crystal struck its surface. More golems pushed through behind it. Three werewolves went down before elven arrows found their mark amongst the Spellcasters. The undead continued their march through it all.

"Their magic is too strong." Dreese, beside Kael, his voice stripped of everything but the fact of it. "We can't break through with force alone."

From the hilltop, Cearan's shout carried the strain of hours. "We can't keep this up much longer!"

The ground past the outer market was theirs, paid for in what lay around her. Elven arrow paths crossed where the werewolf lines had driven through, the pattern they'd built together written in the dirt. Around her, no one met anyone else's eyes.

It would not be enough.

"Hold," Dreese's voice, level. Nothing in it but the word and what it required. "Maintain pressure."

The lines held.

Her gaze slid back toward the warehouse district.

The battle moved around her. Blade up. Move. Reset. Following the rhythm the body learns, so the mind does not have to think.

Somewhere behind her, past the outer streets where the smoke thinned, Stric would be underground. Below the city's skin, in the dark with whatever waited between him and the throne room.

"Left flank, hold your position." Her order was carried outward before she had closed her mouth.

The left flank was holding. The right was not.

Teela reset her grip. Set her feet.

The ground moved.

Something deeper. A tremor that climbed through cobblestone and boot-sole and bone before it reached the surface, as though whatever caused it had begun below.

Across the market district, a building's upper storey folded inward. The crash arrived a breath after the fall, the way sound always ran late when distance was involved.

Structural damage from the battle. A consequence of the violence moving through streets built for commerce, not war.

That was what it was.

The approaching line filled her vision.

Chapter 24

Darkness Falls

The tunnel swallowed Stric whole.

Darkness pressed against the Powerstaff's dim glow from every side, damp stone close enough to graze both shoulders. Each footfall carried him deeper into the palace's belly, walls holding stories carved in bedrock, centuries of them, running beneath Stric's fingers as he moved.

The air thickened as he advanced, heavy with moisture and the metallic tang of old magic. His training at the Guild had prepared him for theoretical challenges and scholarly pursuits conducted in lamp-lit libraries, where danger came from difficult translations rather than from death. The tunnel curved ahead, swallowing the glow of his staff, patient as only stone could be.

He reached the junction, where a shimmer of wrongness halted him. Barok's first trap hung before him: translucent threads woven across the passage in intricate, lethal geometry. Each strand pulsed, the air between them thin and cold as drawn wire, waiting for careless flesh to brush against its structure. Stric's chest tightened, breath catching as he traced the spell's architecture. One mistake could be his last.

Talnar shifted against his chest.

Third thread from the left, the word hurried across the page. That is where the weaving begins. Barok studied under Master Erevan; Erevan always anchored from the left.

Stric's fingers moved through the air, drawing counter-runes with the precision his masters had drilled into him through endless repetition. Sweat gathered at his temples and rolled past his eyes. The trap resisted, its magic coiled tight, but he found its heart and twisted. The ward flickered, bursting apart in a shower of light that dissolved like frost under a summer sun. His shoulders dropped, breath releasing in a rush. The remnants crackled behind him as he slipped through.

The tunnel kept turning. Stone pressed in on both sides, soaking through his sleeves until the seams lay dark and cold against his skin, and the Powerstaff's glow had risen and thinned and risen again across walls that never widened.

The second ward had come apart in a spit of cold sparks that left the smell of scorched iron in the air.

The third had taken longer. Long enough for his forearm to shake around the staff, for sweat to track down his spine despite the chill. Its pattern demanded stillness. A steady thread of power held in place while grit sifted from the ceiling onto his hair and lashes. It had been worked into the mortar itself, stubborn as old bone, and it had yielded by inches rather than all at once.

The air had changed with every stretch of ground. Sewer-stink giving way to wet mineral cold. Wet mineral cold giving way to rot. Sweet now. Closer. His knees no longer carried the clean spring they had when he entered from the warehouse district. The cold had sunk deeper, the kind that came only when stone had had hours to leach the warmth from a body.

The battle above had gone on without him all this time, grinding forward while he fought stone, wards, and the dark. Teela's face flashed across his mind. Dreese. Kael. Aelith. His jaw locked until his muscles burned, a coin-sharp film of the same old magic coating his tongue. He kept moving.

Then the corridor gave him up.

He passed beneath a servant's arch no broader than a cellar door and stepped into the palace. Once, gilded accents were now dulled to the colour of old ash. Gold clung in scabs to the stone, flaking away in curls like dead skin. Marble floors lay cracked beneath a skin of grime and old stains. Dust-covered tapestries sagged in strips, their woven kings and councils half-eaten by mould. The palace had not merely rotted. Stone faces in the carving had slumped, mouths and eyes dragged down as if something heavy pressed on them from above. Seams along the walls rose and fell in a slow, wrong rhythm, as though the building itself were breathing under a hand it could not throw off. Rot hung thicker in the air here, fouler than in the tunnel. Feeding.

Movement ahead pinned him against the wall. Figures emerged from the shadows. Servants moving with vacant expressions, eyes registering nothing, feet carrying them through routines their bodies remembered but their minds no longer commanded. His throat constricted. These were victims, not enemies. People whose only crime had been serving in the wrong palace when evil came calling.

His Powerstaff warmed in his grip as he channelled a subtle enchantment, letting it spread outward like a breath through tall grass. The magic brushed them gently, a murmur in their enslaved minds, and they swayed before settling back into hollow obedience, their paths altered just enough for him to pass unseen. His stride slowed without intent. How many more had Barok stolen? How many souls had he trapped in their own flesh?

The corridors had been built for servants to move invisibly. Narrow with low ceilings. Every arch calibrated to keep those who worked here beneath notice, out of sight of the grandeur they maintained. Barok had needed to change none of that. He had only needed to fill them. The portraits lining the upper passage watched with the fixed attention of those who had seen too much and been unable to look away. In every frame, the shoulders dropped, and the gaze went level. Too level. Aimed at nothing, as though looking away from something just outside the canvas's edge. These halls had known what was coming long before it arrived.

Talnar's charcoal drawings of this place in its glory lived beside the ruin. Light pouring through stained glass to paint the floors in colour, laughter filling these halls during festivals, the King and Queen walking these very stones with their infant son. All of it ground beneath Barok's heel.

A shape lurched into his path, broad as a doorway. Stone shoulders. Sand packed into the seams. Fragments of rusted armour hung half-swallowed in its bulk, as though the palace had tried to dress the thing in what it had once devoured. Light burned deep behind cracks in its head. A trapped soul, pushing against the stone. The air around it carried dust, rot, and a warm, overripe tang that had no place. Its arm rose. A blade jutted from one fist, fused there, metal swallowed by rock.

Stric raised his Powerstaff, magic gathering at the crystal tip. Violence would draw more attention, more golems, more enslaved servants forced to die for a master they had not chosen. His incantation came as breath rather than command, magic sliding through the seams of the construct, searching the spirit bound inside. The golem shuddered, and a sigh escaped from the trapped spirit. Stone grated on stone. Its raised arm sagged by inches, then more, until he guided its bulk toward a shadowed alcove and left it there, stilled but not broken, the fused blade resting against the floor.

Talnar fluttered in his pocket again, demanding his attention.

Efficient, Talnar wrote. *And quieter than your usual approach. You have improved.*

"Don't sound so surprised."

I sound exactly as surprised as the situation warrants. The throne room is just around that corner.

Talnar's pages turned. Not urgently. Slowly, deliberately.

Then they stopped. Words appeared large and rushed. *He is in there. What is it that is in there. I cannot name. Go carefully, young Stric.*

Talnar fell silent as Stric returned the tome to his inner pocket.

The throne room doors rose before him, massive and carved with runes that hurt to perceive. They pulsed with the cold of absence. A void where warmth should live, where light should fall. Stric's pulse beat hard in his throat. He drew a breath, another.

Beyond the doors, something vast and lightless waited.

His hand pressed against the leather binding through his shirt. The warmth that was always present, that familiar weight against his ribs that had been with him since the forest outside the timesling, flowed into his palm.

He closed his eyes. Beneath his sternum, where the three traditions had learned to sit together, the vampyre cold rose first. Then the fairy hum, faint as roots in stone. His own power followed. The thing Thrakmar and Twill had spent weeks teaching his body to carry.

He channelled his newfound power through the Powerstaff, energy igniting in its depths before surging toward the intricate wards guarding the doorway. The air cracked, a bone-deep sound that ran through stone and chest alike. His magic struck the ward hard enough to jar bone and staff alike, and the ward burst inward, dissolving at the edges as the cold air rushed through. The doors swung wide.

Cold came through first. The kind that pressed against the chest and made the lungs work harder, a chill with no source and no bottom to it. Then the smell. Sweet underneath, overripe, coating the back of his throat before he had taken a full breath. The throne room had been built for spectacle. High-vaulted, crystal-lit, loud with the echo of a living court. Every trace of that was gone. Shadows moved across walls that should have blazed with tapestries and light. No fire in the grate. No shuffle of feet, no murmured counsel. A silence so complete it pressed against his ears.

And there, seated upon a throne that defied natural law, waited the thing that had once been Barok Tana.

Shadows churned beneath Barok's weight, forms that reached and grasped with movements born of desperate hunger. Perhaps fragments of souls too broken to escape. They pulsed in rhythm with the crimson light bleeding from the Powerstaff clutched in grey-veined hands.

The corrupted crystal atop its Powerstaff blazed. Below it, the crimson Master Deathseed Crystal absorbed darkness like a hungry mouth, the two working together in a perverted harmony.

The creature on the throne wore Barok Tana's face like an ill-fitting mask. Skin the colour of ash stretched over bones that shifted beneath the surface, as if the flesh had forgotten its relationship with the skeleton it clothed. Dark veins mapped corruption through tissue that failed to move with the inhalation beneath it, each thread pulsing with a sickly light, its pulse slow and irregular against the dark. Whatever human mask he had worn for the world, he had set it aside for this moment.

His eyes held the worst wrongness. Human at first glance, the right shape and proper placement. Behind them lived nothing. A void wearing the memory of what eyes should hold. Their surface reflected without registering. When those eyes fixed on Stric, the air curdled.

"So you have reached me at last." The voice scraped along the throne room walls like grinding stones, but underneath it, other tones bled through. Like multiple voices speaking through one throat that had forgotten how human speech should sound. "Did you truly think you would not be seen?"

Stric's grip locked on the Powerstaff, knuckles driving against the wood. Oil catching flame in his chest, sudden and airless. His feet carried him forward. "You've perverted everything you once stood for. You were a monster then, and now you are just an abomination."

The shape his face made, an approximation of a smile, held the mechanical performance of an expression it had once observed, the eyes uninvolved in what the mouth was doing. "Monster? Abomination?" The words emerged without offence. "Empty sounds." His gaze did not shift. "You are only a human magician." A second voice bled through beneath the first, lower, almost sorrowful, gone before it had fully arrived. "I am more than you can endure."

The Powerstaff in those corrupted hands surged with a dark energy, the Master Deathseed Crystal blazing brighter as Barok rose from his throne. His movements defied proper anatomy. The joints bent at angles a human body could not allow. The spine curving at the midpoint past any angle living vertebrae could hold, and holding it without tremor.

With a gesture that cost him nothing, Barok unleashed a devastating wave of black energy. It rushed toward Stric like a tidal surge of shadow, cold and mechanical, the pace of something that had already decided the outcome.

Stric raised his Powerstaff and drove every ounce of energy he possessed into a defensive counter. Magic met darkness. The impact snapped through bone and staff alike, a single hard crack that ran from crystal to shoulder. Light and shadow crashed together between them, hair lifting as the air turned thin and sharp. The throne room shook with the force of it.

Stric stood in the heart of Talnaress, the throne room pressing down under Barok's monstrous rule. Darkness had spread into every corner like an infection through healthy tissue, embedding itself in stone and emitting a chill that pierced flesh and marrow alike.

The thing observing him across the ruined chamber stood with its weight forward, the void gaze fixed. Its shape recalled Barok Tana the way a corpse recalls the person it once was. Where living flesh moved with the unconscious grace of muscle and tendon, this moved with deliberate calculation. The Master Deathseed Crystal throbbed atop its Powerstaff like a grotesque heartbeat, feeding on the death and blood permeating the city beyond these walls.

"You think yourself a hero. A hero. A hero." The third iteration arrived in a different register entirely, too high, not his, before the grinding control came back down over it. "Your blood is already on this floor."

Stric held his Powerstaff before him and met that empty gaze across the throne room's ruins. "You underestimated us. We will prove you wrong again."

White-blue energy surged from his crystal, a lance of hard light driving toward Barok.

The throne room broke into chaos as his strike hit. Shadows ripped away from the walls, flinching from the burst of light.

Stric's assault sliced through them, forcing the creature back a step toward its churning throne. The mechanical sound it had been making, dry and hollow. A rhythm that clicked at the back of the throat, cut off as it raised its Powerstaff to counter.

"You cling to your hope. It will change nothing!" Control strained now in that grinding voice. Corrupted red-black magic surged forth, a furious current driving against Stric's resolve. Barok's power oozed decay, pressing cold through the Powerstaff into Stric's hands, threatening to consume everything it touched. Stric's magic held bright and fierce, the blue-white light driving the shadows back across the walls, but his feet slid backward across cracked marble as the force built.

The impact reverberated through the palace. The few remaining stained-glass windows exploded outward in a spray of coloured fragments. The creature pressed further into the Master Deathseed Crystal, drawing power from the turmoil beyond these walls. The artefact throbbed with ravenous energy, growing stronger with each death that fed its hunger.

"Do you feel that?" The grey face attempted triumph, the expression cracking and reforming. "Your rebellion crumbles. The more of my constructs they defeat, the more lives they lose, the stronger I grow." Magic lashed out in a narrow red-black lance, driving Stric to his limits.

The force lifted him off his feet.

Cold marble met him hard, pain knifing through his body, breath torn out in a ragged gasp. The force of it pressed through his bones. Too strong. Too far beyond anything human. Blood warmed his lips. Muscles screamed as he pushed up and rose to face the monster before him.

The creature's head tilted. Its grip on the Powerstaff adjusted, its fingers repositioning slowly and precisely.

Blue-white light burst from his Powerstaff. Beyond the creature. Past this moment. Everyone who had marched to Talnaress pressed against him. Teela, Dreese, Whhrll, the fairies, all of them.

Marble cracked underfoot. Dust rained from above in thin, continuous falls, as though the ceiling were trying to decide whether to hold.

He pressed forward. Arc after arc. Each exchange drove fresh fractures through the floor. Outward from every point of contact. Like ice giving way underfoot.

The thing that was Barok turned its wrist. Another wave of power surged out, wide and cold and patient, a force that did not need to hurry because it had already decided the outcome.

Stric's feet held. Barely.

The ground beneath them fractured from the strain. That hollow sound cut through the air again. "I will see your hope fade." The words came out layered, each syllable carrying more than one voice, scraping against the throne room walls.

Stric refused to stop. His magic lanced toward Barok in arc after arc, seeking weakness in the armour of shadows. Each attempt turned aside, the Master Deathseed Crystal blazing crimson-black, its light pressing hard and cold against his own. Yet a shift came. A flicker across the void like features, a fractional hesitation, the crystal's output stuttering for one pulse of Stric's heart.

Time stretched. The struggle, an eternity of blinding light and smothering darkness. Each breath tore at his lungs, the Deathseed Crystal's cold already moving past his knuckles, up the back of his hand. Teela, beyond these walls. Thrakmar. Whhrll. Twill. Kael. His grip steadied.

Stric's Powerstaff blazed against the cold weight driving in from the creature's crimson-black centre. His energy surged, and the room flooded with light so intense that his vision went white at the edges.

Each arc landed closer than the last. The creature's defences yielded inch by inch. Under pressure it had not anticipated. The approximation of triumph on that grey face slipped, replaced by a stiffening along the jaw, the crystal flaring in shorter, sharper pulses. It channelled the Master Deathseed Crystal once more, drawing everything it held in a desperate attempt to crush Stric's spirit.

Stric's Powerstaff shifted in his grip, brightening before he willed it. He was not fighting alone. He had never fought alone. Thrakmar's words returned. *Bridge-mages appear in times of greatest need, when barriers between peoples must be torn down.* He closed his eyes and reached into the very foundations of what he had become.

Vampyre blood magic rose first, silver radiance emerging from his crystal's depths, cutting clean through the throne room's purple light. It entered him cold, spreading from crystal to palm to wrist, settling into his joints like something ancient recognising where it belonged.

Twill's earth-song magic followed, deep green threads coiling around the silver like roots finding purchase. Warmth followed the cold, rising the way heat rises through stone that has had all day to gather it, up from his toes, through his shins and knees, settling finally in his chest. The stone floor beneath his feet pulsed in response, and his awareness ran outward along unseen lines through the palace's living things; even those held under corrupt control still carried sparks of their true selves within.

His own human magic rose to meet them both, the strength that had been with him since childhood. It wrapped silver and green together and held where they should have torn him apart. Where vampyre magic whispered of endings, carrying the long, cold weight of centuries, and fairy magic sang toward beginnings, reaching for the living green of every growing thing, his own human magic did neither. It held them. Steadied them against each other. Made them impossibly one.

"This cannot be!" the creature snarled, its form pulling back a half-step as the convergence strengthened. The very air around Stric changed.

Breath tore in and out, shallow and burning. Too much. His ribs had forgotten how to be wide enough. Sweat gathered across his forehead despite the throne room's chill. Magic pressed against the boundaries of what his mortal frame could endure. The trembling in his hands had stopped. Vrill's face. Ink-stained. Certain.

Against his chest, Talnar lay still and silent.

Those void-like eyes fixed on the Powerstaff. On the silver at its core. The green threaded through it. On Stric.

The thing facing Stric went still.

Words forced their way out of its throat, layers echoing over one another. "Vethra Tar."

The power had nowhere else to go. It jammed through him, white at the edges of his sight, every channel in his body pulled too wide. His teeth locked. Breath tore shallow through his throat. One more heartbeat. Maybe all he had.

Teela flashed through him. Her hand in his. Her mouth softening around promises made in the dark. Then the city beyond these walls. The dead feeding the crystal. The living paying for every breath.

Stric drove the Powerstaff forward and let its power go.

Light crossed the throne room in a single, hard note. It hit Barok full in the chest.

The defence came late. Too late. The Master Deathseed Crystal flared crimson-black and caught the strike with a scream that seemed to come from inside the stone, but the force still drove the creature back into the throne.

Shadows lashed outward.

Stric moved. He lunged.

As he crossed the space between them, the magical energy reached its absolute peak. The crystal sang in a single, pure note. The air itself changed with the power, and ancient stones in the throne room walls glowed in answer to the resonance.

Every choice that had brought him here pressed its weight against him. Battle pressed at him from outside, a pressure at the edge of breath and bone. Teela's voice rang in that pressure. The hopes of countless innocents sat on his shoulders like a weight he could not put down.

The magic had reached a crescendo that threatened to tear him apart from within. White swallowed the edges of the room. His knuckles had gone white on the staff. The crystal's heat had moved past his wrist to his elbow. The ringing in his ears had swallowed everything else. Instinct screamed for release before it destroyed him, but he held on for one more heartbeat, gathering every last fragment of force he possessed.

Stric swung his transformed Powerstaff in a direct strike. Two feet of air between his crystal and the creature's head. One. The crystal atop his staff burned with a light as fierce and new as a just-born star.

In a frantic attempt to counter the unexpected assault, the thing that had been Barok could only raise its Powerstaff. The Master Deathseed Crystal throbbed wildly, eager to defend its host. Then, for just a heartbeat, the crimson flickered. Pale gold beneath it. One heartbeat only, and then gone. The weapons clashed with a force that rocked the palace to its core.

Magic erupted from the impact point in a blazing surge, an outpouring of energy so intense it blinded both. The room filled with light and a scream from somewhere inside the stone, high and unbroken, driving into the base of his skull. The concussive force drove through his boots and into the stone beneath.

Everything slowed. Crystals' energies clashed for dominance, power grinding together in a single, shuddering point. The magic poured from his Powerstaff, ripping apart Barok's. Both corrupted crystals shattered, their dark energies collapsing under the force of his assault. The end of corruption's power dissolving in cascades of colour, he had no names for.

The explosion tore through the throne room, sparing nothing in its path. The blast lifted him off the ground. Spinning the world around him, crystal fragments and stone filling the air, heat driving through his robes.

He struck a pillar. The impact jarred him to his core. His body crumpled to the ground like a broken marionette. Every breath came in jagged agony. He lay there, vision contracting toward a crack in the stone directly before his face. Sound reached him through something thicker than air. The battlefield beyond these walls. Silence or battle, he could not tell.

The throne room lay in ruins, every surface marked by the violent release of power. The screaming stopped. All of it. Voices that had not been stilled in twenty years fell silent, a hush so complete it seemed to press against his ears. A void where darkness had been. It pulsed and trembled. The sweetness of decay that had hung in the chamber was gone.

Through the haze of pain, the thing that had been Barok Tana sprawled across its throne. It disintegrated. The absence of its dark artefacts tore through it with merciless efficiency, revealing what lay underneath. An emptiness animated by stolen power. A shell that should have stopped moving years ago but had not been permitted to rest.

The corruption that had sustained it for two decades unravelled like rotting cloth. Grey skin flaked away like ash, dark veins collapsing inward. Where flesh had been, only absence remained. The seven spirits trapped in the shattered crystal finally tore free, their escape ripping fragments of their prison with them as they fled toward whatever peace awaited them beyond.

"No!" The scream tore through the shattered chamber, multiple voices speaking at once. The thing's denial mingled with the spirits' cry of liberation. "I am..."

Dark energy coiled around the crumbling form before the words could finish, a vortex consuming everything it touched. What remained of Barok Tana flickered and faded, collapsing into nothingness.

A howling force of released power filled the throne room with a storm of destruction. The last moments were swallowed by it, leaving behind only empty robes and shattered fragments of a Powerstaff around the throne, which itself had dissolved, the shadows losing coherence without their master to sustain them.

As darkness claimed Stric's vision, Talnar stirred against his chest.

He pressed his hand to it. Fingers that had stopped obeying him, that fumbled and shook, found the cold leather binding through his shirt. He pulled at it. The weight of his own arm became too much.

The ceiling of the throne room swam, dust still falling through air that had forgotten how to be still. The floor had gone. His hands were somewhere distant, past the reach of anything he could send after them.

Then the warmth came back.

The book slipped from his fingers. Its pages falling open, blank and still.

Letters formed, slow, one at a time.

You did it, Grandmaster Stric.

The darkness took him.

Outside the palace, the shockwave hit Teela before she understood it, a pulse moving up through the soles of her boots, spreading across the battlefield like a stone dropped into still water. All at once. Golems halted mid-motion, their massive stone limbs suspended in one last act of violence before crumbling. She stood with the rest, sword arm still raised to a threat that no longer existed, as the constructs fell, rock and earth spilling uselessly to the ground. Undead soldiers dropped in waves, bones and bodies scattering like brittle autumn leaves.

The collapse came suddenly. A last grinding crash of stone across the field, then nothing. Enemy lines disintegrated in an instant, soldiers who had been under corrupt control dropping their weapons as the influence over them broke apart. Hands released their grips without deciding to. Men stopped in place.

"What's happening?" a voice rang out, the question cracking at its end.

Dreese's voice rose above the chaos. "They're free! Barok is defeated!" His sword gleamed in the morning light, held high.

The allied soldiers cheered, the sound ragged and unsteady, voices breaking open mid-cry. Howls erupted from the werewolves, while the drumming of fairy wings added rhythmic punctuation to the celebration. Enemy Spellcasters, their crystals gone dark in sequence, looked at one another before many dropped their staffs in surrender.

"Spare those who surrender! Show them the mercy they never showed us!" Dreese's words carried above the noise, and the line held.

A pale light moved in one of the upper windows, winding through a cloud of dust or smoke. Something that drifted upward through the cloud with a slowness that had nothing to do with the wind. There and then not there. She stared at the space where it had been.

Her sword hand would not unclench.

She stood. The cheering moved around her. Eyes already on the palace entrance, the cracked façade, the doors hanging wrong, that upper window still pulling at the edge of her attention, while the rest of the field erupted into relief. Kael's voice behind her, steady and practiced. "Tend to the wounded! We need to save those we can!" His hand moved once across a fallen Royal Guard's insignia as she passed him, a gesture she didn't stop to read.

She was already running.

The bodies of fallen elves, fairies, werewolves, vampyres, and soldiers lay scattered under the paling sky. She ran past them. Past the celebrating allies, past the surrendering Spellcasters, past all of it. The palace entrance swallowed the distance between them faster than her breathing could settle.

Rubble under her boots. Smoke in her throat. The smell of spent magic, of stone cracked open by something that had burned too hard and too fast. She went through the entrance without slowing, angling toward the part of the palace where that light had been.

"Stric!"

The corridor threw her voice back.

Each corner opened onto new wreckage. Dust rained from the ceiling. Marble split along cracks that hadn't existed this morning. A tapestry half fallen from the wall. She stepped over a scatter of stone that had been a golem and kept moving, one hand brushing the wall where the passage narrowed, the stone warm beneath her palm.

Her jaw ached. She'd been clenching it since the shockwave.

"Stric!" Louder. Harder. The word cost her more than she had accounted for.

Nothing came back.

The cold thing she'd been holding at the edge of her thoughts all morning pressed closer. She shoved it back the only way she knew. Another step, another corner, another length of ruined corridor crossed. She would not stop. Stopping meant considering. Considering meant the thing she refused to name.

"Please be alive." Under her breath.

The throne room doors stood wide open ahead of her.

She went through.

Stric lay amid the ruins, barely conscious but alive. She dropped to her knees beside him. Her hands found his face, his shoulders, checking for wounds with a touch that trembled. Dust streaked his skin. Blood at the corner of his mouth. His chest rose, shallow but steady.

"Stric." His name left her differently than she'd thrown it down the corridor.

His eyes cracked open, searching before they focused on her. A weak breath stirred dust against her cheek. One corner of his mouth twitched, almost a smile. "You found me," he managed, the words rasped more than spoken.

"Of course I did." Her jaw ached around the answer. Her fingers brushed the fallen book at his side, then returned to his shoulder. "You're not rid of me that easily."

She eased an arm under his shoulders, lifting just enough to get him out of the worst of the debris, his weight heavy and solid and blessedly there. Blood smeared across the edge of her breastplate;

she tightened her grip. The broken throne loomed behind them, its shadows gone without their master.

The world beyond the doorway went on shouting and cheering. Here, only the sound of his breathing and the soft fall of dust from a ceiling that still hadn't decided whether it would stay up.

Chapter 25

Dawn of Peace

Dust hung thick in the ruined throne room, coating everything in pale grey. Scattered stones. Scorched marble. The shattered remnants of what had been Barok Tana.

Stric was still breathing. That fact arrived slowly, like a word in a language he'd half forgotten. Teela's arm was under his shoulders. The floor was cold through his robe. Both were real.

Inside him, where power usually hummed and sparked, sat only a hollow silence. Depleted had a texture. Ache in the palms, the drag of reserves run empty. This had none of it.

He tried to speak. Nothing came. His tongue lay heavy in his mouth.

"Don't try to move." Her voice, close. She shifted her weight, easing him further upright against the cracked pillar, and the world tilted once and settled. "The battle's over. We won."

The Powerstaff lay on the floor beside him. He closed his fingers around it. The silver wood pressed its grooves into his palm. No pulse came back through them.

Through the gaping hole where the great windows had exploded outward, afternoon light moved across Talnaress. The city lay battered but standing. In the courtyard below, shapes moved among the fallen. Too far to make out. The silence up here sat heavy, nothing like the silence out there.

Out there, things were beginning again.

A groan of stone somewhere above. Dust sifted down, soft as breath, settling across his hands, his robe, the empty robes where Barok had sat. He reached inside himself again, searching for even a spark. Nothing answered. The exhaustion went beyond muscle and bone, beyond even the crushing weight of spent magic. The channels had burned out, leaving him hollow.

Teela hadn't moved from beside him.

The broken throne loomed behind them, its shadows now gone. The crystals ground to shards on the floor caught what light came in from the courtyard, a dull glitter in the dust. No warmth left in them. No voices trapped inside.

Seven of them. Seven names in stone and silence.

Thrakmar's face arrived in his mind, uninvited. What the vampyre mage would say when he understood what had happened here. What Lysara would say. He'd carried their grief into this room. He owed them the answer.

Talnar lay still against his ribs, where Teela had tucked the ancient tome. No flutter. No warmth.

The world beyond the doorway had begun cheering. Faint still, muffled by corridors and rubble, but building. The sound of people understanding, all at once, that it was over.

His chest rose. Shallow. Steady.

Teela's fingers tightened once on his shoulder, then eased. A confirmation, nothing more.

He was still there. So was she.

He tipped his head back against the pillar and closed his eyes. Rubble pressed beneath him, grit and broken marble, and somewhere in the wreckage the faint scent of scorched wood and something older, the stagnant cold of a darkness that had finally run out of room.

The cheering grew louder.

Footsteps echoed across the marble in the corridor beyond.

The prince. The king now. Appeared in the doorway, sword still drawn, flanked by Kael and Cearan. Blood spattered their armour.

"Seven hells." Kael's hand went to his sword hilt before the instinct had finished arriving, then stilled. His eyes moved across the room, taking in the scene. The broken throne and the empty robes. The Powerstaff fragments ground to pale dust across the floor.

Dreese crossed the room in three strides and dropped to one knee in front of him. His eyes moved across Stric's face, his hands, the Powerstaff. The king taking account of the cost.

"What did you do to yourself?"

Cearan was already beside him, boots crunching on debris. He studied Stric's face with the unhurried attention of a man used to reading damage.

"You wielded powerful magic." Quiet. Clinical. "The strain alone should have killed you."

"Feels like it did." The words scraped out of him.

A breath.

"We won, though."

Cearan's gaze moved to the Powerstaff. He reached out and closed his hand around it, steady and deliberate, and drew it from Stric's grip. Stric let it go. Harder than it should have been.

Between them, Teela and Kael got him upright. His legs had nothing left in them. Only their grip kept the floor where it was.

Outside, the courtyard had become a field hospital. Fairy healers moved between the fallen, their earth-song cool as water on burns, pressing palms to elven and human wounds alike without pause. Werewolves worked beside vampyre mages, holding bodies still while hands glowing silver drew infection from gashes too deep for bandaging. Elven warriors knelt at the stretchers of soldiers they had fought next to that morning, checking pulses with shaking hands. Dreese passed Cearan his sword and moved out into it, stopping at every face that turned upward. Nobody was left to stare at nothing alone.

Around the courtyard, the cheering had thinned. What remained was the quieter sound of people beginning to count.

Teela and Kael got Stric down onto a stretcher. His legs gave without argument. Cearan set the Powerstaff down beside him, close enough that the back of his hand rested against it. The contact steadied his breathing.

From across the courtyard, Thrakmar approached with the deliberate step of a man who had been waiting for the noise to settle. The battle's aftermath moved around him, and he moved through it without pausing until he reached Stric.

He crouched beside him for a moment without speaking. His violet eyes moved across Stric's face. Taking the full measure of a thing before naming it.

"You should know what happened." His voice was low. "When the crystal broke, we felt it. Every vampyre in this field. A pressure we had carried so long we stopped knowing it was there, and then it was gone." His jaw worked beneath the grey fur. "They passed in that moment. All seven. We felt them go."

Stric said nothing. There was nothing to say.

Thrakmar's claws pressed together at his chest, a gesture Stric had not seen him make before.

"Morvath." A breath. "Sethara. Vyxara. Dravesh. Kaethis. Mythara. Zorven." Each name set down the way a man sets something down after carrying it a very long time. "Twenty-two years. They deserved better than what they were given. You gave them what we could not."

He inclined his head.

Stric tried to find words and did not. He returned the gesture as best he could from where he lay and hoped it was enough.

Thrakmar straightened. His gaze moved once across the courtyard, the five races working side by side among the wounded. The set of his shoulders altered by a fraction. A loosening, small and visible.

He left without another word.

Something fluttered against Stric's chest. Weak. Barely there.

He got his hand to his inner pocket. His fingers would not close properly. Teela reached across without a word and drew Talnar out for him, and held it open.

The pages were still for a long moment. Then a single line formed, the letters uneven, slower than usual, as though the writing itself cost something.

They are free. Veltak is free. Vrill would be proud.

The page turned white.

Stric's vision blurred. The world tilted again. Teela's grip tightened around his hand.

"I've got you." Her voice came from very far away. "I've got you."

The last scraps of light at the edge of his sight crumbled like ash. The hum that had always lived under his skin thinned to nothing, leaving a clean, cold quiet where it had been. He let the quiet take him, knowing they were safe. The battle was done. The dead were free. Everything else could wait.

Stric's recovery came in fragments, like circulation returning to frost-numbed fingers.

The fever came first. He surfaced through it in scattered moments. Cearan's weathered face above him, muttering incantations that did nothing for the hollow ache inside. Teela's hand gripping his, her thumb tracing circles on his palm; fairy healers surrounding his bed, their earth-magic soothing the burns but unable to touch the deeper wound where his power had lived.

One morning, he woke fully enough to sit up. Teela slept in the chair beside him, dark circles beneath her eyes, still wearing the blood-stained tunic from the battle. His Powerstaff leaned against the bedpost within reach. He took it without thinking, an old habit, the motion of years. The crystal sat dull at its tip, the same grey as ash.

He reached inside himself.

Nothing. Only a void where his power had lived, as absolute and final as a room stripped bare. He turned his hand over and stared at his palm. Still the same hand. The same calluses from years of staff work. Everything was the same, except for the pull at the centre of his hand that had preceded every working.

He set the staff back against the bedpost. Carefully. As though it belonged to someone else, and he was merely minding it.

When true consciousness finally claimed him, weakness came with it. He could barely lift his head. His body was in borrowed, ill-fitting clothing, the weight of it wrong across the shoulders. Teela leaned forward. The breath came out of her long and slow. Her jaw unclenched by degrees.

"How long?"

"A week." She shifted closer. "You scared me."

"It's gone." Not a question. A statement that tasted like ash.

Teela's hand tightened on his. "Cearan says the channels that carry magic were burned. Seared away." She paused, choosing words with care. "He doesn't know if they'll heal."

Stric lay back against the pillows. Outside his window, Talnaress stirred with new life: workers clearing rubble, craftspeople repairing damage, citizens reclaiming their city from twenty years of darkness. The hammers rang like bells, each strike marking time in the stone. Scaffolds had begun to climb the palace walls, thin wooden bones against stone. He listened to it, and his fingers stayed flat on the blanket.

"I'm alive," he said, because it seemed like something he should acknowledge.

"You are." Teela shifted closer. "And I need you to stay that way."

His legs shook as he went to the window. He stood there, gripping the sill, breathing against the effort of it, cold stone beneath his palms.

The palace walls still bore their scars. Decades-old soot clung where fire had licked the carved marble, black sunk deep into grooves that had once gleamed white. Brushes and rags had carved pale paths through it in places. Thin, clean streaks running between scaffolds where workers scraped at stone, one block at a time.

Outside his window, gardens were being planted where golems had stood. The city was being rebuilt before his eyes.

A sound behind him. A soft thump, sharp in the quiet.

He turned. Talnar lay on the small table beside the bed. Its cover had flipped itself open. The pages lay pale in the thin light across the room, nothing moving on them. He let go of the sill and made his unsteady way back, each step careful.

The pages did not move. They lay open, warm against the air, and he sat on the edge of the mattress and reached out to rest his fingers on the page.

Then text appeared, in the book's characteristic impatient hand.

About time you woke properly. I was beginning to think you planned to spend the rest of the year sleeping.

Despite everything, Stric smiled. "Nearly died, you know."

I'm aware. I was there. A pause, then the words shifted tone, slower and more deliberate, the way Talnar wrote when choosing carefully. *You did well, young Stric. The seven are freed. Barok is destroyed. The victory is complete.*

"Doesn't feel complete." Stric's fingers traced the page's edge. "Feels like something's missing."

Of course it does. You've spent months in battle, focused on a single goal. Now that the goal has been achieved, you must determine what comes next. That uncertainty is normal, not ominous.

"The healers say the magic may not come back."

And if it doesn't? The words held a challenge. *Will you cease being yourself? Will all you've learned, all you've become, vanish because one tool is removed from your hand?*

Stric sat with those words, turning them over like stones. Outside his window, new-planted beds waited in neat lines where churned mud had been. The city was rebuilding itself, one stone at a time.

He made it to the gardens on his own at last. By the time he reached the bench, his breath came short, and the autumn air bit cold through his robes. Leaves had begun to turn along the palace walls, a scatter of gold against grey stone. In the courtyard, Teela and Aelith were training new guard recruits. Young men and women, some former soldiers under Barok's control, others citizens who had hidden and now wanted to protect what they had nearly lost.

She did not change her training style for observers. She drilled them through defensive stances and attack combinations, correcting form with a firm hand on a shoulder, demonstrating footwork with economy of movement that made complex techniques look effortless. Sunlight caught in her hair. Sweat darkened her tunic. She never once glanced toward the bench.

When the session ended and the recruits departed, she crossed the garden to where he sat on a stone bench. She dropped beside him without ceremony, breathing hard from exertion.

Her gaze moved over him, unhurried. "You're looking stronger."

"Compared to a corpse, perhaps."

She snorted. "You're always so dramatic."

"Sorry."

"Don't be." Her hand found his, fingers intertwining. "You did what needed doing. No one else could have." She paused, choosing words with the same care she used when teaching blade work. "The magic may never return, Stric. Cearan thinks the channels might heal, but he cannot promise it."

"I know."

"I fell in love with you, not your magic." No waver in her voice. No hesitation. "It was useful, I will not deny it. But it is not why I am here. You are still you. Still, the man who walked into Eldoria not knowing if the elves would shoot first and ask questions later. Still the one who earned Thrakmar's trust when no human had in decades." She leaned against his shoulder. "I do not need a magician. I just need you."

Something tight in Stric's chest loosened.

"I love you," he said.

"I know." She squeezed his hand. "Now come inside before you catch a cold. You are still recovering, and I did not drag you from that throne room alive just to have you die of autumn chill in a garden."

The first flicker came without warning.

He was running his fingers over the Powerstaff's familiar grooves. A ghost of sensation, like blood flow returning to a sleeping limb. There and gone so quickly, he could not be certain it had been real at all.

His breath caught. He tried again. Reached deeper, searching. Nothing. Only the same hollow void.

"The channels are healing." Cearan stood in the doorway, eyes level, jaw easy. He crossed the room and gestured for Stric to hand him the Powerstaff. His fingers traced the carved grooves as if listening. The crystal's dull surface caught no light at all.

"You should be dead," he said at last.

He turned the staff once more before passing it back, then glanced at Stric, eyes narrowing as if reading something under the skin. His thumb pressed lightly along the inside of Stric's wrist, where magic had once run strongest.

"Whatever you pulled through yourself burned the channels nearly clean." His thumb did not lift. Voice flat. Unhurried. "Most who push that far never get up again. The rest spend their lives as ghosts of what they were."

Stric swallowed. "And me?"

Cearan released his wrist. The faintest twitch moved in his jaw, the only sign of what he saw.

"You are different," he said. "I have no precedent for how you will heal, so I won't write you off yet. Bone and muscle remember how to knit after a break. Sometimes the paths magic uses remember too."

Stric clutched the staff with both hands. "It will come back?"

"I believe so." Cearan's weathered face creased in something approaching a smile. "You destroyed a powerful magician and survived. Your body is learning to carry that power safely. Be patient. Your power recognises you."

His magic returned in increments. The trickle became a stream as warmth spread through channels that had been cold and dead.

He attempted a simple spell one morning. Light, the most basic exercise from his apprentice days. The crystal in his Powerstaff flickered. Dimmed. Then caught, blazing with pale blue radiance that lit the room.

Stric laughed. The sound emerged half-broken. His power flowed again.

That night, the dream seized him.

Stone closed around him, ancient rock beaded with a sheen that was not water. Whatever light existed in that place fell short of the walls. It reached toward them and vanished, swallowed without a trace. Carvings ran along the stone in lines that refused to stay still, angles that slipped away the longer he looked. The air tasted of metal left too long in the rain. Corruption on his tongue, in his throat, settling in his lungs with every breath.

Cold gathered at his ankles. A thin, deliberate band that crept higher with each heartbeat, as if something unseen were winding itself around his legs. This was the cold of a place that nothing living had ever warmed. The cold between stars, given weight.

A figure waited ahead.

At first, it was only a patch where even this half-light could not exist. It was like peering into the gap where a wall should have been and finding nothing there at all. Then the edges moved. Darkness flowed inward toward a centre that never quite resolved. Strips of shadow folded over one another, clinging close like wet cloth in some places, lifting away in slow, underwater motions in others. No line stayed fixed long enough to be named. No surface remained long enough to call it a face or a hand.

Shadows that should have stretched away from it instead drew in. Threads of thin grey light in the air drifted too near and frayed, unravelling as though chewed apart. Wherever the thing stood, the world lost definition. The stone beneath it blurred, as if his eyes could not remember what had been there a moment ago.

Silence thickened. The weight of it pressed out every small noise until only his own pulse remained, beating hard against his ribs, too loud in his head.

The voice arrived without crossing the distance.

"Bearer of Talnar."

It did not strike his ears. It bloomed inside his skull and the stone at the same time, a vibration in bone and rock. Several tones rode on top of one another: a dry whisper, a deeper note that made his teeth ache, a thin, high thread that lagged a fraction behind the others as if uncertain whether it wanted to be part of them at all. The words scraped along the raw places where his magic had only just begun to mend.

"Did you think destroying one corrupted soul would end what I have set in motion?"

Stric tried to speak. His throat locked. Air went nowhere. Metallic taste thickened, as though he had bitten through his own tongue.

Something in the mass of shadow shifted sideways, like smoke caught by a wind that did not touch him. For an instant, the darkness thinned, and the hint of an outline suggested itself. A tilt where a head might be, the impression of breadth where shoulders might have spread. His mind supplied shapes his eyes could not see, and his skin crawled at its own guesses.

"Barok Tana served his purpose."

No change of pitch. No catch before his name.

"What mattered was what rose through him."

The darkness around the thing loosened at its base. The shapes reaching out across the stone in thin tendrils, like ink poured into water. They did not follow the ground's uneven rise and fall. They passed over cracks and ridges without altering, as if the floor itself meant nothing. Where those tendrils went, the faint sense of rough stone beneath his bare feet faltered. A moment of weightlessness, as though the ground had taken one step back.

"Every choice he made. Every soul he broke. Every door he forced open."

The pause that followed pressed close to his skin. The air right beside his ear cooled, though the figure had not moved. Breath that was not breath at all.

"All of it clearing the way for you."

The cold had climbed to his knees now, bones aching as if the heat were being drawn out from the inside. Muscles clenched against a weight bearing down from above as much as rising from below.

"**Vethra Tar.**"

The figure now stood just beyond arm's reach, or seemed to. Between one heartbeat and the next, it was closer. The shadows wrapped tighter, thinning in one small place where two points of reflection looked back at him. Light caught on the surface of deep water, something far below watching from beneath a skin of darkness. The longer he stared, the more pressure built at the base of his skull, as though unseen fingers had settled there, testing the shape of him.

"I have been waiting for you far longer than you know."

The nightmare shattered. Stric jerked upright in bed, gasping, hand closing around his Powerstaff where it leaned against the bedpost. Sweat soaked his nightshirt. His pulse slammed against his ribs.

Beside him, Teela stirred. "Another nightmare?"

He crossed to the window, needing to see the real world. Talnaress spread below, dark and quiet in the small hours. Beyond the city, unseen mountains rose against the star-scattered sky. North, where something waited and watched.

"Not just a dream." His hand tightened on the windowsill, the wood solid beneath his fingers, real, present, its grain pressing into his palm. "Something was there. Reaching across the distance."

Teela rose, wrapped a blanket around her shoulders, and joined him at the window. "The thing that made Barok what he became?"

"Yes." His breath came out slow. "It knows my power has returned. It is watching."

She took his hand. "Then we will face it when the time comes. Together."

He turned back to her, to the blanket around her shoulders and her hand warm in his. "Together," he agreed. "Always."

They returned to bed. Teela's breathing soon steadied into sleep's rhythm. Stric lay awake longer, the newly returned magic a quiet hum through healed channels. Outside, the wind moved from the north, pressing against the glass.

From the courtyard below, a watch bell rang the hour. Once, and then twice. The city was quiet in between.

In the days that followed, the city's rhythm changed.

Dreese claimed his father's throne and wore his crown, though both sat uncertain on a young man thrust into kingship before the weight of either had grown familiar in his hands. The council that gathered around him no longer looked like the line of human nobles Stric remembered from old Guild tales. Whhrll sat beside Aelith, while fairy wings caught torchlight at the same table. Kael's dented armour scraped the chair back. Voices from forest, mountain, sky, and city argued and agreed in the same vaulted hall.

They met there to make practical decisions about food distribution, rebuilding priorities, and justice for those who had served Barok willingly versus those who had been forced to serve. Most of Barok's surviving Spellcasters had surrendered and now sat in cells beneath the palace while councils questioned them; those whose answers revealed coercion or clear disgust at the lives they'd been forced into were released to help rebuild the city under careful watch, while the few who clung to Barok's cause remained imprisoned to face judgment.

The undead had collapsed with the master crystal's shattering, leaving only bodies to burn, and mixed patrols rode the roads beyond Talnaress, sweeping for stragglers who'd fled the final battle instead of surrendering.

Stric, now Grandmaster of a Guild that existed more in promise than in stone, took his place at the table as advisor. The council had heard him speak twice in the first week, on matters of magical precedent and how a rebuilt academy might serve all five races. The third time a debate broke open over jurisdiction in the outer districts, he leaned back and let Thrakmar carry it, listening as the vampyre elder's measured voice found the thread of reason in the argument and drew it smooth.

Stric walked the palace corridors beside Dreese and Kael, the three of them moving without a guard of scribes or attendants. Stone underfoot shifted from newly laid blocks to older slabs worn smooth by decades of boots. The air cooled as they turned into a narrower passage. Here, the walls still held much of the siege. Faint scorch marks in the mortar, hairline cracks that spidered away from old impacts.

Kael slowed first. His hand drifted to his sword hilt, fingers finding the grooves. He stopped beside a shallow alcove with a small window set into the outer wall. The glass was new. The surrounding stone was not. Soot had sunk deep into the carved edge, thin black veins the brushes had not entirely chased out.

"I stood here the night the palace fell," Kael said. His voice had the flat steadiness he used for battlefield reports. "Watched the city burn before I fought my way to the nursery. Before I carried you out."

Dreese stepped into the alcove. The stone pressed against the young king's shoulders, narrowing the space until he filled it. Outside the glass, Talnaress lay in the late-afternoon light. Scaffolds wrapped around towers, new roofs catching the sun, gardens where rubble had been. Dreese set his palm on the sill.

"My first kingdom," Dreese murmured. "I slept through it."

Kael's jaw tightened. He did not answer.

Cold bled from old stone into the corridor air. Smoke and screams lived in these blocks as much as mortar and lime. For a heartbeat, Talnar's pages and Kael's rare stories pressed over what lay in front of him. Night instead of autumn light, flames instead of banners, a guard with ash in his lungs and an infant held tight against his chest.

"We leave these," Dreese said. His thumb traced one of the soot-black veins along the carved edge. "The palace should remember."

Kael inclined his head. Some measure of tension eased from his shoulders, his gaze settling on Dreese's face rather than the stone behind him.

On the walk back toward the great hall, Dreese did not speak again. He didn't need to. The set of his jaw, the way his gaze moved across stone and window and scar, told Stric enough. The crown still sat heavy. But it sat on a man who now knew it in the walls around him, in the silver threading his temples and the worn leather of his father's sword grip.

At the moon's close, as the first planting since Barok's defeat began, Dreese stood before the assembled court and announced Stric and Teela's engagement. His voice carried the full width of the hall, unhesitating now in the way of a man who had grown into his authority.

Werewolves threw back their heads and howled approval, the sound echoing off the rebuilt rafters. Fairies released luminous pollen that drifted through the air, pale green against the crystal-lit stone. Thrakmar clasped Stric's shoulder with careful claws and spoke of blood given and what had been asked of it.

Teela stood beside Stric, uncomfortable in a dress but bearing it with good grace, her hand warm in his. A breath went out of him that he hadn't known he'd been holding.

That night, as they walked back to their chambers through palace corridors lit by torchlight, the temperature dropped. Candle flames guttered in unison despite still air. A presence pressed against the magical protections around Talnaress, testing. Announcing its attention.

The Powerstaff grew taut in Stric's grip, wood and crystal holding a tension that was not his. Against his ribs, where Talnar rested beneath his robe, something gave a faint, involuntary shudder, as if the old tome had drawn in a breath and held it.

Then it passed. Warmth returned. Stric's hand had moved to his Powerstaff, and Teela's fingers had searched for her sword hilt without either of them deciding to do it.

"It is still out there," she said.

"Yes." He looked north through a narrow window, toward mountains lost in darkness. "But we will be ready when it comes."

They continued to their chambers. Tonight, they had peace.

Stric fell asleep with Teela warm against his side and his magic a low pulse through newly healed channels, felt in the ribs rather than heard. Outside, the stars wheeled overhead in their ancient patterns. The city slept. Guards walked their rounds.

Far to the north, in the mountains where no living thing returned, something watched from the ancient darkness.

The magician's power burned bright again.

A beacon in the void.

The watchers patience was eternal.

Acknowledgements

Some books take months. Some take years. This one took the better part of thirty years, picked up, worked on, set down, and picked up again, before it finally became what it was always trying to be. In that time, the story changed shape more times than I can count. Characters arrived who refused to leave. Plots that seemed certain unravelled and rebuilt themselves into something better. A world that existed only in my head slowly learned to exist on the page. If you are holding it now, you are holding the proof that some stories are simply worth the wait.

This book was shaped, in no small part, by the authors who made me fall in love with epic fantasy in the first place. Tolkien showed me that a world could feel ancient and real. Raymond Feist showed me that an ordinary person could walk into something vast and find themselves equal to it. David Eddings showed me that the people beside you on the road matter as much as the destination. Terry Goodkind showed me that a story could ask hard questions and not flinch from the answers. If there is any echo of their work in these pages, I consider that an honour.

To my beta readers, Bálint Makai, Laurie Robertson, Cindy Lawrence, Mark Lawford, and Lee Sharp, your honesty made this a better book. You told me where the story earned its moments and where it didn't. The prologue became what it is because of your attention, and the mid-book pacing is tighter for your patience in flagging it. I am grateful to every one of you.

To the team at 100 Covers, thank you for taking the world inside these pages and giving it a face worth putting on a shelf. You did a brilliant job.

To the elves, werewolves, vampyres, and fairies who arrived on the page with opinions of their own, you were at times genuinely inconvenient. I wouldn't have it any other way.

About the author

Stacy Hall grew up in Shepparton, Victoria, and has been living inside fantasy worlds since the age of twelve, when a hobbit walked out of a door in a hillside and ruined him for ordinary fiction forever. He is a father of four, grandfather of three, and spends his spare time crafting handmade art knives, which, when you think about it, is entirely consistent with a lifelong love of worlds where blades matter and craftsmanship is respected.

The Oracle's Bridge is his debut full-length novel and the first book in the Bridges of Magic series, thirty years in the making, which he considers a perfectly reasonable timeline for building a world from scratch. Readers who want to know how the villain became what he is will find the answer in *The Scholar's Shadow*, a prequel novella set in Veltak before the storm. He has also published *The Dreamers*, a middle grade fantasy for younger readers looking for their first adventure.

Stacy now lives "just down the road" from where he was born in Victoria, Australia, and can be found either at his workbench or somewhere in Veltak, depending on the day.

Glossary & World Guide

A reference for readers new to Veltak and its peoples.

People of Veltak

Acher, Grandmaster — The first elected Grandmaster of the Magicians Guild, chosen by the original thirteen council members after King Balthor's founding decree. Remembered as the first leader to seek genuine cooperation between the races, a legacy held as a model of what the Guild once was.

Aelith — An Elven warrior-sentry of Eldoria. Lethal in combat and philosophical in instruction, she becomes a mentor and guide to Teela during the company's stay in the Elven forest.

Aeloria, Queen — Queen of the elves of Eldoria. She governs with unhurried certainty and represents her people on the multi-racial council formed after the liberation of Veltak.

Barok Tana — The tyrant of Veltak. A former Guild magician exiled to Lormir Island, who returned with armies of golems and undead to seize the throne. His twenty-year occupation transformed him utterly, and he was not the only force behind his rise.

Balthor, King — The historical king of Veltak who founded the Magicians Guild following the Time of Magical Chaos. His founding vision was genuine but flawed: he built his council of thirteen from humans alone, and that insularity had consequences his successors could not foresee.

Cearan, Master — A Guild magician who carried infant Prince Dreese to safety on the night of Barok's coup, and spent twenty years protecting him on Earth. A healer and advisor, his steady competence is the quiet backbone of the alliance.

Deamara, Stric — The protagonist. An apprentice magician found wandering the woods near the Academy at age ten, with no memory of his past. He carries Talnar, holds an unusual magical signature no one can quite explain, and discovers over the course of the quest that the word for what he is has not been spoken aloud in a thousand years.

Dreese, Prince — The son and heir of the slain King Caelric and Queen Elendra, sent through the Darmoor Island wormhole as an infant for safety. He spent twenty years on Earth, his memories of Veltak reframed as symptoms of illness. Bringing him home and helping him become who he was born to be is the heart of the quest.

Kael — A royal guard who survived the fall of Talnaress and carried Prince Dreese to safety alongside Cearan. Twenty years later, he is still standing, still loyal, still steady, still the man you want on your side when things go wrong.

Marka — The elderly caretaker and guardian of the wormholes on Darmoor Island. Three generations of his family have served in this role. He kept the crystal attuned to Earth's wormhole for twenty years, waiting for whoever would eventually come.

Morvath, Sethara, Mythara, Zorven — Four of the seven vampyre elders murdered by Barok at Drakenholt Mountain. Their names are spoken, and their silence is never forgotten.

Reyna, Teela — The female lead. A survivor of Barok's occupation, she is a fighter of exceptional skill, sharp instinct, and hard-won pragmatism. The emotional foundation of everything Stric builds.

Thrakmar — One of three surviving vampyre elders at Drakenholt. A scholar of extraordinary knowledge and precision, he leads the vampyre mages and carries the grief of his people with a stillness that rarely breaks.

Thrakul — One of three surviving vampyre elders at Drakenholt. A warrior. Brief. Decisive. Done waiting.

Twill — The leader of the fairy groves of Veltak. Small, ancient, and connected to everything simultaneously. She carries the grief of sixty-three dead in the earth beneath every step.

Valkan — Barok's most trusted field commander. Unlike his master, he is capable of accurate tactical thinking and genuine strategic assessment. That doesn't make him good. It makes him dangerous.

Vince — A man Stric and Teela meet on Earth. He helps them because they offer him food and gemstones. He is wiser and kinder than he pretends to be.

Vrill, Grandmaster — The Grandmaster of the Magicians Guild at the time of Barok's attack, and the man who devised the plan to send Stric forward in time. His final act was an act of faith in people he would never meet.

Whhrll — A young werewolf of Pack Grraall, freed from an obedience collar by an accident neither he nor Stric intended.

Proud, principled, and fiercely loyal to those who have earned his trust. He becomes the coalition's werewolf chieftain.

Races of Veltak

Elves — The ancient race of Eldoria. Their magic works through invitation and harmony, not command, a tradition that reflects how they engage with the world. Their forest is hidden behind wards that cause enemies to doubt, forget, and walk away convinced they made a wrong turn.

Fairies — Small in stature and connected to everything. Practitioners of earth-speaking, a tradition of communication with stone, soil, and the crystal veins running deep beneath Veltak. What one fairy knows in the grove, all fairies know.

Humans — Practitioners of Guild magic, structured, incantation-based, and built on command and control. The most numerous of Veltak's races, and the most divided by twenty years of occupation.

Vampyres — An ancient race whose understanding of life-death energies predates the Magicians Guild by centuries. They live in Drakenholt Mountain's cave system, carry a deep and careful culture, and are still paying the cost of trusting the wrong scholar.

Werewolves — A sentient, shapeshifting race governed by pack structures and elder councils. They communicate in part through a rich sensory language of scent, reading trustworthiness, intent, and history in a way no other race quite understands. Pack-memory does not forget.

Places of Veltak

Academy, the — The Magicians Guild's primary centre of learning, located in Treast. Destroyed in Barok's coordinated attacks on the night of his coup.

Darmoor Island — A remote island scattered with thousands of wormholes, vertical tears in reality navigable only through individually attuned crystals. Three generations of one family have served as its guardians.

Drakenholt Mountain — The mountain home of the vampyre civilisation. The air presses thick before you understand why. Inside, bioluminescent fungi light passages of carved beauty, and a council chamber bears seven permanently empty chairs.

Earth — The world to which Prince Dreese was sent for safety. Dense cities, engine-powered carriages, glass towers, and no magic whatsoever. The people are not unkind. They simply cannot see what is right in front of them.

Eldoria — The hidden forest kingdom of the elves. Its wards don't show attackers a false image; they make searchers question themselves until they turn back, convinced they made a navigation error.

Lormir Island — A place of exile where magic dies. The Guild banished Barok here, considered the matter settled, and stopped watching. They should not have stopped watching.

Talnaress — The capital city of Veltak and seat of the royal palace. Under Barok's twenty-year occupation: golems at every intersection, undead soldiers on patrol, windows shuttered in daylight, and a faint sweetness of decay the wind could not carry away.

Treast — The location of the Magicians Guild Academy.

Veltak — The kingdom in which the story is set, and the seat of the stolen throne.

Magic of Veltak

Bridge-mage *(Vethra Tar)* — An ancient vampyre term meaning *born to all*. A bridge-mage is an extraordinarily rare individual, born perhaps once every thousand years, whose soul can harmonise with the magical traditions of all races simultaneously. The same open pathways that make this possible also make a bridge-mage uniquely vulnerable to corruption. It finds more open doors.

Compass spell — A directional locating spell cast through a Powerstaff. Useful for finding someone on a world you have never visited before. Costly over long periods.

Deathseed crystal — A vampyre meditation aid that can be corrupted when violent death occurs near it, darkening into a vessel for captured anguish. Barok created one of unprecedented power. It became the anchor of everything he was.

Earth-speaking — The fairy tradition of magical communication with stone and soil, conducted through whisper-songs that ask rather than command. Barok stole this knowledge. He was not gentle about it.

Golden-green magic — The distinctive hybrid magical signature of Stric's spellcasting, the visible trace of something in him that doesn't fit any single tradition.

Golems — Massive constructs of sand, stone, and dark magic. Each one animated by a trapped spirit, screaming in perpetual agony. Fairies can hear them through the earth's crystal veins.

Grove-mind — The fairy collective consciousness through which all fairies share awareness simultaneously. In fairy self-reference: the deep paths. What one knows, all know, instantaneously, across any distance.

Harmonic resonance — An unusual phenomenon observed when Stric casts spells, noted by trained observers from his earliest work. The explanation takes some time to arrive.

Illusion magic — The conjuring of convincing false perceptions. Three dragons, complete with heat shimmer, footfall weight, and the smell of sulphur, can clear a building faster than any other spell.

Obedience collar — A magical restraint placed around a werewolf's neck to compel obedience, paired with a control crystal held by the supervising Spellcaster. What it forces a werewolf to do leaves a mark that does not fade when the collar is removed.

Pack-magic — A form of collective werewolf magic older than shapeshifting, running in blood and howl and bone. Rarely invoked. Rarely spoken of outside the den.

Powerstaff — The primary magical tool of Guild magicians. A wooden staff topped with a crystal that channels and amplifies the wielder's power, brightening when magic flows freely and dimming to darkness when reserves are spent. Each one carries its wielder's history.

Primal magic — A magical frequency older than any racial tradition, the raw force of life itself, running beneath all other magics like a heartbeat the world forgot it had. It does not command. It asks.

Spirit-binding — A forbidden magical technique that captures dying spirits before they can enter the Great Cycle. What Barok built his power upon.

Timesling — Grandmaster Vrill's most closely guarded secret. A device that hurls its traveller across distances so vast that time bends around the passage. One-way. Irreversible. The path heals behind you.

Transmutation spell — A spell allowing the caster to transform one material into another. River stones into rubies. Useful on a world that uses money.

Translator crystals — Small magical gems fashioned by Cearan that bridge the language barrier between Veltak's tongue and Earth's languages. Automatic. Continuous. The difference between being understood and being stared at.

Tri-harmonic magic — The simultaneous casting of three distinct magical traditions, human discipline, vampyre blood-magic, and fairy earth-song, in full resonance. Not channelled in sequence. All three at once. The cost is significant.

Undead — Reanimated corpses deployed as soldiers. They do not tire. They do not question. They advance with the patient certainty of beings to whom time carries no cost.

Wormhole — A portal between worlds, accessible only during a celestial alignment. The one connecting Veltak to Earth opens for eleven days every two years. Navigation requires a crystal individually attuned to the desired destination. Without one, the other wormholes on Darmoor Island will take you somewhere else entirely.

Vethra Tar *(*Bridge-mage*)* — An ancient vampyre term meaning *born to all*. A Vethra Tar is an extraordinarily rare individual, born perhaps once every thousand years, whose soul can harmonise with the magical traditions of all races simultaneously. The same open pathways that make this possible also make a bridge-mage uniquely vulnerable to corruption. It finds more open doors.

Werewolf Cultural Terms

Alpha-bond — A formal leadership compact that enables a single chieftain to unite multiple packs under one command structure, linking them in something closer to a shared will than a mere social arrangement.

Dark hunt — Werewolf term for being compelled under a collar to hunt one's own pack-brothers.

Den — The werewolf equivalent of a home or settlement.

Den-warmth — A sensory-memory term for the experience of home, family, and safety. Not a place. A feeling that has a smell.

Honour-scent — A scent-word denoting trustworthiness and integrity. It cannot be faked.

Hunt-bond — A formal alliance or sworn obligation between a pack and an outside party. Pack Grraall holds ancient hunt-bonds to the bearers of Talnar, documented across generations of pack-memory, binding regardless of how much time passes between contacts.

Moon-gathering — A regular assembly of pack elders from multiple packs.

Pack — The primary social unit of werewolf society. Not simply a group. The foundation of identity.

Pack-brother / pack-sister — The address used by werewolves for members of allied groups, or trusted individuals outside their biological pack. It means something.

Pack-memory — The collective, multi-generational store of knowledge, experience, and lore carried through werewolf culture. It does not forget betrayal. It does not forget loyalty either.

Pack-scent / scent-words — The werewolf sensory-language system through which identity, trustworthiness, and intent are read through smell. The most honest language on Veltak.

Power-scent — The specific scent-word associated with the presence of legitimate Guild magic.

Pup — A young werewolf. The equivalent of a child.

Talnar-bearer / Talnar-chosen — The designation given by werewolf pack-memory to the legitimate holder of Talnar. A title carried in memory across every generation.

Fairy Cultural Terms

Deep paths, the — The fairy term for the grove-mind network. The crystal-vein connections beneath the earth through which all fairies share awareness. What narration calls the grove-mind, fairies call the deep paths.

Great Ceremony — The annual fairy harvest celebration. Barok came to it wearing the face of a scholar.

Great Cycle — The fairy belief that spirits naturally return to a cycle of renewal upon death. The basis of fairy mourning, fairy hope, and fairy fury at what Barok did with the dead.

Keeper of the Trees — The leader of fairy spiritual practice. Chir held this title until Barok came to the Great Ceremony.

A Brief History of Veltak

Great Separation, the — The historical period during which the various magical traditions of Veltak's races diverged and alliances collapsed. The wound Stric's quest begins to heal.

Time of Magical Chaos — A period of uncontrolled magic and widespread destruction preceding the founding of the Magicians

Guild. King Balthor's solution was order. The question was: whose order, and at whose expense?

The Shadow — Something older than Barok. Something that watched. Something that fed on what he became. The war may be over. The Shadow is not finished.

COMING SOON

Bridges of Magic, Book Two

The war is over. Veltak is free. A new council sits at the table in Talnaress, and five races are learning, slowly and imperfectly, what it means to build something together.

But something older than Barok Tana is still watching.

It has waited before. It knows how to be patient. It knows how to find the desperate, the grieving, the ambitious, the afraid. It has been searching for its next investment for a very long time.

And it's gaze has fallen to Stric.

Book Two of the Bridges of Magic series is coming.

To be the first to know when it arrives, sign up for Stacy's newsletter at:

books.stacyhallauthor.com/freeshadow

Also by

Bridges of Magic Series:
The Scholar's Shadow ***(Prequel Novella)***
The Oracle's Bridge ***(Book One)***

For Younger Readers:
The Dreamers

Connect with the Author

If you'd like to know when Book Two of the Bridges of Magic series is coming, or simply want to talk about werewolves, sentient books, and the ethics of time travel, here's where to find Stacy:

Website
stacyhallauthor.com

Email
stacy@stacyhallauthor.com

TikTok
@stacyhall.author

Newsletter
Sign up at books.stacyhallauthor.com/freeshadow
(Subscribers receive exclusive content and will be the first to know when Book Two arrives.)

www.ingramcontent.com/pod-product-compliance
Lightning Source LLC
LaVergne TN
LVHW030907080826
845145LV00010B/2793

* 9 7 8 1 7 6 4 6 5 6 0 0 9 *